12.34

The Hidden War

DAVID FIDDIMORE was born in 1944 in Yorkshire and is married with two children. He worked for five years at the Royal Veterinary College before joining HM Customs and Excise, where his work included postings to the investigation and intelligence divisions. *The Hidden War* is the fourth novel in the Charlie Bassett series following *Tuesday's War*, *Charlie's War* and *The Forgotten War*.

Also by David Fiddimore

TUESDAY'S WAR

CHARLIE'S WAR

THE FORGOTTEN WAR

DAVID FIDDIMORE

The Hidden War

PAN BOOKS

First published 2009 by Pan Books
an imprint of Pan Macmillan Ltd
Pan Macmillan, 20 New Wharf Road, London N1 9RR
Basingstoke and Oxford
Associated companies throughout the world
www.panmacmillan.com

ISBN 978-0-330-45448-3

1 3 5 7 9 8 6 4 2

A CIP catalogue record for this book is available from
the British Library.

Typeset by SetSystems Ltd, Saffron Walden, Essex
Printed and bound in Great Britain by
CPI Mackays, Chatham ME5 8TD

For Johnny's and the crew of *HMS Harpy*,
the finest ship that sailed

Acknowledgements

The last pages of this book could not have been written without Jane Howell and Jo Hamill, the best guides in the business, who took me up a hill to meet *The Diamond Bomber*, and down a mountain. They are the best and safest of walking companions . . . and I must not forget the Vipers Skiffle Group, whose recordings keep me sane as the world around goes irreversably mad. Bless you all.

PART ONE

The Bus Conductor

Chapter One

'Do you actually believe in God?' I asked my pal Fergal.

That was Father Fergal. He'd watched *Boy's Town* too often, and ended up at a parish in Liverpool after the war.

'You mean the old fellah with the white beard? That sort of ting?'

'That sort of *thing*.'

'They taught me about that kind of question at the seminary.'

'What kind of question?'

'The damned if you do and damned if you don't sort of question. Getting damned is important to us Catholics you know. If I answer *Yes* you'll think your old friend is off his head. If I answer *No* you'll ask me what I'm doing masquerading as a priest.'

'I always liked the word *masquerading*, didn't you? I'm going to Berlin again on Sunday. Do you want to come along for the trip?'

Fergal and I had been to Berlin a few times in 1944. We used to call it the *Big City* in those days, although it wasn't so big by the time we'd finished with it. I thought Fergal had been the best flight engineer in the business, in a Lancaster bomber named *Tuesday's Child*. I had been the W/Op. For those of you brought up to use wartime slang I'll explain that wop doesn't mean Italian for once: it means wireless operator. I was their radio man.

'I don't think my Boss would like that. Not on a Sunday. He's a bit keen on Sundays.'

'So you *do* believe in Him then?'

'Of course I do: but probably not in the way you think. I believe in the God principle I suppose.'

'What does that mean?'

'That the God I believe in is unknowable and unimaginable . . . so I don't try. But that doesn't mean He's not there.'

'Absence of evidence isn't evidence of absence, as far as you're concerned?'

'Yes. That's rather good, Charlie. Where did you come across it?'

'A whore in Paris last week. We were talking about VD.'

'*He* wouldn't like to hear you talking like that.'

'Sure. He created VD just the same as He created us. The pox must have a divine purpose; it's just that to us it's unknowable and unimaginable.'

'Let's go and have that drink, Charlie.'

Later I asked him, 'Don't you suppose that somewhere there's a holy gonococcus preaching to all the other little gonococci, that God created them in his own image?'

Fergal fell off the bar stool while he was laughing, and two pretty girls came across to help me get him to his feet again. Maybe my luck was changing.

It was, and the joke was on me as it turned out, because a week later I began to itch.

I'd had the chance to look Fergal up because I had flown into Liverpool Speke Airport and, you guessed it, by early 1948 the silly beggars were already beginning to call it Speke International. I was in *Dorothy*, the company's Avro York, and had a couple of days kicking my heels whilst they did an engine-out job on one of its four Merlins. The owner had a thing about *The Wizard of Oz*, and named all his aircraft after characters from it. I should have run away as soon as I learned that. We'd hauled *Dot* up to Speke with a load of Dutch rivets for a small car manufacturer, and next year's tulip bulbs for the municipal parks. For an aircraft that was only six months old it was already clapped out: she was being flown to death.

Fergal went into the priest's school at the end of our tour in 1944. I don't know how he ended up at a poor parish in Liverpool, with a children's home full of war orphans. I asked him if he had a choice about where God posted him.

'No, Charlie. God's agents in Dublin sent me here to make me humble. As I remember, it was a case of *Speke, or for ever hold your peace.*' He'd made me smile.

'Has it made you humble?'

'Liverpool would make anyone humble, Charlie. Where I live is a bombed-out human sewer.'

'Come away with me then: I'll get you a job.'

'God's already given me one.'

'But you hate every arse-wiping minute of it.'

'That's the point, Charlie. I'll explain it one day.'

'Fancy a beer then?'

'Thank you, Charlie. Why not?'

I had already met the nice old guys teaching Fergal his trade. Liverpool seemed to attract Irish priests like old dog deposits attract flies . . . and Fergal was right about the districts around the docks: they were full of holes, gifts from creative German flyers in the early Forties. I had a curious conversation with one of the priests whilst waiting for Fergal to finish work one evening. He had tufty wings of red hair, and a ruddy complexion. We sat in a large study, and he poured me an Irish whiskey.

He said, 'In the old days we would have called this the Chapter House.'

'And now?'

'Just Church House. Sad, isn't it? You flew with young Fergal during the war, didn't you?'

'Yes. I was his wireless operator.'

'What do you do now?'

'Same thing, but not for the RAF. I was civilianized. Just like a bus conductor really: I fly with a small freight outfit in Kent. Last week I actually flew a load of coal from northern France to Newcastle. We take it to Germany as well.'

The conversation stalled, then he said, 'I hear that things are really bad in Newcastle.'

'Better than it was. I met someone who told me about entire families freezing to death on his street in the last winter. They don't report that in the papers.' I wanted to ask, *Where was your God then, when they needed him*? But we'd all just got through a war, so we knew the score. Instead I asked him, 'Did you learn to be a priest here, as well?'

'No. I went to a seminary in Spain. The Scottish School . . . and that's where I found my calling, and stayed . . . until Franco chased me out.'

'I have a friend who fought over there. He was chased out as well. He was probably a Communist, so you wouldn't have got on with him.'

'And why not? At least they stood and fought when God deserted us.' He said this without blinking. He wanted to be sure I understood him. Another pause, and then he asked me, 'What do you know about our Church's procedure of *confession*, Charlie?'

'Precious little, Father. Why?'

'I wanted to talk to you about Fergal's confession.'

'Are you supposed to do that?'

'No.'

'Well . . . ?'

'Don't worry about it, Charlie. I have always excused myself by choosing to believe that God is not a personality at all: maybe He's something more like an animated, but complex, set of rules . . .'

'I don't understand.'

'Rules are for the obedience of fools, Charlie, and for the guidance of wise men.'

'And we're the wise men?'

'We wouldn't be here if we weren't, Charlie. Only there's just the two of us.'

'What was your problem again?'

Don't ask me how I knew. It was just like being in the RAF. If an officer butters you up it's always because there's a problem that he wants to pass on to you.

'He confesses your flights over Germany. Twenty-eight of them, wasn't it?'

'That's right. I try not to think about them myself. We had some interesting experiences, but from your viewpoint we probably did pretty ghastly things to nice people.'

'Does that worry you?'

'No. Not any more. I don't know why.'

'It worries Fergal.'

'It always did. Situation normal.'

'That's not the way it works for a Catholic, Charlie . . . do you want another drink?' I must have been slinging it back.

'No thank you, please carry on . . .'

'A Catholic confesses their sins to a priest, repents and asks for forgiveness. The priest gives them penances, usually prayers to recite, and then absolves their sins in God's name . . . and they are forgiven. Their sins have been taken from them, and they are no longer sinners . . . ready for Heaven.'

'Whiter than the shriven snow?'

'That's right.'

'Just li' that?' I said it the way that comedian does. Father Leakey didn't rise to it.

'Yes. Just like that.'

'I must get a bit of that one day.'

'I'll introduce you to a good priest when the time comes.' I've always liked these buggers who had a quick return of serve. 'The difficulty with Fergal is that he kept coming back with the same sins. He confessed your flights over Germany again and again. Countlessly . . . as if the memory of them was eating into him somehow.'

'As if the absolution hadn't taken? Perhaps he knows God better than you do.'

'That's not the problem, Charlie.'

'Then what is?'

'He stopped confessing the flights two weeks ago.'

'There you go then: *alles ist vergeben*.'

'No, Charlie. That's not it. I think he believes he'll never be forgiven. He's given up.'

'What do you want me to do about it?'

'I don't know. Whatever you can, I suppose.'

I awoke flat on my back on a stone slab. When I opened my eyes the universe was above me. There was the constellation of Orion, its belt like a finger pointing into the sky. It must have been about three in the morning. Fergal was six feet away; alongside me on another table grave. He was alert, and had probably been awake longer. The girls had gone. He asked me, 'You OK, Charlie?'

I yawned. I was cold, and my back was stiff, but I felt disinclined to move.

'Yeah; great. I spoke to your mucker when you were finishing up in the church tonight. He's worried about you . . .'

'*Mucker*. You've only been up here a couple of days, Charlie, but you're already picking up the lingo.'

'It's a talent I seem to have; or a disease.' But I wasn't prepared to let him get away from it. 'He's worried about all you've been saying about bombing Germany.'

'He's not supposed to tell you, the louse: there's something called the sanctity of the confessional.'

'He told me that was cancelled out by God being a set of rules . . .'

'Yes; for the obedience of fools, but the guidance of wise men. I've heard that one; he uses it on all of us. It's his excuse for making up his faith as he goes along. He's an old renegade, and will be in trouble with the bishop before long. Apparently he forgot himself once in Spain, got lost, and ended up fighting in the International Brigade. He says he's one of God's backsliders.'

'Like you, and that rule about chastity a couple of hours ago? She was very noisy.'

'You're right. I'll need to confess that.'

'He's worried that you banged on about it for so long, and then suddenly stopped.'

Neither of us said anything for a couple of minutes. I recognized Cygnus, the Swan, low in the sky and counted her stars.

'Do you ever worry about what we did to Germany, Charlie?'

'Is it on my conscience, you mean?'

'Yes.'

'No. Not any more. I'd find it difficult to look at the faces in your orphanage and feel bad about what we did to Jerry. Besides, there's another thing . . .'

'What?'

'When I remember going to Germany in *Tuesday* now, it doesn't feel like it was anything that *men* did. It seems more like an act of nature. Like something terrible but inevitable; like something I wasn't responsible for . . .'

I didn't tell him about the nightmares.

'I worry about it.'

'I know. That's why they're worried about *you*.'

I spotted a bright star about thirty degrees to my starboard, and billions of miles away. I thought that it could be Betelgeuse. Fergal spoke quietly and without passion – quite the old Fergal I knew.

'I won't do anything silly, Charlie. If it gets too bad I'll come looking for you, and take that job you suggested.'

'Good. Can we go back now?'

'Yes; we can.'

'In that case you'll have to pull me up. My back isn't working any more; that whore must have done for me.'

'*Were* they whores?'

'I paid them anyway . . .'

'What was yours like?'

'Very soft and firm at the same time: like lying on one of those blow-up beds. *Consider the Li-Los of the field . . .*'

'. . . they toil not, neither do they spin. And yet I say unto you that even Solomon in his glory was not arrayed like one of these.' Then he said, 'Mary Magdalene was said to be a whore . . .' He had a gentle, faraway smile on his face.

'Why did we come to this terrible graveyard in the first place, Fergal . . . couldn't we have found somewhere more comfortable?' I asked him.

'Remember Marty?'

'Of course I do.' Marty Weir had been our bomb aimer. When the crew had split Marty had organized all of our signatures in a Gideon Bible he'd swiped from a hotel, and given it to Fergal for luck.

'I thought that you'd like to visit him. He's lying over against that wall.'

There were about twenty service headstones over there. I

hadn't given them a second glance. I sat up suddenly, leaned over and was sick. It was probably something to do with all the beer I had drunk.

We flew into Berlin on the Sunday morning with a load of coal, and arrived as black as miners, covered by the dust from the sacks. Without making it obvious the American military governor of the western part of the city was trying to stockpile fuel for a hard winter; there was already a heady black market in coal. Sorry about the pun. This was purely a civilian operation: a charity was paying for the shipment. Berlin was still an open city.

It was a longer stay this time – we were opening up an office there. Old Man Halton, who owned us, flew in as our passenger. He coughed the whole way like someone in the terminal stages of TB. The Red Cross doughnut van followed us around the perimeter: Marthe, its driver, had recognized the red-liveried York as we crossed the boundary, and as usual was determined to let no one get to us before she did. The first time I had met her, a year ago, she was driving an identical wagon in Hamburg, selling hotdogs to tired aircrew. She parked at the fuselage door, so it was impossible to ignore her.

'Doughnut, Charlie?'

'Not this time, Marthe.'

'What you bring me this trip?'

'You sleep with me tonight?'

'No I don't!'

'Then I bring you nothing.'

'You English all the same: cheap arses.'

The little green and white Customs VW saloon turned in our direction, so I quickly tossed her the package I'd wrapped before I'd set off. It disappeared instantly beneath the counter. Three pairs of stockings, some cigarettes, and a bar of chocolate I'd swapped from the Yanks. Marthe wouldn't use them; she'd sell or trade them for what she really wanted, food for herself and her daughter.

'See you at the club tonight?'

'Sure thing, Charlie. Say eight-thirty.'

'Fine.'

Life goes on, doesn't it?

The club was called the *Leihhaus*, which means pawnshop, so at least you knew what you were getting into. It was an *open* club on one of the zone boundaries. Every nationality in the world fetched up there, most of them looking for a deal. The police patrols tended to give the open clubs a miss: they were like an unofficial no man's land. A fortnight before, I'd got into a fight with a Russian there. He had taken a bite from my left ear. Now he was my best friend. His name was Gregor something, which finished with about six *avitches*. We called him Greg. He said that he had a couple of tons of amber to sell, looted from some imperial palace. That was way out of my league, so I agreed to introduce him to my pal Tommo. It wouldn't be out of *his* league.

Dave Thomsett was an American sergeant I knew. He worked for an acquisitions department of the United States Army Air Force down in Frankfurt. They acquired houses in Germany for his top brass to live in, and kraut servants and chocoladies to run them, that sort of thing. A chocolady was a girl who would do it for a bar of chocolate. I know that's difficult for you to believe, but maybe you've never been that hungry. Tommo had spent a couple of weeks in Iceland in '47. He told me they had hotdogoladies there. It made a change for them, from all the fish.

I'll tell you about Greg, as well. You've all heard these stories about nine feet tall Russians as broad as bears. He wasn't one of those. He was the only man in uniform I've ever met who was smaller than me. I think that there was probably something the matter with him, because his head was large: out of all proportion to the rest of him. When he walked in with his cap on, it looked as if he was wearing an umbrella on his bonce, and you wanted to laugh. That was not a good thing to do, because when people laughed at him he either took a shot at them or tried to bite their ears off. He didn't have a girlfriend; he had a boyfriend. The boyfriend was an American deserter, but a great cook. He cooked the greatest omelettes, but that was Americans for you: in Germany in '48, they had most of the eggs.

The amber deal wasn't all that it was cooked up to be either. Red Greg didn't sell the amber to Tommo. He sold Tommo the *location* of the amber. That was under a hundred and fifty feet of water in a lake in Germany. As it happened he'd come to the right person. Tommo was the only man I knew with the organizing ability to recover it. It was in the Russian Zone, which I thought could be a problem. Tommo thought it was cool. Anyway, it was their business, not mine. Greg the Red gave me a hundred and fifty occupation dollars for the introduction, and Tommo gave me the same for the business. Look, don't let this worry you. We were all at it.

People started dancing when the radio began to pump out Artie Shaw's version of 'the Beguine'. Greg had a new chocolady at his table. He probably had the franchise on her. He waved me over.

'Here, Charlie. You wan' a drink?'

'Ta. Who's your new pal?'

'Magda. She's a countess. You wan' her?' An improbable number of the chocoladies were countesses. The Russians, in particular, liked the idea. I shook my head. She was probably already poxed. I told you that I itched a bit, so who knows: maybe I was as well. The bottle on the table was French brandy . . . they came out from under the bar for anyone who could afford them. Magda polished a wineglass on her mothy fox fur, and sloshed some of the spirit into it for me.

'What you bring?' Greg demanded.

'Coal, but it was all manifested.'

'Pity. What else?'

'American dollars and three parachutes.'

'Used or unused?'

'Unused. What do you think I am, Greg . . . some sort of black marketeer?'

He thought that that was funny, and bellowed out a great laugh. As he did that he glared around the smoky room. Everyone he made eye contact with laughed for him; he had that sort of effect on people. Scared them shitless.

'I take the parachutes. Give the dollars to the Austrian: he's short. He'll give you a better price than me.'

I liked to get the business done at the start of the evening. Then I could relax.

My pilot, Dave Scroton, mooched in an hour later. He was new to Berlin and looked unsure of himself. He'd flown Dakotas over Arnhem and survived, and appeared to know what he was doing . . . I'd flown three trips with him and had no complaints so far. He was bunking in one of the accommodation huts on the far side of the airfield; I hadn't made my mind up where to sleep yet. I introduced him around. Red Greg asked him about his name.

'You got an unfortunate name, Dave Scroton,' he said. 'People could mistake it for something else. Maybe you should change it.'

'I already did. I used to be called William — I just never did like that.'

That's exactly when I began to like him. Greg bellowed his laugh again. Half the room joined him without knowing what they were laughing at.

'You like girls or boys? We got both.'

'Girls.'

'You wanna countess? Magda's a countess.'

Magda moved an unlit cigarette in Dave's direction, looking for a light, and she smiled. She was short an incisor, which was a pity, because it spoiled the picture – for a countess, that is.

One thing I always liked about Marthe was her punctuality. She came up behind me, leaned down, put her arm around my shoulders and kissed me behind the ear. I could feel her breast against my back.

'Missed me, lover?'

'Of course I have.'

Her next kiss was on my cheek and close to, but not quite at, the corner of my mouth. Our mutual affection must have been affecting and quite obvious to anyone looking. They would have been wrong, of course, but that was the point. Marthe and I had a non-aggression pact. As long as I didn't push her too hard for a shag, I could sleep on a made-up bed on her sofa, and when she was with me the other men didn't bother her, so she had a short holiday from whoring. At the same time, when I was with her, I didn't get the chocoladies all trying to hit on me.

Dave went outside with Magda an hour later. I saw him give Greg five US dollars . . . which was far too much. Magda would probably wheedle another three from him before they came back inside. I asked Marthe, 'You want to eat here?'

'There's a new little Bavarian cafe just inside their zone: I think we'd be OK there.'

Greg shook his head.

'No. Dog meat. They have *real* dog meat. You don' wanna eat there.'

Marthe shrugged; then smiled . . .

'OK. Here's fine.'

While we were waiting for a couple of plates of spiced vegetable stew Magda got up to go to wherever the girls go forty times a night. The music changed. Mary Martin's heart suddenly belonged to daddy. I gestured at the radio and said, 'This is good. What is it?'

'The Cole Porter Hour . . . comes in from Frankfurt. Decadent Western propaganda.' But Greg was grinning. The grin disappeared like it had never been there: he leaned over and grabbed my arm. He whispered, 'I lied. That cafe will be hit by the Patrol tonight. They forgot to buy their bullets. You wouldn't want to be there then with the wrong papers. Maybe your little woman gets locked up by the Patrol. Maybe worse.'

The cafes and clubs all *bought bullets* from an International Patrol; in other words paid protection money on the side. If they didn't pay, they got raided until they did. A number of raids on the same premises tended to discourage the customers, and the proprietors usually got the message. Greg was right; their use of Marthe, or any chocolady they picked up there, would not have been gentlemanly.

'Thank you, Greg.'

'Think nothing. Empty bottle.' He turned the brandy upside down. 'Your turn.' The waiter brought another bottle as soon as I looked at him. Greg asked, 'You fly to the Middle East? Palestine or Istanbul?'

'Not yet. Why?'

'You bring back all the spices you can get in your aeroplane. Everyone wants spices to put in the shit we eat. We'll clean up.'

'Really?'

'Yes; really. Better than cigarettes.'

Greg's boyfriend came out and sat with us after the joint had stopped serving. He sat in his grubby white chef's outfit. Nobody seemed to mind. They held hands.

Eventually Marthe and I walked home. The cobbles were wet, there were still precious few street lights and we gave a wide berth to an enormous bomb site on which a couple of cooking fires burned. Shadows moved around them. I had one arm around Marthe's waist. My other hand, in the pocket of my flying jacket, grasped the butt of my revolver. It makes me smile today when the wankers on the TV talk of districts of Glasgow or Manchester as being *rough*. They don't know they've been born.

I got the sofa bed I told you about. Marthe shared her double with her daughter – Lottie was about five or six, I suppose. Halfway through the night Marthe came back into the sitting room. She was wearing men's silk pyjamas with someone else's embroidered monogram on the pocket. Her face looked softer with her hair combed out. She wrapped a blanket around herself and curled into my back. There was never anything more than that to it. Half an hour later the child squeezed between us. Everybody was looking for a family in 1948.

Chapter Two

I probably should have reminded you that I already had two children, neither of whom was mine . . . in a biological sense that is. Another thing about 1948 was that people were adopting each other like it was going out of fashion. In most cases responsible adults adopted the children. Trust me to get it back to front; as far as I could see my boys had adopted *me*. Dieter was about eight now — I wasn't too sure: he was a German kid I'd found on a battlefield, holding tight on to the hand of his fourteen-year-old brother. The brother had probably been dead a day when I met them. Dieter adopted me soon after that. The other boy was Grace's child. Grace was a girl I used to love; she'd abandoned her baby in a hospital in Bremen. What had I been supposed to do? Leave them in Germany on their own? They lived with my old Major and his woman in a south coast port called Bosham, and after a few false starts I saw them as often as I could. Sometimes they broke my heart: before my last trip Dieter had parcelled up all of his toys — which wasn't that many — and asked me to take them to German kids who'd lost theirs. I couldn't let him down, so I handed them in to the Red Cross station at Gatow. The gratitude of the German nation was pathetic. Dieter had the makings of a better man than me.

When we flew back into Croydon Old Man Halton gave me a few days off. I rode the rattler down to Chichester, sharing the carriage compartment with a beautiful, stylishly dressed woman who defended herself with a bible. It was open on her lap throughout the trip. At least she didn't mind me smoking. I was learning to love my pipe; whether I'd ever find a woman that loved it as much was another question. Now and again the woman crossed her legs, and smoked a cigarette, and I could see her stocking tops. She smiled to herself, but never took her eyes from the book, and flipped the pages. There was a spring in my step when I left the train. I caught the Green Line bus along the coast, got off at the Bosham junction, and walked in with my pack over one shoulder.

I found James – Major James England – and Maggs walking hand in hand along the shingle. Little Carlo trailed them, towing a long piece of seaweed. He was singing a nursery song. Sometimes Maggs joined him in the chorus. He was the first to see me, turned, and ran with his arms outstretched. James and Maggs waited for me to scoop him up and reach them. Do you remember how good the faces of people pleased to see you are? Maggs kissed me on each cheek. She'd spent the war in Paris. James put his arm around my shoulders, and we all lurched back to their pub joined to each other.

I asked, 'Where's Dieter?'

Maggs said, 'School, Charlie. It's Thursday.'

'How's he doing?'

'Very well, Charlie. Same as a fortnight ago. Don't worry; I'll tell you if he has a problem.'

'I know you will,' I told her, and gave her a squeeze.

'Why don't you walk up to the crossroads in a couple of hours, and meet him off the bus?'

I did, and you should have seen his face.

I gave James the sterling equivalent of the dollars I'd changed for him. He bought them from hard-up Americans in Chichester and

I sold them on in Berlin. I'd never worked out precisely how the value increased every time they changed hands, but by each time I returned from Europe they had grown by about 15 per cent.

Someone was building one of those funny little prefabs next door to the pub and restaurant.

'You're going to have neighbours soon,' I told him.

'Yes, Charlie.'

'Do you know them?'

He nodded. 'Some ex-RAF type with a couple of orphaned kids . . . I haven't told him about it yet.'

It took me a few moments to cotton on: James and Maggs were building me a house. I hugged him because I didn't know what else to do, and felt stupid. 'Might as well, old fellow,' he added. 'We're coining it in between us; didn't you realize?'

I probably sniffed before I asked, 'Everything's coming up roses?'

' 'bout time, I'd say.'

Maggs could always bring us down to earth again.

There was one other thing. Kate was parked between the pub and the pieces of the new house. She was a battle-scarred old Humber staff car, named after our driver's wife, and James had criss-crossed Europe several times in her in 1944 and 1945. Theoretically she belonged to the army.

'How did Kate get here?'

'Les brought her down on his last visit.'

'Don't the army want her back?'

'I don't think they know she's in the country yet . . . Les switched her plates with a wreck . . .'

'So she's legal?'

'More or less. The papers I have pass for originals.'

Good old Kate. I drove her and the kids up to Arundel for a picnic on Saturday: and walked a short section of the Roman road, and Dieter turned out to know more about the Romans than I did. I suppose that Kate wasn't altogether a good thing. Carlo and Dieter slept in the back seat as we returned. The smell of Kate and the wash of the road noise had me remembering some of the things I'd seen in her in '45, and some of the people who were no longer around. It sort of quietened me. James picked up on that when I got back, and after we'd put the boys to bed we drank until we fell off the bar stools. I'd always been quite good at that.

A few days later it was time to pick up the pieces, and go back to Germany for the Old Man. We went back to cold old Europe in a draughty old Dakota the Old Man had probably got free with a packet of cornflakes. She was slow and she rattled. Scroton loved every rivet of her: he'd been flying things like that for years. She carried enough dents to distort the airflow, and one of her engines – they were Double Wasps I think, although I might be wrong – misfired now and again. When one of those big Yankee jobs misses it feels as if a giant has taken hold of a wingtip and given you a gentle shake. And the radio was crap. Scroton said that she was so perfect an example of her type that it was as if she was fresh off the production line.

For me it had been hate at first sight. She still bore the wartime camouflage paint she'd started life with, although the national insignia had been painted out, and she bore our civilian registration in big, untidy black letters. They looked as if a child had scrawled them on. She had a faded squadron painting of a bint wearing a black conical hat, and nothing else, on her blunt nose.

I've told you before that the Old Man had a name painted on all of his aircraft. This one just had three beautifully italicized *W*s under one of her curves, and everyone called her *Whisky*, after the phonetic. I hated the way my radio shack filled with airborne dust particles every time someone opened the cargo door, I hated the silly little canvas seat I had to sit on, and I hated the way she flew with an exaggerated rocking motion that would have made Sir Francis Drake seasick. *Whisky*, I thought, was a right cow.

Our engineer/nav on that trip was Crazy Eddie. I never learned his proper name.

Pilots and radio men tended to swap around aircraft a lot; the engineers tended to stick to one. That made a lot of sense if you think about it. I was separated from the office they flew in, up front, by a threadbare curtain, which I pulled back and shouted at Eddie, 'What's the *WWW* mean then?'

We were in front of the control tower running up the engines. They sounded rough to me, as if they were about to fall out of the wings. Dave and Eddie looked at each other's faces, smiled rapturously and nodded a lot. They obviously had seriously lowered expectations as far as aircraft were concerned.

'Work it out yourself, Charlie. I'll give you a clue. The popsie on the nose never had a hat when she arrived. The Old Man painted that on personally. Sounds good though, doesn't she?'

Oh, I thought. *I get it. I'm back in* Wizard of Oz *country, and we're all sitting in the Wicked Witch of the West*. I could have done without that.

I said, 'She sounds as if she's dying. She sounds worse than the Old Man. Can we go home now, and try again tomorrow?'

Scroton just said, 'Oh ye of little faith,' and pushed the throttles forward.

I thought that the props would come off, but they didn't: *Whisky* began to move. *Sideways*. I'm sure that it was sideways. I closed my eyes.

Take-off speed for a C-47 is somewhere between a gentle jog-trot and an amble, for a reasonably fit octogenarian. When I felt her tail come up I opened my eyes again. Scroton was not looking at where we were going, and the hedge rumbling towards us. He was looking back over his shoulder at me. He had concern all over his face.

'You OK, Charlie?'

I screamed, 'Look where you're fucking well going!'

'Oh, that,' he said, without taking his eyes off me, and pulled the yoke back into his stomach, and gave it some rudder to counteract the yaw. *Whisky* cleared the perimeter fence like a blown horse finishing last in the National. Scroton said, 'Great old girl isn't she?' Then he looked forward again, but it no longer mattered: we were over the sea anyway. Just. I knew another pilot who used to take his eye off the ball like that. What was the matter with these guys?

Our field at Lympne was all grass, except for its perimeter tracking, and almost looked out over the Channel. One became airborne by the simple act of flying an aeroplane off the edge of England. I never got used to the bastard place.

Mother Nature did the rest. Usually you dropped about fifty feet towards the sea, in a great lurch, before the air flowing over the planes was sufficient for flying speed and a bit of lift. *Whisky* was worse than most: I'll swear that her wheels kissed the little wavelets below us before Dave powered away.

Eddie said, 'You look a bit green, Charlie. Were you always as windy as this, or is it something we did?'

They both found that amazingly funny, and cackled like hens for miles. Eventually I grinned back at them. We were taking a cargo of tinned bully to the Americans at Frankfurt, and then going on to Celle to haul whatever the next customer wanted for the good people of Berlin. The next customer was either HMG or the Americans, hiding behind a charity and still pretending to the world that we didn't yet have a problem with Berlin. Served us right, I suppose: it hadn't been so long ago that I had been bombing shit out of the place, and killing their kids. Looking back on it from today it's hard to understand why we agreed with the Russians that the line which was to divide Germany in two after the war was so far to the west of Berlin. It was probably some sort of tactical decision, based on the fact that if they had decided to keep coming it's where we would have fought and stopped them anyway. That left the rubble of Berlin marooned in Russian Germany, and shared between the Yanks, the Reds, the Frogs and us . . . although what the Frogs did to deserve their bit I still don't know. We supplied the Allied sectors of the city through the roads, canals and airfields, but you didn't have to be Einstein to work out that the Reds could cut those threads any time they pleased.

There was money in this airline business. The outward trip for the Yanks alone would pay for this operation. Anything we trucked to Berlin for the Brits would be sheer profit; as would be a return load if we could find one. Halfway to Frankfurt I smelled a strong stench of burning, clapped on my parachute and ran around shouting until they told me that it was the heater port. Apparently Daks often smelled as if they were on fire. I had a prejudice against burning aircraft because I had become too intimately acquainted with a couple of them. What it meant was that Eddie and Scroton laughed at me again, and the *Wicked Witch* was living up to her name. I vowed never to turn my back on her again.

Dave let down more than fifty miles from Frankfurt, and we skimmed across the old Reich at about two hundred feet, crossing significantly buggered towns and villages. A lot of Jerries still flinched at the sound of an Allied aero engine overhead, so a lot of the pilots flew as low as they dared just to spite them. A man ploughing a field shook his fist at us, as his horses skittered away from the parallels: I saw his grey Wehrmacht cap and jacket quite clearly. I'll bet he wished he still had his machine gun. One of the villages looked completely burned out, and deserted. *Who'd lived there?* I wondered, and, *did I overfly it, unseen, at night in 1944?* Like the poor, you see, the war was ever with us. If you'd ever been there you'd understand.

My mate Tommo was there to meet us. He drove a jeep up to *Whisky*, behind the five-tonner they sent to unload her tinned-meat cargo. Both the lorry-driver and his mate were Negroes.

'In 1944 they were flying fighter planes and invading Okinawa.' I told Tommo. 'Now that the war's ended all they're allowed to do is carry things for white people.'

'If they weren't carrying things for white folk they wouldn't have a job at all. You want me to cry about it?'

'No, Tommo. You know what I mean.' I had climbed into the hard front passenger seat, which was on the wrong side of the jeep. Tommo turned to look at me. He always did that when he wanted you to listen to him. He pulled his cigar from his mouth.

'Remember, when you were a kid, just how long time seemed to take to pass? You remember how summers seemed to last for ever, and Christmas never came?'

I smiled at the memory despite myself: days down the rec playing cricket. 'Yes. So what?'

'The human race is like you were when you were a kid, Charlie. It's a very *young* race. That's why things seem to take so long to change. The Negro's day is coming . . . don't get me wrong about that . . . only it will be *some while* coming. They got some difficult times to get through first.' He looked suddenly embarrassed. His black cigar had gone out, and he fiddled for a lighter. He asked me, 'Your people want a lift anywhere?'

'No. They're walking up to the Mess; they're booked in overnight. I think they were officers.'

'How can they live with themselves?'

I chuckled. Same old Tommo. He thought that anyone who hadn't once worn the stripes was just so much dogshit to be scraped off your shoe. That thought reminded me of Fergal again, and I wondered if he'd stopped flying over Germany in his head yet.

Tommo broke in, 'A drink or a broad?'

'You got a place where they both come together?' OK – so that can mean more than one thing.

'That's my boy!'

Good old Tommo. He'd fitted a really dinky radio alongside the jeep's small dashboard and tinny music came out when he turned it on. AFRO. American Forces Radio Overseas, not a haircut – what goes around comes around. He said, 'It came outta Kesselring's staff car. You think ordinary folk'll want music radios in family cars one day? I was thinking of patenting the idea if no one's already got there first.'

I looked out across the airfield. It was a great day. The windsock hung on its pole as limp as a used johnny. We bore down on the airfield gate guard house, with Bunny Berigan blistering the air with his old cracked trumpet, and 'I Can't Get Started'. He'd been dead for five years or more, so it must have been one of those new record programmes.

When the war ended in 1945 Tommo was camped out in German Germany, having got in there in front of anyone else. By some complicated sort of arrangement he'd never adequately explained he had already been living in Hamm for a month when the Germans surrendered. Then he'd moved smartly over to Frankfurt. It's why the Americans already had all the best places to live by the time the rest of us got there. He bought some houses for the US, requisitioned many others, and bought some for himself. He sold one of those to me, and the Yanks paid me to rent it back to them. I've told you before: what goes around comes around. Nothing was simple when you were dealing with Tommo.

'The good news,' he told me, 'is that your rent just went up.

You get thirty per cent more than you used to, because prices are going up all the time. They call it inflation. Remember that word, Charlie; you're going to hear it a lot in the future. The bad news is that you give some of the rise to me, because I fixed it for you.'

'OK, Tommo. Anything you say.'

We were in a small drinkery in Kaiserstrasse. Tommo sat at the end of the bar in a white jacket, white shirt, black trousers and a smart bow tie, looking like he owned the joint. I thought of asking him when he'd last seen *Casablanca*, but decided against it: he usually had a job to laugh at himself. Instead, I asked, 'You have gambling in the back room?'

'Natch. Just craps: nothing flash. You stay outta trouble if you do nothing flash. You want to throw some cubes?'

'No thanks, Tommo.'

'Why'd'y' ask then?' But Tommo had always been quick on the uptake, so he stuck in, 'Oh. I see. *Casablanca*.'

'Sorry, Tommo.'

'Don't be. I think that I look kinda tacky myself, but my customers like it.'

So: he *did* own the joint. The customers, bar me, appeared to be exclusively US servicemen and their women. A man with a guitar sat on a stool in the corner and strummed sad tunes. Tommo asked me, 'You ever been to see the place that Uncle Sam's paying you top dollar for?'

'No. Why?'

'You should. It'd be polite. You got German tenants too. You should give them a look at their landlord's face.'

'Next trip, maybe.' I didn't mean it.

Some couples wanted to dance, but there was no space, so they danced close to the bar and brushed us as they turned. Tommo said, 'You got something on your mind.'

'Yeah. Marty Weir. You remember him?'

'No.'

'He was our bomb aimer; bit of a chancer . . . and you remember Fergal, the engineer?'

'Uh-huh. He was the Mick wasn't he?'

'Yes. Fergal took me drinking in Liverpool a couple of weeks ago, and we got a couple of ladies – for old times' sake. We took them to a cemetery he knew. After they'd gone, he told me that Marty was lying in the corner; six feet under.'

'Upset ya?'

'I threw up, but it didn't at the time: it does now. I always thought that the *Tuesdays* would make it. Now Marty's gone, and Pete . . .'

Tommo looked uncomfortable. Pete had been the rear gunner, and latterly a pal of Tommo's.

'I know whatcha mean.' Then he asked me, 'You going to Celle tomorrow?'

'That's the idea. Then Berlin.'

'Light?'

'So far.'

'You take some unofficial sugar up for me, and on to the Big City? Seven sacks.'

Flying sugar into Berlin was like being asked to fly in gold dust. He could name his own price.

'What's in it for us?'

'Fifty bucks for you and your mates, and I give you the name of a club in Berlin where you can drink free for the rest of your life . . . from next month, that is.'

'Why should anywhere let me drink free for the rest of my life?'

'Maybe because I own it, old man. Maybe I'll invite you to come in on the deal wi' me.' We shook on it: I'd carry the sugar.

'Marty and Pete would have liked that.'

'Yeah. You ready for the broads yet?'

He held a hand up, and squeezed something metal in it that

gave out an odd double clicking sound, like a metallic frog. He didn't even look round as two women came through the bead curtain behind the bar. One was a small blonde, my size. The other was dark with legs so long that if she didn't sit down I'd end up talking to her navel. She was very beautiful. Tommo chuckled and said, 'Know what you're thinking, Charlie, but once her legs are around you, you won't notice how long they are.' Then he turned to the girls, and in fluent local Kraut asked them what they'd like to drink. He told me, 'They're both called Elise. They're twins.'

I thought, *First Fergal, and now Tommo: it's about time that you started picking up girls for yourself again Charlie.*

'I suppose that they're both countesses?'

'Elise is,' Tommo said.

We flew a half-load of military cleaning products from Celle into Berlin Gatow. I had a hangover, and Crazy Eddie slept all the way. He didn't even wake up when a Russian Lavochkin fighter buzzed us on the approach. The Reds had taken to flying their aircraft unpainted since the war: silver bullets with red stars on the wings. I was disturbed to see this one was painted a drab olive green all over – as if it was ready to fight. If the Reds got awkward, and the city wasn't topped up with food and fuel, it would starve or freeze next winter . . . and *we* flew in the cleaning products. We had to overfly two cemeteries on the approach to Gatow, and over one of them I saw *Whisky*'s port wing navigation light literally fall off.

I clicked the radio, and told Scroton, 'Charlie, Skipper. I just saw a bit of us bloody well fall off. It fell off the port wing.'

'Not an important bit, Charlie. Now shut up a min while I have my hands full, there's a good chap.'

I walked around the aircraft after we had landed, and on the left wingtip found the hole that the light had once lived in. Two wires had pulled clear, and dangled in the sunlight. Scroton wandered up and said, 'Get on to the Yanks at Tempelhof as soon as we're in the office, and find us someone who'll sell us a spare. I'll fit it.'

I was worried about something else. It was the tenth time I'd landed at Gatow, and the first time Marthe hadn't met the aircraft. I pushed the small parcel I'd brought her deep into my pack, and hoped that the Customs patrol wouldn't pull me. There was something about the way the new German Customs guys looked at you . . . as if they'd all been in the SS in earlier lives. Only this was the New Germany, remember? *Neu Deutschland*. There had never been an SS, and none of our new neighbours had ever been Nazis. The Nazis all lived in the Russian Zone apparently.

I was wrong about the Customs. The big guy in his dark green uniform picked up my pack unopened and handed it back to me. I had put it on the ground outside our office when I went searching for my papers. He handed me those back without looking at them either. He said, 'Thank you for coming here, Mr Bassett. What you are doing will feed thousands if things get bad. We are all very grateful.'

I could see Marthe's little cafe lorry parked up against the terminal building. I tried, 'Where's the little Hotdog Lady? I missed her.'

'You speak good German, Mr Bassett.'

'Not really, but thank you anyway.'

'She hasn't shown up for a few days. She must be careful or she will lose her licence; you know what these Allies are like.'

Despite what we were always told about the Jerry, this one actually had a sense of humour. I ought to get a photograph of him so that everyone would believe me.

'Yes,' I grinned back. 'I know what these Allies are like.'

I wondered what he'd done in the war. I wondered if he and I had ever looked at each other across the cold night sky. As I walked into the small Visitors office it did occur to me to ask myself how he knew my name without looking at my papers.

Crazy Eddie was behind the single flimsy desk, an opened envelope with my name on it in front of him. He was reading my letter.

'It's from someone called Greg,' he told me. 'He addresses you as Comrade and writes like a Red. He says to go to a pawn-shop before you visit your cousin. You mixing with some funny people, Charlie?'

'No. I'm flying with them . . . gimme that . . .' and I grabbed for the paper.

A waitress with a magnificent figure and a disturbing moustache poured me a drink, while Russian Greg talked with me. The drink was a very fine St Petersburg Tokai. He said, 'I want to talk about some sugar, and you want to talk about your girl. You first . . .'

'Tell me.'

'She was picked up by the International Patrol maybe three days ago. They dropped her outside the door here yesterday. She was in a bad way.'

'Where is she?'

'I got her into the American Red Cross place. I used your friend Thomsett's name. Will that be all right?'

'Probably. He wouldn't mind. What happened to her daughter?'

'I didn't know she had a kid . . .'

He must have seen my reaction, because he shouted at the door to the kitchen, and told someone to bring the GAZ jeep he used around to the front. As we walked out to it I asked him, 'What about your sugar?'

'Tell me on the way, English. OK?'

'OK.'

'Was it Marthe's papers?'

'I don't think so. It seems that her papers are kosher . . .' It was a word that we used a lot to annoy the Berliners. 'She didn't buy her bullets . . .'

'Are they making whores buy bullets now? Since when?'

'Since a few days. She was the first to say *no* I think. Probably the last too.'

He drove the GAZ as if he had his hands on the steering levers of a tank: you wouldn't want to be in his way.

It's funny, the things that you notice. There was a bomb crack in the wall of Marthe's bedroom. You could see it from the outside if you looked up as you climbed the outside steps. I always glanced to see if it had worsened. I looked up now by force of habit. It hadn't opened any further. I always meant to bring her a sack of cement to plug it with: she had jammed the crack with newspapers. We ran up the internal stair – the neighbours must have thought it was the Patrol coming back. I used my key. It turned, but the door wouldn't open more than a few inches. I rattled it. I thought I heard movement, but couldn't be sure. I rattled it again, and shouted, 'It's Charlie. It's Mr Charlie.'

At first nothing happened, and then I heard a dragging sound as something was moved away. It seemed to go on for ever. Because of the cant of the bomb-damaged building, the door had always swung open on its own once the lock was tripped. Marthe's place had been ransacked, but that was all right. It was all right because the child was standing in the middle of the mess. She had a dirty tear-stained face. I squatted down and held out my arms. She came to me, looking down, and taking small deliberate steps. She made absolutely no noise, not until the last minute when she threw herself at me. I hugged her. I could feel her trembling, and said, 'It's all right now, Lottie; it's all right now,' again and again, because I couldn't think of anything else to say.

Marthe was sitting up in bed in a short-sleeved hospital gown. Her face was bruised and puffy. Her forearms were also bruised. The bruises were days old – they were yellowing already. Lottie climbed onto the bed, and tucked herself alongside her mother. I sat on the end of the bed, Russian Greg took the only chair, and smoked a cigarette. Marthe said, 'Aren't you going to ask me what happened, Charlie?'

'You'll tell me if you want to.'

'Don't you care? Can I have a cigarette?'

'I didn't say that. I just didn't want to make it worse.'

Russian Greg tossed her a packet of American cigarettes, and then leaned forward to light one for her with his Zippo. Her breasts moved beneath the gown, and his eyes followed them. That was interesting. She surprised me by smiling at me – the sun came out.

'Thank you, Charlie. I was being a bitch, and you were the closest man to hand.'

'I know. I didn't know what to ask.'

'You were right. Best ask nothing. There were several men, and it was bad, but not as bad as the weeks just after the Ivans arrived. I'll live, OK?'

'OK.'

'I won't be able to work for a week. That's a problem.'

Russian Greg butted in, 'I take over your coffee wagon at Gatow until you're better. I put one of my countesses in it. You don't lose your licence . . . get you job in the kitchen, when you're up and about.'

She added, 'They say I'll be here for a week. I need to make arrangements for Lottie until I get out . . .' She stopped mid-sentence, as if it had just struck her that she and Lottie had already been adrift for a couple of days, and the five-year-old had managed without her.

'All fixed,' Tommo said as he walked in. 'She stays here with you.'

We all turned on him. I asked, 'When did *you* get in?'

'An hour or so ago: I'm shagged out. When they told me that a Russki had dumped a girl here, and used my name for it, I thought I'd better find out what was going on. Mighta guessed it was one of yourn, Charlie.' He turned to Marthe, removed the odd little khaki cap he wore, and gave her either a small bow or a big nod. I remembered that Pete used to do that. 'David Thomsett, ma'am. Charlie's pal.'

Marthe actually looked coy. She looked down.

'You saved me.'

It was Tommo's turn to look abashed. Then he said, 'No. I *invested* in you. I shouldn't like us to be getting off on the wrong foot.'

'I don't understand that.'

'He doesn't want you to misunderstand him,' I explained gently.

Marthe put down a high card. 'Charlie; I've *never* misunderstood a man since my sixteenth birthday.'

It broke the spell: we all laughed.

The American Red Cross had taken over a huge old house on Trautenaustrasse. It was part administrative HQ, part accommodation block, and part short-stay hospital. They employed German labour, and half the population of free Berlin visited it looking for jobs. There were often vacancies because the personnel were combed through for Nazis in hiding periodically, and they always carted a few away. It was surrounded by a large garden tended by three denazified gardeners. I guessed that its rose beds and lawns would be vegetable plots before long: you could just sense the trouble brewing up around the city.

Tommo and Greg took Lottie for a run in the garden, leaving me with Marthe. She asked me, 'Why is everyone being so kind to me, Charlie? I am only a German whore in a defeated city, and now everyone is being kind to me. I don't understand it.'

'It's the club; I think you joined the club.'

'What club?'

'I don't know what it's called, but it's one I'm in, if that helps. It sort of happens to you by accident. Your life is difficult; dangerous – *impossible*, sometimes – and then suddenly you're *in the club*, and people just like you are helping you out.'

'Your friend Tommo is in the club?'

'I think he was a founder member . . .'

'. . . And Greg?'

'Definitely.'

'. . . And lots of other people?'

'Hundreds, I'd imagine. Maybe thousands.'

'Who are they?'

'Good people who like to pretend to themselves that they're bad . . . that's as much as I've figured out.'

She stared out of the window of the small ward, as if she was deliberately distancing me.

'You will come to see us when you get back?'

'Of course I will. I'll be back within two weeks: I'll bring something for Lottie. What would she like?'

'Could you bring her a doll, a girl doll?'

'I'll try. You'll be up and bouncing by then. You'll drive out to meet me at the plane.'

'I'll bring you the best cup of coffee you ever drank in your life.'

'I know you will, Marthe. I'm betting on it.'

I suddenly saw it then: an expression on her face. She looked tired, hungry, hollow and beaten . . . and yet at the same time stubborn, and determined. It was a survivor's face. Within six months it was all around us: and when we called it *the Berlin look* everyone knew what you were talking about.

That night Tommo took us to a smashed-up bar in an alley in the US sector. It was being renovated, and they were just hoisting its new name, in a red neon snake, above its small door. It was called the Klapperschlange Bar. Scroton was with us. He asked me, 'What's that mean?'

'Rattlesnake,' I told him. 'The Rattlesnake Bar,' and shuddered. I might have bloody guessed.

It was Tommo's new outlet. Inside it was being rebuilt by moonlighting US Pioneers, but work had more or less finished for the day, and a party was warming up. On one end of the long bar was a large Plexiglas box: it contained Alice. Alice was the most reliable woman in my life so far. Unfortunately she was also a diamondback rattlesnake. Alice had followed me all around Europe, and now she'd made it to Berlin. These days we'd call her a stalker. She rattled gently when she spotted me.

'Hello, Alice,' I said. 'Long time no see.'

Chapter Three

Have you ever played one of those blindfold hide and seek games, where people are chanting *warm, warmer, cold* or *red hot* in your ear? The agreed air corridors in and out of old Berlin were a bit like that in '48 and 9. What's more, they were almost as busy as a modern autobahn. We were supposed to fly on one side of them, but nobody liked doing that because all a pilot needed to do was sneeze, and he was in the Soviet Zone. Then you had MiGs all over you. So everyone flew down the centre of the corridor, and it got a bit crowded up there. We were caught by a couple of American jets before we got into the happier side of Germany. They must have come whistling up behind us at our height, and just hopped over us, and down in front. They scared us shitless, and had us bouncing about in their slipstreams for a minute. Crazy Eddie, who never strapped in, fell out of his seat. He looked a bit comical on his knees peering forward through the front screens.

'What the hell was that?' he snarled.

'Yanks. A couple of Shooting Stars showing off, I think. Nippy little beggars aren't they?' Scroton was good at aircraft recognition. It was probably why he had lived so long. I looked out to our port: a silver glint in the sun had caught my attention. I poked my head through the curtain and told Dave, 'There's something about a mile out to port. I think he's pacing us.'

'One of them, or one of us?'

'If it's one of us he's asking for trouble: he's well outside the corridor. It must be one of them.'

'Let's piss him off then . . .' and Scroton turned us towards the outlander in a fat wide arc that didn't lose us too much height. That was good because we'd been plugging along at less than two thou anyway.

Sometimes I hate pilots. Especially the mad ones. I asked, 'What are you doing, Dave?'

The gleaming dot in the sky seemed to be standing still – that was because we were flying towards it. 'If we fly out of the corridor he can shoot us down . . .'

'Stop *worrying*, Charlie: you're an old woman sometimes, you know that?' Scroton did a ninety-degree turn back to starboard this time. We were still in the safe corridor, but only just, and that much closer to the little bastard out there. 'Now watch this . . .' Then he said to Crazy Eddie, 'OK, Ed. Switch the plonker box on . . .'

Crazy Eddie leaned down to his left, and reached out for a khaki-colour metal box under Scroton's seat. It had two small toggle switches that he flipped down, and a bigger blue ridged knob, like a tuner on my radios. The box gave out a low persistent squeal as he turned the knob, increasing in pitch and volume. The screech suddenly ceased, and moderated to a loud hum.

'Got 'im,' Crazy Eddie said.

'Now watch *Whisky* bite,' Scroton told me.

I was watching the Russian. He was almost close enough for me to make out the shape of an aircraft. Then something odd began to happen to him. The gleaming dot began to rise and fall, like one of those roller-coaster rides at Blackpool. Each rise and each fall became progressively larger. After less than a minute he did a wing over and fell away from us, and as he did so appeared to regain control. Eddie shut the box down. It whirred down like an engine shutting off. *Like a gyro*, I thought. I asked, 'What was that?'

Eddie sniffed. He looked pleased with himself. 'Neat. That's very neat. They call it *Xylophone*. It buggers up their electrics, Charlie. It interferes with their radar and other instruments – principally the ASI, the altimeter and his artificial horizon. It really spoils their day.'

'Where did you get it?'

'Oh, it's not ours. Someone fancy in the War Office dreamed it up. The Old Man is just doing them a favour by trying it out for them. We've got a couple of them.'

'We're civilians,' I protested. 'I was demobbed.'

'So?'

'I don't want to fight anyone any more.'

'You're not fighting anyone. You're scaring them away: much better.'

'If the Russians catch us trying out military stuff on them they'll probably shoot us for spying.'

'We won't get caught, Charlie. There's a plastic explosive charge in the box. If *we* get it, *it* gets it. No evidence.'

'So Dave is sitting on a bomb?'

'Never looked at it that way before.' Scroton turned to face me. 'Bit of a laugh, what?' I looked at the box. It had a ring attached to a pin that ended inside it. I guessed that last one out pulled the pin – just like a hand grenade. When I looked up Scroton was still watching my face. I told him, 'Pay attention to where you're going, Dave, there's a bit of a mountain over there.'

'Free Germany in about three minutes, Skip.' That was Crazy Eddie.

'Thanks, Eddie; well done.' Then he said, 'Well done, *Whisky*.'

I never liked it when pilots talked to their aircraft: it meant that they were losing touch.

'What's it like over there?' the Major asked me. Friday night, and the pub was full of yachties up from London for the weekend. I thought that it was still too early in the year for leisure sailing, and anyway the Engineers still hadn't cleared all the beaches of mines – you could still get blown up out there.

'A bit like Blind Man's Buff at times,' I told him. 'Hide and seek. Now you see the Russian; now you don't . . . and I'm in the corridor hoping that Ivan doesn't see *me*, and come nosing over for a butcher's. The trouble is that I'm flying with maniacs who don't seem to care that much.'

'More dangerous than flying for the RAF?'

'I don't know. Sometimes it feels like out of the frying pan and into the fire.'

'The Russians respect the neutral corridors, though?' He was talking about the air corridors we had agreed with the Russians: they had been pretty strict about what routes we could fly between our airfields in West Germany, across the areas they controlled, and into Berlin, and they watched us all the time.

'So far. Although there are a couple of stories going about . . .'

'Yes?'

'About aircraft being buzzed by the Reds *inside* the corridor. It *is* warming up.'

'War?'

'Who knows?' It was the question that everyone asked me. The Major had done his bit for six years, but if the Reds had a go at us he'd have another bit to do. 'Sometimes I think that the politicians just let it all get out of control, and when they do people start getting killed.'

'Time to dust my uniform down, and polish the old brasses?'

'No. Not just yet; and you never polished your brasses anyway, James. You always looked a sight. Just like me. Shall I get us another?' I liked the beer James kept.

We were sitting in his small private snug. A door, curtained off with heavy velvet, led directly behind the bar. I took our glasses through. Maggs was serving the yachties, and flirting at the same time. A local guy who worked as a part-time barman was picking up the difference. The place was packed, and heavy with cigarette smoke and noise. As soon as I appeared something which was almost a man leaned across the bar and pushed two whisky glasses at me, sneered and said, 'Two of the same, please, Junior. As fast as you like.'

It took me a second or two to realize that he was talking to me. I said, '*What?*'

'You heard me, sonny. Two of the same again. Chop-chop.'

It happened before I had time to think. The next moment I had hooked my left hand into the collar of his expensive submariner's jersey – one that had never seen the inside of a submarine – and dragged him over the bar towards me. I pulled my right fist back for the punch. It was Maggs who turned and hung on to that, calling out, 'Major . . .' Maggs never spoke loudly, but when she said *Major* instead of *James* she always got action.

James was through the curtain like a ferret down a rabbit hole. He had always moved quickly and quietly. And he was about a yard taller than me. He grabbed my other wrist, warning, 'Charlie!'

You either do it without thinking about it, or you don't do it at all. I let go of the man's jumper by opening my hand very wide, so that everyone could see it was over. Maggs let go of the fist I'd made. The man slid back across the bar away from me, and the colour started to flood back into his face. He even had a short-cropped pointy black beard like the jolly Jack Tar on

Player's Navy Cut cigarette packets. He ran his hand over it in a nervous gesture. That was interesting. He ignored me, and spoke to James.

'Your man's a bit touchy isn't he?'

'My man?' mused James. Then, 'Yes; I suppose you *could* say that he's my man.' He turned to me and said, 'This is *Captain Valentine*, Charlie. Captain Valentine is the Deputy Vice Commodore of one of the yacht clubs – the Arundel.'

I carefully began to pull myself a pint.

'Captain of what? Small craft or a deep-sea job?'

Thinking back to it I suppose that most of the people in the bar had been looking forward for weeks to what happened next: even months maybe. The buzz that had started again, after the little confrontation, suddenly died. They waited for the reply. James said very clearly, 'Actually I believe it was in the Pay Corps, old man,' and then he began to laugh. James had a horrible, cruel, slow laugh. That wasn't very fair to some particularly good blokes in the Pay Corps I've known.

There was a frozen moment, and then someone else laughed – a rather pretty, black-haired woman a few feet from us – and then nearly everyone else joined in. It was one of those daft occasions when you begin to laugh because someone else has. This time Captain Haddock really coloured up. Then he pushed away from us, and out of the bar. About five others trailed uncomfortably after him. I think that James had just lost the patronage of the Arundel: I hoped that it wasn't crucial for the profits.

My language had moderated the further away from active service I got, but this time I couldn't hold it back. 'What a cunt!' I said to James. Then I looked around, and realized that the rather pretty woman had been pressed forward by the crowd, to fill Valentine's space at the bar. She was the nearest other person to me. I said, 'I'm sorry: you weren't meant to hear that.'

James grinned widely. He always did that when I was in the

shit, and not getting out in a hurry. He said, 'Say hello to Evelyn, Charlie.'

'Hello, Evelyn; pleased to meet you.' I was too: she was quite a looker up close.

'Pleased to meet you too, Charlie.' This definitely wasn't a rebuff. She had a wild gypsyish look about her. She wore a black shirt with a couple of buttons popped, a black pleated skirt, and a wide red leather belt between them. Her lipstick matched it – a great blood-red gash. If I let my eyes follow her shirt buttons I could see just the lace edging of a black bra. Party time.

James knew exactly when to come in with the punch line: he always did.

'Evelyn is married to the man with the beard. I think we've made him very unhappy . . .' Bollocks!

Then James started out with his slow, hollow laugh again, and Evelyn copied him. So that was all right then.

I had her in the dark: standing up against the back of the pub alongside the outside bog. Several men came out, and relieved themselves in the covered stone trough without knowing we were there. She gasped when I came, and let herself go immediately. I liked that. Her voice was muffled by my neck when she said, 'Lovely,' and then, after a heartbeat, 'Gorgeous.'

'You're wonderful. Do you know that?' She didn't reply, just shook her head. 'Can you come back to my room?' She didn't pull away from me. I could still feel her belly pressed against mine. She shook her head again.

'No. I have to go back to the boat or there'll be a scene.'

'I've got to see you again.'

'I know.' She pulled away one of the arms she had looped around my neck, and ran a hand through her hair. She said, '*Christ*: this is fast, isn't it?'

I just nuzzled her neck where the hairline met it. I asked her, 'What's the name of the boat you'll sleep on tonight? I want to wander down to the pool, look at it, and imagine you sleeping there.'

'I won't be sleeping. I'll be remembering you.'

I didn't respond immediately. I was thinking the thought that she had put into words. It was: *Christ: this is fast, isn't it?*

'I want to see you again.' It's what happens when I get close to a woman. My brain begins to short-circuit, and I start to repeat myself.

'I come down on my own some weekends; you might see me then.'

'You didn't tell me what your boat is called . . .'

'*The Lady Grace* . . . it's a twenty-footer; white and red – you can't miss her.' Then she sensed my movement and asked, 'Are you laughing?'

'It's nothing.' I was speaking into her hair, and unromantically realizing that my bum was cold. 'God just played a joke on me. I'll tell you another time.'

I helped James, Maggs, and Jason their helper, wash and dry the glasses, and swept the fag packets out of the bar. People can be pigs. Maggs had a twinkle in her eye when she asked, 'Enjoy your walk, did you, dearie?'

I didn't think that anyone had noticed.

I slipped out again at about 3 a.m., without disturbing anyone, and stood on the jetty not ten yards from where *The Lady Grace* was moored. Its long white and red hull rocked up and down gently on the swell. Leastwise; that's what I told myself was causing it to rock.

Over breakfast in the morning Dieter suddenly said, 'I looked out of the window last night Papa: I wanted to see the moon.'

'And did you see it?'

'Yes; and I saw you talking to that lady up against the wall.'

James looked uncomfortable. He said, 'Maybe you didn't, old man.'

'Yes he did,' I said firmly. 'That's how grown-ups sometimes stand if they need to talk,' I told the boy.

'Martin doesn't call it talking.'

'Who's Martin?'

'Martin's in my class; sometimes we go fishing on the Arun with his dad . . .'

'What does Martin call it then?' Why is it always me that gets to ask the stupid question?

'Martin calls it fucking.'

Maggs laughed through a mouthful of tea, and blew it all over the table.

I couldn't believe the progress they'd made with the prefab. I reckoned I would move in when I next came back. We fired Kate up, and drove into Chichester. Carlo and Dieter wolfed down Knickerbocker Glories and lemonade in the tea shop opposite the cathedral, and then we found a toy shop. They chose Lottie a big floppy doll with yellow pigtails. Carlo wanted a small soft grey donkey, and Dieter a Dinky Toy: he chose a little Austin Seven.

Maggs took us all to the small flint and rubble church on Sunday. It didn't matter that we were unbelievers, she told us – it would do the kids good. Each of the children held one of my hands when we walked into church, and all the old dears turned to smile at us. A couple of children turned to look at Dieter. He grinned back at them. Evelyn Valentine sat near the back with her husband, and a group I assumed they knew – they all had that *together* look. She smiled at me too. He looked as if he wanted me dead.

We picnicked on the strand, and paddled in the afternoon, and before he went to bed Dieter insisted on writing a letter to accompany Lottie's doll. I sat at the dining table with him to watch him write. He held his tongue between his teeth as he concentrated. I couldn't help feeling that his brother would have been proud of him. I explained that I didn't know when I'd be going back to Germany. He wrinkled up his nose in a smile.

'That doesn't matter, Papa, as long as they go together.'

He read Carlo and me a story before they went to bed: Carlo still didn't say all that much – which worried me. Then I packed, and drove back to Kent in my little Singer. It was warm enough to have the lid off all the way, and the moon was high before I arrived at the Nissen hut we sometimes camped in between flights. I think that it had been a store shed during the war . . . all the proper accommodation had been in requisitioned houses. Although the blankets felt damp I was asleep before eleven, and dreaming of my old Lancaster, *Tuesday*. That's often the way: she creeps up on me when I least expect it.

In the morning Scroton threw the door of the small hut open with a bang. Sunlight flooded in. He bellowed, 'Hands on socks . . .' as if we were still in the RAF, and doing our square-bashing.

'Bugger off, Dave.'

'What's the matter with you this morning?'

'I'm not awake yet. Give me a couple of ticks.'

I washed in cold water under the tap outside. I've always loved that first brief skirmish with cold water in the morning. I don't shave. I burned my face a bit in the war, and it no longer does beards. Part of me said that that was handy, but another part said that it would have been nice to have the choice.

Scroton kept up some semblance of conversation with me while I dressed. I asked him, 'What's on the board for us?' Old Man Halton kept an ops board in our office at Lympne; just like the old days.

'Nothing yet. I thought we'd motor over to the Parachute for breakfast.'

'We'll walk: it will be good for us.' The Parachute Cafe was less than a mile away. It had been set up to service the Spitfire and Typhoon pilots who flew from Lympne in the war. It just about clung on with custom from the commercial ops at the airfield, and Sunday afternoon drivers. Its breakfast fry-ups were famous for miles. We waved to Dick Barton as we walked out of the main gate. We called him that, and sang the well-known theme tune whenever we took him drinking, because he always wore a long trench coat and dark trilby hat. He never worked out that the image was destroyed by the upright bicycle he pedalled to work. He was Halton's manager. He'd been a squadron leader in the war, and consequently had zero organizing abilities: the office was always in a mess, and our schedules lurched from week to week. We both were still la-la-ing the radio programme theme music, and laughing, as we strolled into the Parachute.

Dick Barton's private office bore a neatly printed cardboard label which said *Squadron Leader Brunton*. That was his real name: he said that it was an old Scottish clan name, but we didn't believe him. He shot out of the door when we waddled into the General Office, waving a flimsy in the air. He grinned. 'Orders. Your target for tonight.'

'Going back to bomb Germany, boss?'

'No, Coventry. You're to drive up to Croydon. They should have finished the maintenance on *Dorothy* by the time you get there. File papers for Amsterdam: pick up a full load of car parts there, and fly them to Coventry for tomorrow.'

'And after that?'

'I'll phone. Don't worry, Charlie; we won't forget you.'

Dave asked, 'Who'll take *Whisky*?' To tell you the truth he didn't like anyone else flying her.

'I haven't got anything for her today, old boy. If anything crops up Milton can have her. He's around here somewhere.'

That made it worse. Milton had done all of his wartime flying on singles, and was a clumsy sod with anything bigger. Scroton made the upside-down smile.

'Have they got that big runway at Amsterdam cleared for use yet?'

'Don't know, old boy; find out when you're there, and let me know. I'll update the Airfield Notes for everyone else.'

The problem was that Brunton was paid more than the rest of us, so that arguing with him was useless. Besides, he'd promised us all tickets for the London Olympics through some shady contact, and we didn't want to bugger that up. As usual, the fire crew had pulled the tender out of her shed, parked it behind the old maintenance workshop and sloped off to the Parachute themselves. We took my car alongside her and, with a yard of rubber tube, affected the transfer of about six gallons of petrol in just a few minutes. If Halton was too broke or too mean to pay our passage up to London, I didn't see why we should have to bear the cost ourselves.

The bastards had locked the side gate of Croydon Airport – the one on the Purley Road – so we had to trundle around to the main gate, and wait in the queue. Before he lifted the barrier for us I asked the old soldier on the gate why.

'The Customs insisted. They said there was too many watches and fags going out through it. Don't worry, they say they're going to scrap the main gate soon, and you'll be able to drive right up to the terminal building just like before the war.'

It was the new world we made after the war: every time you turned your back someone made up a new rule, or a new law, and there was something else you couldn't do. And new taxes? Scroton once told me if there was a hygienic way of measuring shit, they'd tax that too.

While I was waiting for the barrier to go up I noticed the car waiting to leave on the other side. It was a big brown Austin 12

Saloon with black wings; polished so you could see your face in it. The driver was a young man with a hard face, short hair, a dark suit and a Guards tie. The woman sitting in the back was checking her lipstick in a compact mirror: then she accidentally made eye contact with me. I knew her; or rather we had known each other. Rather too well. She smiled quickly, and then looked away. As far as I was concerned the car still had War Office written all over it. If Dolly was sitting in the back instead of driving it, she must have gone up in the world. That was interesting.

I filed our papers with Flying Control and Customs, and waited for clearance. The Customs clerk had dirty fingernails, and an ink stain on the inside of the index finger of his right hand. That used to be the identifying badge of clerks and schoolboys; you never see it now.

Dorothy's proper engineer was named Mortensen: the same as the Blackpool player who scored in the FA Cup. Because I'm small I hate big guys, and Mortensen was so tall that they'd have to raise Tower Bridge if he wanted to walk underneath: you get the picture. His hair was thinning before its time, and he sweated a lot. He also farted more frequently and pungently than any person I've met before or since. For *Dorothy*'s positioning flip to Amsterdam Scroton quarantined Mortensen in the cargo bay after he'd got her off the ground. I sat in the engineer and co-pilot's seat alongside Dave. I asked him, 'What's your route?'

'Down to the Channel and turn right; no, *left:* that's it. If I turn right we'll end up over the Atlantic. I thought I'd fly over base, and see if that sod Milton is rogering *Whisky*.'

None of the independent cargo carriers were allowed to use the direct corridors between London and the main European capitals, because BOAC and BEA had complained that we were getting in their way. Even so, Scroton was routing us a lot further south than we needed to be.

We roared across the outfield at Lympne at about a hundred feet. *Whisky* was tucked away on a hard standing down in the Dell. Her cargo door was open, but nobody seemed to be about. Brunton ran out of his office as we crossed, and shook his fist at us, although he would have forgotten all about it by the next time we met him: part of his charm. Dave put *Dorothy* into a hard climbing turn to port, her engines roaring like a quartet of lionesses. When she was empty she flew like an angel, and I decided that I loved her very much. I thought that, in *Whisky*, Dave had misplaced his affections.

Scroton asked me, 'Get your end away over the weekend?'

'Yes; as a matter of fact I did. You?'

'No. Funny thing is that I wouldn't have fancied it if it *had* been on offer. I want to see Magda again. I've asked the Old Man to send me back to Berlin.'

'She's a whore, Dave.'

'I know. I can't help it.'

I hadn't been able to help it myself once, when I loved a girl who was a generous, but undiscriminating lover . . . but I wasn't going to encourage him. Mortensen came back up for his seat on the let down to Amsterdam. I strapped into the seat behind them, facing my radios, and introduced us to the Tower.

The way the car-parts scam worked was this. Immediately after the war, when our light industry was changing gear from wartime to peacetime production, there was a shortage of components for products for the domestic market; especially cars – we had never needed chromed door handles during the war, for example, but we needed them now. So when we got going again we imported some items from Europe. The deal was that if the importation was from a war-ravaged country the Customs duty was low – that way we were encouraging the rebuilding of their industries. On the other hand, if the items came from a country that had managed to stay out of the war, and just profit from it, like one of the three Ses – Switzerland, Sweden or Spain – then the duty was high – not to penalize them for being the cowardly, uncommitted money-grubbing neutral bastards that they were, you understand; it was just to encourage the others. The knack for the car companies was to buy their parts from these previously neutral countries, where they were high-quality and cheap, slide them across Europe's porous borders, and then import them from a European airport claiming the reconstruction low rate of duty. Everyone was at it.

I hated the car-parts run anyway. The boxes of metal components pushed *Dorothy* close to her maximum load, and she showed it – crawling around the peritrack on the ground, and wallowing like a hippo once we got her into the air: these loads scared us.

Mid-afternoon. They had cleared and extended the main runway, which wasn't a bad thing because *Dorothy* needed every bleeding inch of it that day. If there had been a house close to the end of the runway we would have sailed slap through it. It took us twenty minutes to put nine thou on the clock, and that was it: *Dorothy* was going no higher. It was a good job that there weren't any mountains between Amsterdam and Coventry because we wouldn't have made it over them. We were over the North Sea – not high enough over it for my liking – when Mortensen tapped the four dials mounted slightly behind him to the right, snorted and said, 'Bloody ridiculous, Skip, but our fuel's marginal.'

I was actually squatting behind and between them. I asked, 'What does *marginal* mean? Marginal for Coventry or marginal for England?'

He laughed. If Mortensen could summon up a laugh our situation can't have been all that bad.

'Marginal for Coventry, Charlie. You'll see England before long.'

'How the fuck did that happen?' Scroton demanded.

'We're just using it up quicker than we should. Either it's these tired old engines, or there's a leak in one of the fuel cells.'

'How much did we load?'

'As much as Brunton authorized us for . . . it should have been enough for the trip and ten per cent . . . now it's not.'

I said, 'These bastards don't float. Not at all.'

'Shut up, Charlie,' Dave replied. 'I'm trying to think . . . and you're not helping.'

We shut up and let him think. It seemed to be a long process. He was better at flying than thinking. Eventually he sighed, and said, 'See if you can speak to Lympne. I don't want to divert to there . . .'

'We may not make it that far anyway,' Mortensen said, and shrugged. 'Sorry.'

'Ask them where they want us to go.'

'Why don't we flop down onto the first piece of concrete we see?' I asked him. 'If there's a leaky fuel cell we could have aviation spirit sloshing about anywhere.'

'There isn't a leak, trust me, Charlie. It's just these bloody old engines. Now do what you're bloody well told.'

'Aye aye, Skip.'

'And not so much of your bloody lip.'

If he was that cranky then he really was windy.

At least the radios worked. I discussed our disappearing fuel load with Halton's chief engineer, another ex-services type. He agreed with Scroton: the engines needed a complete overhaul; they had too many hours on them. He reckoned that Cambridge was more or less on a straight line between Amdam and Coventry, and Mortensen agreed that we'd get that far, so that was that. Cambridge was an airfield run by an engineering company called Marshall's: they'd spent the war rebuilding broken aircraft — maybe they'd be kind to *Dorothy*.

They weren't: fifty miles out Lympne told us that Marshall's couldn't disrupt their flying programme for long enough to let us in. I'm sure that Brunton was lying to us: Marshall's would just be asking for a landing fee, and Halton didn't want to pay it.

'What do you want us to do then?' I asked Brunton. 'We're running short of options.'

'There's an old bomber airfield on care and maintenance a few miles southwest of Cambridge, and on your track. It's called Bawne. Put down there, and we'll get a tanker over to you. Sorry about this.'

He bloody ought to be. The hairs stood up on the back of my neck. I'd flown from Bawne during the war, and had never wanted to go back. He came in again, and asked, 'You still there Gulf Delta? Charlie?'

I took a deep breath.

'Yes, boss. Your message received, and understood. Gulf Delta out.' I found that I was speaking slowly; like an amateur. Worse than an amateur. I switched to talk through and told Scroton. I was going home, and didn't bloody want to.

Chapter Four

Mortensen's alimentary tract came back on line as soon as *Dorothy*'s main wheels kissed Bawne's lumpy runway. He dropped an absolute stunner. It was as if the cabin had been filled with chlorine gas. We opened the side screens to vent it. The fuel situation had been more critical than he'd told us, because the starboard outer shut down of its own accord before they closed the throttles. When Scroton stopped coughing he advised, 'You know, Engineer, that someone wrote a book about you once?'

I came in on cue, and asked, 'What was that called, Skip?'

'The Fart of Darkness. I think some poor beggar died in it with the words *The horror, the horror* on his lips. I think he must have just experienced one of Morty's farts.'

'At least we lived to tell the tale,' I said.

Mortensen smiled, but he didn't laugh. I guess he didn't find it all that funny. Maybe he'd heard them all before.

Scroton had managed to do something that my old skipper had never mastered: he kept *Dorothy* on the ground as we crossed the hump, an old peak in the main runway that the RAF hadn't ironed out. Thinking about it, maybe it was only gravity. Maybe we were just too overloaded to get airborne again without power. We taxied it as close to the buildings as we could, and then sat listening to the engines tick as they cooled. I got out and walked round her: I couldn't smell petrol. That wasn't surprising; I think that Mortensen had temporarily destroyed my senses of smell and taste.

In the distance there was the tatty old airfield control caravan painted in faded red and white squares like a 3D chessboard. I remembered it from my Bawne days, but hadn't realized that it was still in use. Now I watched two men descend its narrow steps to the grass, and get into an equally tatty jeep that had been parked beside it. When it drew up alongside *Dorothy* I saw that its driver was an overweight flight lieutenant with a Groucho Marx moustache, and the other guy was a Navy two-ringer. After wondering what the Navy was doing so far from the sea I reassigned him in my head. It was the bloody Customs.

I was leery of Customs officers, and I'll tell you why. Because the radio operator had the least to do in a Halton aircraft, he also completed, signed and handed in the official documents. That included the Customs General Declaration – or Gen Dec – and one of the things you had to declare was what you were hauling, and where it was from. The severe penalties for making deliber-ately incorrect statements gave me a problem on the car-parts runs, because we were doing it all the time.

The fat man squeezed from behind the wheel of the jeep, and said, 'Hello, old boy. Spot of bother? I had a signal you were coming in.'

'I didn't know that there was anyone here, sir.' I used the word by instinct. 'I would have given you a call up.'

'Forget the *sir*. Just me; a few stupid policemen and my mess servant.'

'We ran out of gas. Stupid really. The owner didn't tank up enough in Amsterdam.'

'Pleased to get the company, old boy. Makes it feel like a proper posting again.'

He had that look that told you he'd been in the RAF for ever.

I didn't realize it, but so must I, because he suddenly said, 'You were in the mob too, weren't you? It's written all over you.'

I grinned. 'You mean the worry lines? Yes. Bombers. What about you?'

'Explosives and Ordnance Officer. I ran the bomb dump. That was in India most of the time.' The skin of his face was vaguely yellowed: that accounted for it.

'Miss it?'

'Yes; I do, oddly enough. Better than being a caretaker of a dead airfield.'

'Have you any idea when our fuel will turn up?'

'Tomorrow apparently. They've had to make some arrangement with Marshall's. I had your gaffer on the line: Old Man Halton. Is he as fierce as everyone says?'

'No. Nothing like. He's a very good employer.'

'He says for you to book in somewhere local, and fly on in the morning.'

'OK.'

'I called the local Customs johnny. I knew that Halton would want everything done by the book.' *That's what you think*, I thought, but said, 'Fine,' and looked at his passenger for the first time.

I didn't have to tell Scroton any of this, because he was hanging out of his sliding window, earwigging. Occasionally his lips moved as he related something back to Mortensen.

The Customs guy was tall and slim, and wore his uniform so well that you'd think it tailor-made. Perhaps it was – there were some odd types in the Customs just after the war. His cap was tipped jauntily to one side, showing you a thatch of stiff, light-coloured hair. His face was long and squared off, and it smiled and smiled and smiled. He said nothing. He was the Customs man you never wanted to meet when you had an overnight case full of duty-free fags. It was as I took this in that I recognized his attitude. I said, 'You were in the job too.' Not a question; a statement.

He smiled and shook his head, but it was a distant smile, and it wasn't an emphatic shake.

'No; not quite. I was in Coastal.' Coastal Command: the bit of the RAF which flew over miles of ocean for days at a time. They used to joke that it was the boredom which killed them. It wasn't; it was usually the sea of course. They never quite saw themselves as the same as the rest of us.

'What were you on, Sunderlands?'

Sunderlands were giant seaplanes with more domestic accommodation than a Hamburg brothel: my girl Grace delivered them in the early days. He shook his head, and smiled again. His easy smile made you realize that he thought life was a bit of a joke. 'No. Liberators: I was at St Mawgan.'

'What was it like?'

'Back of bloody beyond. The locals tried to make us welcome, but there were precious few women. What about you?'

'Lancasters. I flew from here, actually. I never thought I'd come back again.'

There was one of those ten-beat gaps in the conversation. Then he asked, 'Shall we have a wander around? See what's left?'

I'd known from the start that I'd have to do it, but I hadn't wanted to. It was good of him to offer me his company. What was odd was that the sun, low in the west, was still shining. Warm on my face. In my memory Bawne had become one of those places where it always rained.

We walked up to one of the big hangars – there were only two. They had dragged my old Lancaster *Tuesday* into there, when her bomb doors fell off after one particular shaky do. In my mind I could still hear my old skipper, Grease, singing out *Bomb doors gone* over Germany . . . as if it had been some bloody great joke. I told the Customs man the story as we walked, then I asked him, 'Where are you based?'

'Thurleigh. The Americans are still there, but not for long. Do you know it?'

'I was there once.'

'You wouldn't recognize it now. There have been big changes . . .'

'Didn't you mind the CO here calling you *the Customs Johnny?*'

'Why should I give a bugger?'

'I'm Charlie . . .'

'Bob Holland.'

We shook hands as we walked.

The door to the big T shed still slid easily aside on greased rollers. I don't know what I expected to find inside. Not an aeroplane at any rate. It was a bleeding car park. There were about thirty RAF lorries, up on blocks with their tyres deflated. Out on the apron again, and in the sun, I could see the Grease Pit – which is what we'd named the Nissen hut I'd lived in for months when I flew from here in 1944. It nestled up against the fences and woods, closer to the administration and domestic blocks. I don't know why I was so reluctant to go down there.

The Customs man asked me, 'What have you brought in this time?'

'Personally, or *Dorothy*'s cargo? Do you want a Gen Dec?'

'Yes please; I'll stamp it up here, and you can carry it on to Coventry. I meant what cargo?'

'Car parts for William Lyons. That's Jaguar, isn't it?'

He nodded, and asked me, 'Reconstruction parts, are they? Come from the Low Countries or Germany?'

Decision time.

'I shouldn't think so; but that's what will be on the Customs papers eventually. There was a great fat Swiss C-54 on the next stand, and I saw the boxes transferred across from it.'

Decision time again. For him but not for me: like the bells of hell in that song. I'd just told him the parts would be misdeclared. He was good at the ten-beat pause. Then he said, 'Thank you, Charlie. You didn't have to tell me that.'

'I don't know why I did. What will you do now?'

'Nothing for the moment. It's nice to know though,' and that was it. And we were standing in front of the Grease Pit: the place I knew too well.

He left me there. There was a padlock on the door. I could have asked for the key, I suppose, but it was actually a bit of a relief. Pete, the tail gunner, and Marty the bomb aimer both were dead. I didn't want to think about the others, in case some of *them* were. Sergeants all: stars. I walked around to the back of the hut where the fence stood on the Bawne Road. The gap we'd once cut for late-night expeditions to the flesh pots of St Neots had only been roughly repaired with twists of wire – in fact it looked as if someone might still be using it. Eventually I walked away, and didn't look back. Going back to somewhere that once was important in your life is always a mistake.

Lieutenant Swan – such was his name – had actually offered us accommodation before I got back to them, and Scroton had already accepted. What goes around comes around: I was going to live in the Officers' Mess of the station I had flown from as a sergeant. We ate with him, and his senior policeman, in a dining hall full of echoes of the past. If you listened carefully you could hear all the dead men sitting down for supper. There were white lawn tablecloths and the best Mess silver . . . but not quite alone in the huge space we soon found ourselves whispering. The food was fucking awful: some things never change.

Then Swan took us on the skite to Bawne pubs I knew better

than he did. Between the meal and the pubs I slipped away for another trip of my own, in the twilight. I went out through the hole in the wire, and along the metalled road to a house I remembered. It had been lived in by a WAAF I knew. She had been kind to me. The small garden was overgrown, and a window pane had been broken. No one home. I had been right the first time; it was best not to go back. Listen, I have a piece of advice for you: stay away from empty airfields – they're full of ghosts.

The next morning I awoke without much of a hangover, although Dave Scroton didn't look too good. I don't know what had been in the Brown Windsor Soup we'd been served the night before, but it tightened up Mortensen's sphincter miraculously. There wasn't a squeak from him until after we landed at Coventry. The refuelling bowser from Marshall's had been standing alongside *Dorothy* when we trooped out to her after breakfast, and the top-up took a bare half-hour. Once Mortensen had signed for the fuel, and declared himself satisfied, it was time to go.

Old Man Halton's two-tone grey Rolls-Royce was sitting alongside the cargo shed at Coventry Airport. His matching grey chauffeur opened the back door of the vehicle so that he could speak to us.

'Everything OK, lads?'

'Yes, Mr Halton.'

'Go over and lodge the papers please, Charlie; then you and Pilot Scroton will return with me. I want you to take *Whisky* to Germany tonight.' He always called his pilots *Pilot*; almost as if it was a rank.

In the Customs office the one officer looked like a child of about fifteen in a navy blue uniform. He said, 'Thank you, Mr Bassett. Mr Holland called me about you.'

'Mr Holland?'

'Holland, the officer at Thurleigh. He asked me to give you this.'

This was a tin of fifty Senior Service export cigarettes with an export seal. He pushed them into the small pack I always carried for my gear. Then he turned away before I had time to ask why. Now I was a paid informant. A grass. I told you: everyone was at it in '48. It wasn't only the airfield that was on care and maintenance.

In the car the Old Man mostly ignored us, and concentrated on a great file of paperwork he ploughed through. I was amused to see that his mouth moved as he read. Dave and I had one of those inconsequential conversations that you have when the boss is in earshot. Now and again the Old Man joined in, with an acidic comment that would make us laugh. He was still coughing a lot. I do remember that at one point he leaned over, tapped me on the knee to fully engage my attention, and said, 'Come and see me next week, boy. Brunton will schedule you an appointment.'

'OK, sir. What have I done this time?'

'Nothing to worry about. We just have to talk about your next career. I went to an exhibition of radio technology last week. The new radios are so small and so simple that even our fools of pilots will be able to operate them.' He smiled at Scroton to take the sting out of it. 'The radio operator's days in commercial flying are numbered. We'll have to find you something else to do.'

I suppose that it was nice to feel wanted.

I phoned the Major from Lympne. He asked, 'Where are you?'

'Sussex. I'm off to the Fatherland again. Tell Dieter that his letter to Lottie is on its way.'

'Will do.'

'What's my house looking like?'

'It has a roof on it, running water and electricity. Almost there.'

'Did I ever say thank you?'

'All the time. Time you stopped. The Valentines were here last night. He still thinks that you work for me, and advised me to sack you. Apparently he's a Special Constable in the City in his spare time, and they've been giving him lectures about Communists and freethinkers. He definitely thinks you're a freethinker.' He laughed. I didn't see the joke.

'He *doesn't* think; that's his problem. I wonder what *Mrs* Valentine thinks.'

'She thinks that she's coming back on her own soon, for a few days' grass widowing, and asked me to remind you that you owed her a chess game. I didn't know that you played chess.'

'Schoolboy stuff.' We both laughed.

As I put the phone down Brunton put his head around the office door.

'That's *Whisky* all loaded and ready to roll, Charlie. Do you want to nip over and check your radios?'

I didn't particularly; but, what the hell – it's what I was being paid for. *Whisky* was still on the hard standing down by the Dell. I walked down to her because I needed the exercise, and to keep the buggers waiting. Her big cargo door was open when I arrived – noticing that almost distracted my attention from the patch of new oil on the concrete under the port engine. I hated this bloody aircraft. She had about half a load in the hold.

'What have we got?' I asked Crazy Eddie.

'Gold dust. Fifty-eight cases of tinned hams, and eight cases of ready-ground coffee. But for that, read *fifty-nine* and *nine*. We've got one of each extra. I gave the crew chief that brought them down a fiver. You can bung me your share later: OK?'

'Frankfurt again?'

'S'right. Then we do the odd part.'

'What odd part?'

'Taking the passengers on to an RAF station at Fassberg, that's north of Celle. Then we take them on to GGW.' GGW was one of the call signs for Gatow; that was the British airfield in Berlin. '. . . leave them there, and come back a couple of days later via Lübeck. The Old Man said he'd speak to you before we left.'

Hoo-bloody-ray. I should have noticed it as I climbed aboard. I would have done if it hadn't been for the oil leak: there were two new seats bolted in side by side on universal mounts down at the tail.

'What passengers?'

It seemed to me that Dave Scroton deliberately turned his back to us before Eddie replied, 'Old Man Halton is doing a favour for someone. The Skipper's gone all huffy about it, and won't talk.'

I could understand why; we weren't the tossers in BOAC with long-legged canapés and free air stewardesses. You probably think that I got that back to front, but I didn't: think about it. What would we do with the buggers for three hours' flying time? So much for keeping my people waiting; someone was keeping me hanging about instead. I sat on the lip of the cargo door with my legs dangling, smoked my pipe, and browsed an old book of Scottish poetry I'd found in the ready room. There was an endless verse about the Battle of Flodden by an old dog named Aytoun. Halton's Roller crawled around the peritrack to us. It seemed to take about a day. When the Old Man got out and hobbled over to me his coughing was worse than ever, and up close his voice smelt like cancer.

'Charlie . . .'

I hopped down to meet him halfway. 'Guv'nor.' He smiled. I guess he liked that. I asked him, 'The engineer hinted you wanted me to do something over there this trip.'

'I want you to keep your eyes open, and deliver our passengers safely. I want you to have a poke around Fassberg, which is an RAF station, and Lübeck if they let you, and tell me how much kit, or people, we'd have to ship into either if we were to contemplate regular runs to Berlin from there if we were asked to.'

'Are we going to be asked to?'

'You never know, do you?'

Maybe this was my new career. Poking around places. His eyes sparkled, until he started to shudder in another paroxysm of coughing. He smothered it with a handkerchief, and then spat, 'I want a written report when you get back. One I can use as a shopping list if I need to.'

Halton's chauffeur handed me up two hefty suitcases for stowing. When I turned back he was turning away to open the rear door of the big car for our passengers. The man emerged first. He still had a brown suit the colour of yesterday's shit, and a haircut like a toilet brush. He had a messenger bag handcuffed to one wrist and one of those new Stirling sub-machine guns carried almost casually in the other. From his crewcut hair to his brown suede shoes, he looked very twitchy. The woman showed about four yards of leg, and dark stocking tops as she followed him. I'd have known those legs anywhere.

Dolly Wayne, bless her, still carrying an old gas-mask case. If I still knew my Dolly then it contained noting more sinister than a clean change of smalls, her lipstick, handkerchief and a couple of French letters. Happy days!

Chapter Five

Dolly Wayne had been allocated the General's suite in the American HQ meeting house on Rossmarkt. There had been a Rossmarkt in most German cities and towns until the '20s. I think that it meant horse market . . . there aren't that many left now, because we bombed most of them. You can't de-nazify a horse; all you can do is eat it.

It wasn't really a house; it was a pocket palace, and relatively unscathed. Tommo once told me that we marked out the buildings we were going to occupy, and deliberately didn't bomb them. Jerry should have noticed that, and worked out what was coming. Privately I didn't think that our bombing was that good. If Marty Weir, our bomb aimer, had got within half a mile of what he aimed at we were satisfied.

She lay face down, sprawled over the huge old bed wearing nothing but her dark stockings. God had achieved His design peak in creating Dolly's behind – I'm going to tell Him that if I ever get to Heaven. Her bum had a gentle splash of freckles I never tired of kissing and counting. One stocking had slipped about three inches, and had wrinkled. I smoothed it up again, and asked her, 'What are you doing over here?'

Her reply was, 'Fucking you, I think. That wasn't half bad, Charlie; you're getting better at it.' Talking dirty never sounded

65

dirty when Dolly did it. What she meant was *I'm damned if I'm going to tell you*.

'You're not so bad yourself. Do you want me to find you a meal? You always used to provide the condemned man with a hearty meal after you'd shagged him half to death.' She smiled a smile as wide as the battered Brandenburg Gate; then a thought occurred to me. 'Where's your man? The one you brought in with you.'

'Angus is in his kennel in the basement, counting his bullets. He's very serious about bullets. He's supposed to look after me, and do the unpleasant stuff when it's called for.'

She'd already told me more than I expected.

'Will he be hungry too?'

'He's Scottish and doesn't eat: I think that he lives on fresh air, and runs up and down mountains for afters: he's the most boring man I've ever met.'

'But good at his job, I'll bet.'

'Don't know, Honeybunch: I've never asked him to do it.'

There was an old exchange of information still dividing us, and now was as good a time as any, I thought, to put it straight.

'If you're in charge now, Dolly, why didn't you come looking for me when Piers died?'

Piers had been her boss once, and for a while, I think, mine too. I'd held his hand while he died. She rested her chin on her hand, and extended a forefinger so that it crossed her lips. There was nothing about her face that was smiling, and yet everything was. That was it. She said, 'Turn away now, while I dress.'

'I like watching you dress.'

'I know you do. That's why you should turn away.'

I didn't, and halfway through we started all over again of course. She said she was glad to see that I had my appetite back.

They had given her a nice neat 4x4 command car with big

wheels. I drove it clumsily, heading for the Leihhaus. We had to present our papers at an American checkpoint, but Dolly got a great salute from the corporal of the guard. She'd let her skirt ride up so high he could see her breakfast. I didn't know if there would be any food at the Leihhaus, but if push came to shove we could always slope over to Tommo's place and eat Alice.

In the car Dolly told me, 'I was temporarily promoted when Piers died, and nobody's bothered to unpromote me yet. It can't last.' Only Dolly could take the word *unpromote*, and roll it around her mouth like that to give it a positively sexual charge.

'Well done. So you're in charge now?'

'Looks like it . . . but only for the time being.'

They've probably got an acronym of about thirty letters and numbers for her job now, and nobody talks about *The War Office* any more of course, because everyone knows that we Brits are a peace-loving bunch of sods. We call it the *Ministry of Defence*, but that fools nobody. Dolly Wayne was an RAF intelligence officer: and believe me, they are the very worst kind.

I asked, 'Still hungry?'

'Starving. You'd better be worth it.'

She slipped her arm through mine. We had once walked to a Sunday service at the Scottish church in Pont Street linked like that. It was a good memory. I had almost loved her then. She changed the subject.

'Where do you put up when you're over here?'

'With a woman you'll meet in about an hour.'

'You might have told me before we . . .'

'I don't sleep with her. I just stay at her place. She used to drive the coffee and doughnuts van up to the aircraft when I arrived.'

'Why don't you sleep with her?'

'Dunno. It never came up really. She's a very strong personality . . . you'll see.'

'She's saving it for Mr Wonderful then . . . poor Charlie.'

'Not really. She was a *Dankeschoen* girl long before *I* showed up.'

'Sorry . . . ?'

'A *Dankeschoen* . . . a girl you shag, give a bar of chocolate or a pair of nylons, and some money to afterwards . . . and she says *Dankeschoen.*'

'A whore, you mean?'

'Nearly . . . not quite.'

She worked it through and said, 'You know, Charlie, you have very unusual relationships with women.'

'No, I'm just lucky.'

'That too.' Her hand found mine on the steering wheel, and gave it a squeeze. It was my turn to work it through. I decided to tell her the truth.

'I don't think I understand the word *relationship* very well. I suspect it's a word that doesn't really mean anything.'

She gave my hand another squeeze. That could have meant anything, I suppose. Women are good at that sort of thing.

At the Leihhaus Marthe came to the table with her apron still on, and gave me a smacker. Russian Greg applauded. At first the two women sized each up like the mongoose and the cobra. *Rikki-Tikki-Tavi.* I introduced them. Then Marthe asked me, 'So, Dolly is your girlfriend?'

I said, 'No,' and Dolly said, 'Yes,' at the same time. Pause.

'Sort of,' I said, and, 'but you're my girlfriend too. I brought you some things.'

'I didn't tell Lottie you might bring her something too, in case you forgot.'

'I didn't forget. There's a bag in the car. Can I walk you home when we're finished?'

'OK. I suppose that you, and Dolly who's not your girlfriend, want to eat?'

'Yes please.'

'Omelettes do? Real eggs.'

'Yes please. Spot on.'

'*Spot on*,' she echoed laughing at me, and ruffled my hair. People only do that because I'm small. She swung her hips so wide as she sashayed away from us that I was afraid she would smack the guys at the tables either side as she passed. I realized that the women hadn't actually spoken to each other. I didn't like that.

'I didn't follow all that. When did you learn to speak good German?' Dolly asked me.

Greg snorted. He said, 'The only good one's a dead one; didn't they tell you that, English girl?' Then to me, 'Where you find this li'l girl, Charlie?' That was good, coming from him. Dolly was probably a foot taller than him.

'She's my passenger, and an old friend.' Then I told Dolly, 'My German's not all that good: barely adequate. It may sound silly but I actually don't know how the languages happen. I just seem to be able to pick them up. Greg's even taught me bits and pieces of Russian.'

'What do you know in Russian?'

'I know how to say *I surrender*, *please don't hurt me* and *your breasts remind me of sweet apples*. I can say that in a dozen different languages now.' Then I asked Russian Greg where he got all the eggs.

'From that American, Tommo. You wanna know where he gets them?'

'Yes.'

'From England somewhere; an' now two English people are eating them. What goes around comes around.' He must have caught that from me.

'International trade,' I told him. 'I'm all for it.'

*

69

We didn't walk home that night as it happened. Dolly gave us a lift. The two women still didn't address each other directly, which was a bit of a pisser. Lottie was asleep in Marthe's bed when I peeked in. I laid the doll on the pillow alongside her, and placed Dieter's letter under one of its arms. I could do that because Marthe stood alongside my sofa bed and announced, 'I sleep in here tonight,' and then asked, 'Why've you never had me, Charlie? All you got to do is ask.'

'I know. The subject just never came up.'

Marthe had a great laugh; a whore's laugh. Men like women who have a whore's laugh. And she knew a good pun when she heard one. The subject didn't come up that night either, but neither of us seemed to mind. I usually slept deeply and without dreaming at Marthe's place. When we woke up in the morning Lottie was jammed between us. So was the doll. We whispered across her; I reached out and touched Marthe's hair. It was heavy. She put her hand over mine and held it there. I asked, 'If I got used to the idea, do you think the subject might come up on my next trip?'

She pulled my hand down to her mouth, and kissed it. Lottie stirred but didn't wake.

'We don't love each other yet, Charlie, do we?'

'No, but when we're together we are rather formidable, aren't we?'

She repeated, 'Formidable' — in German gewaltig — as if she'd just discovered the word, and rather liked it. Lottie opened her eyes, and yawned. She smiled, and wriggled up to plant a kiss on my cheek.

'Thank you for Ilse, Uncle Charlie. I love her already.'

'Good. We saw her in a shop window in England, and she told us she wanted to come to a little girl in Berlin. Why have you called her Ilse?'

'The boy who wrote to me asked me to call her Ilse. He had a sister called Ilse; she died.'

I've said it before. You learn something new every day. All along Dieter and I had more in common than we realized: we each had a dead sister.

Before I left, I emptied my pack on Marthe's kitchen table. Four tins of hams, four of ground coffee and that tin of fifty Seniors. She squealed when she saw the coffee, kissed me, put two tins in her kitchen cupboard and pushed the other two to one side: she would sell those. The oddly shaped tins of ham were unlabelled. She asked, 'What are these?'

'Hams; whole hams. *Schinken*. Ready to eat.'

'Truly?'

'Truly.'

She kissed me again.

'Wonderful. I keep one, and sell three to Greg in the kitchen.'

'You keep two, and sell two. I want meat on your bones when I get back,' and I kissed her back. It was the first time a woman had treated me as if I was a good provider.

I had time to walk with them in the local park. Lottie carried Ilse as carefully as she would have done a newborn baby. Most of the women promenading in the weak sunshine had a man on their arm. Most of the men were in uniform, but none of the uniforms were German. A man in khaki and a woman leaned against a blasted tree, and everybody pretended not to notice. She had her eyes closed. I wondered who she was thinking of. A boy and an American captain flew a kite. Immediately after the war ended this would have been called *fratting*. I wondered when they'd stopped asking the sixty-five-dollar question. What the hell; I was a civilian and their rules didn't apply to me anyway.

We split at the park gates, underneath an equestrian statue scarred with bomb shrapnel and decapitated by an artillery round.

They walked off in one direction, and I another. Marthe had kissed me goodbye and said, 'I know that I am the luckiest woman in the city.'

I hated that. I hate it when people around me start talking about luck. That's when it usually starts to run out.

There was a battered small Auto Union at one of the cab ranks that were starting to reappear, and the driver cheered up when I offered to pay him in dollars. He said that he had a boot full of Deutschmarks which wouldn't even get him a tank of petrol. We stopped talking as we approached the rubble fields closer to Gatow; I don't think that I would have wanted to make small talk with an Englishman in the ruins of my own bombed city either.

Whisky was parked way over the far side of the field at Gatow, out close to its western perimeter. The Countess gave us a lift to her in the Hotdog wagon. Scroton rode up front with her, while Crazy Eddie and I were in the back. Eddie looked as if he had been crying, which meant that he would have been on an absolute bender the night before. We would have to watch his work until he straightened up. The big cargo door was open, but *Whisky* was empty this time. Except for two more bloody passengers. Two thin men in makeshift civilian clothes and peaked, black wool peasant's caps. They sat in the two seats near the tail. They had the thin European face that looked about a hundred years old. As I climbed up they offered me a scrap of paper each. Two railway tickets on which the word *Bahnhof* – railway station – had been neatly ruled through, and replaced by the name *Fliegerhorst*, neatly printed in ink. *Fliegerhorst* means airfield.

I told Scroton, 'I believe that *they* believe that someone's sold them a plane ticket.'

'That's all right then.'

'No it's not. This probably isn't legal.'

'Any sod who wants to get out of Germany is OK with me. Who are they? DPs?'

Both men gabbled at me in turn in a meaningless babble of sounds . . .

'They're Hungarian Jews,' Magda told us. I looked round to find her at my shoulder, which wasn't a bad thing, because, faced with the noises our passengers were making, my language skills folded their blankets and crept away.

'Thank you, Countess. What are they doing in our aircraft?'

She spat words at them, and they spat back. Maybe they weren't all that keen on countesses. She told me, 'They bought tickets. They are going to Israel.'

'But we're not. Tell them they're on the wrong plane. We're going the other way.'

Magda didn't even bother to consult them. She told me, 'Easier to get to Israel from England. They will fly to England with you.'

I was interested despite myself, because my best girlfriend had thumbed a lift to Palestine on a tramp ship the year before. 'What then?'

'They cross the Channel, and walk through France and Spain. Then they get a ship to Israel. Everyone knows that.'

'I didn't.'

'It's the old escape route set up for shot-down English airmen. The Jews took it over . . . they even use the same safe houses. Everyone knows that.'

'I told you; I didn't.' Then I asked the obvious: my speciality. 'Who sold them their tickets?'

'I saw your American friend talking to your engineer last night; after you left.' She gave me her come-hither smile. Except for the missing tooth it was a rather good one. When she inhaled on a cigarette the air whistled through the gap where the tooth had been.

Bloody Tommo and bloody Eddie! I swung on the latter. He still looked ill, but now he was blushing as well. I hadn't the heart to kick his backside for him. He said, 'You'd better make your mind up. The Customs are coming over for our papers.' He nodded towards a small green and white car moving away from the admin buildings, and beetling towards us.

I told him, 'Shut the bloody cargo door. We'll sort this out ourselves.' Just saying it made my mind up, didn't it?

I gave each Customs guy a packet of cigarettes with our outward clearance documents. *De Reszkes* I think. When they left they had smiling faces, anyway. We made small talk until they were a couple of hundred yards away.

Scroton was chain-smoking – never a good sign – and Eddie tugged my sleeve to get my attention. He said, 'It's going to be cold back there for them.'

I wrestled the cargo door open, and Magda did the talking. She gave each of them a small aluminium pot of coffee, a hot dog and a doughnut. They wolfed the hotdogs immediately. We hugged Magda. Then we mounted up, and I dogged the hold door behind us. As I pulled the curtain around my seat I leaned out, and held my thumb up to our passengers. I remembered that at Tempsford we called our passengers *Joes*. Each held a thumb up, and repeated the signal back to me. Not a bloody smile. I reckoned that I had three hours to work out how to get them off the bloody plane at Lympne without Brunton or Old Man Halton getting wind of it.

Whisky gave me the willies. We had to turn downwind after our landfall, and fly about thirty miles down the Channel. We were descending over the cold wet stuff and racing the twilight when the old girl's starboard engine gave out a colossal bang and started to stream a thin thread of white smoke. Scroton ignored it. Crazy Eddie didn't even look up. I was standing behind and between them, holding on to their seat frames for balance. I shouted, 'Shouldn't you *do* something?'

Dave said, 'Who? *Me?*' as if it was the last thing that would occur to him. I had this feeling that if he *didn't* do something it was the last thing that would occur to any of us.

Eddie asked, 'What do you *want* us to do?'

I glanced over my shoulder at the Joes. All I could see was two pale faces back in the shadow. The engines were definitely noisier; I had to shout.

'Something about the bloody engine . . .'

'Christ man, *no*. Either it'll keep running, or it won't.'

'What happens if it won't?'

Eddie seemed to consider the question for an age. Then he asked me, 'Can you swim?'

It came down to a race between us and the sun. Which we won, otherwise I wouldn't be here telling you the story, would I? Scroton hauled the old bitch over the headland, and into the valley. After that all he had to do was land her uphill, in a crosswind, across the field in the gathering twilight. We weren't authorized for night operations at Lympne because there wasn't a proper flare path yet – just a few goose-neck flare pots the RAF had left behind. When *Whisky*'s wheels started swishing through the grass it was already dark enough for the lights to be on in the Admin block . . . later Dave told me he just aimed for them. Both the Joes began to clap their hands as we touched down: maybe they were brighter than I took them for. We stopped for a couple of seconds on the peritrack on the way down into the Dell, popped open the hold door, and pushed them out into the hedge. As Eddie shut down the engines a minute later a great streak of flame poured out of the starboard exhaust and frightened the life out of me.

'I *hate* this aircraft,' I told nobody in particular.

'Aw, don't say that,' Eddie responded. 'She loves you; can't you tell?'

Brunton and his secretary, a neither pretty nor plain girl named

Elaine, were listening to the radio in his office, sharing a cheese sandwich and having a laugh. Brunton phoned the Customs office at Folkestone, and was told that it was OK for me to leave our papers in their postbox. They had an office in our block that they used, but they weren't coming out to clear an empty aircraft with no passengers at this time of day. Their loss, wasn't it? When Brunton left us I pinched one of Elaine's cheese sandwiches, and told her I'd like to pinch part of her. She told me that that wasn't the way to a girl's heart. It wasn't her heart I was thinking about, and we both knew it. Eddie and Scroton checked the board; they were on for a run to Beauvais the next day. I wasn't. Scroton ruffled my hair as they left, as if I was his fucking dog: I've already told you about that.

I was just working out whether Brunton would leave us alone long enough for me to ask Elaine for a date when the Old Man looked into the office. He coughed, beckoned to me, and asked, 'A minute, Mr Bassett.'

Old Man Halton knew how to do it right. He had the biggest office in the building, which was kitted out to double as a boardroom . . . even although, as far as I knew, we didn't have a Board. Perhaps he was just aiming high. He had his desk, a couple of leather armchairs, and his cupboards at one end of the room . . . and a table for twelve at the other. It was to the table he waved me, and we sat at adjacent seats. He coughed, and wiped his mouth with one of his big red handkerchiefs. I'd never asked him about his cough but he told me anyway.

'I was gassed in 1915. At Loos. They told me I had ten years if I was lucky. I've had more than thirty.'

'Then you were lucky, sir.'

'Luck's got nothing to do with it, boy; it's sheer cussedness, and we both know it.' I'm glad that we'd got that out of the way. He muttered, 'If you want to stay with me in the long run you're going to have to do something other than swan around in my aeroplanes, talking to bods on the radio. Wireless operators are for the dark, apart from the long-haul jobs – and we do precious few of them.' I was glad we'd got that out of the way as well. I couldn't fault him for straight talking, could I?

'*Well*? Do you want to? Stay here, I mean?'

'I rather think that I do,' I told him, and forgot the *sir*.

He didn't seem to notice. He grunted, 'Good,' coughed, and wiped again. The cough went on a bit.

'So what do you want me to do, sir?'

'Stay on as a radio officer in the short term, until we don't need those any more: I've already told you I can see that coming. Once the aircraft captains are running their own communications you can run the radio base station from here: it will be crucial to my operation – you can supervise that. You'll still be required in the aircraft for particular occasional flights of course, but I'm not looking for that sort of business at the moment . . .'

'OK.'

'. . . and I hear that you have an ear for languages, and seem to be able to handle the police and the Customs pretty well wherever you go. So whenever we set up a new office you'll be the first person in. It means you'll be away from home for a few weeks every now and again. Is that a problem?'

I thought about Dieter. He could come with me in his school holidays.

'No, none at all.'

The old man sighed.

'You're being promoted, Charlie: you're allowed to say *thank you*.'

I had a history of not being much good at being promoted. I probably grinned.

'Thank you sir. Sorry. I was thinking.'

'That's one of the few things I like about you, Charlie; you never seem to stop. How many radio officers have we?'

I could count to three.

'Three including me,' I told him.

'You can call yourself Senior Radio Officer from now on, and tell Mr Brunton to give you another fiver a week. You're going to earn it.'

Twenty quid a month is another two hundred and forty pounds a year. Rolling in it. This time I came in on cue. 'Thank you, sir.'

He waved a hand as if weary. 'You can start tomorrow by driving me to Fairleigh.' Fairleigh was another Battle of Britain station about twenty miles away — but still in RAF hands, I thought. 'My driver, Perry, has got to take his little boy into hospital: appendix. Get to know him; you'll find him useful. Zero nine thirty here. OK?'

So, for another two hundred and forty pounds a year I got to be a chauffeur. I wondered if I got the grey uniform and silly hat to go with it.

'Fine, sir.'

I don't know whether she'd planned it that way, but when I walked back into the general office Elaine was bending down, facing away from me, picking up something from the floor. She might as well have painted a bull's-eye on her derriere. At least it made me make up my mind quickly. I asked her, 'Where's Dick Barton?'

'Cycling home to mummy.'

'Isn't he married?'

'Same thing.'

She looked away as soon as she said it, and started to lock the office down for the night. She had a ring on her finger too. Just my luck. One of the boys working with the airfield crew came in to hand over his keys. The bunch was large enough to have a ceremony with. I finished the sandwich I had started before the Old Man grabbed me, and a half cup of coffee that Brunton had left. It was tepid, and too sweet. Elaine asked, 'Are you hungry?'

'No, not really. I was in Germany at the end of the war. Grabbing it while you can is a habit I got into.' I helped her on with her light coat, and waited until she'd locked the office door behind us. She had a cycle, like Brunton, because she only lived in the village. She asked me, 'What are you going to do tonight? Go to the pub?'

'First I'm going to walk down to *Whisky*, and make sure she's tucked up for the night.'

Actually, that was Crazy Eddie's job. I wanted to make sure that our two Joes were no longer in the hedge. Elaine leaned her bike back against the office wall.

'It's a lovely night for this early in the year. I think I'll come with you; all right?'

'Smashing. I'll be pleased if you do.' Actually *no*; that could be a problem.

Bad decision, Charlie: possibly dangerous. After five minutes I grabbed her hand when she stumbled on one of the small potholes in the peritrack, and I didn't let go again. I liked the feeling of her fingers curled about mine. There was no moon, but billions of stars. We didn't say much, and at one point I heard a huge sigh go out of her.

'Anything the matter?'

'No, I'm happy that's all.' It sounded like sitting at a traffic light and getting a green.

I could see that the hedge looked disturbed where the Joes had scrambled through it, but you would have to know it was there to spot it. We walked on down to *Whisky*. She looked a bit sinister by night; bloody old witch. *I'll put a spell on you.* I wandered around her with Elaine, touching the things I'd seen Scroton touch on his walk-rounds, but not knowing what the hell I was doing. That bloody navigation light was missing again. Finally we were at the cargo door, and I tried the handle.

Then I pushed Elaine against *Whisky*'s flank, kissed her, and inched her dress up. She was a great, soft kisser.

I said, 'I thought *you* were supposed to be married,' between hazy damp kisses.

I bloody knew she was, but I always liked to get them to say it if I could. That's a bad one, Charlie. She nipped my lower lip in revenge, and then sucked on it to take away the pain.

'So what?' It wasn't much more than a breathy whisper. 'I was here at the end of the war too. Grabbing it while I can is a habit I got into too.'

When we came up for breath again she still whispered.

'I always wanted to do it in an aeroplane, but never have until now.'

'I'm sorry love, we can't. Not inside. It's bad form. Shagging in aeroplanes makes people die in them. I saw that too often on the squadron.'

She bit my ear, gently,

'The only way you're going to get inside my knickers tonight, Charlie Bassett, is if *I* get inside your smelly old aeroplane. *Capisce?*'

Second bad decision, Charlie. I opened the hold door, and helped her to scramble over the sill, hoping that she wouldn't ladder her stockings. Inside in the dark we must have reached out for each other simultaneously, because I found myself, ludicrously, holding on to her thumb. Elaine giggled, found my neck and my ear, cuddled into me and whispered into them, '*This old man, he played one, he played nick nack on my thumb . . .*'

We explored every verse of the old song, and then some more. It's remarkable just how many words more or less rhyme with *one*. It was the first time I realized what the rhyme was really about. Every filthy verse of it. It's lovely: you try it.

Chapter Six

Driving the Roller was easier than I'd imagined. I suppose that if you pay that much for a car you wouldn't expect it to be impossible to drive. The only things that worried me were the narrow country lanes around Fairleigh. There was no room for a slow waltz if a maniac with a horse and cart came tearing round some of the corners at you. I couldn't communicate with the Old Man because he sat twenty yards away, in the back, with a briefcase full of papers. From time to time he rattled away with a small wooden abacus – it was the first time I'd seen one since primary school. I'd checked the route on an old Bartholomew's map I'd found in the office, and was pleased to get us there in under the hour. If he was pleased to see me wearing a smart grey suit, polished brown brogues and an RAF tie, he didn't say so.

There were cars parked everywhere along the lane leading to the Fairleigh gate. Halton urged me forward, and the RAF policeman on the barrier gave him a great salute as he waved us through. There was a big empty parking space in front of the Officers' Quarters. I had the feeling it had been left for us. The problem, of course, was the aircraft – there were bloody hundreds of them. I'd never seen anything like it before.

Fairleigh had been a fighter section station until 1943, when they'd built a 4,000-foot concrete runway across it. After that it was an emergency landfall for wounded bombers coming back from the Fatherland. Later still it became an invasion springboard for D-Day. Now it was full of aircraft again. I didn't open the door for Old Man Halton – I wasn't that sort of chauffeur. He frowned, but quickly worked out how to do it for himself.

'What the hell's going on here?' I asked him. He frowned again. Don't swear, Charlie, and remember the *sir* . . . 'Sir.'

'It's an aircraft sale, Charlie. Hosted by our good friends the RAF, because, coincidentally, most of the aircraft for sale happen to be theirs. War surplus.'

'And we . . . ?'

'. . . are going to buy some aeroplanes. Yes.' He gave me a handful of his business cards. 'Wander off, and pick me out some good ones: make yourself useful. I'm going inside to meet my good friend Reg Waite.'

'What do you want, sir?'

'Two heavy-lift cargo-carriers and one or two smaller ones. Brunton talked me into our last buy, *Dorothy*, and she's proved a bit of a disaster. See if you can do any better.'

It was as crowded as Brighton beach out there, but it didn't take me long to work out that most of the potential purchasers were scrap metal merchants. A tired old Mk II Lancaster with Hercules engines had more than a hundred mission markings painted under her cockpit, poor cow. I watched a scrappy buy her. After all that they'd been through these wonderful old ladies were going to be cut up and melted down. Wandering among them was like walking around a graveyard where the corpses have been left to rot above the ground. I hadn't bought an aircraft before, and under these circumstances found it a vaguely distressing experience. I suppose I twigged that when a country dumps its war materials it has also dumped the men who used them.

I picked him out two Lancastrians, and put a marker on them – that was giving the RAF corporal in charge a couple of Halton's cards. The corporal chalked *Halton Air* above their fuselage doors with heavy red crayon, and locked them up. That was two I'd saved from the knacker's yard, anyway. Lancastrians were civilianized Lancaster bombers, which had been converted in the factory by Avro before being supplied to the RAF. They could haul people or things. The RAF was switching to Avro Yorks for its transport needs. With *Dorothy* in mind, I came to the conclusion that the RAF had made a mistake. The Lancastrians' light grey paint was worn from standing outside for all their brief lives, but inside they looked almost unflown, and they were going for not much more than the cost of a new family car. There's nothing much peaceful you can do with a Spit, a Tiffie or a Beau, and there were plenty of those as well, but finding him something smaller was not going to be as easy. Not until I met Randall, that is.

Randall was sitting on the wing root of an olive drab Airspeed Oxford. An Oxford was like a scaled-down version of *Whisky*. Two engines, but still pretty small all the same. And actually, not very pretty either. We used Oxfords to train bomber pilots and crews when we still had Germany to bomb. But they could also be cheaply converted to haul a few passengers, or small amounts of freight.

Randall was a competent American who had flown, mysteriously, for our government — *very important people in a hurry*, he used to say — and his first love was this battered old aircraft. He'd flown me in it a few times in the last few years, although I could fairly be described as neither. Physically Randall was one of the largest men I'd ever met. Shaking his hand was like doing one-arm press-ups. Usually he looked happier than this.

I said, 'Hi, Randall. What ho.'

He must have seen me coming because he didn't even look up.

'Fuck off, Charlie.'

'Nice to see you too, sir. What are you here to buy? One of these?'

'Nope.'

'Don't tell me they're flogging you along with the aircraft?'

'Don't try to be funny. I came along to see her go to a good home.'

He'd always been a stronger man than me, in every sense, until then. Now there was something hollow and hurt in him. He must have known that chances were that his aircraft would be going for scrap, so I spoke quietly.

'Sorry, Randall. You know what I'm like, don't you?'

'Yes. You're an arsehole. You're an arsehole who always needs me to fly you out of trouble . . . which won't happen any more.'

Randall was another non-swearer so he must have been letting the pressure get to him.

People just hate it when I come up with ideas of my own. 'Won't it just, though?' I asked him.

I found Old Man Halton sitting in the Officers' Mess bar, reading *The Times* and drinking gin. I stood back at the door with Randall, playing the family retainer bit, until he looked up, saw me and beckoned us forward. He stood up to meet Randall: he had that sort of class, even if his hand disappeared inside the American's. I reckon Randall's bulk exceeded Halton's and mine put together . . . he certainly occupied more space. For once Randall looked more or less respectable: he wore clean USAAF chinos and shirt, but no tie . . . and an old leather bomber jacket which must have been privately made, because no company makes anything that size deliberately.

I said, 'Randall; this is Mr Halton, my boss. He owns Halton Airways.' I should have said *Sir Somebody Somebody Halton*, but I always got that wrong. To the Old Man I said, 'This is Randall Claywell Junior, sir. He's an American pilot, and a friend of mine.'

Friend was actually pushing it a bit.

'Good morning, Mr Claywell.' He smiled then he asked me, 'Did you buy us anything?'

'Yes sir. I reserved two Lancastrians for you. They're almost new, and having Merlin engines like *Dorothy* means that you won't need to engage or retrain ground crew for them. They're almost giving them away.'

'Anything else?'

'Two Airspeeds. They're as strong as oxen, and will last you years if Milton doesn't drop them.' (I've already told you Milton was another of our pilots. He was famed for his clumsiness.)

I couldn't work out if he was being a patronizing git when he said, 'Well done, Charlie . . .'

'And I bought you something else,' I told him. 'Used my initiative.'

He didn't frown or anything like that. He had a coughing fit which lasted minutes. When he looked up his face still wore a quizzical, friendly look.

'I bought Randall for you as well. He's just received a *Dear John* letter from the War Office, and they're selling his aircraft. You've just bought it. I decided to buy him with it.'

The quizzical look didn't waver, but I was suddenly rather aware of a dangerous old sod behind it weighing up his options.

'I don't think I need another pilot, Charlie.' He sounded a bit like a schoolmaster saying, *See me after school, boy*.

'You need *this* one. Randall can land an Oxford on a bit of grass not much bigger than your handkerchief. At night without lights. And take off again uphill, with eight passengers on board. If we're being smart, sir, you need him more than you need me.'

There was one of those long frozen silences where no one wants to be the first to break it, and then Halton said, '. . . and don't call me *sir* when you don't really mean it, Charlie.'

'No, boss. It would mean that you could get rid of that wanker Milton before he breaks something, or kills somebody.'

'I can't do that.' That was quick. Then he said, 'You've got it all worked out, Charlie, haven't you?'

'Not quite, boss.' What I had worked out was that he *did* need me; although I didn't know what for. He laughed, then coughed and then laughed again. Several conversations at nearby tables stopped to watch him. He didn't give a damn.

'Sit down, Mr Claywell. Go and find a Mess boy, Charlie. Let's have some lunch.'

He offered Randall a six-months contract. That may sound a bit dodgy to you, but we were all on six-month contracts, so it meant that Randall was in. The Old Man asked him, 'Where do you live?'

'I have a small flat up in town, sir.'

'You'll be based at Croydon, OK?'

'Fine, sir.'

'Fly one of the Oxfords up there today; come back tomorrow for the other one. You'll do most of the maintenance yourself.'

'Fine, sir.'

'Charlie?'

'Yes, boss?'

'Find a telephone, and call Elaine. Tell her to book some hangar space for the Oxfords at Croydon. There's plenty to spare over on the far side. And tell her we have another pilot on the books.'

'What about the Lancs?'

'I'm still thinking about that. Can we get them into Lympne like *Dorothy*?'

'I don't see why not. But you should really ask a pilot.'

He turned away, said, 'Mr Claywell . . . ?'

Randall looked up, but I butted in before he had a chance.

'No, boss. Not Randall. Randall would try to land a B-17 in a tennis court. You'll have to ask a normal pilot.'

The old man went into a prolonged bout of coughing again;

then he went into a prolonged bout of laughing again. They didn't sound all that different.

He kicked us out so that he could have another meeting with his pal, Air Commodore Reginald Waite to you and me. They were up to something, and I didn't know what. That always got to me. I hate it when the bosses start plotting. Randall and I wandered out among the beautiful old girls who were soon to end up as cubes of aluminium and bundles of electrical cable. It was all so bloody sad.

There was a young businessman over near half a dozen late-mark Spits – probably mark fourteens – he had a smart black suit, a regimental tie, and was chatting up the RAF engineering lieutenant charged with selling them off. They shook hands, and the man turned away. *Done deal*, I thought. There was something familiar about the way he moved. He joined someone identically attired, who was obviously closing a purchase on three tired Marauder light bombers. Click. They were my two Joes. Maybe they'd changed their minds: instead of bumming their way to Israel they'd decided to buy a small air force. Mazeltov.

Even although the words which passed between Elaine and me were nothing but professional and cool, I received a tremendous sexual shock from the conversation, and I knew immediately that the same thing was happening to her. It was as if the telephone had come alive in my hand. I couldn't wait to have her again – sorry to put it as bluntly as that, but it was interesting.

The Old Man was saying goodbye to a senior RAF officer as I made my way back to the Rolls. He introduced me. If I had been his gardener he still would have introduced me: I think that they call that 'old-fashioned charm'. Then he said, 'This is Air Commodore Waite, Charlie. The Air Commodore has had a heretical idea.' I grinned, and shook his hand. What else was I supposed to do? Halton's eyes twinkled. He went on, 'The city of Glasgow has two airfields, Charlie – Glasgow Renfrew, and

Glasgow Abbotsinch. The Air Commodore believes that if, for some reason, the road, railway and sea routes into Glasgow were completely closed down, we could easily supply the entire needs of the civilian population indefinitely by air. Using those two airfields.'

I went cold. I clasped my hands behind my back, because I didn't want anyone to see that they were trembling. I can read the newspapers the same as anyone else, and what's more I could take the hints that Russian Greg dropped from time to time. The bastards weren't talking about Glasgow; they were talking about somewhere a lot bigger and further away. They were talking about *Berlin*.

Milton had curly brown hair that stuck up from his scalp like a hedge. It was almost red. He was younger than me, I think, and his face was smothered with freckles. He looked as if he had stepped from the pages of the *Beano* or the *Dandy*. We sat outside the ops block on deckchairs. Behind and above us, the office window was open, and we could hear Elaine singing along with an American called Dean Martin. *Once in Love with Amy*. The way he sang it, I could have fallen in love with Amy myself. I had changed back into my work clothes, and felt very comfortable in the sun . . . it shouldn't have been that warm at the start of April.

In for a penny; in for a pound: I said, 'I gave the Old Man the opportunity to sack you this morning, and he wouldn't do it. I thought that was interesting.'

'He wouldn't. He once knew my mother rather well.' Milton had one of those irritating Surrey nasal drawls.

'When was that?'

'Twenny-three, twenny-four years ago.'

'How old *are* you, Colin?'

'Twenny-two or three. You?'

'Twenty-four.'

We had a bottle of beer each. No flying. *Whisky* was still away with Scroton and Crazy Eddie. God knows where *Dorothy* was. A big column of black smoke was drifting back from a burning car down in the Dip, at the lowest end of the field. The Fire and Maintenance Gang had put a match to an old Austin in order to practise extinguishing fires. They weren't having much luck. The car had burned like a torch for half an hour so far. I made a mental note not to be inside a burning aircraft around here.

Milton was nothing if not direct. 'Why did you try to get rid of me?'

'. . . because you're such a goddamned awful pilot. Everyone says so. Everyone says a little prayer when you take a kite up, because they don't think they'll see it again.'

Elaine was singing with Jo Stafford now: *The Best Things in Life Are Free*.

'You're beginning to sound like a company man, you know,' Milton yawned. 'Anyway it's not wholly true; I'm very good with singles. It's just that I've been a bit slow on the uptake with twins and multis.' He meant twin-engined and multi-engined aircraft.

'But all of our aircraft *are* twins or multis.'

He yawned again. 'You have a point, old son, but fear not . . . you'll find I'm very good in a crisis. All my flying skills come to the fore then.' Then he added, 'When I next get you fired I'll tell *you*, as well.'

'Why should you want to do that?'

''Cos you've made away with the fair Elaine, whom I rather fancied myself.'

'Why would you think that?'

'Dunno. Everyone's talking about it. The Squadron Leader's going to be pretty teed off when he finds out.'

Above our heads the window slammed shut, and I said, 'Shit.'

'Any good, was she?'

I said, 'I haven't a clue what you're talking about,' but it sounded unconvincing, even to me; I probably blushed.

Later I learned that one of the fitters had found a pair of smalls in the back of *Whisky*, and the others quickly worked out that Elaine and I were the last off station. Two and two: in the original sense probably. *How the hell can a girl go home without her knickers, and not know it?*

'Just how good were you flying fighters?'

'*Very*, old man – particularly Hurricanes: the good old *Hurrie*. T P F F.'

Same day, same people, same sun, but later. We were on a seat outside Lympne's only pub.

'What's that? T P F F?'

'Take-off check list for the Hurrie. Trim; prop; fuel and flaps. I can still remember them.'

'I should bloody well hope so; we're not that drunk.'

He held up his beer, and squinted down the road through it. It was slightly cloudy.

'Lo. The fair Elaine cometh.'

She was walking, pushing her bicycle and smiling. The sun sparkled in her hair. Before she was in earshot he asked me, 'So you didn't couple with the fair lady?'

'Wouldn't tell you if I had. Flattering of you to think of me, though.'

He sighed, then admitted, 'I'd better uncirculate the rumour I started then.'

'. . . and apologize to the fair lady,' I said as Elaine flopped onto the seat alongside him, and smiled.

'Don't bother. I've already taken my revenge.' When we didn't ask, she informed Milton, 'I've told everyone the knickers are probably yours – that you wear girl's knicks under your flying clothes. No one will want to fly with you after that. Get me drink: a Pink Lady if they've the makings.'

Milton looked suitably hangdog. 'No one wants to fly with me as it is.'

'There you are then. That's fixed you properly.'

'I'll fly with you, Colin,' I said.

He said, 'Good God!' before he left to fetch her some alcohol.

Elaine told me, 'I think you're madder than he is.' She slipped over and gave my arm a quick squeeze.

'Why aren't you angry any longer? You were pretty mad when you slammed the window on us.'

'I'm used to it, I suppose. If you believed all you heard I've slept with every man at the airfield. There's a different one every week.'

'Why?'

'Something to do with being the only presentable female in the middle of a herd of unpresentable men. Wishful thinking. It's something girls have to put up with.'

'I thought that maybe you were Brunton's girl.'

'I once thought that maybe I was going to be.' She looked out towards the war memorial at the road junction. There were new names on it. There was regret in her face, I thought. Then she said, 'This arrangement's much better. I say; you *are* single, aren't you?'

'Yes. Of course. No one would have me.'

'I would.' Maybe she'd already said too much.

'You'd change your mind,' I told her. 'Before long you'd find me too much of a good thing.' That seemed to take the heat out of the conversation. I started to wonder where Milton had got to.

'Are you staying on tonight?' Elaine asked me.

'Yes. I'm in the accommodation hut. On my own I think.'

'Good. They *weren't* my knickers, by the way. That's not a mistake I'd make so easily.'

So who, for God's sake, had lost them?

Milton appeared just in time. He had two pints and two pink ladies; he obviously expected Elaine to catch up with us. Everyone knew that her husband Terry was a long-distance lorry-driver flogging big Fodens up and down the Great North Road. He was home at weekends. After the first time I never asked again about her being married and she didn't quiz me about being single. It seemed to work.

That night, squeezed into the narrow bed alongside me, she told me, 'You can go home tomorrow if you like. Don't come back until next Thursday. Every aircraft will be in and out of the workshops for days . . . just like yo-yos. Halton's having them all painted in a company livery.'

'What will that be?'

'*All Day Permanent Red*.' That was an advertisement for Max Factor lipstick I think. It came back years later.

'Seriously?' I could feel her breasts rubbery against my chest, and knew that if we were still awake in twenty minutes I would want her again.

'Seriously. Like half the newspaper joke.'

'I'm sorry love, I haven't heard that one.'

She laughed quietly, and kissed my chest a couple of times before she responded. Like a dog gnawing on a nice old bone.

'What's black and white and red all over?'

'Ah, that one: a newspaper.'

'Your aeroplanes are going to be red all over. Like *Dorothy*.'

'*Whisky* will look like a run-down butcher's shop.'

'Only on the outside, Charlie.'

She humped up about six inches, and kissed me on the mouth until we stopped talking.

*

92

Carlo sat on my lap, and read a very simple book to me. I hadn't realized that three-year-olds could read. Maggs looked as pleased as punch, and told me, 'Dieter's been learnin' him. He's very forward for his age: a proper little Albert.' It was a phrase that everyone was using; she meant *Einstein*. Dieter looked properly gratified as well. He was reading a Penguin aircraft recognition book, and grinned at me over his new specs.

'Which one?' I asked Maggs. 'Which one is forward for his age?'

'Boaf of 'em,' she pronounced triumphantly.

'You're doing very well,' I told her.

'A potter's only as good as 'is clay,' she explained.

If you said kind things about the boys you didn't need to bring her presents. I did anyway. It was a lace shawl from Alsace. She turned away when she took it from me: tears in her eyes.

'If I didn't have my Major,' she told me, 'there's no way any other woman'd get anywhere near you, Charlie Bassett.' Whenever she felt particularly fond of me she used both my names, which was a little bit odd. My present to James was $3600. It had been $2800 when I had set out from England ten days earlier.

'Doesn't the bank ever say anything?' I asked him.

'Yes, Charlie. Usually it says *thank you*.'

I told you before: everybody was at it in 1948.

Friday afternoon. James's place had a new pub sign. He took me outside to admire it. It showed three raggedy-looking soldiers clustered around an equally raggedy-looking khaki staff car, and the words *Happy Returns*.

'You're a sentimental old twerp,' I told him.

'You like it then?'

'Of course I do. Les will love it as well. It may put off any German sailing types though.'

'Haven't seen any of those yet.'

'No, I think we stole all their yachts. I saw one sailing through Belgium on the back of a three-tonner.'

'Can't help thinking it served them right. The Jerry was a frightful beggar when it came down to it, wasn't he?'

I thought about Marthe and Lottie. 'Not all of them.'

James picked me up wrongly. 'I didn't mean Dieter. He's one of us now.'

I had driven down in my old Singer, and abandoned it in James's car park. It had a few dents and scrapes, and one small cut in the canvas hood, but still looked like a class act. James had a gravel car park which took about eight cars. He could always expand it if he needed to, but most of his customers at the weekends walked up the quay from their boats anyway, so why would he bother?

Evelyn Valentine swept in in a new Sunbeam Talbot sports car. It was powder blue, and had a long sweeping tail for sweeping in to places with. She was wearing about a hundred pounds' worth of clothes; a pair of slinky sea-green silk trousers, and a natural wool sweater three sizes too large for most of her. Dark glasses and a headscarf which matched her trews. Make that a thousand pounds. It was the first time it occurred to me that Mr and Mrs V weren't short of a bob or two.

'Hello, Charlie; hello, James.' She removed the sun specs, and frowned. 'Do you prefer *Charlie* or *Charles*?'

'Charlie.'

'I forgot; I'm sorry. I'm always forgetting things.'

Was that a warning off, or just a warning?

'So do I. I think I owe your husband an apology, don't I? I don't know why I wanted to thump him.'

'I do: happens all the time. You'll have to wait anyway: he's gone to Birmingham for the weekend to play a golf competition against some tiresome man with no legs. I'm a grass widow for a few days.'

No, it hadn't been a warning off. She dropped her eyes, and then looked up again in exactly the right places in the speech. Dieter had been watching her, a finger in his mouth and spellbound, from the restaurant door on the side of the building. The thought occurred to me again: maybe he and I had more in common than we knew. I lifted her bag from the boot of her car – it was the first time I'd seen a sports car with a boot large enough to climb into. I also carried the bag down the quay for her, to where *The Lady Grace* was now lashed alongside. She removed her shoes to climb down to the yacht, and moved competently around on its decks. Her feet were very white, her lipstick, finger- and toenails very red. Probably that *All Day Permanent Red* Elaine had told me about. The grin she gave me when I handed her case down to her was very cheeky.

'See you tonight in the bar, maybe.'

Now, God doesn't often drop life's little prizes straight into your lap. When he does my advice to you is to accept them with gratitude. And immediately. What was that phrase again? *Grabbing it while you can becomes a habit:* something like that.

I sat with the boys in the evening, watching them scoff their teas. Maggs had put a fry-up in front of them. Both came back for more fried white bread. My function was to provide the entertainment; the stuff that Charlie Chester was doing on the radio was a bit too sophisticated for them. I drank a pint of beer and started a round of I-Spy, and Maggs cautioned them for speaking with their mouths full. After they had readied themselves for bed I read Carlo a story – the same book he'd read to me on the day I arrived – and Dieter surprised me by sitting on the arm of my chair to share it. They chanted *The Grand Old Duke of York* as they stumped up the steep, narrow staircase to their bedroom. Maggs was making a rather splendid job of them. I still wasn't a proper parent, but maybe I was moving closer to it.

I ate supper with James and Maggs in the bar before it opened. James's new chef Jules served us a beef stew topped off with baked slices of potato. I wondered why nobody ever called James *Jim*. Jules and Jim sounded all right to me. He was originally French, ex-Catering Corps, a bit of a bruiser and a bit of a find. He didn't particularly want to return to France. Anyone could understand that. He sat in the bar, and smoked a French cigarette while we ate: the scent took me back a couple of years. James told me he was living in a caravan until they could make a more permanent arrangement. That was when I realized he was waiting for my room upstairs when I took the prefab.

As far as women were concerned I had never hidden much from James, and couldn't from Maggs anyway.

'My love life,' I told them, 'can be really bloody confusing. Sometimes I don't know if I'm on my head or my heels.'

Maggs had run a small brothel in Paris during the war. She sniffed and said, 'My girls knew some o' them tricks too.'

'No, that's not what I mean, Maggs. What happens is that I have no girlfriends for weeks and weeks, and then two or three come along at the same time . . .'

'Just like buses,' James said. 'Yes, I know what you mean, although I don't know why you're complaining.'

'It's inefficient,' I told them. 'I always hated inefficiency . . .'

'If I was you I'd grab it while you can, Charlie love.' That was Maggs of course.

Then someone rattled the bar door from the outside. The Frenchman sighed, stubbed out his cigarette, looked at his wristwatch then moved to unlock it. Through the glass panes I could see Evelyn's face. She looked hungry.

By the time Evelyn drove away on Monday morning my balls ached. She worked me like a navvy. The forepart of *The Lady*

Grace's accommodation was one large bed, and I got to know it from most angles. Its ornate decoration and hangings told me that the vessel didn't go to sea all that often.

When I wasn't with her I was with the boys. They wanted to walk up the Roman road the other side of Chichester again, and we did so, under the trees and hiding from the drizzle. Going to church again on Sunday morning worried me a bit, but I spent the time there thinking about Fergal, and wondering how he was getting on. After that we all ran out on the shingle, and flew a kite that James said had been his when he was a boy.

I was there on Monday morning to lift Evelyn's case back into her car. Her hair shone in the overcast like the oiled black of a crow's wings. Despite the hard red slash of her lipstick across her pale face you could have almost taken her for a happy woman. On Monday night I relieved James's bartender in the small bar, and got a bit sideways from the drinks the customers bought me. On Tuesday I washed up the crocks for Jules in the restaurant, but Tuesday night turned bad.

That was because he phoned me on Tuesday night. He must have got my number from the office. Old Man Halton. I knew that it was him when the phone coughed at me. I said, 'Yes, boss?'

'Can you come down on Thursday, Charlie? We have to get things moving.'

'I was going to anyway. What things?'

'Haven't you listened to the News today?'

'No, what's happened?'

'The Russians have shot down a BEA Viking in one of the air corridors. It was full of passengers.'

'Any survivors?'

'No.'

'*Fuck* it.' Say it with feeling.

Halton said, 'You know that I don't like people swearing, Charlie . . .'

'Yes, boss; sorry, boss . . .'

'. . . but on this occasion I happen to agree with you. Winston's warning us that the Reds will have closed down all access to Berlin by road, rail or canal before the summer's out. For once I agree with him too . . . So yes; *fuck* it . . .' and he put the receiver down at his end. Then it happened again: my hand was shaking. One of these days I was going to wake up brave, just like everyone else.

I decided to drive across on the Wednesday, following the coastal road, but that still left time for me and Carlo to raid the Chichester bookshop before it closed for its half-day. I always loved English towns on Wednesday afternoons after the shops had all closed: it was as if a sprinkling of fairy dust had put the population to sleep. Dieter wanted a Biggles book. I bought him two because I didn't know when I would be back — and later told Maggs to hold one back for a week or so. Carlo wanted a picture book about a cat that flew an open-cockpit aeroplane and delivered the airmail. The aircraft was completely red, like a GPO delivery van . . . and the aircraft I would be flying for the next few months . . . and it seemed to crash a lot. I suppose that having nine lives makes a cat an over-confident pilot. They were always worse than the cautious ones.

James and Maggs came out to see me off. It was as if we all knew that something was starting to happen again, but didn't want to bring it up. I had the hood down because, even though the sun wasn't showing through, it was still an unseasonably warm day. Maggs reached in, and ruffled my hair. I didn't mind *her* doing it. She said, 'I been thinking about what you said about the women you go wiv.'

'What is it, Maggs?'

'You get your share right enough, but what's worrying is that none of 'em like you enough to stick around fer long . . . you gotta work harder at it, Charlie.'

Trust a woman to put the blame back on me. I said, 'I love you, Maggs.'

She leant over, and gave me a peck on my cheek. James put his hand on my shoulder when he said goodbye. He didn't usually touch people. That's when I realized that maybe they thought they'd never see me again. I looked out along the quay, and noticed that *The Lady Grace* was flying a small flag quartered in white and blood red squares. I might have been wrong, but a fading signal from my memory seemed to be telling me it was the naval signal flag for the letter U. Flown alone it meant *You are standing into danger*.

Chapter Seven

Two hours, and the further I drove the colder it became. Eventually I stopped and fished my flying helmet and split-lens goggles from my pack. I must have looked quite the thing – like the racer Reg Parnell maybe.

Someone must have told them I was coming, because the stove in the small accommodation hut was burning. I was hungry, so I roared it up, and stuck a tin of baked beans and a tin of Spam on top – after piercing them with my knife of course. They were ready in an hour, and washed down well with a couple of bottles of Worthington. I could have gone on to the pub, or found Elaine, but I just wanted a couple of hours without the pressure of people I knew around me. Do you know what I mean?

Eventually I jumped back in the car and went down to the Odeon at Sandigate Road in Folkestone. It was showing *The Brasher Doubloon* with Nancy Guild. Just before I went in I remembered that she could be a bit of a shrieker; not my type at all.

It was the Movietone News before the feature that really grabbed my attention; they ran an item on the Vickers Viking incident in Germany. They showed some grainy, shadowy images of smouldering wreckage that the Soviets had handed over, because the aircraft had fallen out of the corridor and into their sector. It was a scheduled BEA passenger flight in a nearly new aircraft. It hadn't been shot down; it had collided with a

Communist Yak fighter. The Russians were saying that it was all our fault of course. They flashed up a publicity still of the Viking's crew. BEA was still heavily into radio officers, and this one was Charlie Mamser. I knew him because we had been on the same course. It was the moment I realized that we were at war again. Funnily enough, after seeing that I didn't get the shakes again until 1949.

'Hands off cocks; hands on socks!'

The door bounced with his blows. Bloody Scroton again. He was getting bolder. He always stayed up in the village; I never worked out with whom. He'd brought my breakfast from the Parachute on the way: a fried egg sarnie, with lashings of salt and sauce. The warm yolk splattered and ran down my chin. Brilliant. Halton Airways was on parade on the grass in front of the little brick admin block. That was *Dorothy*, old before her time, *Whisky*, and the two new Avro Lancastrians. They were all painted red.

'Christ,' Crazy Eddie muttered. 'Custer's last stand!'

The two Lancastrians had *Tin Man* and *Scarecrow* lettered neatly in black on their great red noses . . . and I do mean *great* red noses. A Lancastrian had a nose like Schnozzle Durante; if you can still remember who he was. The Old Man had even been able to wangle appropriate registrations for them: *Tin Man* was G-HATM. You could read that as Halton Airways *Tin Man;* she was *Tommy Mother* when we were on air of course; *Tommy* for short. I can't say that red is my favourite colour. I think that most men who've been to war would tell you the same thing. *Whisky* looked awful; they'd painted around the naked bint on her nose: she was still perched on a trio of black *W*s with an evil smile on her face. She still wore nothing but a black, pointed witch's hat.

'Where did you spring from?' I asked Ed.

'I came down on the milk train this morning; special request. I always knew that it was a mistake to give the office a telephone number.'

'How long have you had a telephone?'

Ed sniffed. I suddenly realized that he sniffed a lot. 'Don't. It's my auntie's. She has to come down the street for me.'

'Eddie lives in Earlsfield,' Scroton told me. 'It's the posh end of Wandsworth.'

'Where are we going today then?'

'*You're* not, Charlie. The boss has left you a brown envelope that doesn't look like a pay packet. We've got to air test *Jasta 11*.' He motioned to the aircraft behind him by jerking his thumb over his shoulder.

At first I didn't get him, and then a misspent boyhood with Biggles kicked in, and I remembered that Jasta 11 was the Red Baron's squadron in 1918, and that they painted all their bloody aircraft bloody red. It didn't cheer me up, because you know what happened to poor old Manfred, don't you? The bloody colonials shot him, and they're still arguing about by whom.

I sat in the front office with Elaine, and fingered my envelope. I opened it when I saw she wasn't in the mood for a chat. Old Man Halton had a thing about *shopping lists*. He'd used the phrase before. He wanted me to go to Celle, the memo said, and Lübeck and Gatow. I was to examine a small office at each airfield, give the RAF a shopping list of the furniture and fittings to put in them. He thought that if we could get in before the other airlines we could get our own accommodation . . . with his friends pulling the strings, I got the feeling that anything was possible. Very good of the RAF, wasn't it? I was also to make a contact at each place who could arrange overnight accommodation for our crews if pinch came to shove. *Mine not to reason why*, although I did wonder. How many other private airlines were already asking for facilities at airfields in Germany? How many would get them? Pretty few, I'd guess. Maybe none.

Apart from the Yak hitting the Viking passenger flight in the corridor, all of the rest of the traffic – along the autobahn, railway and canals – was getting through to the Big City OK as far as I knew. It was almost as if Halton was planning for a worst-case for Berlin . . . not that it would be worst-case for him: anyone with an aircraft to spare would be coining it in. We'd need more loaves and fishes than Jesus if we planned to feed the five thousand down there. I got the feeling that the commercial airline business was limbering up to get its snout into a trough.

'How am I supposed to get there?' I asked Elaine.

'Apparently Mr Claywell's coming down from Croydon for you.' Then she sniffed. What had I said wrong this time?

What a bloody relief. Randall's Airspeed Oxford had not received the *all day permanent red* treatment. It was its usual horrid colour of drabby green, and bore no registration mark. I told him, 'You're going to have to put her Reg letters and airframe number on it. Some of these fancy civvy airfields will turn you away if you aren't doing it from the book.'

'I'll get round to it when they make me, son.'

'How did you get away without being painted all over red, like the rest of them?'

'I convinced the Old Man that it would be useful to have at least one kite that was so nondescript that no one would pay any attention to it. He spent the day with me on Tuesday. Feisty old bird, isn't he?'

'I like him.'

'So we got somethin' in common, Charlie. Maybe our marriage will work out after all.'

I grinned. You couldn't do anything else with Randall. He carried a whole small-pack full of one-liners.

'Nice to see you again, Randall.'

'And you, Tiny Tim. Thanks for getting me my job back.'

I suppose that was technically correct. The rest of Halton's small fleet would haul the freight, whilst Randall would end up with the odd jobs. He was very good at odd jobs, and irregular work suited him.

'I knew that I'd need a taxi in this job, and I didn't trust anyone else . . .'

'Ah, Charlie. *Put not thy trust in princes . . .*'

'Are you a prince?'

'I am, actually. I bought a beat-up castle in Germany from one of my compatriots a year ago. A title went with it. *Prince of Thüringen and Saxony.*'

'I think that title actually belonged to the Kaiser.'

'Not any more it don't; it belongs to the Claywells. You ready to go?'

I flung my pack into the back of his aircraft between the passenger seats, and followed him forward. The Oxford was the old trainer twin, and still had a radio rig for trainee wireless operators. I fired it up, and tuned it almost by instinct while he was taxiing. The old lady's Cheetah engines purred like contented pussy cats. As soon as I strapped myself alongside him Prince Randall Claywell Jnr opened up the throttles and let her go. It was good to be back . . .

It was also good to cross the old Reich border in daylight, and with no one shooting at us. The American girl controller sounded familiar to me, but that's a knack all American girls have. She told us to turn right if we wanted to go to Frankfurt. Randall turned right.

Randall rarely flew with a navigator: I don't think that he trusted them that much. He flew with a couple of maps tucked into the top of each flying boot, and always seemed to know which one to pick without looking. Maybe he couldn't read maps anyway, so it didn't matter. I told him, 'We're not going to Frankfurt, Randall.'

'We are now, Charlie.'

'We're not fuelled for Frankfurt, Randall.'

'We are now.'

There was no point in arguing with the only man up there who knew how to fly the damned thing. I thought that it was going to put another day on my trip. So what? But what was the bugger up to?

I think that Randall made the longest, straightest, lowest approach to Frankfurt ever – he was going for the record book. Two women working in a field clearing stones paused, straightened up and waved to us. *That's new*, I thought. Randall had half slid back the little Perspex side window beside him. The cabin temperature dropped by ten degrees immediately. He threw out a small, well-wrapped package, and slammed the window shut.

'What's that?' I asked him. 'Some sort of contraband?'

He shrugged, and didn't answer immediately. Then he said, 'Chocolate for their kids. Several of us are doing it.'

'You're all heart after all.'

'Not all of the time, Charlie.'

I didn't think we'd diverted south just so he could fling some bars of chocolate to a farmer's wife: I was correct. We were directed off Frankfurt's runway on to the peritrack, and Randall took us around to a hard standing as far from the main airfield buildings as possible. It was already occupied by a gasoline truck and a jeep.

The jeep was also occupied. Tommo sat alongside the US officer who drove it. She had light-coloured hair secured in a stylish French roll. They'd brought our lunch out to the aircraft. Thermoses of tomato soup and coffee, and pastrami sandwiches made with that coarse white German bread with the hard bits in.

'*Wotcha*, Charlie,' Tommo said, and hugged me. I wished he wouldn't do that.

'That's an English word, mate.'

'I know. I'm anglophilic. That's another one. This is Wendy . . .'

'I know,' I told him. 'We've met. She was running the caravan at an airfield called Fécamp in France, and we split a bottle of her wine . . .'

'. . . and you're Charlie,' she said. 'You were with that maniac David Clifford.'

'I left him in Germany after the surrender, but he stole my girl. Have you seen him since?'

She bit her lip, and looked away. 'No . . . and he was killed a few weeks later, I think. Knifed in an argument with some Russian.'

We sat on the grass and picnicked close to the Yanks refuelling the Oxford: they finished before we did. Tommo had greeted Randall by now. A quick handshake and, 'Hail to the prince!'

Randall grinned, but I beat him to it with, 'Didn't know you two were acquainted. Should have guessed.'

Tommo said, 'I know everybody. Ain't you worked that out for yerself yet?'

The tomato soup was very good. American tomato soup always is: they should teach us how to make it. I kept from staring at Wendy's tits the way I first had at Fécamp in '45. Well; most of the time. Tommo caught me at it, rolled his eyes to the sky, grinned and shook his head.

When she drove away again she was alone, because Tommo was coming with us. He had a big pack, just like me, so he must have been expecting to be away for a few days. He told me, 'Don't look so downcast, Charlie. This is a properly accounted, paid-for official flight. The US army's funding it, and it has a high degree of legality.' The problem with that was Tommo's understanding of the word *legality*.

*

The officer I found myself doing business with at Celle was a competent Flight Lieutenant WAAF of about forty. They may have been calling them something like the WRAF by then, but I never could see a difference. There was just a touch of grey in her stiff black hair. She didn't laugh much, didn't smile much either. She showed me an office in the office block, and a spare control caravan, and asked me to choose. I took the latter because it was roomier, and didn't smell of damp and piss. She gave me a quick look which seemed to tell me I'd made the right choice. Then she made up a list of things that I'd need to run a small air force from there, and made me sign for it. I wasn't sure that I liked that bit. I still don't like putting my name to bits of paper that mean things to other people. I asked her about accommodation.

'We've got a terrace of requisitioned cottages we don't use – just down the road. I'll pick you a good one. OK?'

'Thank you.' I felt awkward about what I asked next, and that probably showed in my voice. 'Look, do you know what this is all about?'

'I haven't been told, if that's what you mean. But I can bloody well work it out the same as you can: something bad is coming. I hope I'm back in Blighty before the fucking balloon goes up; I don't want to be in this dump when that happens.' Her swearing was absolutely conversational, as if it came naturally.

I'd bombed Celle, or tried to, in 1944. We hadn't made much of a job of it, but a Tiffie squadron came back six months later and buggered up their railway yards. I asked her, '*Is* Celle a dump? It doesn't look too badly knocked about to me.'

'It's not Celle that's the dump, it's bloody *Germany*. I hate the damned place: it's still full of bloody Nazis. We should have emptied it and started again.'

We found Tommo and Randall sitting on upturned oil drums, taking in the last of the sun. Randall had a mug of cold-looking coffee, and Tommo a bottle of one of those pale beers the Jerry likes so much. The wind was whistling across the airfield the way winds do: I think they were impervious to it.

Tommo said, 'Finished? Good. We wondered where you'd got to.'

'I had a job to do. That's why I came here.'

'You didn't tell me it was with Vera. You be careful with her, or she'll eat you alive. Hello, Vera.'

'Hello, Tommo.'

'. . . and don't ask *is that a promise?*' Tommo swung back at me, '. . . or it *will* be, an' you'll in more trouble than I can get you outta.'

She reached up, touched his face lightly with one hand, and suddenly smiled for all of us. It was a terrific radiant smile. She was like a film star – the most attractive woman in the world. Where had that come from?

'You're a lovely man, Tommo,' she said.

As we climbed back into the Oxford Tommo grumbled, 'I thought I told you to stay away from people like that, Charlie.'

That was interesting.

I sat up front with Randall, and to keep him awake fed him coffee from a thermos all the way to Berlin. Tommo slept in the back and snored like a sow giving birth. I wondered if his volume had anything to do with the fact that he never hung on to his girlfriends for long. Then I remembered what Maggs had said about me: neither did I. I smoked my pipe, filling the cabin with the scent of Sweet Chestnut, until it was time to help Randall hold on to the radio beacons in the corridor to Gatow. The Russians had started to try to disrupt them, and you could find yourself flying over somewhere from which they'd have a pot at you.

*

I didn't tell you about the coffin nails, did I? Cigarettes, that is. We had ten boxes each containing ten thousand cigarettes to deliver to the Military Police at Gatow. That's why Randall hadn't strayed far from the aircraft. Actually we'd signed for ten boxes but had ended up with eleven. Just like playing crib: one for his nob. One for us, that is. It didn't come cheap, but in Germany it was worth ten times what we'd given for it. Randall parked up close to the buildings at Gatow, and we unloaded the ten boxes onto the tarmac ourselves, shutting the cabin door on the eleventh just as coppers drove up. They had four men and a sergeant, a jeep and a three-tonner. That was going a bit over the odds. Randall and I helped them load the boxes into the lorry, whilst Tommo leaned against our aircraft door and looked unfriendly. He was good at that. The sergeant signed the paperwork. It said that we'd carried and delivered *nine* boxes. I told you: everyone was at it. He pushed a roll of notes into my jacket pocket with, 'Thanks, mate. You didn't bring anything else with you?'

'No, just a passenger.'

'I'll tell the Customs. They won't bother you.'

Then he saluted and they all mounted up. That was odd. I was flying in a set of grubby coveralls that I felt comfortable in, and my old leather flying jacket. Maybe I'd begun to look like an officer at last. Maybe it creeps up on you before you notice. Now we had ten thousand coffin nails to flog, and, I found after we counted it, already two hundred and twenty occupation dollars to spend. The guy who wrote that song almost got it right: sometimes life is just a bowl of cherries.

I went round to Marthe's place, and let myself in. There was no one there, and the flat had that indefinable stale air of not having hosted humans for a couple of days. It was cold. As usual the water coming into the basin was just a rusty trickle. But I drew enough for a decent stand-up wash, changed, and went out again. I had put on my old, but clean service trousers and battledress blouse – having replaced the buttons with plain dark blues, and removed the rank flashes – and put my jacket on over the top. I had liked Randall's description of his aircraft: *nondescript*. I thought that I matched it.

At the Leihhaus I found Russian Greg. Someone put a bottle of PX beer in front of me, and I stuck my legs under the table. He said, 'You're too late for eats. You wanna a sandwich?'

'That would be good, Greg. Thank you.' Then I switched to German and asked, 'Where's Marthe?'

'She went to visit her parents. They're at Fürstenwalde.'

'Isn't that in your half?'

'Yes, Charlie, it is. I fixed her a visiting ticket to get in.'

'Is that a ticket out as well?'

'No. She fixes that for herself when she's ready. I can't help; another department.' I wasn't sure that I believed that, although he might have meant a different geographical area. The Russians sometimes used the word like that. 'What you got?'

'Eight thousand cigarettes. But I have only a half-share in them, and Tommo's already hinted that he wants them. We'll have to wait for my pilot.'

Randall walks in on cue, doesn't he? Spots me at the table and shambles over. I can see that he disturbs people: it's a bit like having a small grizzly bear walking up to you on its hind legs. He hadn't changed; you could still smell the aircraft from him.

'Charlie's pilot,' Red Greg greeted him in English. He pulled a chair out neatly with one booted foot, and slid it in Randall's direction. 'Welcome to the Leihhaus. Hungry?'

'Thanks pal; starving.'

'Soon everyone in this city will be starving . . .' The Russian put a bit of a dampener on it. He always did say exactly what he thought once he had booze in him. Then he shouted, 'Make that *two* sandwiches, please . . .' at the kitchen.

'This is Red Greg,' I told Randall. 'This is my pilot, Randall,' I told Greg. Randall frowned momentarily. It was just a fleeting thing. That was his hard luck: if he'd wanted another name he should have told me. The Russian asked him, 'You sell me your share of Charlie's cigarettes?'

It was nice seeing Randall discomfited for once. He squirmed, then he answered, 'I don't know. Someone else wants them.'

'You mean Sergeant Thomsett? I know that. We auction them maybe.'

'You know Tommo?'

'Try it the other way round, Randall,' I interrupted. 'Tommo knows everyone.'

Randall suddenly relaxed and grinned. 'I guess he does. Is someone going to get me a beer, or does a man buy his own round here?'

A waitress appeared from the kitchen with two plates. On each were two sandwiches: one thick with fatty bacon, and one of cold German sausage. She gave him a ghastly smile and said, 'Some men do, honey.'

It was nice to see Randall discomfited again. Twenty minutes later we were beating up one of the Russian's bottles of cheap brandy when Magda strolled in. After the introductions I explained to her that Randall was a prince. You could see the reappraisal occurring behind her eyes. I translated her for Randall because I thought he had little German.

'She says that she is a countess.'

'Is that right?'

'I believe so: Russian Greg collects people with titles.' Magda cut across the conversation again, so I told him, 'She says that you and she have that in common.'

'She a whore?'

'A *chocolady*; which is something like. But you're some kind of fucking bandit, so don't get snotty about it.'

Randall laughed, Magda laughed, and when Tommo came by he and the Russian bid each other up for the fags until there was no profit left for either of them: it was just a matter of pride. Then they agreed upon half each, and we gave them the price they were always looking for: it was nice to see the Allies agreeing about something for a change.

Chapter Eight

If Tommo had told me at Frankfurt that he was flying into Berlin to start a fight in his own bar I wouldn't have believed him. Later he told me that he took Randall along because he reckoned Randall was a bit of a roundhouse brawler, and me because I was clever. *Even if you have a yeller streak.* When I thought that through I decided that I'd had the best of it, and I was flattered.

Tommo had had problems at the Klapperschlange for a week or more. A couple of fellow sergeants had set up a bar nearby, and coveted Tommo's customers. They call that a turf war these days. The opposition had taken the services of a PFC hoodlum called Tiny, who came round to the Rattlesnake most nights and insulted or roughed up a couple of customers. The MPs steered clear of Tiny; he was a crazy. The customers had started to drift away to places where they could drink without getting into a fight. Tommo was very tight-lipped about the whole thing, which meant that he was pretty mad. I never liked him when he was feeling mean: there was steel in him.

He'd driven us there in a very nice Mercedes saloon. It was black, and still had the small holes in the front wings where the little Nazi flagpoles had been. He would have to do something about the holes in each of the rear passenger doors where an uninvited cannon shell had said *Hello Sailor!* on its way in and out.

On the way there I'd asked him if he had a gambling room in the back, like his other place.

'No, Charlie. We couldn't work it out. The footprint of the place is just too small. I gotta couple of rooms I fixed up upstairs.'

'You have the gambling up there?'

He looked a little uncomfortable. That was almost a first in my experience of Tommo.

'No, Charlie.' Then he paused. Then he said, 'There's a couple of girls up there.' I didn't say anything. I glanced back at Randall. He was looking out on Berlin as if he hadn't heard anything. Tommo said, 'I ain't a pimp.'

'I didn't say you were.'

'You were thinking it. I can always tell when you're thinking dirty.'

'I wasn't.'

'I don't charge them no rent. I just take a commission from them . . .' He wrenched the car around a corner too quickly, and without changing down. We skidded, but he held the skid, although he nearly ran down an International Patrol crossing the road. I don't know if it was the Russian or the Frenchman he was aiming for.

'It doesn't matter, Tommo. It's just a business I didn't expect to see you in; it was a surprise.'

What Tommo said next he almost whispered. I'm sure that Randall didn't pick it up. He said, 'I'm just nuts about one of them, Charlie, that's all.' He looked anguished and dejected. 'What was I supposed to do?'

'Whatever you did, that's OK by me, Tommo.'

When a pal cries out for help you don't walk by him, do you? I don't know: maybe you lot see things differently.

It was just as I remembered: the steep, narrow street of cobbles slick with rain, and the bar front wore its sign of a red and deadly worm like a crown. That looked almost pink in the thin drizzle which had grabbed Berlin for the night. The long, narrow bar inside had been finished since my last visit. It was faced by small semicircular red velvet settees. They formed booths built one onto the other, and were about shoulder-high when you were seated. There were a couple of round rustic tables with straight chairs if you didn't want to be an intimate drinker. The guitar player in the corner was the guy from Tommo's Frankfurt joint – he must have been moonlighting – and I don't reckon the circular area for dancing could satisfy two couples at the same time. Alice was in her box at the end of the bar. I think she was pleased to see me, but she looked kinda cranky and restless. When Tommo took off his trench coat he was wearing his *Casablanca* outfit underneath, only he was a whole lot bigger than old Bogey.

First proper surprise was Dolly sitting at one of the round tables. I walked up to her but didn't say anything in case I wasn't supposed to know her. She smiled and said, 'Hello, Charlie. I expected you an hour ago.' She was wearing a royal blue dress, and had an ankle-length, black leather, SS top coat wrapped around her shoulders. Its epaulet shoulder straps had been neatly removed: she'd probably bought it in the market that had sprung up by the old Reichstag. She was smoking an American cigarette in a short holder: I'd seen that before. She always reminded me of Doris Day, but I said, 'I thought that it was Marlene Dietrich sitting here; you look very beautiful.'

She had crossed her legs, and they were there for all the bar to see.

'Thank you, Charlie.'

'You haven't moved in upstairs, by any chance?'

'No; of course not. What's upstairs?'

I shook my head. 'Never mind. Can I sit with you?'

'Please.'

The place was eventually about a quarter full, the guitar player perked up, and Dolly gave me a nice slow dance resting her cheek against the top of my head. There was a tension in the air, and the party atmosphere necessary to a successful drinking enterprise was woefully lacking because everyone was waiting for a nice evening to be spoiled.

Randall had waited outside, dozing in the car at the end of the road. Whatever he and Tommo had set up had not included me. I had just waved the waiter for another bottle when Tiny's giant shadow fell across the outside door. I still don't know how he managed to squeeze through it. I don't know what I had expected, but it wasn't this sensationally ugly creature who made Randall seem like a dwarf. I suppose that his being scared of mice was too much to hope for. He stood at the bar, as far from Alice as he could manage – which was interesting – having bounced a quiet couple out of his way, and pinched their drinks. He was a big man in a smart US army uniform and carried a silvered .45 in a buttoned holster worn prominently on his belt. Now *that* wasn't regular. He held himself well, but I somehow got the impression that he was already slightly oiled.

I had my own gun in my pocket of course, but I wondered at its ability to stop this man mountain if he came my way. Oddly enough I didn't actually shy away from the thought of shooting someone. I had had to do that before, and it had opened a box in my brain that should have remained closed. It would have to be a head shot, and I didn't know that I was that good. When I looked over at Tommo he gave me just the smallest of smiles, and shook his head. How could the bastard actually enjoy this sort of thing?

Tommo walked up to Tiny, and stopped just short of arm's reach. Tommo's barman matched him pace for pace, but behind the bar. A pincers attack. Then Tommo asked the rest of us in the bar, 'Do you folks think this thing had a human mother, or did we jest find it in some Alabammy swamp some place?' Tommo's voice and accent had changed. He now had that high nasal Southern drawl. The sort that sounds insulting even when it's saying *Thank you, sir*. There were a couple of nervous laughs, but not from Dolly.

She laughed out loud; almost a man's laugh. King Kong blinked down at Tommo, and put his right hand on his holster flap. Then he stared hard at Dolly, who laughed at him again. Then he took a step towards her. I stood up, but that was completely unnecessary because Tommo was between us again, with a half step as neat as a ballet dancer's. Tiny blinked at him again. This time I was sure that he was already juiced. Then the main door behind Tiny opened, and he must have felt the cool air flow in: the rest of us did.

Randall stepped just inside holding an old-fashioned shotgun across his chest at the port. Tiny now had a problem. He needed to know what was going on behind him, but at the same time he didn't want to turn his back on Tommo. Randall cocked the hammers of the shotgun. It was not a quiet sound in the silence that had fallen on the room, so Tiny made up his mind. He spun round to see. He was lifting the holster flap now. Fumbling.

As he turned away from Tommo the latter held out his right hand to the barman and the barman placed a baseball bat into it. Taking the bat and bringing it down on Tiny's head was a single flowing movement. I heard the *crack* from where I stood twenty feet away, and winced. Randall was stepping out of the way, and gently letting back the shotgun hammers before the man hit the floor in front of him. What you always forget about violence afterwards is how *fast* it is, and how much of an immediate anticlimax. A bit like some sex, I suppose. Silence.

I broke it by asking, 'Did you kill him?' My voice sounded croaky.

'Naw. 'nother inch down would a done. I can do without that.' His voice was the normal old Tommo again. Just like that.

Conversation and buzz started up again. Tommo nodded to the guitar player, who started up with a fast number, 'What Is

This Thing Called Love?' Then I suddenly realized that I'd also seen the bartender before. In Tommo's bar in Frankfurt. My American friend had brought him down here, and what we'd witnessed was a set-up: a choreographed piece from the theatre of violence. They'd done it before.

Tommo took Tiny's pistol and belt. Then he and Randall took an arm each, and the barkeep and I a foot each, dragged him out into the alley and manhandled him into the Mercedes's boot for dumping. The guitar player launched into a rather jaunty version of Chopin's march for the dead: I thought that was kind of neat. When Tommo came back with us he fished Alice out of her box using a stick with a curious looped end, and dropped her in a dark canvas drawstring bag. Alice kicked up a lot, and was rattling, hissing and spitting before she gave up. She was one pretty mad snake.

'Where are you two going with her?' I asked Tommo.

'She's going visiting. You don't wanna know. OK?'

'OK.'

He looked around the room. The guitar player was doing 'On Green Dolphin Street', one of my favourites since I'd heard it the year before. When Tommo said, 'Drinks on the house till I get back. Nothin' happened, OK?' it was in a conversational tone, but nobody missed it. The waiter began to line up glasses along the bar, and an hour later it began to feel like a party.

When Tommo returned he dumped Alice unceremoniously from her bag into her box. She had a big lump nearly a foot down from her head, and a long piece of string trailed from her mouth. She wriggled about some, blinked at me, but forgot to rattle.

'Has Alice swallowed a giant Tampax?' I asked him.

'Naw. She's eaten a rat on the end of a yard o' string. It helps get her back in the bag when she's pissed off. Dead rat on a string. She hits the rat and swallows it. You can manoeuvre her some if you got her on a yard o' string. She's gotta be hungry a' course. If she's hungry you just dangles the rat, and *bang*; she don't even think about it.' Tommo looked tired and satisfied. The way a man looks after a successful combat. Alice looked pretty much the same.

'What did you want her for, anyway?'

'You ever see how fast a bar clears when someone empties a rattler onta the dance floor?'

'No, but I can imagine.' I would have smiled even if I hadn't drunk too much.

Dolly wrinkled up her snub nose, and asked, 'What do you smell of?'

'Kerosene. We had a fire there. Good job Alice cleared the bar first. People might have got burned.'

'Tiny?'

'Left on the Aid Station steps. Maybe he had a thinner skull than I thought. He might get shipped home after this . . . all's well that ends well.'

'I think you've said that to me before.'

I pushed him. 'This is real hardball stuff, isn't it? Gangster versus gangster?'

Tommo sighed and said, 'No, Charlie, it's *business*. Business is nothing more than the continuation of war by other means.'

'Didn't Clausewitz say something about that?'

'I said it better.'

I persuaded Dolly to let me share her bed, because I didn't want to go back to Marthe's place on my own. We shared a cab. In bed Dolly turned her back to me. The last things said before we slept were me asking, 'Where's that Scotsman who's supposed to be looking after you?'

Pause, then Dolly muttering, 'Angus. I've bloody lost him, haven't I? That's why I'm still here. There's going to be hell to pay when I get back.'

That gave me something to think about.

Waking up beside Dolly in the morning, without having made love felt like being married . . . and I rather liked it. I wasn't going to tell her that, and give her ideas. We ate breakfast in the communal canteen downstairs. Dolly wasn't unfriendly but she was still preoccupied: she had dressed in uniform, and looked rather fetching. The cooks didn't look too happy to be serving someone as scruffy as me at all. Scrambled eggs and grilled tomatoes. The American scrambled egg is sloppier than ours. I asked her, 'Are you going to tell me what you're here for?'

'No. How long are you staying?'

'Today and tonight. Flying out in the morning.'

'Are you going to tell me what *you're* here for?'

'No. Trade secret. Business-in-confidence.' We grinned at each other. 'Have you really lost your partner?'

'I didn't realize I'd told you that.'

'You probably didn't mean to. You were sleepy. I know some people here . . . I could ask around.'

'Only if you can be discreet. We don't want to be embarrassed.' I nodded. I still think that other nationalities don't understand how dangerous it is to embarrass the English. I wasn't going to push it. 'Have you found a club called the Leihhaus yet?'

'Of course. Everyone has; didn't you take me there? That's where I last saw Gus, you know.'

'Join me there tonight if you like. I'll buy you a meal if they're serving. At least they don't keep a snake.'

The RAF Regiment corporal at Gatow was hardly accommodating. Maybe Old Man Halton's writ didn't extend this far. All I was offered was a scrubby space off the peritrack, marked out for what he called a *temporary build*. What was that when it was at home; a bus shelter? There was a piece of land marked off with string – he assured me that it was fifteen yards by ten. A small label on a wooden peg driven into the ground bore the words *Halton Airways*. I couldn't help noticing six similar peg-outs with no names in them yet. It wasn't much but at least we were ahead of the game as usual.

The airfield had that unhealthily purposeful air about it which somehow spelled out *war footing*. I could see Meteor and Vampire jet fighters, and some REME Pioneers and DPs close by were building a series of huge three-sided bays, with walls of sandbags and old railway sleepers. I asked the corp, 'What are they; stands for our aircraft?'

'No sir, they're the coal bunkers . . . and we're sinking a row of petrol tanks over there. Didn't anyone tell you?' He pointed to the other side of the airfield. Nobody tells me anything, son.

I had to sign for it, of course . . . and for a short shopping list, more or less identical to the one I'd seen the day before. It did occur to me to wonder if Halton Airways was good for what I was spending. I got him to drop me off at the hotdog wagon; he told me to come over to his office later on, and he'd show me a book with pictures of the things I'd signed for. Big deal.

The Countess still wore last night's make-up, and Randall was leaning on the counter. They looked over-friendly. Randall's hands and wrists were black with oil. When he saw me he said, 'Changing her plugs; OK?' I nodded. I assumed he was talking about our aircraft. '. . . and I'll get a new main wheel tyre if I can. One of them's beginning to creep . . .'

'What's creep?'

'What it says. The tyre is beginning to creep around the wheel, instead of staying where it was put on.'

'How can you tell?'

He looked exasperated: amateurs like me shouldn't ask questions.

'You put a spot of paint on the tyre, and another just under it on the wheel rim. When the spots start to move apart you got creep. It means the tyre wall's getting soft and stretching. Not too many landings left on it.'

'Can you do anything about it?'

'Just be tender with her for the time being; like undressing a sensitive broad.'

I don't think that I'd met many of them yet, but I got the point. The Countess's coffee was better than Marthe's. She probably had better sources. We left her, and went to sit on the concrete in the sun, with our backs against an arseholed bunker of some sort. I asked him, 'Where did you get to last night?'

He smirked. I hadn't known that he could smirk. 'Furthering US–Polish relations. Working hard at it in fact.' He smiled at the memory.

'Polish?'

'Magda. She was born in Poland; that's what Russian Greg has over her – he can always send her back.'

'Even though she lives on our patch?'

'She seems to think so.'

I thought about it for a moment, and then asked him, 'Do you know one of our pilots called Dave Scroton? Thin, ugly guy with a scar on his forehead?'

Randall thought about it for a moment.

'Yes. I met him once. Flies a Dakota, doesn't he?'

'Flies anything: he's a maniac.'

Another one of those damned pauses. Two men tiptoeing around a conversation.

'What of him?'

'If you're doing what that grin on your face says you're doing, then you're sharing his German girl with him. I wouldn't fetch up in this town at the same time as him if I was you, unless you wanted complications. He could be in love: he's daft enough.'

He had an angry red weal on the back of one hand: I could see it through the grime. I asked him, 'What did you do to get that?'

'That Alice . . .'

'She didn't bite you?'

'No: she gave me a kind of kiss: a scrape . . . I just got my hand clear in time. I don't think she broke the skin. Anyway, she wouldn't bite a fellow American.' Obviously no one had told him her story yet: Alice had more notches on her rattle than Curly Bill Brocius.

'Are you OK?'

'Sure; it stung for an hour, but now it's only an itch. I'm fine.'

'One day someone's going to have to do something about that snake,' I told him.

Because I had little else to do I mooched around a bit to try to find someone I knew, and inevitably ended up at the Leihhaus soon after it opened up. Empty drinking places always feel as if they're haunted, and you can smell the cigarette smoke and disinfectant in a way you never can when there's a shindig going on. They are the ghosts of parties past. The Riesling I drank had the same label as that in Tommo's bar. Someone must have cut a deal. Russian Greg grabbed a glass and another bottle from the bar as he walked over an hour later.

'English or German?' he asked me.

'Russian: I need to practise.'

'You can't talk Russian for shit Charlie. We be here all night before you say your own name.'

'German then.'

We spoke German. I asked him, 'A friend of mine has lost a military Scotsman. Where would I go to find him?'

'What's he look like, this Scotsman?'

I described him and added, 'A soldier. He definitely looks like a soldier; but in civilian clothes. He was wearing a brown suit the last time I saw him . . . and he's probably got a soldier's weapons: a machine gun and a pistol. He probably came here on his own.'

Russian Greg stroked his chin. He had a heavy growth, and it never seemed to shave properly. His hand rasped. I had seen that gesture before and knew what it meant. It wasn't that he was deciding whether or not to tell me the truth; it was whether he was going to tell me anything at all. Eventually he swallowed his wine and poured another glass. Then he gave an exaggerated shrug, and sighed. It was all a production.

'I'd look for him somewhere in the Lower Havel, Charlie . . . the Scharfe Lanke or the Jungfernsee. I heard about someone there . . . somewhere like that. With a knife between his shoulder blades of course.'

Bugger it. The Lower Havel was part of the river and lake complex that flowed through Berlin.

'Did your lot kill him?'

'No.'

'Who then?'

'He was dead before you flew out last trip. He probably smells now. We think the Jews did it.'

It was my turn to sigh.

'You can't blame *them* for everything. What's the matter with this country?'

'Nothing's the matter with this country; nor mine neither. The Jews done it. Accept it. It is always them.'

'What do you mean?'

'They are like the butlers in your English detective stories; the Jews *always* do it.'

'Why?'

'Because he came out here to find them.'

I didn't know what to say next, but Greg did.

'If you don't believe me, Charlie; I won't tell you any more.' Then he changed the subject, just like that. A few minutes later he said, 'As a special favour I could arrange for the body to be recovered in your sector, or the Americans'. That's all I will do.'

There was never any point in beating about the bush with Greg. I asked him, 'What do you want?'

'An English passport. A kosher one.' No, it wasn't a joke.

'I'll have to ask someone.'

'I trust you, Charlie.'

Dolly didn't come to find me, so I went to find her. I found her eating alone in that same canteen. The food looked bulky and unappetizing.

'I knew a Scottish squaddie who made something that looked like that,' I told her as I flopped into a seat opposite. 'Corned beef and mashed potato and their skins. You found your Scotsman yet? Did you have any luck?'

'No. I spent the day at the Control Commission. I must have read all the magazines and newspapers in the place, waiting for a twenty-minute interview.'

'Who with?'

'A French officer who had a German clerk. The clerk kept smirking all the time. I thought that he looked like a Nazi.'

'That's no longer an issue, my friends tell me. The issue is whether he is one of *our* Nazis, or one of *their* Nazis. Flashing your legs didn't work?'

'No. Gus hasn't been lost long enough to be officially lost yet.'

'Did you actually call him *Gus*?'

'Not to his face. I went to his wedding only a month ago.'

Sometimes it's hard to resist giving someone both barrels, isn't it?

'Then you can tell his blushing bride that she's a blushing widow. He was knifed the day before I last left Berlin.'

Dolly put her fork down, and pushed the plate away. Sometimes bad news really does for your appetite. She looked away. She didn't want to look at me, which gave me a peculiarly powerful feeling. She lit up a Senior Service, and pulled the aluminium ashtray towards her, and whispered, 'Sure?'

'I haven't seen the body; it's in one of the lakes – but there's an element of trust involved here. Friends told me he's there, and I believe them. They recognized the description I gave them, although it was vague.' I used the plural deliberately: no names, no pack drill. No drill for ever, for poor old Gus.

'Did they tell you who did it?'

'Yes; but that I *didn't* believe. They said the Jews did it. People have been saying that sort of thing in Germany for fifty years: it was never true. They also said that they can arrange for the body to be recovered, and found in an Allied sector. You can have the remains back, but for a consideration . . .'

Throughout the conversation she hadn't raised her voice, and it was almost as if it hadn't occurred to her to doubt me. Just as it hadn't occurred to me to doubt Greg . . .

'. . . that element of trust, I suppose?'

'Yes. A Russian I know wants a British passport. Can you arrange it?'

'Yes, but it will take a few days, and Gus . . .'

'Gus is already moving. You'll probably be notified by the Control Commission or the police tomorrow. I told you . . . an element of trust was involved. You can leave the passport in a plain envelope behind the bar at the Leihhaus. OK?'

She finished her cigarette, and lit another from its stub.

'OK . . . Do you know, Charlie; I can't make myself say *Thank you* to you. Isn't that strange? What do you want to do now?'

'To fuck you.' I said it fast without thinking about it. It sounded even uglier than it reads here. 'I want to take you upstairs and fuck you. Part of me loves Berlin because she always makes me feel dirty. Tonight I want to fuck you until I feel clean again.' The words were coming out staccato now; like machine-gun fire. They had unnatural gaps between them.

Dolly said, 'OK.' She still hadn't lifted her eyes to look at me.

We were brutal with each other. If it hadn't been a coupling it would have been a fight. Afterwards, before we slept, I shared a cigarette with her because I couldn't be bothered to get up and fill and light a pipe. As I took the fag from her she said, 'You probably have scratches on your back. I hope that you won't have to explain that to anyone back home.'

'If there had been someone I needed to explain to, I wouldn't have been here. I expect you've got a new collection of bruises as well. I'm sorry about that; it's been an odd few days, and all sorts of dark things inside me seemed to burst out just now.'

She took the cigarette back. 'Ditto. Don't worry about it. Sometimes I almost get to the point of loving you, Charlie . . . did you know that? Then it never quite happens.'

We lay in silence. Moonlight through the open curtains made beautiful patterns on her body. A last tram rattled towards the Tiergarten and the burned-out Reichstag – the tram stop they now called Black Market. I had one of those strange moments when old memories collide with the present, and join up. I said to her, 'I should have guessed what you were up to. You were chasing Israeli immigrants when I met you in London last year. You're still doing it.'

'I prefer to think of them as terrorists actually. Irgun. The Stern Gang . . . yes . . . you're right, of course.'

'Why bother?'

'I'm here because they were going to try to smuggle a couple of men from Berlin into the UK. They have funds to buy weapons for their people in Palestine; they even want their own navy and air force now . . . and when they've done that, they're going to assassinate Bevin.'

'Nye Bevan? You cannot be serious?'

'No. Ernie Bevin. Isn't that sad? They believe he's an anti-Semite, and excessively pro-Arab. He's going to be blown to kingdom come: made an example of. Gus and I were supposed to make sure these men were stopped before they got to England. If we couldn't arrest them Gus was supposed to stop them any other way he could. He was a specialist . . . we heard a couple of rumours, that was all. Gus went off to check them out, and then nothing: no Gus; no assassins.'

'I'd go home if I was you; once you've got Gus back.'

But I wasn't prepared to tell her why. I was in enough trouble already. The Joes I'd smuggled into Lympne had already turned up at an auction buying Spitfires, hadn't they?

I went back to Marthe's place on the way to Gatow. It was still unlived in. The last thing I did was hide two cartons of cigarettes under a loose floorboard in her kitchen. Then I moved a chair over it. She would notice the chair out of place as soon as she walked in, and guess that there was something there.

I had more or less worked out how the money racket operated. Marthe could sell a carton of fags at ten dollars a pack in the Tiergarten . . . and she would insist on the real dollar. So she's got a hundred dollars . . . on the black market she could get a thousand occupation marks for each dollar – you can work it out from there. There wasn't a Berliner over twelve years old who wasn't an expert at exchange control, and how to get round it. You remember that Tommy Dorsey number 'The Music Goes 'Round and Around'? Well; money was like that in Berlin in '48. Not that it always meant a lot: inflation could wipe it all out before the song ended.

Germany in 1948 was the first place I heard the word *inflation*. It only took you two trips to Berlin to find out what it meant. I once saw a woman office worker pushing her week's pay in a pram. No one bothered to rob her because it was virtually worthless by the time she got it home.

PART TWO

Back To Berlin

Chapter Nine

Randall banked the Oxford round, and down towards Lympne. That glorious consistent purr of the little aircraft's seven-cylinder engines was like sweet music; I know why he loved her so much. The sun was just dropping away over the edge of the ocean, and its light reflected under the layer above us, changing the colour of the clouds to orange and gold. It was a staggeringly beautiful sight . . . one of the occasional gifts of flying that you can never truly explain. Beneath us there were yachts out from Folkestone and Hythe. The light made their sails glow red, and reminded me of that old Guy Lombardo song. It was one of Milton's favourites; he always sang it when he was juiced.

The harassed squadron leader I met at Lübeck had been a doddle compared to the Celle witch, and Gatow's twitchy little corporal. I hadn't said much to Randall on the flight home since then, nor him to me. He had a cob on; or its Anglo-American equivalent. He hadn't liked being told that Magda already had a boyfriend. Everyone hates the messenger who brings bad news. When we had landed, and taxied up to the office, he shouldered his way out of the aircraft in front of me, showed me his back and walked off.

There was no other Halton aircraft on the field, and Old Man Halton stood in the office door to cough a greeting at me. He'd given me a leather music case for his working documents, and he took it back immediately.

'Any problems?'

'Depends whether they give us our own space at Gatow, boss . . . but I'd say no; no problems.'

'Good man. Do you want a couple of days off?'

I felt as if I hadn't done much in the last five days. Nothing that could explain why I felt so drained.

'Yes; I should go over and see the kids, but I actually fancy a couple of days on my own. Up in the Smoke maybe.'

'Bring the children here for a visit some time. Boys love aeroplanes.'

I couldn't remember telling him I had sons. Perhaps it was in my papers somewhere.

I probably forgot to mention it – and you'll find it hard to believe in these days of putting fences around everywhere, and locks on every door – but the road to Lympne village ran through the north of the airfield. There was a traffic-light system when the airfield was flying. Nobody thought that strange at the time. After I turned left on to it I came across Crazy Eddie weaving along the road in front of me dragging a small but heavy suitcase. He was sauced. He didn't notice me until I drove past and stopped.

He stopped as well, swayed from side to side, and then sat on the suitcase.

'Where are you going, Ed?'

'Home.'

'You missed the last train.'

'Spent too long in the bar. Daft. I'll sleep on the station, or maybe walk.'

He wouldn't get much out of a 48 if he walked all the way.

'No you won't. I'll give you a lift. I'm going that way.'

He heaved his case into the back seat and followed, slumping and then fumbling in his pockets for a cigarette. I gave him one, and filled and lit my pipe. After his first fag Eddie slept all the way to London, until I woke him at Wandsworth and asked for directions. It was after one when we drove into a street of small nineteen thirties mock-Tudors which old Jerry had left standing. Ed insisted that his aunty would still be up.

I propped him up against the door with his case at his feet. Then I rang the doorbell and stepped back a couple of paces. If aunty appeared with rollers in her hair and a rolling pin in her hand I was ready for a swift exit.

OK so she surprised me. Aunty was a stunner: long blonde hair like Carole Lombard, silk shift and a cigarette burning at the end of a long cigarette holder. Hollywood comes to Wandsworth. She had a nice smile and a soft, middle-class South London accent.

'Edward's plastered again I suppose.'

'Sorry. I think so.' Who was I kidding? I knew so.

Ed had slumped down against the door jamb, and appeared to have gone to sleep. He wore an exceedingly contented smile. So would I if my aunty looked like that.

Between us we hauled him upstairs to a small bedroom. He reeked of old beer and stale cigarette smoke. When we returned to the door I lifted his suitcase over the threshold for her. I needed both hands for it. She closed the door behind me as I set it down, but that was only for privacy.

I said, ''Strewth. What's he got in here?'

'Shall we have a look?'

She knelt and opened a suitcase full of wristwatches and clocks. Hundreds of them. *Bollocks.* I stood up from where I had bent over it, heard myself say it aloud, and apologized.

'Sorry. I spend too much time in male company.'

She had lifted a couple of the watches. When she handed the watches up to me she took my hand, and used the leverage to help her to stand. She was no bigger than me.

'Keep them. Eddie won't notice.'

I remembered the watches in my jacket pocket the next

morning. They were beautiful chunky Swiss jobs, and possibly exceptionally valuable. And profoundly illegal. The thought of having driven from Lympne with a suitcase full of them scared me to death.

When I had known Dolly the year before, I sometimes stayed in her mews flat when I was up in town. She shared it with an Australian girl named Denys, and they'd given me a key to come and go. I'd even met their landlord, a dentist with a soft handshake who drank wine for breakfast. His name had been Stephen. I headed there now, not wanting to face booking into a hotel at two in the morning.

Even so I was signalled down by a lonely patrolling copper who wanted to see my identity card, and shone his torch in my face. He didn't apologize; they never do – but he did give my car the once-over, and observed, 'Lovely car, the old Singer. I 'ad one before the war.'

'I like her. What do you have now?'

'A bicycle,' he said flatly and turned away, looking for a better prospect than me.

The girls' flat was above a couple of lock-up garages where Stephen kept his cars. The ground-floor door gave onto a narrow steep stair – I remembered a surprisingly commodious cupboard in the wall halfway up where they kept their booze. My hand found the light switch by memory. The cupboard was still full of booze. I lifted out the first bottle to hand as I ascended. Bourbon. The girls must have been targeting the Americans again. In one respect it was like Marthe's ramshackle place in Berlin: I knew immediately that no one had been there for days. The milk in the cold cabinet had curdled so I drank Camp coffee topped off with the bourbon until I slept, wrapped in a Royal Navy greatcoat I found hanging behind the door, on Dolly's cold bed.

I dreamed of burning aeroplanes over Germany – that still happens occasionally – and woke in a cold sweat. If there was the

echo of a noise hanging in the room it was probably my screams.
I had been disturbed by the noise of the United Dairies milkman
in the mews, raced down and bought a bottle from him. An hour
later I repeated the trick with the Co-Op baker, and came away
with a cut white loaf of bread I paid three times over the odds
for. The girls' butter was a bit on the old side, but we weren't
as picky about butter when you couldn't get it that easily . . .
so what it meant was I had the makings of a toast breakfast. I
was feasting on that, and a tin of PX strawberry jam I'd found,
when Stephen trod daintily up the stairs. He hadn't seen me for a
year, but didn't bat an eyelid. He said, 'Hello. Nice to see you
again . . . ?'

'Charlie . . .'

'That's right; *Charlie*.' I always hate it when someone congrat-
ulates me for remembering my own name. 'Weren't you going
out with Den? Or was it Dolly?'

'Both. Sorry; where are they?'

'Den's up in Scotland with her American. I never know where
Dolly gets to. Terribly hush-hush I think. Best not to ask.'

'I think so too.' I was doing what my mother had always
cautioned me against: talking with my mouth full. If Stephen
noticed the discourtesy all it provoked was, 'I say, that looks
rather good, even if the jam will do for your enamel . . . not
enough for two by any chance?' I pushed the loaf at him: he could
toast his own. When I asked him about the dentistry business he
told me he was giving up on it.

'I'm absolutely fed up with sticking things in people's mouths,
even if it does pay well. Dentistry is only upside-down gynaecol-
ogy. Ughh!' He shuddered theatrically.

'What will you do?'

'I fancy retraining as a chiropractor, and learning to play the
piano.' I didn't see the connection, but he hurried on, 'All the
best folk have their own chiropractor these days. The royals have

so many that they throw garden parties exclusively for them.'
What was pleasant was that he felt good about his decision. It was
a pity it all went tits-up fifteen years later.

I didn't want Stephen to know my business so I telephoned the
Customs office at Thurleigh from a callbox. The operator took
about an hour to find me the number. The woman's voice which
answered the telephone sounded both guarded and intelligent,
but you can always be wrong. I asked for Officer Holland.

'PO Holland's not here at present, sir. Can I help?'

'It's not an official matter,' I told her. 'I'm civilian aircrew; I
met him recently and he asked me to look him up when I was
nearby. I can be nearby today or tomorrow.' Then I asked, 'Who
am I talking to, anyway: sorry?'

'Woman Search Officer Search . . . and please don't make a
joke about that. I'm sure I've heard them all.' She must have been
in the office alone to be speaking to a stranger like that, and if she
was in the office alone then it was probably a small office. Good
thinking, Charlie.

'I'm Charlie Bassett. I can tell you every liquorice allsorts joke
in the world, so perhaps I know how you feel.'

'Have you heard the one about . . . ?'

I was smiling now. I reckoned this woman was ex-services. I
told her, 'Don't even think about it.'

A pause, and then she asked me, 'Are you speaking from
London by any chance?'

'Yes I am.'

'Bob's gone up to town to get some injections and to see the
Waterguard Superintendent . . .'

'Who's *he* when he's at home?'

'He's also the chairman of his local council as it happens, but
he's our boss as well. Bob's bound to go to a pub called the
Canterbury on Fish Street Hill, just opposite Billingsgate market;

he always does – creature of habit. He'll get there for lunch, and stay until he catches a girl or the train back. You could see him there if you can find it.'

'I will, and I'll tell him you're a gem.'

She laughed, '. . . and he won't believe you; he knows me too well.'

'Thanks anyway.'

'That's OK.'

One of those odd conversations where neither of you knows how to hang up. The pips did it for us. We both said goodbye hurriedly, and maybe a little embarrassed, and then the line was gone.

I parked the bus on Lower Thames Street between two fish lorries, and hoped that the smell wouldn't rub off. I put the hood up because there was that sense of rain in the air. The Custom House on the bank of the Thames was a Georgian building as big as a battleship. It was a honey colour, and not bashed about too much by the Kraut. It reminded me of my girl Grace's place in Bedford. I was angry with myself for still thinking of her as *my girl Grace*, because she hadn't been for a few years.

I backtracked towards the old London Bridge site, and then turned right up Fish Street Hill. In minutes I was walking into the Canterbury Arms, a low dark pub with wood-panelled bars and a rich aroma of tobacco and Whitbread's beers. If you want my opinion, when I get to heaven it's going to look something like that. There was a bloody great stone column in the road outside. I'd paused before ducking into the low doorway and squinted up at it. I suppose that it had been grey once, but it was stained and pitted with smoke now – sinister somehow. Our man was sitting on a stool at the bar, and a barmaid with tumbling falls of chestnut hair was giving him her full attention. They were both laughing as I walked up and hopped on to the stool alongside him.

Enter a gooseberry, stage right.

'Hello,' I said. 'Remember me?'

'Yes. Charlie Bassett. You fly with Halton. Want a drink?'

'Thank you. Bitter please. Your name was Holland.'

'Still is. Is this meeting coincidental?'

The girl came back with my beer, and Bob paid her. She blushed. I thanked her, and then said, 'No. Not entirely. I telephoned Thurleigh, and a funny girl told me where to find you. Cheers.'

'Funny amusing or funny peculiar?'

'Amusing. She made me laugh.'

It was very good beer. The barmaid was a very pretty woman. I began to think that Holland had very good taste in all the things that counted. It took that long to settle him, then he turned to face me properly. When the girl moved away he asked me, 'OK, so what's the problem?' The transformation from playboy to officer was absolute and immediate, and unnerving.

I took a gulp of the sharp hoppy stuff first, then, 'I have some information to pass on, and you're the only one I knew.'

'You could have tried your locals, or the police.'

'No. I don't know the locals, and the one time I walked into a police station I was arrested and locked up for three months: I avoid them now.'

He chuckled. He still looked like a film star when he smiled. The barmaid had given us space but she still couldn't keep her eyes off him.

'What had you done?'

'Forgot to come home after the war: it's a long story.'

He shook his head, but was still smiling. 'What do you want to talk about?'

I'd been putting it off by filling and lighting a pipe. I'd sloshed through my pint too quickly, but waved for another round from the girl.

'What if I started by talking about the smuggling of a couple of DPs from Germany to an airfield in the UK?'

He looked relieved, waved a hand dismissively, reached for his new pint and said, 'Thanks by the way. That's happening all the time. We can't sit on every little airfield or bay — we just don't have the manpower. Were they going to stay here, or just use us as a staging post for a jump to the US?'

'No; to Israel. That's the way the story was told to me, anyway.'

'That's a bit different, old son. A lot of people are pretty fed up with what's going on over there . . . official policy is to intercept them if we can.'

'What if I went on to tell you that I saw the same DPs a week ago at a war surplus aircraft sale at Fairleigh?'

'What were they doing?'

'Buying late-mark Spitfires and a couple of Marauders. I think they're tooling up for a serious little war.'

'Are the aircraft still here?'

'I don't know. I thought that should be your end of the business.'

He nodded broodily. Then he said, 'Let's go and sit at that table in the corner, and go over it again.'

I had decided not to tell him about an attempt on Bevin's life, and the murder of a British soldier in Berlin, but, even so, it had been good to get even a bit of it off my chest. In the end I gave him two decent descriptions of the Joes. The hard agreement we came to was that regardless of what he did with anything I told him, he wouldn't reveal my identity to anyone. When we had finished he leaned across the table, shook my hand and said, with some irony, 'This could be the beginning of a wonderful friendship,' as if I had suddenly woken up in the last scene of *Casablanca*. I briefly wondered what Tommo was up to.

The pub was shutting up around us by then anyway, and wouldn't reopen until half past five. I admired a brand-new dark green Mk IV Jaguar saloon parked outside: it had been there when I walked in. It had wire wheels and looked sleek and fast.

He offered me a fag, but I shook my head, and started to fill my pipe again. I suggested we slope off to find a bar that was open, but he refused. He said he had a prior arrangement. The barmaid came from the bar towards us, and Bob steered her towards the passenger side of the Jag and let her in; perfect bloody gentleman. He gave me a cheeky grin across the roof of the car before he, too, disappeared inside. His partner had said he was on the train. That was interesting.

London's not the worst of cities in which to be at a loose end. I had a day and a bit for myself, hadn't planned what to do with them, and there was money in my pocket. I parked up on Soho Square and took a cup of thick tea with the cabbies in their green wooden kiosk. Then I walked to a big toy shop on Oxford Street, where I bought a painted wooden aeroplane for Carlo and a Kiel Kraft glider kit for Dieter: the sooner we started him with the old balsa wood, paper and glue the better. Then I went mad, and booked myself a night in the best suite at the Regent Palace; the truth was I didn't want to go back to Dolly's place.

After I had eaten at the grill, I strolled out to a Soho pub my old Lancaster crew used to favour on our trips up to the Smoke. What happened there was odd; I found that I couldn't cross the threshold. There was another piece of my life the other side of that door, and I wasn't ready to face it yet. I went back to the Regent, and drank at the bar there until decision-making became problematic.

I called the airfield just before I checked out the next morning, just to find out what was going on. Elaine answered, and the thought that came straight into my head was, *You've been crying.*

Brunton must have quickly taken the telephone from her. He said, 'Charlie?'

'Yes, boss.'

'Where are you?'

'London: just booking out.'

'You'd better get down here. Milton's bought it.'

Chapter Ten

The Russians gave us the body back a week later. They were pretty good at giving bodies back I remember . . . as long as there were no incriminating wounds on them.

The Old Man had arranged a week's buckshee instruction on Lancastrians for Milton with a company called Flight Refuelling. They specialized in converting freight aircraft for the transport of fuel: each carried tanks containing 1500 gallons of petrol or diesel. Milton had done three trips as a second pilot, and was looking good. Even fully laden their nimbler Lancastrian suited him better than our lumbering York and Dak.

He was trucking a routine load of petrol along the corridor, for the garrison at Gatow, when his aircraft reconfigured itself into a fireball. The explosion was heard five miles away apparently. For once no one blamed the Reds. They hadn't been anywhere near him. The sad fact is that if you overload aircraft with tanks of gasoline and fly them up and down the country you're doing something that God did not intend you to do, and occasionally it's going to end in tears. Milton's body had been blown clear and according to the American army pathologist who did the needful, was burned black, and saturated with petrol. It's customary to tell relatives and loved ones that the dead man *wouldn't have felt a thing*. Who do they think we're kidding?

I went out with Old Man Halton to recover the body. Randall

flew us over in the other Oxford that had been painted in Halton's livery: it looked very smart. So did Randall. He was wearing black trousers and flying boots, and had a new dark grey leather flying jacket with a narrow collar. Randall being Randall, it was big enough for me to have slept in, of course. Apparently his was the new flight crew uniform and we were all going to get them. I wore my old flying jacket over a sober suit, and the old man was in black.

We collected Milton from Wunstorf, an RAF station west of Celle. It was new to me because it hadn't been on my Cook's Tour itinerary. We stopped overnight in a concrete olive drab block labelled Aircrew Accommodation. It was like a hostel for the homeless, with narrow twin-bunked rooms, and two large communal bathrooms on each corridor. It occurred to me that they could have housed hundreds of aircrew in there. Then it occurred to me that they probably intended to. We had a room each, but it was a chill and cheerless place, and it stank of damp . . . and overloaded toilets. Flying into Wunstorf, the dark forest had seemed to stretch to the horizon in all directions . . . the long approach over miles of dense pine and fir seemed to go on for ever.

Randall and I sat up at the guest bar, and started to talk to each other again. He said, 'Sorry, partner,' and sighed.

'So am I. I just thought I ought to tell you.' That was it. We didn't mention Scroton or the Countess again.

I had never heard him talk about his own country or countrymen before, but he must have been feeling broody, because he asked me, 'What do you think about America, and Americans?'

'Do I include the fact that War Loans mean we owe you everything we can earn between now and the next century?'

'Stop messing around. You know what I mean.'

'I think two things, Randall. The first is that when a country is as powerful as the States it's easy to dislike its policies, and the things that it does. Then when you come across individual Americans you find them to be among the most courteous and brave folk you'll ever meet.'

He signalled the barkeep for another round.

'OK. Thanks for that. What was the other thing?'

'Whenever anything goes wrong in the world, the first question anyone asks is, *What are the Americans going to do about it?* Half the fucking world looks to you for leadership now: haven't you noticed that?'

'Yeah; it will be a heavy load to carry.'

'My lot carried it for three hundred years. Perhaps it's just your turn. Think about it that way and get used to it.'

Randall smiled into his drink. I didn't know what the hell the conversation was actually about, but he seemed to have arrived somewhere. Then he got me to tell him all I knew about Milton. It wasn't much. Then we talked about Berlin, and the places to go. It turned out I'd been there more often than Randall. Old Man Halton sat in the corner at a small table, and read a Somerset Maugham novel. And drank an entire bottle of whisky. Then he stood up, bade the bar *Goodnight*, and walked steadily to his room.

In the morning we collected Milton from the station mortuary. The RAF Regiment got it right; they always do in my opinion. They are a very professional outfit. Milton's coffin was a plain, narrow, rough pine box: he'd get a proper job when we'd got him home. The Regiment surprised us by providing a colour party and honour guard, and you couldn't see Milton's box because they covered it with the RAF flag. At the aircraft they folded the flag and gave it to the old man – he was crying by then – and they insisted that we mount up, and let them load the box after us. As we taxied out they came to the alert, and saluted. I felt a lump in my throat, and looked away.

What goes around comes around. Not far from where we loaded Milton for his last ride, another colour party was loading a second box onto an RAF York. Dolly followed it into the aircraft; she was taking someone back. The same as us. I don't think that she noticed me. I hoped that her reception was to be a kind one.

I sat in the Oxford behind Randall, and alongside Old Man Halton. He held the flag in his lap, his hands twisted into it. He hadn't coughed once since we'd arrived at Wunstorf. Milton was behind us. His box wasn't a particularly good box, and soon into the flight the aircraft was pervaded by the smell of raw gasoline and scorched flesh. I'll never forget the smell in that aeroplane that day. None of us remarked on it. The only thing the Old Man said to me, an hour into the journey, was, 'I'm bringing my *son* home.'

I said, 'I know, sir.'

For once the *sir* was intended, and he didn't tick me off. He nodded. As Randall spiralled us smoothly down into Lympne that afternoon, I noticed that the house flag above the ops block was flying at half mast. Milton would have laughed his socks off.

That's how we took him home.

If Milton had been a bit of a crisis for us all then I guess May and June of 1948 were full of crises of one kind or another. In the middle of it the office had a call for me from Winchelsea. A thick, slow shower was blowing over Lympne, splattering the car park with large, spaced out drops of rain. Broken low cumulus, and plenty of blue.

I'd already done a trip to France in *Whisky* trying a new small radio that Halton had bought: the pilot and engineer could operate it from small paddles on their spade grips – just like gun buttons. I suppose that you could call that a peace dividend. I sat up front alongside Scroton, whilst Ed slept at my post behind us. Scroton whistled 'Blue Moon' between clenched teeth: I thought that he and *Whisky* had lost some of their mutual affection. When he put her on the deck at Beauvais he ran too close to the hedge at the edge of the field and collected a small branch of hawthorn in her starboard aileron – it waved like a flag as he taxied over the bumpy grass to airfield control. It was as if his mind wasn't on the job.

I cadged a lift back with Randall, who was out in the red Oxford, delivering some electrical parts for a power station which the Frogs were desperately trying to bring back on line. It had been sabotaged by *La Résistance* in the war. That says it all about the French in my opinion: they'd spent half the war blowing up their own power stations, factories and railway lines. If they'd tried to do that to Germany's own infrastructure instead, and a bit earlier, we'd all have had a better war. Randall whistled between his teeth all the way back, and irritated me. It was that bloody 'Blue Moon' of course: those two bastards had too much in common.

He and I had sprinted, laughing, for the offices when the rain started to clatter down. The big drops bounced off the concrete like small armour-piercing rounds, lifting fine puffs of dust. Elaine was just putting the telephone receiver down. Her face looked ashen. *Shit*, I thought, *again*! Old man Halton stood in the door to the corridor. Brunton had stepped out to his office door too. The Old Man spoke first. He coughed after the first syllable, and then everyone waited for him to get started again. Eventually he got out, 'Go home, Charlie. Your boys need you. Go home now, and sort it out please . . .'

'Sort what out?' No time for the niceties.

'There was a Mrs Maggs telephoning,' Elaine said. 'Your sons are missing. They went out last night, and haven't come back yet. The Police and the C.D.Vs are out looking for them.'

I didn't respond immediately. My face grew hot. And then cold. Then I felt fear: the sort that dissolves your bowel.

The Old Man grunted, 'Go . . .' again, and turned away, waving a hand, and stifling a cough and whatever he was going to say next in his handkerchief. I should have remembered that I'd just helped him bring his only child home.

Elaine said, 'I'm so sorry, Charlie. Would you like me to come with you?'

For a moment my brain wouldn't work at all, then I managed, 'No. It will be all right. I'll manage . . .' I wasn't sure that I could. 'Where was she telephoning from? I ought to call back.'

I called the Major's place. I spoke to him and I spoke to Maggs. His tones were calm and measured. Her tones were calm and measured. I knew immediately that they were panicking like fuck. Before I walked out of the office the Old Man came back and gave me a hug. Oddly enough I didn't mind. Then he pulled out his wallet, and made me take it. It was stuffed with money. I told him, 'I won't need this . . .'

'You may . . .' the words disappeared into his handkerchief with a great hacking. When he had his breath back he finished, '. . . and if you need any more go into your bank, and ask them to phone me.'

'Thank you, sir.' There; I did it again, and just like the last time, I meant it.

Randall was waiting outside for me, kicking at the concrete. The sharp shower had blown over; the concrete didn't even show it. He grabbed me just like the old man had done.

'Put me down please, Randall. I can't breathe.'

'Do you want me along with you?'

These bastards could melt you, couldn't they? I hated the emotionfest; always have.

'No, Randall. I can handle it, one way or the other. But thanks for offering. I won't forget it.'

'Yes you will. Jest like I do.'

'How about if I call the office when I have some news? I'll tell them if I need you.'

'OK, partner.'

I've only known one other man in my life address me as *partner*. I liked them both enormously. In the accommodation I stuffed my clothes and my cleaning kit into the big pack, and threw them into the back seats of the Singer along with the brown paper carrier bag with the kids' toys I'd bought in London. I just prayed to God that I was going to need them.

Old men think more clearly than young men when the crisis hits; did you know that? . . . When I reached Worthing the car had an empty tank, and was running on petrol fumes and wishes. I found that although I had my coupons, I had no money, and paid for a tank of National Benzole from Halton's wallet.

It was dark when I pulled up alongside the prefab. Every light in James's place was on, and the car park was full. So was the bar. It fell silent as I shouldered my way inside, which can't have been good news, can it?

There was a uniformed police constable with his notebook in his hand. He seemed to be writing down everyone's name and address. He licked his pencil between entries: you don't see that any more. When I walked up to him he asked me who I was, and when I told him he asked to see my identity card.

'Why?'

'You can't be too careful these days, sir.'

'Stop being a cunt. Have you found my boys yet?'

'I couldn't answer that question, sir, until after I've verified your identity.'

The man who pulled me off him was Les. Time stopped. I was momentarily three years younger, driving across Holland or Germany somewhere with him.

'Hello, Les. Where did you spring from?'

'The Major telephoned me. I've been here since this morning. Put the officer down now, Charlie, and let's go through and talk about it.'

I always did what Les told me. Force of habit. The policeman started to make threatening noises once he got his breath back, but Les gave him the look, which shut him up. I've seen Les do that to people before.

Council of war. That was like three years ago as well. Me, Les and the Major. Maggs sat in a deep chair in the corner and kept her neb out, unless she was asked . . . although at one point she sniffed and said, 'Three bleeding musketeers, ain't you?'

Les poured us three whiskies from a bottle which had already had a hammering. Maggs nursed a giant glass of her favourite port: Cockburn's from Edinburgh. Eventually she told me, 'I s'pose it was my fault. Carlo was being a proper little monster – getting into anything. I warned 'im. At the end he reached up to a saucepan of peeled potatoes on the stove when me back was turned, and pulled it down all over himself.' I winced, and she hurried on, 'Don't fret. The water was cold, but it coulda been boiling, an' it scared me to think about it.' I nodded. So far so good. Maggs finished her bit, 'So I gave 'im a clout round the ear, didn't I?'

'Is that all?'

'Till Dieter came in from school. Carlo must 'ave told him, an' 'e started laying into me about slapping a defenceless kid. I never heard anything like it before . . .'e sounded like some sort o' bleedin' lawyer.'

'So?'

'. . . So I gave 'im one as well. These kids 'ave got to learn from someone.'

'Then what happened?'

'Dieter just looked at me. He went white, and looked at me. Then 'e just turned about and walked out. It was the way 'e looked at me . . .'

'Like what?' Les asked. Then he lit one of his pungent little roll-ups.

'Like he was so sad. I coulda stood it if 'e was angry at me; but no. 'e just looked sad. I 'eard them go out to play before tea. I always let 'em out fer an hour. When I went to call 'em they never came back.'

When I looked up she was dabbing her eyes with the edge of her pinny. I had never seen Maggs cry before. I went over and hugged her.

'I can't say Don't worry, Maggs, because we're all worried stiff. What I mean is that I might have done the same as you. It could have happened with me or the Major. So whatever you do, don't take it personally. I need you to be thinking straight at the moment.'

She nodded, and gave a weak smile through her tears. Seeing Maggs like this was just as worrying as the bald facts. I asked James, 'Tell me what your worst assessment is.'

He gulped his whisky, and held out his glass to Les for another.

'It depends on where they went, Charlie. If they were caught up the estuary with the tide coming in . . . it can be a right bugger. Dieter can swim, but Carlo can't yet.'

'But you don't think they've been stolen? Gypsies or something?'

Les made a very dismissive sound.

'That's an old wives' tale Charlie. It never happened. Gypsies stole horses, not kids. No, the Major's right . . . they've run away. Either they got caught on the shore an' got into trouble, or they ran away and are being very serious about it. One o' mine fell out with his ma once, an' did the same. Caught him hitching a lift to Brighton.'

I turned away from them, and looked out of the window. There was a line of lights on the water, leading away from the estuary. James came over, followed my glance, and told me, 'The yacht club's out for you. They're sweeping the estuary in parallel lines – been out there all day. They'll have to come in soon.'

'Who organized that?'

'Coastguard. Your Mrs Valentine is out there somewhere. She came down from London deliberately. She took Jules out with her.'

There was something I still couldn't quite understand.

'If Dieter's run away, why did he take Carlo with him? That would only hamper him.'

Maggs answered me from the corner of the room. 'You still don't get it, Charlie, do you? Dieter took Carlo to get 'im away from me. 'e couldn't stop me givin' 'im a slap so 'e did the next-best thing . . . they scarpered.'

I felt worse than I did the day my father had told me that my sister was dead; isn't that odd? So I put my head in my hands, but I didn't cry, even though I felt like it. Les came over, and didn't say anything stupid like *It will all work out in the end*. What he did was rest a hand on my shoulder, which was, I suppose, the same thing.

I slept in the prefab for the first time. It wasn't the celebration I once thought it would be: first night in my own place. It was a small efficient house that had been designed to scale for someone my size. Maggs and the Major had furnished it from junk shops, and the furniture repository in Chichester: most of the furniture was thousands of years old, and *hadn't* been made to scale for someone my size. Canute would have recognized it. They'd even opted for an old heavy double bed with a carved headboard in wood that was almost black, and a solid horse-hair mattress. The bedspread and bedroom curtains were a heavy velour red – just like the rooms I remembered from Maggs's brothel in Paris.

Evelyn Valentine spent the night with me. We made love with a savage energy which was a bit unnerving. Her skin tasted of salt. Each of our bodies bore the impression of the other when we rolled apart. Afterwards she lit a cigarette and said, 'There; *that* was all right, wasn't it?'

'Did I hurt you?'

'No, silly. You were fine. I don't mind that kind of hurt.'

I couldn't find an ashtray for her, and eventually padded to the kitchen and brought her back a saucer. She asked me, 'Why didn't you turn the light on?'

'I wasn't sure where it was. Anyway, I was naked.'

I'll always remember her gentle laugh then. She said, 'Silly,' again, and then, 'Who would see you?'

'Thank you for taking your boat out to look for the boys.'

'Thank Tanty – he's the Coastguard who organized it. Thank Jules as well; he's a big strong man, isn't he? I couldn't have handled *Grace* without him . . . and he's very easy to get on with.'

'Are you telling me something there?'

There was a long pause before she answered, 'Maybe.'

I knew that she was smiling in the dark. I've always liked honest women; haven't you?

I was up before seven the next morning, and was quietly exploring the house. I had left Evelyn sleeping; sprawled across the bed like the Rokeby Venus. The other bedroom contained two bunks for the boys to use when I was at home. They must have already tried it out, because the beds were made, and had a change of clothes folded neatly on each of them. That was Dieter. I think that in a quiet way he had taken on Carlo's practical education. There were a few toys scattered about, cardboard boxes that had been cut down into square sheets of corrugated cardboard, and a shoe box containing a few pieces of silver foil, glue and string. The silver paper looked like wrappers from food or chocolate. I slipped out quietly, without waking her, and sloped over to the pub kitchen to see what Maggs was cooking up. She was always an early riser.

We shared a plate of fried bread and sugar, and drank fiery mugs of real black coffee.

'When I was in France in the war I used to long for a taste of real coffee. 'ere we are free years later, and I still can't get enough of it,' she told me.

'We never had coffee at home when I was a boy; only tea. My mother kept it in a silver tea caddy my old man brought back from France. It was the Americans who showed me coffee.'

'Tanty's comin' 'ere this mornin'. Meeting up with Mr 'orrocks from the Civil Defence. They're going to plan wiv the Major what to do next.'

We ate in companionable silence: I had known Maggs for three years, and felt very comfortable with her. She was like an amiable, criminal aunt. She was probably thinking the same as me. *What comes next?* And, *How long can two children last out there on their own?* At last I told her, 'I found a load of cardboard and silver paper in their room. What was that for?'

'Dieter's doing the Romans at school. He made them both shields an' swords an' armour: so they could play.'

'Ah. Where's Les?'

'Out already; walkin' the shoreline. He said I wasn't to get you fer that.' Les never flinched from anything bad the whole time that I knew him.

I went up the narrow stair to the bedroom the boys usually shared in the pub. The bunks were squared away Bristol fashion; just like those in the prefab. I looked in their wardrobe, and their chest of drawers. Their clothes were all folded, or hanging – unnaturally neatly for boys. I'd have to have a word with Dieter about that, I thought – and then caught myself: I was no longer sure that I'd have that chance. Dieter's school books were piled on a small desk beneath the window, with his pens and pencils. Almost as if he knew that he wouldn't need them any more. *Where was his school bag?* He didn't have a leather satchel like the other kids. He had one of my old RAF Small Packs, and he was very proud of it. The other things I couldn't find were cardboard swords and armour. That was something.

Hope is a dreadful thing: it is like a distant lantern flickering in the dark – now you see it, now you don't. I gave Maggs a brief peck as I left. The skin of her cheek was dry; an old lady's skin. I hadn't noticed that before.

'Try not to worry, Maggs; we'll need you as soon as we get them back.' I didn't tell her that I was going out on a long shot myself.

I don't know why I chose Kate instead of the Singer, but I did, and she must have been worried about the boys too, because she crackled into life immediately. As I pulled away I saw Maggs's face at the kitchen window. I smiled and waved. The hand she waved back to me with was holding a handkerchief. I turned back down the road to Chichester.

There was room for three cars in the small lay-by on the coast road where we stopped. I remembered the crooked footpath sign with the words Roman Road pointing off into the woods. The sun was shining, but the ground was still damp and steaming: there must have been a shower overnight. The road was like a track through the forest: mainly oak trees and ash. Cobbles and stones poked through the grass, and felt hard under my boots. My feet slipped a couple of times, and I struggled for balance. If you looked carefully you could see the ruts in the stones worn down by centuries of chariots and carts. I recalled from my school books that even now the gauge of our railways is determined by the width of a Roman chariot. The raised military *agger* roadway tailed off into overgrown ditches on either side. In places the ditch had nearly disappeared, but in others it was four feet deep in unfriendly brambles. I cheered up because I've always loved the smell of woods after rain, and, like I told you, hope had raised its hoary little head. As I struck north and up the old straight track I called out *Dieter*, and *Carlo* every hundred yards or so. Sometimes I carried on talking to them, as if they were with me. At first I felt foolish, but I wouldn't feel foolish if I was right. Occasionally I heard small animals moving, or disturbed clattering birds.

After about four miles I thought that there was more light ahead of me. The woods seemed less dense. The road would eventually climb out onto the South Downs. Arundel Castle was probably miles off to my right – the east. I was thinking about that, and calling to the boys when I should have been looking where I was going. That's why my foot slipped off an oddly prominent round stone, and I turned my ankle. I distinctly heard it click. It wasn't a break, but it was something all right. I lost my balance and tumbled into the ditch and a clump of briars: real man-eaters. I probably began to shout before I came to rest.

'*Balls*! Bollocks!' My ankle hurt like hell when I tried to straighten myself and sit up, so I rolled onto my side. 'Fucking *bollocks*!'

An animal moved in the wood not far from me. The Duke of Norfolk's deer. Wasn't someone chased for poaching those, in a Kipling poem? You think of the oddest things when you're in pain; I've noticed that before. But it wasn't a deer.

'You swear too much, Papa,' Dieter said from somewhere nearby.

At first I couldn't say anything. Then I laughed. Could you have thought of anything better to do?

The boys stepped out onto the *agger*. Their cardboard swords looked very past their best; they were bent, but the shields and cardboard and silver paper breastplates had held up pretty well . . . and for two children who'd seen their second night out in the open they looked in pretty fair condition. Carlo threw away his sword and shield, and dived straight into the ditch to hug me. I kept trying to hold him clear of the brambles.

'Mind,' I said, 'mind . . .'

Dieter lifted him clear, and then helped me roll on to my hands and knees and crawl up to the roadway. My right foot wasn't much help. When we rolled my trouser leg up and my sock down, I could see the ankle was already swelling. Dieter squatted down and put a hand on my shoulder.

'Can you walk, Papa?'

It probably wasn't the time to remind him that I'd told him to call me *Dad*.

'Probably. Let me get my breath back.'

Carlo asked, 'Are you hurt?'

'A little,' I told him, 'but I'm going to be all right now that you and Dieter are here to rescue me.'

He hugged me again, and that moved my leg, and sent fire into my brain. Dieter was studying my face, and smiled when I managed not to swear. It was a close-run thing though. I could see that he was thinking. Then he said, 'Wait here; I won't be long,' and plunged back into the woods. I called, 'Dieter. No . . .' but he was gone, leaving his armour and shield on the road.

When he came back five minutes later he had a freshly cut stave with V arms at the top in one hand, and a clasp knife I had given him at Christmas in the other. I always knew that it would come in handy. In the meantime Carlo had told me that the game of Roman soldiers in the woods had gone on too long, and he was cold and hungry. He was probably pretty tired as well. I smiled, and put my arm around his thin shoulders. Dieter helped me to my feet, and put my new crutch under my arm. It pinched, but it worked, and that's how we came back to Kate. Two small Roman soldiers, and a second-hand airman.

They told me about their two days, which appeared to be a cross between a make-believe game, an adventure and a bit of serious running away. It would take me some effort to sort it out.

It took us nearly two hours to make it. I was supported by the crutch on one side and Dieter on the other. Carlo held tightly onto Dieter's free hand. At the end of it, although it's hard to explain how, I felt as if we three knew each other better. Dieter slowed our pace momentarily as Kate came in sight.

'Mrs Maggs can punish *me*, but must not smack Carly again. He is too small.' It was the first time I had heard him use a personal diminutive.

'She knows that now. I don't think it will happen again. She was scared when he tipped the pot; it could have been full of hot water. She's even more scared now.'

'Last night I told Carly not to play in the kitchen again; that it can be dangerous. He understands now.'

'Thanks, old man . . .'

'We were coming back anyway. Nearly all the food was gone.' He touched his school bag lightly. 'We have only three cold sausages, and a piece of cheese left.' For a moment I thought he was telling me I was a fool to have bothered. No. He was just a deep one; none deeper.

The odd thing was that tucked up in my new bed later that evening, with my ankle in a strap, watching Evelyn as we talked by firelight – and listening to the murmur of the boys from the room next door – I felt as if after all the worry and excitement and pain, I had come out ahead. It was almost as if it had been worth it. She glanced in the direction of their voices, got up from the small armchair by the fire and said, 'I'd better go then. Val's coming down tonight. He says that he was sorry he missed all the fun.'

'I'm not sorry. I didn't miss it. Particularly the fun last night.'

She bent over, and kissed me. It was a nice soft kiss that said absolutely nothing. No other parts of our bodies touched.

'See you soon?'

She did it again. After a pause she said, 'I don't know. Maybe.'

I can't stand these honest women, can you?

I'd always wondered what it was that triggered my dreams of being in Lancasters over Germany again. I worked it out later that night. The dream usually came after I had had a bad time, but was then safe. When I awoke the small fire in the bedroom was on its last legs, but still flickering. Dieter was standing in the doorway in those hideous striped flannel pyjamas we could never get away from, rubbing the sleep from his eyes with his hands. He said, 'You were shouting. It woke me. Carlo is still asleep.'

'Sorry, Dieter. It was only a nightmare.'

'Was it about Germany?'

'Yes.'

'Sometimes I dream about Germany too.' As he turned away he added, 'You don't need to worry now, Papa, we will always be here to look after you.'

Then it was my turn to turn away, because there was a lump in my throat.

Chapter Eleven

Two days later Les drove me back to Lympne. As usual he drove my car too fast, and easily outran a police car that gonged us from a distance. It was just like old times.

Maggs had gone back to the junk shop, and found me a rattan cane – I have it still. My ankle was bound up, and only really hurt like hell if I let it bend under me. I had wanted to keep the crutch as a reminder, but Maggs claimed it, and hung it above the bar. She wanted it for a reminder as well.

All of the kites were out, but Berlin wasn't on yet, despite Halton's preparations and the screaming headlines from the newspapers. Perhaps the politicians would sort it out for once without anyone having to die. After I'd told the tale, Les chatted Elaine up. I'd seen Les in action before: he wasted no time once he'd made his mind up. Old Man Halton appeared from somewhere. I gave him back his wallet. He hardly acknowledged it. I also gave him an envelope that Dieter had asked me to pass on. The Old Man looked at it quizzically, and wrinkled his nose. That might have been a smile. He coughed, and asked, 'From your son, you said?'

'Yes. One of the runaways. He asked me to deliver it.'

It was addressed to Halton in a neat, boyish script; Dieter's best handwriting. When the Old Man opened it, it contained a drawing which had been folded twice. The drawing was of a man

recognizable as the Old Man himself; an equally recognizable
civilianized Dakota sat on an airstrip in the background.

'How did he do this?'

I glanced at it.

'From a newspaper or magazine photograph probably. He
keeps a scrapbook of anything to do with me, or the RAF.
Someone must have told him I was working for you now, and he
cut your picture from somewhere.' What I didn't tell him was
that a different boy, in a different place, had once given a similar
drawing to me – and I thought it had brought me luck.

The Old Man said, 'Mm . . .' as he turned away with the
paper in his hand, and, 'I told you to bring them down one
weekend, didn't I? Boys like aircraft.'

'Yes you did, boss.' The problem was that I was no longer sure
that *I* did. 'Thank you.'

Sometime weeks later, when I happened to be in his office, I
noticed that Dieter's picture had been framed, and was up on the
wall alongside those Halton had commissioned and paid hundreds
for. Dieter's sketch hung alongside one of Milton by Cuthbert
Orde; he would be pleased to know that.

Elaine drove Les down to the station to catch a train. I sat in
the office, and waited for her. Brunton wasn't there, but occasionally I could hear someone moving around close by – probably the
Old Man – and there was a periodic clatter from the maintenance
team, when they came into their domestic rooms to get their
char.

Everything was curiously peaceful. There was a storm gathering, just like early 1939, but nobody wanted to face it. I made a
cup of black stuff from the bottle of Camp on the table behind
Elaine's desk. Then I sat and read her *Mirror*, and found I was in
for a treat. Jane was naked in all four of the windows of her comic
strip. Maybe she was so tired of losing her clothes every day she
couldn't be bothered to put them on. I looked at Jane, and

wondered if there was anything I could do about getting a proper girlfriend for once. Jane looked back at me; the message I got back from her was that I couldn't.

The Old Man shuffled in preceded by his thunderous coughs. He dropped a folder of papers in front of me. It had a dog-eared card cover, not far off RAF blue.

'Look through this, would you, Charlie. You might need to help Mr Brunton, and this is the quickest way to get you up to date.'

I suppose that I could have done the meek and loyal employee thing, nodded and kept my mouth shut, but that's not me, is it?

'What is it, boss?'

'Correspondence; and pre-contract flimsies between us and Mr Attlee. He suddenly finds he might need a bigger air force than the one he has left.'

'He doesn't want us to help by dropping bombs on people again?'

'No, just food. Food and fuel and clothes, and whatever else it needs to keep our bit of Berlin going.'

'It's on then?'

'Not officially. They're still trying to avoid it.'

'I had a friend once: Pete. He was Polish. He said that the Russians were worse than Jerry. He hated Stalin more than he hated Hitler.'

The Old Man stifled another massive coughing fit with his handkerchief. I'd noticed that occasionally when he pulled the cloth away it was stained dark with flecks of blood. I wondered how long he could go on. He must have picked up on that, because he said, 'Do you know the worst thing about my lungs, Charlie?'

I shook my head, and said, 'No, boss,' even though I didn't want to know.

'Can't smoke. I used to love a cigarette, or a good cigar. If I did that now, the docs say, I'd be dead in a month. I really miss that. There are a hundred things like that I can hate the Hun for, and now it looks like I'm going to be the one feeding him. *Funny*, what?'

'Ironic,' I told him. 'There's nothing funny about it as far as I'm concerned: or if there *is* I don't know who's laughing.'

'The Commies, Charlie, and I suppose we'll all have to get used to that.'

I'd joined the CP myself, by accident, the year before. Not many people knew that. I wondered if Halton did, or if I should find a way of breaking it to him.

I was still in the papers when I heard the company car pull up outside. It was a ten-year-old Rover saloon on its last legs. We called it the Passion Wagon . . . that's what most of the aircrew borrowed it for, and its saggy back seat had been battered into submission. You had to watch out for a vengeful spring or two. Elaine had been faster than I expected. She looked over my shoulder, and asked, 'Where did you get those papers?'

I was just about finished anyway, so I closed the folder. 'The Old Man asked me to read them. He said it would get me up to date.'

She looked out of the window, across the airfield. Pensive and sad. 'Do you think we're going to war again? I'm not sure that I could bear it.'

There had always been the suggestion that Elaine had lost someone very close to her in the war; it would have been surprising if she hadn't – most of us did.

'No. Not that kind of war, anyway. I think that we're all too used up to slug it out again for another few years. It wouldn't surprise me if my sons had to fight the Russians one day though.'

When she turned back she had softened.

'Tell me again. How are your sons?'

'Partly proud of themselves, and partly very ashamed . . . and more than a bit frightened when they found out just how many people had risked life and limb looking for them. The question of punishment *did* crop up – we're big on punishment, we English, aren't we?'

'What's going to happen to them?'

'The Commodore of the Yacht Club came up with the suggestion that they be sentenced to clean and help on people's yachts, for the next so many Saturdays. I accepted for them, and when I told the boys the smiles on their faces were like Christmas had come: I think that they'd wanted to get on those boats for months!'

'So, all's well that ends well?'

'I suppose so. Over and out, for the time being, anyway.'

She sat on the edge of the desk and asked, 'How old were you when you became a father, Charlie?'

'First of all I was twenty-one, I think . . . but then I was never a father at all, really. They are other people's kids. We became attached in the war, and never got unattached again.'

'You're their legal guardian?'

'Not that either. I've signed some papers for the school and the council, but I don't think that's the same . . .'

'You'll have to sort that out properly. I think that you and I should have a long talk about them some time . . .'

'Sorry, love.' I reached out, and touched her leg as if I had her permission to do it. She stepped quickly away. 'I only talk about that sort of thing in bed. What are we doing after work?' To be honest that sounded crass, even to me.

It was her turn to say *sorry*.

'Sorry, Charlie. This is Friday. My Terry will be home by seven.'

I did the two-can trick on the stove again; there was a pile of split birch logs outside. It was big enough to fuel the *Queen Mary*. This time I used a tin of corned beef, and a tin of processed peas. I still washed them down with beer. Then in the twilight I hobbled manfully around the peritrack, because the docs in Havant – the small hospital near Chichester – had told me to keep the ankle exercised. Down in the dip, and up against the hedge at the edge of the field, were five small aeroplane-shaped humps, each lashed down under a tarpaulin. You couldn't see them from the admin buildings up on the ridge. In fact you'd have to be in the know to know they were there at all. I had a peek under one. It was a very nice late-mark Spit: hardly used. I had the feeling that I'd seen it before. A specific blasphemous word came to mind – one I'd been using too frequently recently.

I had gone too far for my weak ankle, and took twice as long to get back up the slope. I tried a short cut across the grass, but it was hopeless because my stick dug in. It was dark before I was within a hundred yards of the welcoming light from the windows of our pro tem accommodation hut. The only problem was that I hadn't left the light on when I went out. I hoped that Elaine's old man hadn't found out she was playing at outside left, and tossed her out.

Fergal was sitting on one of the other beds, a big cheap suitcase alongside him. He looked weary.

'Hello, Charlie.'

I was actually as tired as he looked, and my ankle throbbed. I sat down heavily on my own bed.

'Hello, Fergal; run away?'

'You were always good at keeping the stove in, Charlie. You must have a knack with them. No. I haven't run away. I *feel* like running away, but I haven't. You, me and a Nissen hut. Quite like old times isn't it?'

'It's not as big as the Grease Pit, but it's not as draughty either. Our aircrews use it if they're only here for a night, and haven't a floozy up in the village to sleep on.' The Grease Pit was what we'd called the hut we slept in when we were on the squadron.

Grease had been our pilot. I told you before, *Sergeants all*. 'So what are you doing down here? Checking up on me?'

'No. I'm a shepherd between flocks. They've given me a new orphanage. It's four times the size of the Liverpool one, and I'm going to be in charge.'

'Is that a promotion?'

'I think so, Charlie, but don't congratulate me until you've heard the rest.'

'Why?'

'Because it's in Berlin; and your mob is going to fly me out there apparently. My boss has spoken to your boss, and fixed it up.'

My initial response was *Fuck it*! But I actually observed, 'Fergal, *your* boss is the Pope.'

'I know. Impressive, isn't it? Even if he *was* a bit of an old Nazi. Is that what they mean when they say *friends in high places?*'

'Has anyone hinted that the Big City may not be the most comfortable place in the world for the next few months?'

'Everyone. All the time.' He did what he always did when he didn't want to talk about something: he switched on a brilliant smile which made him look momentarily about fourteen years old. 'I'm starving, Charlie. Have you got any scoff in this place, or will I be reduced to eating the blankets?' *Good practice for Berlin*, I thought, but I didn't tell him that.

'Spam and beans, or bully and peas?'

'How about both? Then you can show me to your pub. God won't mind just this once.'

Later we sat in the bar, and drank gently towards oblivion. Fergal's black garb drew some glances, but no one had the nerve to say anything. Elaine was sitting in the corner with a man who looked like Desperate Dan. Brunton was at another table with an improbably pretty redhead. When Elaine smiled to him he pretended he hadn't seen, and turned away. Elaine's husband picked that up, and frowned. I could smell the trouble on the air like brimstone.

On Monday morning, after we'd shaved, I asked Fergal to drive us up to The Parachute for breakfast. My ankle still didn't like the changes of direction my car's pedals demanded of it. There was a small crowd of groundies outside the office. We stopped alongside them. I asked the maintenance Chiefy, 'What's up? Nowhere to go?'

'The office ain't unlocked yet; Mr Brunton didn't get in yet. We can't get in to our locker room.'

I looked at my watch. Nine twenty. Brunton was an eight ack emma man. Damn.

'What about Elaine? Mrs Curtis?'

'Her neither.' He sniffed, and wiped his nose on his sleeve. Chiefies are made, not born. Double damn.

'Have you got a spare key?'

He glanced from one side to the other before he replied, 'Maybe . . .'

'Then use it, fer chrissake. OK? *My* authority . . .'

Then something strange happened. He straightened a little from his habitual hunch, and touched his forehead in something that once was a salute, years ago.

'OK, Mr Bassett. Thank you, Mr Bassett.' *Mr Bassett*. Me. As Fergal eased the Singer away from them he murmured, 'Less of the *for Christ's sake*, Charlie. He might hear you, and then we'll both get into trouble.'

I still couldn't get over being called *Mr Bassett* by a man twice my age. Neither could I work out if that constituted a good start to the day, or a bad.

When we got back Halton was behind Elaine's desk, and both her telephones were ringing.

'Where have you been? What do you think I pay you for?' He was not a happy man.

'Radios mostly, boss. Do you want me to take over?'

Instead of snarling *Yes* at me he lost himself in a cough. Then he nodded his head fiercely. As he got it back under control I asked, 'Where are the others?'

I had to wait for the bell between another two rounds.

'The squadron leader's in hospital, and our secretary is in a cell at Dymchurch. So is her husband. Mrs Brunton's on a train back to Auchtermuchty, or wherever she once came from. These are not unconnected events.'

'Has the squadron leader been being a wicked old squadron leader, boss?'

'No, Charlie . . . that's *your* role in life's little drama, isn't it? Don't think I don't know what's going on around here – Brunton got blamed for it, that's all.'

I looked away. I never like getting caught out.

'Badly hurt?'

'Broken jaw; two teeth. Then Elaine stabbed her husband with a fork. Terry Curtis has been charged with assault, and Elaine has been charged with stabbing *him*: we'll be lucky to keep her out of prison.' He seemed to notice Fergal for the first time. 'Is this the priest?' he asked me.

'Yes, boss.'

He smiled thinly at Fergal, and kept his hacking lungs in check.

'Welcome to Lympne, Father. I understand that you were on Lancasters in the war?'

'That would be correct, sur. Flight engineer.' Fergal was pulling the tow-headed yokel trick.

'Good. One of my pilots is ferrying a Lancastrian across to Wunstorf this afternoon for Airworks, you can cadge a lift, and work your passage.'

'My pleasure, sur. It will be quite like old times.'

The Old Man avoided the coughs, and shot back in an icy tone, '*Old times* are precisely what we're hoping to avoid, Father.'

'Aye aye, sur.' Fergal was smiling. He knew the score all right.

'Do you want me to go over as well?' I asked Halton.

'No, Charlie, you can stay here, and run the damned office until we get some of our staff back. It was probably all your fault anyway.'

Old Man Halton was rumoured to be Plymouth Brethren, so the word *damned* revealed the depth of his anger and frustration. He'd probably have to confess to having used it to whatever god his lot bowed down to. Perhaps I'd ask Fergal to intervene for him; these bloody religions all seemed much of a muchness to me.

Elaine stooged in after lunch. I asked her, 'You all right?'

'Yes. Terry won't bring any charges. He told them it was an accident.'

'Was it my fault? Halton seems to think so.'

'Of course not, darling. Terry bashed Mr Brunton for looking at me the wrong way in the pub. Then Mrs Brunton kicked him when he was down: she must have agreed. I got angry and slapped Terry. Unfortunately I still had my fork in my hand. I'll pop up and tell the Old Man, and apologize for getting in so late.'

'Don't bother.' That was Halton's voice from the door way. 'The *Old Man* heard you.' Elaine blushed. I'd never seen that before. She looked younger. 'Open the day's mail as quick as you like, and bring it in . . .'

'Yes, sir.'

'When can I have my manager back?'

Elaine replied, 'Friday week at the earliest, I'm afraid, sir. He can't speak yet.'

There was a short lull in the interchange, and then Halton

stepped fully into the room: a light, neat step for a light, neat man. No coughs. He looked at me.

'You know that I don't approve of bad language, Charlie?'

'Yes, boss . . .' What had I said now? 'I . . .'

He waved me to silence. 'The problem is that there's no direct way of saying what I want to say to you without it.'

In for a penny. I asked, 'What's that, boss?'

His little dark eyes bored into me. I was sure that this was the sack. Then he sighed, 'You finally fucked your way to the top, Charlie. Take over until Brunton is back; all right? But no more hanky panky. Understood?'

I think that what he meant was, *Don't get caught*. I gulped and nodded.

'Understood, boss . . . and thank you.'

'Briefing in the boardroom in an hour. Elaine will have put the papers together by then. OK?'

We both probably nodded in reply. I couldn't have said anything if I'd wanted to.

I went into Brunton's small office, tried his desk for size, and let his big old leather chair swallow me. He had a small mirror above a shelf – he was that kind of squadron leader, if you know what I mean – and I caught a glimpse of my grinning face in it. I was thinking about what my mum would have thought if she could have seen me now . . . her little Charlie, running an airline. A small one maybe, and only for a week, but everyone has to start somewhere.

In the outer office Elaine turned on the radio, and sang along with Aaron Aaronson. The song was 'Let's Misbehave'.

One of the first calls I took was from the Customs. In reality Elaine answered all the calls, and had a gadget on her telephones which enabled her to switch a call through to telephones that lodged with Halton, the engineers or Brunton. It seemed like bloody magic to me.

Holland said, 'Hello, Charlie. Have you gone up in the world?'

'It's only temporary. Our manager got into a fight last Friday, and I'm sitting in his chair until he gets back.'

'I hope you've got a fat cushion, so you can see over the desk.' What is it with these tall guys?

'What do you want?'

'Your bill: in print that is. I have to get the chitties in by the end of the month. Your Mr Brunton was going to invoice me by today.'

'For what?'

'Storing the King's aeroplanes. I hope you still have my five Spits parked on your lawn. I seized them last week.'

'Yes, they're still there. How *do* you seize an aircraft?'

'You lay your hand on it, and solemnly declare it seized in the names of the Commissioners of Customs and Excise . . . it's almost like muttering a spell. Then you explain to its previous owner, if you have him to hand, that it now belongs to the King . . . or in the case of one of those Spits, that it now belongs to the King *again*.'

'I thought it was tactless of you to bring them here.'

'I have to use the nearest operational civvy airport, old boy; the opposition would have smelled a rat if I'd taken them anywhere else. Thank you, by the way – we are in your debt.'

I almost said, *I'd prefer not to talk about it here*, before something occurred to me.

'Did you catch up with the . . . the . . . new owners?'

'No. A pity about that. We got the pilot who was taking them out, poor sod. He'd already got one away.'

'What will happen to him?'

'Prison probably, unless he legs it. He was out of work. There must be thousands like him.'

'Yeah; poor sod,' I echoed. 'What happens to the aircraft?'

'After we've been to court we'll sell them again.'

'. . . And what happens to you; a gold star in your exercise book?'

The pause told me I'd offended him.

'No, old boy; better than that. Money. We get paid seizure rewards, just for doing our jobs . . . and aeroplanes come pretty high up the list. Thanks to you, I've five of them. I must remember to buy you a lollipop some time.'

'What will you do with the money?'

The pause this time was reflective. He was genuinely striving for a reply I'd understand.

'I've always had a hankering to take Mrs Holland on a really long motoring holiday: caravanning. I'll probably buy a brand-new caravan to tow behind the Jaguar.'

I hadn't forgotten that I'd won him that either.

'You must enjoy your work . . .'

'Funnily enough old boy, I do. Laugh a minute . . .'

I told him that I'd get someone to send him his bloody invoice, and put the phone down before he did.

Then Fergal called me from Wunstorf. He was stuck there, but thought he could get a lift into Berlin on an RAF Hastings in a couple of days. They'd put him into that huge accommodation block.

'This is a horrible fucking country, Charlie. I hate it already. Me mam asked me to bring her back a Dresden china shepherdess.'

'Dresden doesn't exist any more in a meaningful sense. Didn't we knock it down and burn the bits in 1945? You'll probably have to get half a dozen shepherdesses, and stick one together from all the bits: it will give you something to do while you wait. Anyway, Fergal, you're not supposed to swear. Priests aren't supposed to swear; Mr Halton doesn't like it either.'

'Living in the remains of Germany would make anyone swear.'

'You'll feel much better once you've got your orphanage to look after.'

There is something I like about ex-servicemen: they don't duck the issue, do they? There was a gap, into which he quietly asked, 'Am I going to be able to feed these children when things get tough, Charlie . . . or will I just have to sit there and watch them starve?'

It was my turn to fill a gap: Fergal always put the screws on you without you realizing it. I replied, 'You'll always be able to feed them, Fergal. You have my word. I promise. Go and get drunk now, with some nice accommodating American girl: they really go for clergymen. Everything will look better in the morning.'

'I'll be seeing you, Charlie.'

'Sooner than you think. Bye, Fergal.'

Chapter Twelve

They announced the shutdown of Berlin and the official start of the Airlift a few days later, but no one invited Halton Airways to the party. The newspapers said that our bold RAF and USAF boys could handle it alone: only the *Daily Mirror* had the wit to ask if they actually had enough aircraft any more — but even the *Mirror* buried the query at the bottom of page three. Most tabloid newspapers have better things to do with page three these days. The name they gave the British end of the show was Operation Plainfare. I've also seen that spelled Planefare, which was a nice pun if you're into that sort of thing. Old Man Halton didn't seem all that worried. He just went out, and bought another rustbucket of a Dakota to chum up with *Whisky*. He was spending most of his time in his London club, entertaining pals from the RAF and the Air Ministry.

Unfortunately for him the commercial paint shops had run out of red paint. I know that the idea of running out of paint is a bit of a novelty to you, but if you'd been around in the Forties you'd have had the experience of running out of all sorts of ordinary things. The Kirbigrip crisis of 1949 is a good example; it led to women fastening their hair in place with pipe cleaners. Within a fortnight we'd exhausted the pipe-cleaner supply, and men were cleaning their pipes with stalks of grass, and so it goes. Luckily we've never been all that short of grass. Anyway they had to paint the new C-47 with the nearest bloody colour they could get, which turned out to be a very deep reddish pink. It looked absolutely bloody disgusting – like a flying boudoir. Before the Old Man could dig into his *Wizard of Oz* bag again someone called it *The Pink Pig*, and that stuck. She even ended up with a PP registration, and a fat black porker painted on her snout.

The blockade of West Berlin by the Soviets had been finally provoked by the Allied imposition of a new currency that the Reds couldn't control, forge or manipulate. Whatever the Russian phrase for throwing the rattle out of the pram is . . . they did it. Although it's worth asking why, however often we manage to blame the enemy, the ultimate provocation to war – or its declaration – is usually down to the British. Truly we are not the peace-loving nation we would like to be taken for. The Russians had been planning it for months of course, but then so had we – which is why we had enough planes and materials in place before long. Not many people knew that. As far as they were concerned it was Berlin Airlift sudden shock horror.

When the Reds shut down the roads, the canals and the railways we still had two functioning airfields, Gatow and the Tempelhof – although we opened up another in the French Zone later – and the air corridors between them and the West had already been guaranteed inviolable by treaty. All that was left was to find out if the Russkis would allow us to fly the corridors in peace, and whether we had the materials and will to supply half a city under siege. Brunton hadn't come back to us, and Mrs Brunton hadn't come back to him. Chiefy said the rumour was that she'd got off the northbound train at Liverpool, went into a pub with a Lascar seaman, and hadn't been seen since. Maybe Brunton would find himself on the market again, once he stopped eating his meals through a straw. I didn't care as much as I should have done, because his office and records were in a shocking mess, and most evenings I found myself back behind the desk, sorting them out. The truth is that the bastard, like most ex-officers, couldn't run a kiddy's train set, let alone a small airline.

James called me up a few days into the crisis. He asked, 'Is this *it*, then?'

'I think so, James. I only hope the people upstairs know what they're doing . . .' Then I told him, 'I may not get home for a few weeks to begin with. Can you tell the boys?'

'Why don't you tell Dieter yourself? He's still up; helping Mrs Maggs with the washing up.' That sounded better; although I wondered how you could call the woman you shared your bed with *Mrs Maggs*. Perhaps I had it wrong.

I had to wait a couple of minutes for Dieter. When he came on he said, 'Sorry, Dad; I had to wipe my hands.' I was a bit choked. I don't think he'd actually called me *Dad* before.

'Don't worry. I'm just sitting in the office adding up petrol bills.'

'*I* could do that for you.'

'You could probably do it better. I just called to tell you that I may not be home for a few weeks. I didn't want you and Carlo to worry about me.'

'I'll tell him. Is it to do with what's happening in Germany?'

'Yes, it is.'

'Major England's newspaper says that people in Berlin will all starve.' Bugger.

'It's wrong. We won't let them.'

He didn't respond immediately, then he said, 'Do you remember the German girl we chose a doll for?'

'Lottie. Of course I do. Do you want me to give her another message?'

'No, but if people begin to die in Berlin again I want you to bring her out. Just like you did me.'

'It won't get that bad, and anyway, her mother may not like that.'

'Her mother too.' I sensed something in the next pause. It was as if he was weighing up whether or not to tell me something. 'You could marry her. You ought to be married.' The little bugger had it all worked out.

I tried to laugh it off. 'She wouldn't want me, Dieter. Anyway, I'm not the marrying kind.'

He did it again. The five-beat pause. 'I think that you are, Dad. In fact I'm sure of it.'

What had started as a simple call to pass on some information had suddenly become a bit deep for me. I said, 'Look, Dieter, can we talk about this when I next come down?'

'Yes. I'll remind you. I'll remember to tell Carlo in the morning. Did you know he can say his alphabet, and write his name and address? I taught him. Mrs Maggs helped me.'

'Give him a hug from me, and tell him *Well done*. I'm proud of him. I'm proud of you too. Are you getting on OK with Mrs Maggs now?'

'Mrs Maggs is like a mother for me,' he said rather formally, 'although I'd rather we had one of our own.' It was something he was not going to let go of easily.

'OK, Dieter,' I sighed. 'I get the message. I'd better speak to James again.'

I told James I'd phone every few days if I could, and that there was an envelope addressed to him under the mattress of my bed in the prefab. He didn't need to ask what was in it. The call went on a bit because Mrs Maggs insisted on getting a word.

'You're doing a grand job with the kids,' I told her. 'Does anyone tell you that?'

'You do. But thank you all the same.'

'Dieter's got me married off already.'

'. . . Time someone did, innit?'

Her quick putdowns always left me smiling. I think that she knew that. It was a good way to leave it.

I stared at the telephone for a minute after I had put it down. It was dark outside, but not cold. I recalled that as late as 1944 I was shy of using a telephone, because we'd never had one in the house. My eight-year-old son had just chatted to me on one for five minutes as if it was the most natural thing in the world. Things were changing. Then I caught the word. I had just thought of Dieter as my *son*. That was a first too. I stood up from the desk, and pulled the office curtains in case Elaine looked in for that spot of hanky panky. When I went back to the desk I saw that I'd doodled the words *Marthe* and *Lottie* on the blotting pad, and drawn a dark circle around them.

Airworks and Flight Refuelling got the call before we did. Five days into the Airlift proper Berlin ran out of petrol, and one of them already had most of that side of the business all sewn up. They'd been buying up Lancastrians like there was no tomorrow, and converting them into flying petrol tankers. We lent them a couple of pilots to ferry them into Germany: every time I saw one I momentarily saw Milton's silly face, and lost my place in the day.

Then I went up to Cardiff in *Dorothy*, with Scroton and Mortensen . . . and after that I nearly bought it.

It was a simple run between Cardiff and Lorient in Brittany. I've sometimes wondered why the French call a port just about as west as they can go in their country, *the orient*. Peculiar sense of direction maybe. We had thirty-five war-surplus US tractors for the Brittany farmers. Scroton had filed a flight plan for Rennes, which was the nearest place with a proper airfield for Customs and freight, but the Old Man vetoed that. He'd taken a door-to-door contract, and didn't want to shell out for road transport at the other end. A local farmer who was fronting the deal assured us that he had a field large enough and firm enough for *Dorothy*'s fat footprint. He'd promised us farmhouse bed-and-breakfast, and a petrol bowser waiting to top her up. Reading between the lines I think that meant *les Douanes* knew nothing at all about the trip.

Mortensen said he no longer farted. He'd been to the Doc when everyone refused to fly with him, and had been dosed up. He sweated instead, and his sweat was more rancid than his farts. He smelled positively unhealthy. The armpits of his white shirt had stiffened to a lemon yellow colour.

One of the tractors broke loose in turbulence over the Channel, and raced around the cargo space like a fighting bull in the Ronda ring. Mortensen and I eventually managed to rope it down, but not before it had dealt *Dorothy*'s flanks some spectacular dents, and it still moved about under its shackles. I couldn't stop myself from going back to check on it every ten minutes. When I went back to report to Scroton I distinctly heard Mortensen drop one, and got the shock of the sickly, sweet smell we were familiar with.

'I'm not due any more linctus for an hour,' he told us. 'You'll bloody well have to put up with it: *I* have to.'

Then there was the rain out of Cardiff so deep we took half an hour to climb out of it. *Dorothy* was cold and clammy, and wallowed around in the wet air as if she was ready to give up. Flights like that can discourage you. We broke clear of the squalls over Torquay, and a couple of Fleet Air Arm Sea Hornets came up to play silly buggers for ten minutes. Anyone would think they hadn't seen a red-painted big job before. They pushed off as soon as the weather began to catch up again. So much for the Navy's vaunted *all-weather fighters*. The precipitation chased us all the way down to Rennes and then across to Lorient, which is where things got a little awkward.

Scroton circled *Dorothy* around the field a couple of times, at about a hundred feet. We'd shared the navigation, and were pretty pleased with ourselves for finding it without too much difficulty. Dave said it was plenty long enough if we touched down in one corner and ran diagonally across it. The Frenchman obviously thought the same, because he'd pinned a big white arrow, made from sheets, at the touch-down corner, and marked the course across the field with half a dozen swan-necked flares – he'd done this before. Each flare burned with a sharp orange light and a narrow plume of black smoke, so the smoke gave us a wind drift as well. Piece of piss really – well, you'd *think* so.

Scroton committed us to the landing with a short flat run, and dropped her just inside the boundary, almost on the arrow, and immediately shut down all four throttles. Then Mortensen said, ''s funny. The hydraulic pressure's . . .'

He didn't get a chance to say anything else, because Dave had tramped on the pedals, and nothing happened. He screamed, '*Fu-u-cked* . . . *no brakes*! . . .' You could have heard that shout back in Cardiff.

The field ran away from us, and we were crossing it like a comet. It dropped a few feet into its far corner, beyond which was a big stone farmhouse, a line of jaunty washing, and about six cottages: there was no way we were going to clear or avoid them. Scroton told me later that he didn't think about what he did next . . . he just selected *undercarriage up*, and dropped the York onto the field in a classic belly flop. Look, Ma, no wheels! Like all the best dancers *Dot* had a nice flat tummy, and we careered across the wet grass on it like a toboggan on Hampstead Heath. Dave hung on to the controls by instinct, but they weren't doing anything any more. The noise was tremendous, and clods of earth and grass billowed around *Dorothy*'s run like a thundercloud. Then she stopped. Mortensen hit his head on the side screen, and closed his eyes. I slammed into the back of his seat.

What followed wasn't silence, it was the pattering and banging of all of the shit we'd flung into the air falling back down onto us again. Then there was the silence, and Scroton began to laugh.

'I think that was my best crash so far,' he told us.

We had lost the crew door, which was on the port side, under the wing. A big Frog wearing one of those smashing small black berets put his head and shoulders through the space. He said, ''allo?'

I was sitting on the floor. My shoulder hurt, and my face was telling me to expect a black eye in the morning. Dave was laughing, and Mortensen was out cold. The Frenchman tried again, ''allo, 'allo?'

''allo,' I responded. I was probably grinning like a fool.

'*Les tracteurs?*'

'*Oui. Tout va bien. Très forts.*' Then I switched wearily to English, because my brain wouldn't work. 'You're supposed to say, *For you the war is over*.'

He shook his head and smiled, and said in better English than my French, 'Welcome to France. Your first visit?'

'No. I was here in '45 and '47.'

'She has changed.'

'So have I. I'm older, and I get hurt more easily.'

'What's the bad smell in your aeroplane?'

That made me smile again. 'That's a long story . . .'

'A glass of wine perhaps?'

'Delighted, old fellow.'

He helped me out. Scroton scrambled after me, dragging Mortensen. We laid him on the grass, but he was having none of it, because he woke up, and sat up.

'If you say, *Where am I?*' I said, 'I'll clout you and lay you out again.'

'Where am I?'

'In France.'

'That's OK. For a moment I thought we were still in Wales. I couldn't bear to be in Wales.'

It wasn't wine, it was bloody cider. Bloody gallons of the

bloody stuff. I phoned Lympne from an odd-shaped public pay phone outside one of the cottages, and explained to Elaine that although our crew and cargo had arrived approximately intact, the same couldn't be said for *Dorothy*: she was going to need some determined nursing.

'Are you all right?'

'Bruised and just a little drunk. *Dorothy* slid on her belly for damned nigh a hundred yards before she stopped. No word on the Squadron Leader coming back?'

'Complications: he's been transferred to the dental hospital in an ambulance.'

'Any decisions you want me to make then? I'm good at that when I'm drunk.'

'Why don't I do it for you, and just put your name to them?'

'OK. Will you tell the boss we had a problem?'

'How big is the problem? Will *Dorothy* fly again?'

'Eventually . . . why don't you get Randall to drop the Chiefy over here to look at her?'

'OK, Charlie . . . you're in charge.' The odd thing was it bloody felt like it as well.

You may not believe this but there was a party going when I found my way back to the farmhouse: someone had produced a whole cask of cider, and half a dozen bottles of clear spirits. The farmer paid me in cash for the tractors, which was a bit nervy. It was a wallet of franc notes that he asked me to give to Halton: I hadn't known that they were his bloody tractors as well. I don't know where all the folk came from, but the farmer, Gaspard, had the best collection of Tommy Dorsey 78s I've ever seen. I danced a couple with a very pretty young wife, but didn't like the way her husband watched us – cleaning his fingernails with a nasty-looking lock knife with black grips. After 'East of the Sun, West of the Moon' I led her back across the floor and gave him her hand, a small bow and a *Merci*. Later we danced to bagpipe music in large rings, just like the Scots, and didn't go out to *Dorothy* again till next morning.

She didn't look all that good in the morning; like your girlfriend without her make-up. I probably didn't look so good myself; I had a hell of a headache, I'll tell you that. If someone from Brittany ever offers you some sloppy white spirits in a greasy bottle, do yourself a favour and say *No*. Randall flew the drab Oxford in at about half past ten. He said that he hadn't wanted to attract attention to us. I think we'd already done that ourselves; we'd left a ruddy great red aeroplane in the middle of someone's best field. Chiefy had brought a fitter with him. They both had overnight bags with them, and got down from Randall's aircraft looking around for the enemy. We left Mortensen with them, and were back in Lympne after lunch.

The Chief phoned me before I jacked it in for the day. He said, 'You've left yon *Dorothy* with a very dirty pair of knickers, Mr Bassett.' *Yon*.

'I didn't think you were a Scottie, Chief.'

'I aren't. I belong to Consett. Why did you think that?'

'Never mind. How's our aeroplane?'

'Not as bad as I thought. These Yorks have a very strong frame, but I'll have to reskin her belly, and you need three new propeller blades. I'll look to her engines tomorrow.'

'What do I tell the boss?'

'Tell him she might fly out of here in a fortnight; there again, she might not. If she's part of his cunning plan, tell him to claim on the insurance and go out and buy another. We can always sell one later.' That's always the problem with engineers: they tend to be too free with other folk's money.

'Where will I find the parts and materials you'll need, Avro's?'

'Leave it to Mrs Curtis. She'll know. I'll send her a telegram.

Is that all for the time being, Mr Bassett? . . . There seems to be some sort of dance starting up, and I don't want to miss anything.'

'Don't they ever bloody stop?'

'I wouldn't know, sir; ask me in a week.'

Elaine assured me that he wouldn't be out there a week. He'd get the work started, then we would send in another erk with the spares and the Chief would come back on the same flight. He'd probably go out with a pilot to get *Dorothy* into the air again. Ground-crew chiefs are like your mother; you don't know where you'd be without them.

Elaine said, 'You've a proper shiner there, Charlie. Did some woman's husband catch up with you at last?'

'You could almost say that, but actually *no*. *Dorothy* did it to me.' If I had a smile, it was at a recent memory. When I walked out to the Oxford with Scroton and Randall, the pretty woman I had danced with, and her husband, accompanied us. They were neighbouring farmers who had bought one of the tractors. She gave me a kiss on each cheek, and he held out his hand for a shake. I felt something pressed into my palm. When I looked down it was his wicked little lock knife. He closed my fist over it, smiled and nodded . . . being one of the first farmers in France to own a tractor was going to give him an edge. I suppose he thought that he was giving me an edge too. It was an evil little thing, and I loved it immediately. I put my hand in my overalls pocket as I spoke to Elaine, just to make sure that it was still there.

Old Man Halton made a flying visit. It's what owners of pocket airlines do. I should have guessed that he could fly, although I wouldn't have liked sitting alongside him for a landing when he started to cough his lungs up. He had a nice shiny new Auster, which he taxied right up to the office as if he owned the place. I walked out to greet him. On its cabin door it had the words *Lionheart* and *Halton Airways* in neat black stencil.

'I couldn't call her plain *Lion*, or *Cowardly Lion*, could I?'

'I suppose not, boss. What will you do when you run out of *Wizard of Oz*?'

'I've thought about that; I thought I'd make a start on *Alice*. Am I going to need a new *Dorothy*?'

'Only if you want her within the next fortnight. Chiefy says she'll be back in the air by then: good as new.' My left hand was behind my back, fingers crossed.

He was shaking his head, and coughing at the same time. 'I won't buy another. She's been nothing but bother.'

I rather liked the way she'd walked away from her first crash landing, but decided to hold that observation for later. He stooged around what was temporarily my office, looked through the clips of clearances and flight dockets, and checked them against the readiness board.

'You're rather good at this, Charlie,' he told me.

'I'm doing Mr Brunton's job, and flying as well. I should get double the pay.'

He laughed. 'Not *that* good.'

I wasn't going to push it. I had a good number and knew it.

'It's not all that difficult, boss. You just need to keep tabs of where our assets are, if they're serviceable, what they're doing . . . and where you want them next.'

'Assets?'

'Sorry: aircraft and crews.'

'You're thinking like a capitalist, Charlie, I don't know whether to be proud or ashamed of you.' We'd just dumped his biggest aircraft in a field in France, and the little bugger was cracking jokes. Even more, they were weak jokes with a little bit of poison inside. I'd have to watch him. Before he left an hour later he told me to jump on the next bus to Celle and Berlin . . . he wanted to be certain that things were ready for us. He always seemed to know that much quicker than the rest of them.

Getting across to Germany at no expense – which is what the

Old Man expected – entailed a delay of nearly two days. A new pilot we'd taken on was due to fly the *Pink Pig* and a load of American PX stores over from an American base in the UK. We arranged for him to flop down at Lympne to pick me up. The Old Man said it would give me a chance to check out both the pilot and the *Pig*.

There was a pilot waiting outside the office for us when I walked up from the hut the next morning, but it wasn't our new man. This one was a stocky young fellow who wore old RAF blue trousers, scuffed lightweight flying boots and an old patched flying jacket. It looked almost as ill used as mine. The man looked almost as ill used as me. The grin he summoned up was strained, but he stuck out a paw. I said, 'Are you looking for a job?'

'I would be if I wasn't under arrest.'

'What for?'

'Smuggling aircraft. I flew a second-hand Spit to France a couple of weeks ago. It ended up in Palestine. The Customs got me as I tried to take another one. Now I'm out on bail.'

'Yeah, but what are you here for?'

'Customs guys told me to report here. They want to photograph me alongside the evidence. It's easier to produce a photograph in court than an aircraft.'

I said, 'Tough break.'

'Yeah. I know, but thanks for saying it.'

He seemed an all right type down on his luck, to me.

'Are you allowed to have a cup of char with me while you wait?'

'Thanks again. Don't see why not. Are you the manager of this outfit?'

I know that you'll think me slow, but it hadn't occurred to me in as many words before.

'Yes. I rather think I am. Come inside, and I'll fix us up.'

In fact, in our small galley I sat at the table while he made the tea. His motions were neat and economic, and when he relaxed he smiled a lot. He said, 'I should have come and asked you for a job before I took the money for the Spits.'

'You should have done. I think that you might have fitted in here. What's your name?'

'Bozey . . . Boswell Borland.'

'I'm Charlie Bassett.'

'Weren't you in the papers last year? Something to do with Germany in 1945.'

'Yes,' I told him, 'but would you mind if we didn't talk about it? It was a load of old cobblers.'

'O . . . K.' He spaced the two letters out. Uncomplicated.

'Look, I know the Customs guy who's dealing with your case. He told me you'd go to prison unless you ran away.'

'Yes, he told me I'd go away.'

'I got the impression that if you *did* run away he wouldn't come looking for you. I think they're satisfied with a shelf full of Spits. The court case is a complication he doesn't need.'

'Do you believe that?'

'Yes, I do . . . and I'll tell you something else. This is a small operation: we work out of here and Croydon. If you can get out of the country, to Germany, we could have office chairs in Celle, Wunstorf, Lübeck and Gatow – especially Gatow – in a fortnight. If you can make your own way there and you're any good, I'll find you a flying job one way or another.'

He wasn't so dumb. He asked me, 'Why?'

'Search me. Something to do with running out of luck a few times myself perhaps.'

'I'll remember it then. Thanks.'

'OK.'

We took our mugs of char into the outer office. Elaine wasn't due in for another ten minutes, and the Old Man was back in London. It had been an unseasonably cold night, and in the sunshine the grass glistened with dew. We were still standing watching it when Holland rolled up in his fancy Jaguar. He had a woman in the passenger seat alongside him. I went round to open the door for her, and she gave me a dark red smile. Her lipstick was as red as Eve Valentine's.

'This is Charlie Bassett,' he told her. 'He runs things around here. This is Patsy,' he told me. 'Patsy works for the *News Chronicle*, but moonlights for us. She's an ace photographer.'

Patsy looked about fourteen years old. She asked me, 'Weren't you in the news last year?'

'Yes. But I'd prefer to forget about it.'

Holland asked me, 'My smuggler turned up yet?'

I said, 'I think your car's much too flash for a servant of the Crown. It's a spiv's car.'

'Has my smuggler . . . ?'

'Yes he has.' That was Borland's voice from the door. 'I was just putting on my make-up for your photos.'

I left them to it. I knew that I'd done the right thing telling Holland about our friends from the Stern Gang buying warplanes to use in Palestine, but I hadn't expected to face the fall guy who was going to answer for it. In particular, I hadn't expected to *like* the fall guy being prosecuted for it. Elaine came in, and I told her what was going on. She made a face. She didn't like it either.

'I'm going to revoke our Bozey's bail.' Holland said when they trooped back in half an hour later.

'What for?'

'For being sarky. Captured smugglers ain't supposed to be sarky; they're supposed to have a humble and contrite heart — just like the hymn says.'

'Can you do that?'

'I'm *going* to. With your permission I'm going to give him a little taste of prison right now, and lock him in your office. Then I'll take you and Patsy up to that cafe for breakfast. I'm famished.'

They must have had words – as we used to say – because Bozey didn't look sarky; he looked bloody angry. That was a good sign. I preceded him into my office, and checked both the catch and latch of the window while he watched me. They worked perfectly. I grinned as I met his eye, and nodded as I locked him in, and gave the key to the Customs man.

I told a few stories that kept them there for half an hour. Bob told a few more and kept us there for another. Patsy laughed at all his jokes, and none of mine. I decided that I didn't fancy her anyway.

When we returned to my office Elaine looked smug. She said, 'Someone's pinched the Passion Wagon. I just turned around, and there it was gone. They must have been very clever.'

Holland unlocked my office door, and handed me the key. Then he opened the door with a flourish. The room was empty of humans, and the open window swung gently in the morning breeze. He said, 'Dearie me,' then after a short pause for breath, 'Dearie, dearie me.'

'I must have forgotten to tell you about the window. Sorry about that.'

That was me.

'Wow!' That was Patsy. 'He's gone on the lam. How exciting. Phone the police.'

Holland gave her a withering look. 'Don't talk daft, woman.' No explanation, no observation, just *Don't talk daft woman*. '. . . and don't tell the bloody rag you work for either. Not if you want any more work from my lot.'

Elaine chipped in with, 'Why don't we all have a nice cup of tea?' She'd been listening to too much radio.

As if she'd picked up on my thought she turned the radio on. Edmundo Ros was singing 'Everybody Loves Saturday Night'. I've always loved that one.

Chapter Thirteen

I felt like bloody royalty. Not that I've ever had much time for that lot: they get paid far too much for holding garden parties and handing out gongs. I felt like royalty because it looked as if they'd sent two planes for me, not one.

The *Pig* made a neat landfall, but was followed in its surge up the slope towards the offices by another Dakota. The second one was a new all-American job; silver all over with the Yanks' big stars, and the words *Camel Caravan to Berlin* painted big on its flanks, above the windows. The words were lettered in the same script used on packets of Camel cigarettes. If it actually majored in fag runs it was destined to become a very popular kite. The pilot was a bit flash, but that's Yanks for you. If I thought about it, Randall's flying always had a touch of Hollywood about it too. By contrast the *Pink Pig* sat alongside it in the colour of fresh steak in a butcher's shop. They kept the props just ticking over, so they didn't intend to hang around for long.

Elaine drove me out to it in the Passion Wagon, which she'd collected from the station where Borland had left it for us. I rode with my hand between her legs, loving the pressure from her thighs. Her cheeks burned red and she was smiling, so I guess that it was all right. She gave me a peck on the cheek just as I got out, and said, 'Come back safe, Charlie.'

'Don't worry. *Take no chances* are my middle names.'

'Liar.' She kissed me again. It was very light, like a spider on your skin. I suddenly realized that I'd seen this movie before: it felt just like going to war.

The *Pig*'s cargo door was open. I flung my bag into her, scrambled over the sill and helped the engineer dog the door shut. The pilot was already turning her into the wind and running her engines up. Through one of the windows I could see *Camel* doing the same, and they took off in parallel, like a couple of fighter planes. There was something about the way our aircraft skipper pulled her off the ground, before I found a seat to strap into, that was disconcertingly familiar. I'd seen flying like this before, but couldn't quite remember where . . . or when. Then I remembered the Yanks of the 306th I'd met at Thurleigh years ago – they flew like this: wrenching an aircraft off the ground like they were riding a bronco. The American Dakota dropped into our airstream, and the two aircraft launched themselves across the Channel.

Our engineer was used to it. He easily clawed his way back to the front. When he disappeared through the curtain I began to move myself. We were in a climbing turn, and it seemed to take me years to clamber over our parcels and crates after him. The engineer turned, grinned and gave me the thumbs up. His agility belied his age – he looked as old as Old Man Halton. He already had a map open on his lap. The pilot had his head turned away. He was only a kid, but I knew that head. I had signed his papers up the day before. His name was not familiar – Rufus Padstow – but I knew that bloody head.

'Hello, Max,' I said. 'How old are you these days?'

He turned and grinned: an older version of the red-haired, freckled boy I remembered.

'Let me see. Sixteen and four. I reckon I'm over twenty – just the same as you when I met you. I must be getting old. Hello yourself, Charlie.'

'Who's *Rufus Padstow*, and where did he come from?'

'Me, Charlie. *Rufus* because of my red hair, and *Padstow* because that's where I was conceived, according to the gardener who was fucking my mother at the time.'

'Padstow in Devon?' I don't even know why I was asking.

'It's in Cornwall actually. No: it's our lot on Cape Cod. The Kennedys are our neighbours.'

'Why can't you still be Louis Maxwell? It was a pretty good name.'

'They sent me to college when I got back to the States and took my flying licence away. I went down to a pilot school in Florida last year and got another, but I needed a new name for it.'

OK, so little Louis had got me up to date. In 1943 he'd joined up in the USAAF about five years too early, a big boy lying about his age – thousands did the same. I'd met him when he was AWOL: he'd run away when he'd found that he wasn't too keen on war after all. It didn't explain why he was piloting one of our aircraft.

'Who hired you?'

'Your owner: my father knows him, and *I* know the secretary my old man is knocking off at the moment. We worked out a deal to keep me quiet, and get me out of the way.'

'What's in it for Halton?'

The *Pig* suddenly found some thin air, and dropped about fifty feet. My stomach heaved, but Maxwell held her up very professionally. Maybe he was a halfway decent pilot. Without looking the engineer reached for the two throttle levers, eased them forward a fraction, and then back as we came out of it.

'Gas. Petrol. At five cents the US gallon less than the

marketplace price. Everybody's happy. Have you met my engineer?'

I turned and made proper eye contact with the guy alongside him for the first time, and was chilled to the marrow.

It took just that one glance to tell me the old man was as mad as a monkey. When you meet the violently deranged for the first time, you know it immediately, don't you? Three hundred years earlier he would have covered his straggly hair with a red bandanna, worn an eyepatch, and carried a cutlass between his teeth. Yo ho fucking ho. When he smiled his teeth didn't look all that good, and I could smell the damage his breath was doing to his mouth from a couple of feet away. His eyes were askew – they moved independently in his head, and then, disconcertingly, would suddenly focus together. He was another Yank, but whereas Max's speaking voice was modulated and the accent was soft, this guy sounded like biting a pumice stone. My teeth are set on edge even thinking about it. He held up his right hand, palm towards me, and said, 'How.'

'How what?'

'It's what the redskins say,' Max told me. 'It means *Hi*.'

'Is he a redskin?'

'He can speak for himself you know.'

'Hell no,' the pirate said. 'I come from Cincinnati.' He fished with one hand in the top pocket of his ovies. They look so threadbare and ragged that you'd think they'd been handed out at a soup kitchen. What he brought out was a rusty four-inch nail suspended at its C of G on a piece of greasy string. He held it up, squinted at it and then asked me, 'Where you wan us to go?'

'Celle. That's in Germany.'

As soon as I spoke he flicked one end of the nail so that it spun horizontally. When it stopped spinning its head was towards Max and its sharp end pointed out of the window alongside the pirate.

'Turn right,' he told Maxwell. 'Gain a bit o' height.'

'He's the navigator as well,' Max told me. 'I flunked all my navigation courses because I couldn't be bothered with the math.' He saw me watching the nail swinging as the aircraft changed heading. 'That's his compass. Neat, ain't it? The best things in life are free.'

I asked the engineer navigator pirate, 'What's your name?'

'Red Ronson.'

'This is Charlie Bassett,' Max told him. 'Now we all know each other.'

'What do you do in this outfit, Charlie?' the engineer asked me.

'At the moment I run it, but I'm beginning to have second thoughts,' I said grumpily.

Red was watching the swinging nail. 'Bring her back ten degrees if you will, Pilot, and watch your heading. You were drifting.'

'. . . and who hired *you*?' I asked him.

'We come as a package,' Max jumped in. 'He's the gardener's cousin. I guess you're stuck with us, Charlie.'

There was something else about Max: we had been in love with the same girl for a while.

We let down for landing three hours later. On the glide path we passed between high blocks of flats, and over a couple of graveyards. These landmarks rang all the wrong kind of bells. I told Max, 'This doesn't look like Celle to me. I think we're in Berlin.'

''s right.' That was Red. 'This is Tempelhof; a little bit of America in the big wicked world. Welcome to American Berlin, boss. We can all go to Celle tomorrow.'

'You filed a flight plan for Celle: so why didn't we go today?'

'Because the *Camel* needed to get to Tempelhof, and it doesn't have a navigator. We said we'd show him the way.'

'. . . and what the *Camel* wants, comes before what your employer wants?'

Max sounded hurt by the question. 'Sure, Charlie. Country before calling. I gotta help a fellow American in trouble.'

Ah bugger it. We'd flown two kites from Lympne to Berlin, guided by a maniac with a nail on a bit of string. That had to count for something, didn't it? I had one last question.

'What's in *Camel* that's so important?'

'Nurses, Charlie. Twenny-six unsullied female nurses with clean undies. The American garrison is going to love you to pieces for getting them here.'

'But I didn't. I didn't know anything about it.'

'Yes you did. You authorized the in-flight change of destination . . . for humanitarian reasons.'

'I never did.'

'You did.' Red turned round to look at me. He winked his right eye. It was a terribly slow wink, like half his face was paralysed. His left eye roamed. 'I forged your signature on the Dec. I'm good at that.'

I got the Kraut Customs to give me a lift over to the terminal buildings: there wasn't much room in the rear seat of their funny little VW car . . . even for me. *Camel*'s pilot was there before me. Some guys were pummelling him on his shoulders. Someone stuffed a fag in his mouth, and a second guy lit it up for him. As I was about to push past he turned and stopped me. He had dark rings under his eyes. He asked, 'Are you Mr Bassett from the Halton C-47?' The Yanks called it C-47. *We* called the Dakota a DC-3. Do try to keep up.

'Yes I am.'

He turned away, and shouted at the scrum, 'Hey guys, this is the guy who led us in!'

I got the cigarette treatment after that, and a waxed paper cup of coffee was shoved into my hand. Eventually I was corralled by an older officer, who told me, 'We're in your debt, son. From now on anything you need, jest ask the army,' and pumped my free hand. I'll swear that he had tears in his eyes. It wasn't until he moved away that I noticed that he wore stars. A general had just fallen in love with me. Not long after that a khaki bus brought the women from the plane, and the focus of attention switched away. They didn't look much like nurses to me.

'Concert party,' Russian Greg explained. 'They manifest concert parties and entertainers as *nurses*, so we won't know. You bring in a big morale boost for our hard-pressed American allies.'

'We aren't your allies any more, Greg. You've shut down the transport network, and are trying to starve us out.'

'Then why you still here? Wanna drink?'

'Yes please. Whatever you're having will do. Anyway, why are *you* here? Isn't the Leihhaus in our zone?'

'No, Charlie. This is the neutral zone. Here. This club is in No Man's Land. If you look at the lines drawn on the map you see this is where the British Zone meets the US Zone, and where they both meet the Soviet Zone. There is a little triangle where the lines meet, and we are sitting in it.' There was a heavy roll of thunder from the south. I think I knew there was a storm coming. My bones ached.

'How's Marthe? Did she get back?'

'Yes I did.' As I heard her voice, I felt her hand on the back of my neck, and then a light kiss there. 'What have you brought me this time?'

'How about me bringing you a sleepless night?'

'That too. You hungry, *Liebe*?'

It was all our act. I've told you that already.

'I could murder an omelette, if anyone feels up to it.'

Magda wandered over from a table where she had failed to get a couple of GIs to buy her a bottle of counterfeit champagne. She blew me a kiss when she sat down. Marthe came back out of the kitchen with a couple of bottles of wine and four glasses. How did she keep her fingers around the stems of four wineglasses?

'Italian white wine.' She pulled out a chair and sat down. 'The kitchen has a contract with some bad men from Sicily. A lorryload came in just before the blockade happened.' She raised a glass to me, and looked me gravely in the eye. 'Prost.'

I was juiced by the time that Max walked in with Red Ronson. Ronson stayed up at the bar for a while. Then he danced with one of the chocoladies. I took Max over to a small table and asked, 'You follow me here?'

'Yes, pard. I wanted to ask you something.'

'What?'

'What happened to that girl Grace? I was nuts about her you know.'

'You were only sixteen.'

'I was in love with her. Weren't you in love when you were sixteen?'

'Sure; with my cricket bat.' Then I knocked over my drink, and said, 'Sod it!'

Maxwell fetched me another. Marthe looked over and smirked; she thought I'd had enough. When he came back I said, 'I was nuts about her myself. I saw her again last year.'

'Are you still nuts about her, Charlie?'

'Probably.'

'So am I. Where is she?'

'She went to Palestine . . . Israel . . . whatever they're calling it this year. She joined the rebs.'

'Hot damn, Charlie! Is she a *Kike*?'

Red danced past. It was the first time I'd seen a man who could look over both of his partner's shoulders at the same time. I concentrated on Max, and asked him, 'Would it matter if she was?'

He stood up and looked down on me, shaking his head and his mop of red hair.

'In the short term, for a quick poke, I guess not . . . but if I tried for anything longer my old man would disinherit me without a second thought. No Jew blood in the Maxwell line . . . and I weren't meant to grow old poor.'

'You call that love?' I snarled, and fell off my chair. I hadn't got so shit-faced for months. That Max was a nice kid, but there was something about him that always brought out the worst in me.

I opened my eyes in a very comfortable bed in a palatial room, pinned to the mattress by a hundredweight of bedclothes and a heavy bedspread. The bed frame was gilded wood, the curtains rich gold brocade, and there was a gold garland pattern on the white walls. My head hurt. I had been disturbed by Red Greg opening the curtains, and letting in a golden day and the air that went with it.

'Where am I?'

'They say that in all of the American gangster movies, don't they? You are in *my* zone in *my* apartment, which happens to be the largest part of one of Hermann Goering's Berlin houses. He kept his mistresses and a horse here. Even after he was too fat to ride either. You like?'

'Grotesque. It's like an Edwardian brothel. It makes my head ache.'

It was as grotesque as the powder-blue uniform and blue suede riding boots that Red Greg was wearing. His row of medals was so extensive that if he fell over he'd be struggling to stand again. The German Iron Cross seemed to figure prominently among them. 'I get it. That's one of Fat Hermann's uniforms, isn't it?'

'From his wardrobe: I found it here. I had it tailored to fit me, and I wear it whenever I am feeling fascist.'

'Are you're feeling fascist this morning?'

'Very fascist. Are you ready for breakfast?'

'If I eat again I'll die.'

'Don't worry about that, it's the effect of the drug. It'll wear off quickly, and you'll be very hungry.'

'What drug?'

'The Mickey I slipped in your drink so we could get you here.'

'Here being the Russian Zone?' I was waking up.

'That's right, Charlie: you're quick this morning. I guess I kidnapped you.'

I didn't feel quick, and was momentarily dizzy when I stood up. I was naked. I was also scared and ashamed, because I didn't know what I'd been up to. There was an eight-hour blank between my ears. Russian Greg read my mind.

'Don' worry, Charlie. You still a virgin. You wan' the bathroom?'

'I want a shower.' Sweat had dried on me, and I stank.

'You'll feel better after breakfast,' the Russian informed me. 'It will give me time to confide in you, and apologize . . . and maybe make mends.' His English wasn't perfect but he always got close to it.

I stood under the shower for ten minutes. It was hard to believe that I was still in Berlin, because the scalding-hot water was endless. I imagined it washing all of the bad stuff out of me, and draining it out through my legs and my toes as a grainy black fluid, and then suffusing my clean new body with a golden buttery glow. That's a trick which works for me. Charlie was himself again when I stepped out. My clothes were laid out on the bed. They had been cleaned, and pressed. My boots gleamed back at me from the floor.

I followed the smell of cooking through suite after suite of enormous beautiful rooms, until I fetched up in a diner. It was dominated by a huge polished dining table that could have seated fifty. Russian Greg sat at a smaller table in a bow window overlooking a beautiful formal garden. He was still wearing Goering's uniform, and had dribbled soft egg down the front. The empty shells of four more littered the tablecloth in front of him. My sheepskin flyer was draped over the back of a chair opposite him. I sat down in it.

'I take the medals off for dinner,' he explained. 'I fall in the soup I drown.' That was accompanied by a great guffawing laugh.

A chef – you know, one of those tall guys in a big white hat and pinny – came in on cue. My tray consisted of enough kippers to feed a small fleet – where the hell had they got those from? – and a plate of scrambled egg, bacon and kidneys. When you thought about what the population outside had to eat, it was obscene. I was about to love every flawless mouthful. Greg was right: I was ravenous.

'OK, shipmate,' I asked when I pushed my plate back, 'what's all this about?'

Russian Greg waved one of his fat fingers in front of my face. His feet didn't reach the floor, and he was swinging his legs lightly from side to side like a child. He always did that when he was happy.

'Starts with you being naughty in an aeroplane last year, Charlie.'

He was just fishing. He can't possibly have known what I was doing before my demob. Red intelligence just wasn't that good.

'That sounds like a good story, Greg. Tell me the rest of it.'

'You think I don't know?'

'There is nothing *to* know. Tell me the rest of this story you made up.'

'Is good story.'

'I'm sure it is.'

'Wait for the coffee.'

The chef brought the coffee in a tall silver coffee pot with a swan-necked spout. It was probably worth hundreds of pounds. The coffee, like the pot, was exquisite.

'This aeroplane,' Russian Greg continued, 'was Avro Lincoln bomber airframe number ED617. You flew from Waddington. I can tell you the names of the crew in there with you if you please . . . and the date in your flying log. You can check.'

'I made a few radio calibration flights on weather spotters before I left the service, Greg. Is that what you mean?'

'This time you fly close to the border: close to Soviet territory.'

I was uncomfortable because the little fag hadn't a fact wrong so far. Maybe he was going to lock me up for spying after all.

'If I was on a flight that strayed into your air space it would have been by accident.'

'No it wouldn't,' Greg admonished me. 'You . . . were . . . spy . . . ing.' He sang the sounds out like that, and wagged a finger in my face. He was grinning. I didn't respond. He made a business of lighting a cigar. He offered me one, and I shook my head. He said, 'On this flight you spoke to a Soviet fighter pilot: aircraft to aircraft.'

I remembered the bizarre encounter now. A woman pilot in one of their new MiG 15 jet fighters had formated on us high in the cold night sky. She had told my pilot that she was *just looking for company; someone to talk to*. She had a voice like Marlene Dietrich, and perfect English. I remembered that she sounded as sad as hell, and that her voice had haunted me for weeks afterwards. She had said that she was about to be arrested. Her husband and children already had been, and this was her last flight. Tim, our pilot, had offered to take her into an Allied base, but she turned us down, and dropped away. The incident had lasted less than five minutes. She must have told her interrogators about us. I can understand our offer pissing off the Soviets: I had told Tim that at the time.

'I don't think that ever happened, Greg.'

He shrugged. 'No matter, Charlie. Just background. I was pleased it was you in that plane when I found out.' I wondered how he had. One of our bastards in blue must be passing operational records to the Soviets.

'Background for what?'

He leaned towards me. 'Background for you, Charlie. The dame's being rehabilitated. She's collecting cowdung on a new collective farm less than fifty mile away. Her husband's in a tank factory near Moscow . . . an' their two boys are being re-educated in a school in Smolensk. I can get them all here together, but only once. It has to work first time: no second chances. *I* get them out of Russia; *you* get them out of Berlin, an' out of Germany to the West . . . just like you did with those two Jews . . . I'm depending on you. That way they stay together, yes?'

I sat back. So they knew about my Joes as well. Had Tommo set me up? Russian Greg was studying the pattern his cigar smoke made as it lifted. Occasionally he moved his hand to put a curl in it.

'Why should I?'

Russian Greg looked at me and said, 'One thousand dollar . . .'

'I don't need the money, Greg . . .'

'Ten thousand dollar. You can buy six houses in England with ten thousand dollars. Rent them out, and you never work again . . .'

I shook my head. Too much bloody risk. What had I told Elaine about *take no chances* being my middle names? I sensed that the mood had changed. When I looked at the Russian again I noticed, with shock, a fat tear running down each of his cheeks.

'*What?*' I asked him.

'Is my sister.'

Bollocks.

Chapter Fourteen

'Suits me to stay another day,' Max said. 'Anyway, I lost Red. God knows how long it will take me to find him again.'

We were in Black Market Gasse, an alley off the main mart, sitting either side of a card table and drinking black tea. The old lady who ran it kept an eye on us, and leapt up to refill our cracked cups every time we looked like leaving. It was good tea. An old man in a decrepit soldier suit stood alongside Max. He had a tray made from a piece of cardboard on a string around his neck. The tray was full of German medals. Maxwell sorted through them. He held up an ornate, royal blue and gold Balkan Kreuz on a black and silver neck ribbon.

'What's this?' he asked me.

'The Pour le Mérite. It was awarded for sustained acts of extreme heroism. Only the bravest of the brave got it. They call it the Blue Max.'

'I like that. Why?'

'Haven't a clue.'

'I'll take it.' He asked the old man, 'How much, Pops?' I translated for him.

The old man said, 'Thirty dollar.'

Max said, 'Ten.'

The old man said, 'Twenty dollar.'

Max said, 'Ten,' and held out the bill. The old man took it

without a word, and handed the medal over. While Max was hanging it around his neck I spotted a tiny enamelled lapel badge, in the shape and colour of a forget-me-not. I'd seen someone with one in London, hundreds of years ago. The old man looked at me without blinking. He had watery eyes. He said, 'Thirty dollar,' in the same hopeless voice.

I gave him a twenty and a ten, and pinned the badge on my jacket. I couldn't believe how quickly the collapse had come: the blockade was only a week or so old, and already they were selling the family medals. By the way, the dollars were the occupation units – ten to the dollar US.

'You just bought the highest award for bravery in the world . . . for a buck,' I said to Max.

'Yeah. My old man will be impressed, won't he?'

'You don't deserve it. You deserted.'

'You got that completely wrong, Charlie. I ran away from dropping bombs on the Kraut, didn't I?' I nodded. 'So it stands to reason that the Kraut would give me a medal for that if he knew about it. Think of all the Krauts I didn't kill. I earned this medal better than anyone else earned theirs.'

It was quite easy to get fed up with the little bastard.

'Look, Max, I don't want to see you for the rest of the day OK? . . . Anywhere, *Capisce*?' It was Max's turn to nod. He blew on his tea to cool it. 'Just meet me out at the *Pig* tomorrow morning, and make sure Ronson's with you or we'll leave him behind.'

'But I can't find my way around without him, Charlie. I told you that.'

'You'll soon work out where you are when the Reds start shooting at you for straying outside the corridor. Now bugger off.'

Marthe had an hour or so before she reported to the kitchen in the Leihhaus. We drank weak coffee in her sitting room. There were two sacks of coal in the corner; everyone in Berlin was laying up stores for later. She wasn't too worried about using the last of the coffee because I had brought her a big bag of it, along with the usual stuff. Cigarettes – some to smoke and some to sell – and a pair of stockings . . . and some safety pins. Half the fucking Continent had run out of safety pins. I'd even found time to get a big bag of PX boiled sweets for Lottie, who was at school now that it had reopened.

I told Marthe what was troubling me. 'There was an old soldier in the Tiergarten, selling his medals.'

'I know him. Don't feel too bad. He steals them from corpses, and their widows. He does all right.'

'How did we all get to this?' She didn't answer me. After a comfortable silence during which I filled my pipe, and she lit a cigarette, I asked, 'Why did you let Greg take me away last night?'

'This is Berlin. I work for him, Charlie. They treat you bad?'

'No, nothing like that. He just wanted to talk. He had a business proposition for me. Something he wanted me to do.'

'His kind of business is usually dangerous: you going to do it?'

'I don't think so. Why do you still work at the Leihhaus? I can easily give you enough.'

'You are not always here, Charlie . . . nor is your friend Tommo. The people there look after me.'

I spoke without thinking: some things are better that way.

'After they were bombed out during the war, my mother and father always kept a suitcase under the bed. It contained a change of clothing for them and my sister, and all their documents . . . in case they needed to run again.'

'Why are you telling me this, Charlie?'

'Because I want you to start keeping a suitcase under the bed.'

'Where would I run to?'

'You would run with me.'

'To England?'

'If that's what you wanted.'

She said, 'So,' breathed out a long stream of tobacco smoke, and stubbed out the butt in a heavy glass ashtray. It was the sort of ashtray that fallen ladies accidentally kill their pimps with in B movies. *So* was such an odd word, and I didn't quite get where it fitted. It was like the full stop in a sentence which had come to a natural conclusion. Then she asked, 'You want to go to bed now?'

I could do pauses as well. Eventually I said, 'Yes please. Tonight, when you've finished your shift.'

She smiled. That was good because Marthe never smiled a lot.

'You are the first man to say *please* . . . in a long time.'

'*Gut*. Good.'

'Do you love me, Charlie?'

'No, but I'm thinking about it.'

'I am thinking about it also.'

I said it again, '*Gut*. Good.'

She said, 'It would be nice to love someone again.'

I realized that I agreed with her. Something cracked.

'Yes. Yes it would.'

That night I slept in the family bed, and Lottie slept on the sofa. It didn't make any difference. When I woke up she was jammed between us. Her floppy rag doll was in her arms.

Maxwell and I waited out by the *Pig* until the gunfight started. It was like the Battle of New Orleans. We dived under a parked ambulance, and stayed there. Soon two Snowdrops joined us, so it got a bit crowded.

'Who is it?' I asked one. 'The Werewolves?'

He loosed off the magazine of his sub-machine gun in the general direction of an old hangar about a quarter of a mile away. Bullets pattered off the road near us in response. Whoever they were could shoot straighter than the Lootwaffe guys lying alongside us.

He grunted, rolled on his side, and changed the gun's mag.

'You seen too many of them Lon Chaney films, bud.'

'There was a bunch of Nazis left over at the end of the war. They called themselves the *Werewolves*, and caused a bit of trouble.'

'Never heard of them, bud.' He let rip with another ten-second burst that went all over the shop. Birds lifted from the long grass between the runways. 'These is the Berliner Kardinals.' He pronounced the word as *Kar–din-arlez*.

'Who they?' Max asked him.

'They used to be a football team. They're trying to steal the flour in that warehouse.'

'We're being attacked by a football team?' That was me. I always got the good question. The policeman probably thought he owed us some sort of explanation,

'You gotta understand, bud; the goddamned Kraut takes his goddamned football goddamned . . . seriously.'

A bullet slammed into the ambulance above us with such force that it rocked on its springs. I lay with my face pressed against the concrete. Welcome back to Germany, Charlie.

It was over as quickly as it blew up. That was because the warehouse did as well. I watched a bazooka crew lined up on it. I think that they only intended to scare the thieves. They aimed high, the charge thumped in close to the top of the tin shed, and a second later its roof came off with a detonation you could have heard in Vienna. I distinctly saw two bodies cartwheeling through the air.

The copper used the phrase I'd picked up from Max a couple of days earlier. 'Hot damn,' he said, 'what had they got in there?'

Max was taking some interest again. He said, 'Just flour. Just like you said. It's the dust. Once it's in the air you're sitting on a bomb. Father had an old flour mill in Poughkeepsie that blew itself to Kingdom Come. He got out of flour after that.'

We followed the cop over to inspect the damage. What was left of the warehouse – the old hangar – was no higher than my shoulder, and burning fiercely. The heavy smoke smelled like burnt porridge. There was one blackened body high in a nearby tree, and another on the peritrack. We walked past a dead GI spread out like Da Vinci's *Man*. He was wearing old khaki ovies and had dropped a spanner: some kind of mechanic. There was a neat hole in his forehead; he wore a gentle, fixed smile. He looked as if he had been a nice guy, but I suppose that you never can tell. The Snowdrop closed his eyes and put a handkerchief over the dead face.

'Who's gonna tell his folks,' he asked us, 'that he was killed by a goddamned Kraut football team?' *No one*, I hoped. Maybe they'd come up with a better story. Maybe the policeman was already working on it. 'What did you say those last Nazis called themselves?'

'Werewolves.'

'*Werewolves.*' He spoke softly. 'Poor kid.' I could tell he was already getting his story straight.

'I've just been attacked by a football team,' I told Old Man Halton on the telephone. 'The *Pink Pig* has a few holes in her, but that's not serious. She also has a flat main wheel, which *is*. They shot the tyre out. I'm negotiating for another, but Dakota tyres are scarcer than hen's teeth over here.'

'Are you all right, Charlie?'

'I'm fine.'

'What are our two new Americans like?'

'*Horrible*. The worst yet, but I doubt you'll get anyone cheaper.'

The line crackled, and his voice drifted away. The last thing he said was that as soon as he could squeeze a place in the schedule he'd send Randall over with spare tyres we could store. *Where?* I wondered. I hadn't told him that I wasn't at Celle yet. It wasn't something that I wanted to explain.

Max had gone for coffee. I sat on the *Pig*'s cargo door sill. There were fewer boxes in the *Pig* than we'd set out with. Either Max and Red were already into a bit of private enterprise, or we'd been visited during the night. I wondered where the bloody engineer was until Greg drove up in his big GAZ jeep. I didn't question how they came to be in the middle of the Berlin US airbase: he seemed to be able to go anywhere – king of the bleeding castle. Red Ronson was in the back, out for the count.

'What did you do to him?'

'Rescued him from a bordello in our zone,' Greg said. 'He was kicking up shit. I don't know how he got there.'

'Why isn't he moving?'

'I got the police doctor to give him a shot. It was the only way we could get him into the car: he's a feisty little bastard. He tell you about Mantell?'

'Who's Mantell?'

'Who *was* Mantell, you mean. Never mind.'

I asked Red Greg, 'Didn't your air force get a load of Dakotas from the Yanks in the war?'

'Yes English. Now we make our own. Just the same, but stronger.'

'Can you get me some tyres?'

I thought that he was going to laugh, but he didn't: quite a little triumph for him.

'Yes, Charlie, I can get you tyres. You gonna fly my sister out of Germany?'

Six-beat intro, and main theme.

'Yes,' I told him.

Then he did laugh, and held his hand up for that *high five* thing the Yank boxers had started to do. It took another thirty years to catch on. Then he did a little gloat dance in a circle. I guess he deserved it.

Two hours later he was back with an old US GMC truck. It had *Red Ball Express* painted on its ragged canvas, so I guess that's why the Russians stole it in the first place. They're keen on red. He had two tyres and a sullen group of fitters, who jacked the *Pig* up and changed both her boots. I love the smell of new rubber. We took our own good tyre, and tied it down in the back.

'Is there anywhere in Berlin you *can't* go?' I asked him.

'I think not, Charlie.'

'Is there anything you *can't* get?'

'I can't get liquorice. My General wants liquorice from when he was a boy – he asks me every time he sees me.'

'Want me to get some for you?'

'That's kind, Charlie.'

'No, Greg; it's what you and Tommo have been teaching me. It's business.'

It was raining in Celle. A soft, warm blanket of water in the air. I wondered if it was raining in Berlin, and damping down the flour fire. The *Pig*'s Russian tyres were more heavily grooved than their Goodyear counterparts, and displaced so much water that we bowled down the runway like an enormous speedboat. Maxwell sang a passable imitation of Benny Goodman's 'On a slow boat to China' and Red, strapped in behind, just groaned. He'd been sick on himself, and it stank of thin, bitter wine. I preferred Mortensen's stench to that.

There was an RAF jeep waiting for us at the end of the runway. It had a large painted signboard on its arse which read *Follow Me!*, so when it set off in front of us, we did. It led us to a hard standing, and there alongside was the old control caravan I'd been promised. It had had a new coat of RAF blue, and the word *Halton* was stencilled in white on its door. Maxwell powered down, and the *Pig*'s props stopped spinning. Then he lifted his medal from where it hung around his neck and kissed it before he let it drop back. That became his routine for successful touchdowns.

We were there for the night. The Officers' Mess had its own small dance floor, and a jazz band of army musicians played there twice a week. A stocky young national serviceman called Derek Webber blew his heart out for us, on jazz bassoon of all things; I reckoned he had a great future if he got the right break.

I ended up on my own in the easy room – a kind of lounge – sobering myself up with cup after cup of black coffee. And I wasn't exactly on my own either; a mess servant was clearing up for the night. When we spoke it was in German. He spoke good German: most Germans do. I just about got by. He asked me, 'Pilot?'

He was a tall thin guy, who would have been good-looking but for a livid scar like a jagged line which ran above his right eye.

'No. Radio operator. Radioman.'

He touched the scar. 'So. *I* was a pilot. *Töpfer*.' He gave that little nod of the head they use to introduce their name. 'Harald; Harry.'

'Charlie Bassett. Would you like a cup of coffee?'

'No. Thank you. I take mine in the kitchen.'

He continued to tidy up. On a low table there was a heap of books and services magazines. Most of the books were those photographic hymns of praise to the British armed services that the WD published just after the war, to justify all the killing and the sacrifice. He picked one up as he stacked them, and turned it so that I could see it. It was *The Battle of Britain*, and had that picture of St Paul's wreathed in vapour trails on its cover.

'A very good story,' he told me with a gentle smile, 'but a sad ending.'

Despite the half-promise of a cottage, we slept in a concrete accommodation block like that at Wunstorf. I had a cell of my own, while Red and Max shared the one alongside. When I awoke facing the wall in the morning I could see the imprint of the wood shuttering from when the concrete had been poured, right in front of my face. It was like sleeping in a bunker. The rain had stopped, and the runways and the concrete steamed in the weak early sunlight.

There was a wide concrete apron around the administration buildings at Celle, and that morning there were two RAF Gloster Meteor jet fighters parked on it. I walked over to have a gander at them. One was unpainted, and the other an overall light grey. They both had those new postwar roundels on their wings, with a narrow band of white separating the red centre from the blue margin. They looked odd to my eye, and even more unsettlingly like an archery target. On the grey aircraft the jet pods in each wing were stained underneath by green streaks: the RAF was getting sloppy since my time. Even so, they looked purposeful, and spoke of the future. As I turned away from it I was attracted to its name, in yellow italic on the nose: *Baster Fastard*.

I went in to breakfast. The German with the scarred face nodded to me from the serving tables. Neither Max nor Red Ronson showed up. They must have been on the skite the night before.

The three-storey tower on the end of the block was what the Americans, and our own papers, had begun to call the Control Tower. In my day we called them the Watch Office. It was topped with a glass box from which the Duty Officer controlled the movements of aircraft on or around the airfield. I climbed the outside iron staircase; it was good for me. Then I talked myself over the threshold. I think that the flight lieutenant and his clerk were getting lonely up there anyway. My excuse was that if I was to operate my company's precious aircraft out of Celle, I wanted a picture of its layout. I wanted to see the goddamned place, so that I could describe it to others. The grey Meteor had left.

'Border patrol,' the AC clerk told me. 'Out high, in low.'

'We only do it to piss Ivan off,' his boss said.

'How low?' I asked.

From the intercom speakers above our heads a crackling squawk intruded. A pilot made all the right sounds and the Duty Officer the right responses. 'See for yourself,' he said. 'That's him back now.'

The Luftwaffe had obviously known how to build Watch Offices. From the goldfish bowl of this one I could see for miles. I could see Max and Red supervising the unloading of the *Pig* into a couple of army Bedfords – maybe I'd been a bit hard on them. Max's medal gleamed at his throat. I could see the peritrack and the taxiways, and the infield of uncut grass. And I could see a black dot, growing instantly larger, thundering at us at treetop height from the northwest.

'That's Peter Dare, but everyone calls him *Dan*.' That was the Duty Officer again. 'Look you, on the pilot of the future!' He was obviously going to buzz the erks unloading the *Pink Pig*. The controller picked up his mic and said emphatically, 'More height Fox Baker, more height.'

From the speakers overhead I heard the pilot laugh, and then he was on us with a shattering scream of jets that rattled the glass. His small jet made more row than a Lanc at full chat. Looking down on him I could see that he was so low that the long grass was being swept aside by his progress. Ripples of green waves flowed away from the aircraft. The erk observed, ''e says 'e judges 'is 'ight, sir, by feeling the grass on the bottom of his aircraft. That's why we never cuts the grass out there.'

Halfway across the field there was a sudden flash of yellow light from the exhaust of his starboard engine, followed by a long and continuous streak of orange flame, and a thin line of dark smoke. Immediately he climbed away to port with, 'Fox Baker . . . bird strike. Immediate pancake.'

'The bird must 'ave stood up!' The erk said.

His boss replied with, 'Shut up, Ivor. Hit the tit,' and into the microphone handset barked, 'Roger Fox Baker. Immediate pancake.' The phonetic alphabet was changing a bit, but at least somewhere in the world they were still using most of the words we went to war with.

The tit the erk hit was a big red knob on the small bench in front of him. It activated a mighty klaxon, and the klaxon activated the fire and rescue teams. They were probably pleased to have something to do, because they jumped to it and were on the apron before the stricken jet had lined up for its touchdown. As it happened all they had to do was trundle down the runway behind it. They made an impressive parade. The erk hit the tit again, and the klaxon ran down to blessed silence.

'It's on the roof above us,' the lieutenant said. 'That's why it makes so much bloody noise. The Jerry hooter is that much less musical than ours, don't you think? I'm sure it's damaging our ears.'

'Your fire crews seem quite good.'

'All done with kindness.'

'You're the second person in a few days to tell me that. Kindness must be catching.'

'That'll be the day, sir,' his erk said. 'Then we can all go 'ome to Blighty an' 'ave a right old knees-up.'

Then the Duty Officer briefed me on the air corridors into

Berlin, and how he expected my people to operate in them under RAF control.

The RAF controlled the northern corridor. Anyone flying in the southern corridor was under the direction of the Yanks. Each corridor was marked at each end by radio and radar beacons — although the Russians were already trying to bugger about with them — and instructions concerning height and separation would be rigorously enforced. *Orders*, he told me, *were to be obeyed without question at all times*. Weren't they saying that sort of thing around here in the 1930s? Luckily, both Gatow and Tempelhof had GCA. That meant that they could talk us in if we couldn't see the bloody runways. When you looked at the prevailing weather patterns, and the frequency with which they were fogged in, that was a reassuring fact. I could see that I was going to love Berlin.

I waved goodbye to the *Pink Pig*. Actually it was a bit of a relief to see the tail of her — Max and Red were a disaster waiting to occur, and I felt less responsible for them when I wasn't with them.

The Halton caravan was a little home from home, with an office, a radio desk from which we could talk with either our aircraft or the tower, a kitchenette with an easy chair, and even a small glass greenhouse on the roof, under a couple of steps. You could poke your head into it, and watch your aircraft chugging along the runway.

For this trip the *Pig* had been overloaded with wooden staves. They were supposed to be for building things like hen houses with, but I liked to think that I was beginning to know the Berliners by now: they'd wait until winter, eat the chickens and then burn the bloody wood. Anyway, that was it. The RAF, for the WD, invoked our contract, and the *Pig* had the honour of flying our first proper load of the Berlin Airlift. Some time later Old Man Halton told me that we were the third commercial outfit to be called up. He seemed to take that as a compliment.

Pig was supposed to run the corridor with a radio operator to spin the beacons, and we didn't have a spare one. The RAF did, and lent us one of their duds . . . this became a not infrequent occurrence. He was a wizened Scots kid with overgrown teeth. Ratlike. His nose lifted slightly, and twitched as he spoke. He was named Patterson — part-way through his national service after the end of a university course. When he was excited his voice came out in a high-pitched quivery Highland squeal. He was bound to end up covered in hair, and teaching his gibberish to gibbering students in a university at the fag end of the universe somewhere. From the moment I first saw him, I mistrusted him . . . and just hoped he knew his business. I had to pay him the difference between his service pay and the commercial rate. I resented every shekel.

Vera drove over. She was smiling as I opened the caravan door. That was a first.

'You look happy.'

'So would you, if you had just been given your ticket out of this palsied dump. I'm off home.'

'Demob?'

'Something like that.' She was carrying a large cardboard tube. 'I thought that you'd like my spare charts; save you buying them.'

'That's kind. Thank you.'

'. . . and I brought you this; why don't we have a look at it.'

This was a single printed piece of paper. It looked like an old-fashioned Wild West 'wanted' poster.

'What is it? It looks a bit like a wanted poster.'

I had forgotten that Vera had first described her job to me as being something like a policeman.

'It is. The Cousins send them to us occasionally.' That was a word we sometimes used for our American allies.

The paper was the description of an American air force engineer on the run. There were four pictures of his head: each side, back and front. *Dangerous and dishonest*, it told us.

'What's Mr Lieter supposed to have done, other than desert? It doesn't say.'

'They rarely do. It's usually what we'd call *treason*. A threat to the State, that sort of thing . . .'

It wasn't his name, but the pictures were definitely of Red Ronson. I said, 'A few days ago he was fished out of a brothel in Berlin, and shanghaied back onto one of my aircraft.'

'Who was this hero that brought him back?'

'I believe that he's a Red Army Intelligence officer.'

It was Vera's turn. '*Fuck* it!'

'You swear too much, for a woman, Vera. You know that?'

'. . . and it's dealing with twerps like you that makes me!'

My blushes were saved by the taxi: Randall came motoring down the runway with the red Oxford. When Vera saw it she started to make her excuses. I asked her, 'Do you want to come back with us? I've got a small job at Lübeck; then I think I can go home.'

She was calm again. The tiger I had seen in her was back in its den. 'You're a sweet man, Charlie.'

'I know.' Also a big-headed one I guess.

'. . . but the RAF has laid on a seat on a Hastings for me. They're going to give me the VIP treatment until they wash their hands of me.'

'When's that going to be?'

'Not soon enough. I can't wait to get out of their clutches.'

'You could come down and see me. I've a small house and a couple of spare kids alongside a pub on the south coast.'

'That would be nice, Charlie. Thank you.' She didn't ask for my address though, and to be honest I was a little relieved. She wasn't the sort of person you collected.

Randall told me, 'We'll need to tank-up before we move on. Lübeck for tonight, and England tomorrow. OK?'

'Fine, Randall. Anything you say. The airlift is on. The *Pink Pig* just flew a load of wood into Gatow. The Old Man's pretty chuffed.'

'I got three *Pig*-sized tyres in the back for you and five metal boxes for the station commander here.'

'We can stick the tyres under the caravan, and cover them up with a tarp.'

'What's the *Pig* taxiing on at present, if *I* have her new tyres?'

'The Russians gave me a couple. She's on new rubber.'

'Don't get me wrong, Charlie, but aren't the Russians supposed to be the bad guys here? Starving us out, and that sort of thing?'

'It's a long story, Randall, and I don't think I'm ready to tell it yet. Shall we walk over to the Watch Office and organize some gas, and transport for your boxes?'

We overflew the outskirts of Hamburg that afternoon. The vis was perfect, and I could see for miles. There was no escaping the utter ruination of large areas of the city. No wind, and already smoke was rising from hundreds of open cooking fires amid the ruins. It made me feel sick. I wanted to look away, but I couldn't. I stared on for what seemed like hours, fascinated by the devastation I had helped to create.

Randall observed, 'I love coming to Hamburg and seeing this. I suppose they'll rebuild it all one day and spoil it for me. Then I'll have to go somewhere else.'

I grunted a reply which caused him to look briefly at me. He asked, 'You don't like this, Charlie?'

'No, I don't. I was in Bremen when the war ended. The people were living in cellars; like animals.'

'It served them damned well right. They spent years behaving like animals before that: I jest hope that we never let them ferget it.'

'What do you think about the Airlift then? If it carries on we'll be shipping food and fuel in next – to keep Jerry alive.'

'I think that it's a waste of time. The Kraut will come back and bite us again as soon as he can.'

'The ones I meet seem to have learnt their lessons.'

'If you'd been this soft in 1944 Charlie, we would have lost . . . an' the Kraut would not be crying salty tears over you.'

Randall's chin was stuck out. I could tell he was looking for a fight over this. I told him, 'I guess so. Get us away from here, Randall.'

'OK, boss.' He turned onto a northern heading. I think that he was relieved as well.

Lübeck wasn't as bad. We had disappeared the old wooden Hanseatic city centre for them on Palm Sunday in 1942, and it was only plastered a few more times after that – mainly the U-boat ship yards on the outskirts: once by me. By 1948 they'd cleaned up most of the mess, although the bones of the wrecked buildings and churches still reached for the sky, and there were more open spaces than Lübeck had started the war with.

Both our Oxfords had the old 1154/1155 radio rigs I'd used in Lancasters and early Lincolns. It was good to get a decent radio under my hands again – it had been several weeks since I'd done the job in anger. The RAF Controller at Lübeck was a laid-back type who asked us to circle at five thou so that he could clear five inbound Yorks. The big silver RAF aircraft looked very impressive as they glided in one after the other. I relayed the information to Randall, who said, 'I wonder if *Dorothy* is back yet. She was standing on her own two feet when I last saw her.'

'When was that?'

'Week past. They were putting a new skin on her bottom, but her knickers were still showing.' Then he asked me, 'Can you wake them up again downstairs, and ask if they're ready to receive us yet.'

They weren't. We had to watch two tiny Vampire jet fighters crawl along the taxiway and launch themselves into the sky. They went like shit off a shovel.

'Ever flown a jet?' I asked Randall.

'Nope.'

'Ever wanted to?'

'Nope. Kids' stuff.'

'What's that mean?'

'When I was a child I spake as a child, I understood as a child, I thought as a child: but when I became a man I put away childish things . . . *those* things aren't aeroplanes, Charlie, they're kids' toys.'

'That's from the Bible, isn't it?'

'One Corinthians thirteen.'

'. . . Where it goes on to talk about seeing *through a glass darkly*.'

'You never fail to surprise me, Charlie. You go to church?'

'No, not really. It's just that's how I see Germany I think: through a glass darkly.'

Chapter Fifteen

Randall obviously knew his way around Lübeck. A lot of flyers are like that: they keep charts and maps in their heads, and bring them out when they think you're not looking. They had less accommodation at the airfield, and needed it for operational fliers. Apart from the RAF Yorks and Dakotas I noted three civvy airlines, including the converted Halifax bombers that had been named after the Old Man. Their bomb bays had been so distended to carry freight that they looked pregnant. I was surprised he hadn't already bought a handful.

Anyway, we were given rooms at a proud old hotel which had probably seen Napoleon ride by years ago. Randall knew where it was, and we borrowed a clapped-out Hillman Tilley to get there. My room had a huge double bed, with massive bedposts; I was surprised they had managed to hang on to it. The place had a Union flag hanging from the front balcony, was managed by the army, but all the servants were Jerries. This was a pattern I was beginning to recognize. I flung my bag on the bed, and went straight back down to the bar.

It was run by a friendly Geordie lance corporal and two Jerries. They both looked too intelligent to be natural bar staff, worried and anxious to please. Each wore a spotless white jacket with a name sewn across the breast pocket. The older, heavier one was *J Wellington Wimpy*, and the other *Sweet Pea*. The young one had a thick, dark lock of hair that flapped over his forehead, and an occasional piercing angry stare. Blue eyes. He had the look of someone whose image we'd lived with for eighteen years. The lance corporal smoked a corn-cob pipe at the port, like General MacArthur. He also had protuberant eyes, a scrawny neck and a prominent Adam's apple. He reminded me of someone, but I couldn't think who. He told me, 'Named 'em miself, sir. I didn't like their Jerry names.'

'Didn't they complain?'

'No: so I reckon they're Nazis in hidin'.'

'I met a woman who thinks they're all Nazis in hiding. Maybe they just like the names you gave them better than their own. What have you got?'

'NAAFI beer. It's getting better.'

'Any pipe tobacco?'

'Royal Navy Flake any good?'

'I'll have both. Thanks.'

'Sit down at a table, sir, and one of the boys will come across. I do things Jerry style in this bar. It helps them to feel at home, and the customers feel as if they're on holiday.'

Randall came down an hour later. He was moving and talking a little slower, and stank of bourbon. I hadn't put him down as a decent drinker before. That was interesting.

'Apparently we're supposed to feel as if we're on holiday,' I told him.

'I haven't had a holiday since 1942.'

'In that case, sending you off on leave is the first thing I'll do when we get back. Cheers.'

Sweet Pea had brought him a beer, and Randall savoured it with genuine pleasure. Whatever the cloud between us had been earlier, it seemed to have blown over. We ate at the table – grilled ham, American style, fried potatoes and cabbage, and processed peas – and then split for an early night. On a table in the large Common Room, I found a Dashiell Hammet book I hadn't read before, and took it up with me.

When I woke up I was still fully clothed and lying on the bed. My book was over my face, and there was a hammering in my ears. The hammering in my ears came from the hammering on my door. My watch told me that it was a quarter to three in the morning. Fuck it.

Randall. He looked pasty-faced, and had beads of sweat on his forehead. He spoke hastily. 'Sorry about this; and sorry I was on bad form earlier, bud.'

'That's all right, Randall, but you could have waited until morning to tell me.'

'No I couldn't. I wanted to tell you that I know this place.'

'I guessed that. You knew the way here.'

'I hate it. I can't stay here again. It's fulla ghosts. I gotta go.'

I yawned. Randall copied me. There has to be an evolutionary reason for infectious yawning.

'Let's find out if the bar's still open.'

Sweet Pea was still at his post, but asleep. He was sleeping bolt-upright on a narrow bar stool. I thought that took some doing. He actually smiled when we bumbled in and disturbed him. He spoke in German. So did I. So did Randall, which surprised me, of course, because he'd never let on before. Of the three of us Randall probably spoke the best German. That surprised me too.

Sweet Pea asked, 'Can't sleep, gentlemen? Too many restless spirits or not enough?' Neat pun.

'That's what my friend says. I haven't met one yet.'

'They need to get to know you first. What can I get you?'

'Thank you. Beer I suppose. Three if you'll join us. What's your proper name? . . . I can't call you Sweet Pea.'

'Reinhardt . . . Reiny. Thank you.' He gave a correct, fast

little bow which finished at the neck. *If you do that too quickly*, I thought, *you'll flick your bleeding head off*. I've thought of him as Herr Flick ever since. He brought six bottles of beer to the small round table so that he wouldn't need to go back for more. We all prosted one another straight from the bottles, and he asked Randall, 'So. Who did you see? Which one?'

'This time I saw an officer, but I've seen other guys here. I woke up when the bastard shook me awake. There was water pouring off of him, and he scared me.'

'This is hard to take in, Randall.' Me again. 'Give me a moment.'

'Feel my sleeve.' He was wearing a thick old khaki mechanic's sweater. I'd seen him in it before: he loved it. I felt the sleeve. It was soaking wet. 'Now taste it.'

'I'm not keen, Randall.'

'Damned well *taste* it!' Now, you may well have noticed that Randall, like Old Man Halton, was not much given to swearing, so this was an indicator of earnestness. Besides, he was bigger than me. I squeezed the wool, and tasted my fingers.

'Salt water.'

'You got it.'

'From condensation or from the roof maybe,' said Reiny helpfully, '. . . after all we are a port city.'

'You know that's not right,' Randall tried. 'Tell us the story.'

'He had a beard, this officer?' It came out as *Offizier*, of course.

'No. Clean-shaven. He was in his sea clothes, and wringing wet.'

'So. The one with the beard is his captain. His head was bombed off. Sometimes people see him without his head. Sometimes the head is all they see.'

'Different guy. No beard. Who's *my* ghost?'

'Thomsen. First or Second Officer. I forget which. He came

223

from a U-boat in the First War. He was killed in an accident: nothing dramatic. First he haunted the boat, then, when it sank, he came back here. Everyone knows him.'

'What about the others? They tramp up and down all night in the corridor. It's still wet in the mornings.'

'Sometimes they sing – have you heard that?'

'No.'

'They are looking for Petersen. Petersen deserted after he found dead Thomsen grinning at him one morning. No one has ever seen Petersen. Good story, yes?'

'It's a good story,' I told him. The German shook his head, and gave a deprecating little smile. 'No story,' he shrugged. 'It's true.'

'Why do they come back here?'

'Kriegsmarine place. This is a U-boat hotel. Same in both wars . . . same again when we start fighting the Reds next year.' I was depressed that so many people I met seemed to expect that. 'If you've got hard money we have a few bottles of schnapps under the bar.'

I sighed, and then yawned. This time no one yawned with me.

'Might as well.'

Eventually we drank two bottles. Randall asked me if he could share my room, and I said *No*. I also heard a child laughing and bouncing a ball in the corridor outside, and some men singing as I drifted off. They sang a sad old German soldiers' song, 'Ich hatt' einen Kameraden', and the first thing I noticed as I stepped out of the room in the morning was the big damp patches on the corridor carpets and the tang of salt in the air. I've told you before that I don't believe in ghosts. But bugger it, I was hungry by then, anyway.

'When were you there before?' I asked Randall. We were out over the North Sea. Randall had cheered up, and was humming

'Stardust'. None of the occasional crackles we heard from the radio were for us. I spotted a formation of three silver dots about five thou above us heading south, about the same time as Randall. His reaction was the same as in wartime – he turned away from them and got closer to the sea. Then he grunted. I think it was a small laugh.

'*What*?' I asked him.

'Sorry. Force of habit.'

'Me too.' I had reached for my earphones, which were around my neck.

He sighed. 'You think the war's ever gonna end, Charlie?'

It was a good question. The war seemed to condition my response to practically anything.

'No. Not for us. Not for anyone who lived through it. Is that what you mean?'

'Guess I do.'

It was a perfect afternoon. The North Sea looked almost mirrorlike – I've only once before seen it that calm, and that was at night. I smoked my pipe, filling the cabin with the tobacco's sweet, nutty aroma. I realized that Randall hadn't answered my first question yet, so I tried again.

'When were you in that hotel before, Randall?'

'That would have been in 1943, Charlie.' I'd always known that there was more to him than met the eye. I suppose that he hadn't needed to tell me; he could always have found a way of avoiding the question. There was a little something in his voice as he said it: as if something had momentarily come between us and the sun. He sighed again, and said, 'Fuck it. Times change, don't they?'

'They do, Randall.'

'Ask me about it some other time, OK?' I opened the thermos I'd brought with us, and gave him the first cup of sweet coffee. Later he said to me, 'That little fellar Reinhardt; he said that the hotel was a U-boat hotel. Did you pick up on that?'

'Yes. I did.'

'. . . But what you don't know is that U-boat can mean more than one thing in Germany.'

'It means submarine.'

'Yes, Charlie . . . but it can also mean Jew. One of the Jews who went into hiding.' It was such a stupid thing to say that I didn't know how to respond. It was as if your English teacher had suddenly told you that the word *cow* also meant *piano*. 'Some Jews didn't answer the knock at the door when the Kraut came to collect them. Hundreds, maybe even thousands, became submarines and submerged: went underground. Some were even hidden by non-Nazi German families . . . more than you'd credit.'

'What happened to them?'

'Nobody knows. The SS hunted a few down in the war, but eventually the camps were full anyway. I read somewhere the cops called them U-boats. The people who slipped under the surface of society. Neat, wasn't it?'

'. . . And you were here in 1943.'

'I told you, Charlie, ask some other time.'

'OK, Randall. Is that England?' I could see a narrow smear of dark grey on the horizon.

'I'll tell you somethin', bud – if it's anywhere else then we're in a helluva lot o' trouble.' I looked at his face. He was grinning. Like all good pilots he never looked at you when he spoke, his head was always on the move as he scanned every patch of sky he could see. I felt myself relax into the seat; I always felt safe flying with Randall. The rest could wait till later. Not long later an air traffic controller from the East Midlands came on air and demanded to know who we were. I liked neither his attitude nor his public school accent. I don't suppose Randall did either because he answered, 'Pinocchio.' Did that make me Gepetto?

After a few splutters in the ether Randall relented, and reverted to the new formality demanded of us by a civilized world. I dozed until we were in the circuit over Croydon.

I had a couple of beers in the Propeller before I called the Old Man from the red box outside. I was worried about something, but hadn't yet worked out what – you know the feeling. The Old Man wasn't worried: he invited me to supper in a small restaurant in Purley Way, only a short walk away.

'Do you know any women in London, Charlie?'

'Yes, I do, boss. Do you need a couple of telephone numbers?'

There was a short pause before he replied – I'd pushed too far. Me and my mouth. Then he chuckled. And then he coughed for a week of course.

'No, Charlie, but thank you. I'll bear it in mind. I wondered if you might bring someone along; company for Freda.'

I didn't chance my arm and ask who Freda was.

'I'll see if I can rustle someone up.'

'Twenty thirty, Charlie . . . and please don't keep me waiting.'

'Yes, boss.' I felt as if the headmaster was giving me a wigging again. When had I been late for anything? Except the end of the war. I was very late for that.

I called Dolly. Her landlord Stephen answered, and said that she was in the bath. I knew what Dolly looked like in the bath.

'Go and get her out. Tell her it's the Chief of Air Staff.' I had to wait about four minutes, and feed the telephone's gob with a tanner and press Button A again . . . that was the problem with this new technology: it wasn't cheap. I heard her pick up the telephone.

'This had better be good, Charlie.'

'How did you know it was me?'

'The Chief of Air Staff wouldn't speak to me: I'm in purdah.'

'Because Angus McDoom, or whatever his name was, got himself killed? He was supposed to be looking after you, not the other way round. He was trying to show off, and must have stuck his neck out . . .'

'Can't talk about it, Charlie. Certainly not on a telephone.'

'Come to supper then. I've been asked out, and need a date with me.'

'Have you just come in from somewhere?'

'Can't talk about it. Certainly not on a telephone.'

'You're not funny, Charlie: not funny at all.'

The pips went again, and I shoved more money in, and punched the button. The hollow rattle in the black box told me that it had recently been emptied.

'Please. Come and meet my boss. You'll like him, he's a millionaire.'

She hit that straight for the boundary.

'Where and when, and what do you want me to wear?'

'Something summery and dressy at the same time. The restaurant is called Bill O'Neal's and it's on Purley Way in Croydon, so you'll have to get your skates on. Take a cab and I'll pay for it.' I heard Stephen's voice in the background, and Dolly giggled. I asked, 'What was that?'

'Stephen told me to put some clothes on; I'm making him feel hungry.' Then she put the phone down. She hadn't said *Yes*, but I thought that it was implied.

Dolly looked the million dollars that Old Man Halton was probably worth. When she stepped out of the cab she knew it, and threw me the Betty Grable smile and a bit of leg. I suddenly realized that I didn't know if Halton was married. We walked in at twenty twenty-nine, and either we were in the wrong place or the Old Man was going to be late. I wasn't sure whether that was one up to us, or not. The place had about ten tables, including one in an alcove that could be screened with a curtain. That's where the waiter showed us when I dropped the old guy's name. The food was Italian. The waiter said his name was Dominici. His accent was as Sheffield as a Fairbairn dagger. He gave us a hand-written menu and asked, 'Will you need help with the menu?'

He seemed to be addressing his question to Dolly's lower neckline. If I had been a ventriloquist I would have thrown my reply back to him from between her breasts. I would have liked to have seen his face. My lack of reply made him look at me instead. He wasn't good at it. Then I said, 'No. Thanks. I know a bit. I was in Italy a few years ago.'

'During the war?' His lip definitely curled.

'No. Not long after. When they were putting things back together again.'

'I never been to Italy.'

Dolly tried to ease the tension. 'Where have you been?'

'I've been to the Isle of Man for six bloody years. My father came to England when he was six years old, you know that?'

How could I? I hadn't seen the bleeder before, had I?

'No, I didn't.'

'I was born and bred in Doncaster, never left England in me life, and they locked me up on the Isle of bloody Man for six bloody years because I got an Italian bloody name.'

I was fed up with this, but when the Eyetie suddenly said something like, 'Pah!' it was all right, because it was a laugh, or that's what his noises degenerated to.

I heard Halton's cough coming along the road outside. When it reached the door a dog came in instead. It was a liver-coloured poodle that needed a haircut. It pulled a vivacious dark-haired beauty into the restaurant behind it, and the Old Man followed them. The woman's dress was dark blue but covered in white polka dots. She was smaller than I first thought, because I could have played billiards with the high heels of her shoes. The dog sat beside me, and lolled its fat grey tongue. And dribbled. I stood anyway, to meet the lady, who wasn't Freda, of course – she was *Frieda*. She spoke English like Lili Marlene.

Halton asked, 'Did you order, Charlie?'

'He ordered nothing,' the waiter said. '*I* give orders around here.'

'Bugger off and bring us a bottle, Dom, before we send you back to the island.'

'Yes, Mr Halton. You wanna eat tonight?'

'Of course we do. Just start serving and I'll tell you when to stop.'

He waved Dominici away. They were both smiling smiles of men who had known each other years.

'I knew his father before the war,' Halton said, and then told me, 'Don't tell him you bombed Italy or he'll spit in your soup.'

'I didn't bomb Italy,' I grumbled. 'I only bombed Germany.'

Frieda spoke up for herself uninvited for the first time, 'Did you bomb Hamm?'

'If I did, ma'am, it was only by accident.'

'Good. I came from Hamm. Now I won't have to spit either.'

The waiter put a basket of odd lumpy grey bread on the table. I had eaten something like that in Siena, and had liked it. Halton helped himself, and passed it round.

'She would too, you know,' he said.

'No she wouldn't, boss. Dolly wouldn't let her. Dolly's been trained to suppress all opposition with a single look.'

That entertaining thought brought him a small hurricane of coughing. The neighbours turned away.

'*Gas!*' He shouted at them. 'Aren't you used to gassed soldiers by now?' Then he apologized in time for the waiter to appear with two bottles.

I asked, 'Wine's appearing in all the restaurants again. Where are they getting it from?'

'Never asked them. Let's have a drink and relax, and you can tell me why you were a day late getting to Celle . . .' He never missed a bloody trick, did he?

He liked the story of the Battle of the Flour Warehouse. He clapped his hands, and laughed, and coughed. Frieda forced a smile, and looked away. I thought she was the most exotic creature I had ever seen. Dolly saw me thinking it, and aimed a kick at me under the table. Unfortunately she hit the dog instead, which yelped, bit its tongue, and skulked around the other tables dripping blood. I thought that it was quite funny, but the animal clearly terrified the other customers. The wine kept on coming, and I wondered if the Old Man was getting us drunk for a purpose. The food was superb, as long as you like spaghetti. I do. And creamed semolina. I do. And cake soaked in wine and spirits. I do. After three decadent courses, and small cups of black coffee you could strip paint with, he came across with a cigar whilst the women went off to do what they always seem to need to do together.

'Frieda's my ward, Charlie.'

'Is that all I need to know, boss?'

'I'm glad that you've understood that. She speaks very good German.'

'Most Germans do, boss. I noticed that a couple of days ago.'

He just watched me smoke. He stopped coughing as soon as I lit up. Funny that.

'You're going back to Germany, Charlie, and you're going to stay for a little while . . . until things are running smoothly, OK? I don't want any bad surprises.'

'I guessed. When?'

'As soon as you have the show at Lympne properly organized. Say in about a week, if you take a couple of days off with your boys. By the time you fly back to Berlin I want an operation in place where the aircrew, ground crews and stores match the aircraft we have in the places we have them. The aircraft will be routed to match the contracts, and the whole set-up is to be flexible enough to respond to rapid changes in those contracts.

Capisce?' Italian restaurants lend themselves to murderous attempts on the language – have you noticed that? The truth is that Caruso and Valentino had a lot to answer for.

'Understood. Anything else?' I probably glanced at the door the girls had disappeared through. I meant *Anything else before they come back?*

'Yes. When you go back to Germany base yourself at Berlin.' Perhaps he thought I missed that the first time, '. . . and fly only as often as you need to keep the operation ticking over smoothly . . .'

'OK. I can do that.'

'I know you can, Charlie . . . and to help you . . .' he looked briefly away for a moment and then drilled me with his fierce little eyes again, '. . . you will take Frieda with you. She has family and friends she wishes to find, and I expect you to look after her.' What I thought was, *Fuck that for a game of soldiers.* What I said was, 'Sure, boss. No sweat.'

He screwed his mouth into a smile. Alice used to smile like that.

I stayed with Dolly. Looking down at her later I thought it was good to have her back where she belonged. You can sing along with that if you like.

In the morning we had mugs of tea and freshly baked bread rolls in one of those new Daisy-boy cafes that were springing up all over West Ken. I felt comfortable with Dolly. In the morning she always had an appetite for three – almost greedy. I loved watching her demolish a breakfast. Women have memories like elephants and they keep our moments of weakness in them, so the conversation, after she'd polished the crumbs from her plate, went something like this. She remembered, 'Some time ago – it seems like years, but it probably wasn't – you asked me if I'd ever want to settle down and have children. I formed the idea that maybe you were talking about you and me.'

'Maybe I was. I can't remember how the subject came up. You said something like *Eventually, but not at the moment*. I got the impression that you were talking about us as well.'

She stared out of the window at red buses full of people going to work. She had a dreamy look on her face that disturbed me. It was not a Dolly look.

'Maybe I was. Would you want me to tell you if I'd changed my mind? If the calendar had moved on?'

'If you wanted me to sod off you mean?'

I can be slow on the uptake sometimes, and her face showed that now.

'No. The other thing, silly: marriage and babies.'

'You're not kidding me?'

'No. I don't think so.'

'Let me think about it for a second. You know that I've already got two kids, more or less?'

'Yes. OK. While you think about it I'll order us up another pot of tea. The tea here is really jolly good.'

I thought about it, and told her, 'Yes, Dolly; I would want you to tell me . . . but you ought to know that I've had a very similar conversation with another woman recently. The one we met in Germany: Marthe. She has a little girl of her own. They may need rescuing if Berlin collapses around our ears.'

Dolly was nothing if not practical. She asked, 'Do you like her more than you like me?'

'No. I more or less like you equally. That is, I like *you* more when I'm with you and *her* more when I'm with her.'

'Not an easy choice then. What do you think might swing it?'

'It could well come down to who actually jumps in with a proper offer first I suppose . . .'

'Mmm . . . Thank you, Charlie, I'll remember that.'

'. . . Or there again I might just panic, run away from you both, and marry someone else on the rebound.'

'. . . And I'll remember that too. Would you like me to drive you to Victoria?'

'Yes please, Dolly. You know I love you.'

'I believe that you believe you do. Sometimes.'

'What does that mean?'

'Not what you think it does, Charlie. Which train did you want to catch?'

Dolly was often hard to read. I loved that about her too.

Chapter Sixteen

We had three new pilots. I didn't think that was enough. The Old Man did. I'd met one of them, a Leither named Hardisty, at a session at the Lympne pub one night. I liked what I remembered of him. He drank large whiskies with half-pint chasers, but never mixed his drink and his flying: one of these solid Scots you could depend on until the end.

Hardisty had volunteered to drive down to the station in the Passion Wagon, to pick me up. I guess that the Wagon had been having a bit of a pounding, because her passenger seat was now as uncomfortable as the squab in the back.

'It seems very quiet at the moment. Odd. It's like a church down here.'

'You go to church?' I asked him.

'Sometimes. I'm a son of the manse. Do you know what that means?'

'No.'

'My father is a church minister. Church of Scotland . . . that's a bit like your Church of England without the frills.'

'Fire and brimstone?'

'Only occasionally. Peace and brotherly love most of the time. He says that Switzerland and Iceland are the only two countries who know what they're doing – they never declare war on anyone.'

I laughed, but I told him, 'I'd like to meet your old man.' And I meant it.

'It was difficult when I joined the RAF. We didn't speak for two years.'

I didn't want to go there, so I asked him, 'What were you on?'

'Wimpies mainly, and Marylands: I flew in India and over the hump into Burma. What about you, sir?'

It took a second or two for that to sink in. *Sir?* I decided to ignore it until I knew how to deal with it. I'd ask Elaine.

'Lancasters out of Bawne in Cambridgeshire, then I made a mistake and ended up in Germany for the last few weeks. I picked up a bit of Jerry lingo whilst I was there, which is why the Old Man has picked me for this job I think.'

Airworks had just converted Hardisty on to Lancastrians for us, and in a couple of days he was flying the *Tin Man* out to Wunstorf with a gash engineer.

'. . . and after that?'

'I'm to crew up with her regular engineer and sparks, fly on to Celle for a load of flour, and then make my first home run.'

'Windy?'

He definitely didn't want to answer that. Eventually he said, 'I suppose that I am. A bit.'

'Good. That's what I wanted to hear. That way you'll stay in one piece, and more important, you'll keep my aircraft and my crew in one piece too.' I caught myself. When had I started thinking of them as *my* aircraft? He was grinning when I glanced at him, which is how I wanted it. All three of our new boys had passed their conversion to the Lancastrian so they were partying in the pub that night. Hardisty invited me to join them. I thought it would give me a chance to give them the once-over.

'Thanks. I'll see what's waiting for me in the office. I'll see you later.'

What was waiting for me in the office was a stack of bills to authorize, and crew and maintenance schedules to agree. I was inclined to just bang my moniker on the bottom of each one and bugger off . . . until I realized that if anything went wrong because I'd missed something, and people were killed, then it would be my fault. I'd never had to think about that before, so I found myself studying fuel and lubricant records for individual aircraft, trying to work out if there was anything to worry about. Elaine came through to my office with a cup of tea for me, and looked over my shoulder.

'What are you doing?'

'Trying to justify the fuel consumptions . . .'

'. . . leave that to Chiefy and the engineers if I was you. They'll soon flag up any rogue to us – that's their job. I'm always checking them anyway. I'll let you know if anything out of the ordinary crops up.'

'You're a gem. Thanks. Why didn't I think of that?'

She flushed, and I wanted to kiss her. I didn't. She said, 'I don't know. My Terry was a driver during the war. He says that officers had their brains scraped out.'

'We used to say that as well. Am I an officer again?'

'That's what it says on your door. Didn't you notice?'

She'd been walking around with that *I know something that you don't* look on her face since I arrived. I walked out to her office to look back at the door I still thought of as Brunton's. A new painted notice on it read *General Manager*. Underneath that in smaller letters was *Lt. C. Bassett*. Bugger me!

'Who did that?'

'One of the fitters. He's a trained sign writer. I think he's called Jim.' She'd told me more than I needed to know, and not enough.

'Who told him to?'

'I did; after the Old Man told me. Pleased?'

'Shocked, I think, but I was never a lieutenant you know. What happened to Brunton?'

'He's out of hospital, but won't come back in case he runs into Terry again. He resigned . . . he's going to train to be a school teacher.'

'What did Halton think?'

'*Halton* was quite pleased, actually.' The Old Man's voice preceded him into the room . . . 'Squadron Leader Brunton is a very brave man, and all that, but when you get down to it, it takes more than bravery to run a commercial airline, doesn't it?'

I turned quickly and said, 'You'll have to stop moving so quietly, boss. How do you expect me to talk about you behind your back if you keep on creeping up on us like this?' I don't know how it had happened, but I had developed the knack of making him laugh. I suppose that it was something he needed.

He laughed and coughed a bit. Then he straightened up and said, 'Now stop messing about, tell me where my aircraft are, and what they're doing.'

I hadn't got that far yet, but I looked up at the operations board above Elaine's desk, and prayed that it was up to date. She smiled. I was OK.

A few hours after that, torpor lay over Lympne like a hot blanket. I looked out of the office window and nothing was moving, not even the windsock. Like a Barcelona brothel on a Wednesday afternoon. Elaine came into my office, came around the desk to stand beside me, yawned and stretched. I do so love the way women's bodies move under their clothes. I ran my hand lightly up the back of her leg until it reached her stocking top, which, for the hedonists among you, is as far as it got. She leaned a hand on my shoulder, and said, 'Terry's home this week. He's got a week's holiday.'

'OK. We could . . .'

'. . . and the other pilots are in the accommodation with you. So I think we'd better forget it for a little while.'

'Then why did you come round here, and stand so close?'

'Teasing,' she said, smoothed her dress down and pushed my hand away with the same motion. God was sending me one of His little messages. As usual, the reception wasn't so good, and I should have listened more bloody closely.

When I walked into the pub the party was in full swing. They'd bussed in a number of nurses from the hospital in Folkestone to get things going. There was a small jazz band tootling away somewhere. I recognized the clarinet break on 'Dippermouth Blues' and promised myself to find out what a dippermouth was one day. Elaine's Terry joined me up at the bar. He still walked with a limp from the stabbing. He looked a bit sheepish. I had to look up to him to hear what he was saying of course. It was like standing alongside a cliff face. He started with, 'I wanted to apologize about the fuss the other night.'

'That's all right . . . Terry, isn't it? All done and dusted.'

' 's right. You won't be givin' her the sack then?'

'Of course not. The place couldn't run without her. They're more likely to sack me than sack her. How's your leg?'

'Still sore. She touched a nerve.'

'Women have a habit of doing that, don't they?' At least that raised a grin.

'I won't be able to work for't least another week.'

'I know. She told me.'

'I don't know what came over me that night. I just didn't like the way he looked at her.'

'I told you, it's finished . . . nothing's going to happen.'

'Thanks. I'll remember this.'

'Don't bother. Buy me a pint instead; I'm parched . . . and if I ask Elaine for a dance later on don't bash me for it!'

He grinned at this, and said, 'No fear; she'd only get the knife into me again.'

Was that an attempt at humour? Knife and fork? I wasn't sure.

I danced one with her, and led her back to him. It was a halfway decent party. Scroton had turned up, and Mortensen, and once I thought I had a glimpse of Milton dancing with one of the nurses, but that was impossible. When I got back to the hut I was the only one without a nurse, and lay awake listening to my pilots mating discreetly in the dark.

Lying there, waiting for sleep to claim me, it struck me that Terry Curtis had just apologized to a man who had been shagging his missus, and for whom his mighty right hand had just won a sizeable promotion. There was a lot of bad karma there; I'd better watch out for myself. And he'd kill me if ever he found out, of course. In fact I thought about myself, and wasn't too keen on how I'd behaved of late. The problem with deciding to turn over a new leaf was that I'd enjoyed the old leaves so much. My life was just like my last school report: *Could do better.* It was a long time before I slept.

There was one other thing. I had tired of the party around midnight, and wandered out into the car park to smoke my pipe and look at the stars. An airliner with all of its lights showing droned overhead on its way to France. Just for a moment there was the trace of a familiar obscene smell in the air. Gasoline and burnt meat. Probably just in my memory, but you never can tell.

Dorothy was sitting outside my office window the next morning. Scroton complained to the Ground Crew Chief about the engines. He only complained about *Dorothy* because he was still a little in love with *Whisky*. There's no telling some men.

The Chief looked hassled. He explained, 'There's bugger all the matter with her, or her engines. It's just the way you operate her.'

'Might have known it would be my fault.' That was Scroton.

'She's too fat, too heavy and too low to operate efficiently from grass strips. When she's laden you just need so much more power from the engines to get her up from grass – particularly if it's wet – and you put more wear on them. Fly her off a patch of concrete and she's a different beast. That's all . . .'

I walked over. 'There's concrete all over Germany, Chief . . .'

'Then get her out there as quick as you can.' He wiped his hands on a petrol-smelling rag. I turned away momentarily because it reminded me of Milton again. '. . . and start making a profit off her.'

I touched his arm. 'Will do, Chief. Let me see her maintenance dockets, and those for the Lancs, sometime today, will you?'

After he had sloped off Scroton said, 'You're getting airs and graces, Charlie. Be careful now.'

'I had a girl named Grace once. I was nuts about her: we all were.'

'That's how I feel about the Countess. When will you send me back to Berlin?'

I wished he hadn't asked me that.

I went down to see the boys on the Friday night. It was staged as a surprise visit, and I made no promises about the next time. There was a patch of flat mown grass behind the bay, and we played cricket on it all weekend, using James's old gear. I avoided Dieter's probing attacks on my matrimonial status . . . rather skilfully I thought.

After Elaine had dropped the portcullis on me I had been looking forward to palling up with Evelyn again, so I was disappointed to run into her old man in the bar early on Friday night. He looked rather grim, but at least he apologized to me.

'We got off on the wrong foot,' he said. 'Thought you were staff. Sorry about that.' I liked him even less for the form of his apology than for his original assumption. '. . . and pleased things worked out fine with your little boys.'

'Thanks. It was just a storm in a teacup. I was choked at the way everyone rallied round.'

'Eve came down as soon as we heard. I couldn't get away.' *Eve.*

'I'll find a way of thanking her properly one day.'

'She'd like that.'

Did I feel like a bit of a bastard? No. I'd never feel bad about putting one over on him. There was something on his mind; I could tell.

'She found your cook a pillar of strength in the boat apparently.'

'Good. I didn't even know he could sail. Probably a quick learner: he looks the type.'

'I dare say. She's been out sailing with him every day this week. Showing him the ropes.' As he said it a picture of a big old-time sailing ship came into my mind, and I realized that it was probably another one of those phrases that the Navy handed down to us. He paused before adding, 'Don't suppose I've anything to worry about, do you?'

No, I thought, *but maybe I* have!

'I wouldn't know. Sorry. Wouldn't have thought so – anyway I'm the wrong person to ask: never here.'

'Quite. Sorry I asked. I just thought . . .'

'Shall we nick a couple of James's scotches before anyone comes back into the bar?'

He took the hint, but it was just as I suspected: my options were closing down.

Maggs cornered me after church. She asked, 'What's the matter, love? You looked pinched.'

'One of those weeks; nobody seems to want to know me.'

'No *woman* wants to know you, you mean.'

'I suppose so.'

'Prob'ly your own fault. I told you to try 'arder.'

'That too.'

'Don't worry, love. Maybe you need the time to get your breath back.'

'That too, too.'

On Sunday evening James and I walked around the bay in the late evening. Jules had finished serving, and was helping Maggs and the potboy behind the bar. James had taken up a pipe, and we discussed tobaccos. The shingle crunched under our feet. From a distance we might have looked like two ships under steam. We realized that my last farewells had been premature, but he asked, 'This is really *it*, this time?'

'I think so, James. The Airlift is on. The Russians seem determined to starve us out, and we seem determined to prove them wrong. The politicians are waffling, as usual, and the papers are just standing at the ringside, holding the coats and egging everyone on.'

'. . . as dangerous as we thought?'

'I don't know. The scary part is that if it turns nasty, it will happen fast. One minute we'll be flying established routes and schedules, albeit under some pressure, and the next they'll be shooting us down.'

'Like dancing an *excuse me* but getting no notice of the change of partners.'

'Precisely.'

'What do you want me to tell Dieter? He reads the newspapers you know.'

'The truth, always the truth. I once promised him that. In some ways he's as grown as we are James, he'll know what to do.'

'You ever wondered if you make too many promises, old boy?'

'Someone else asked me that.'

'Recently?'

'No. Years ago.' I shivered, and said, 'Let's go back in. I'm getting cold.'

I got only as far as Wunstorf in one hop, sitting at the old radio operator's seat in *Whisky*. Scroton and Crazy Eddie had a cargo of powdered milk in tins, which is pretty light for its bulk, so *Whisky* flew like a skittish colt, and Scroton enjoyed himself. One of Chiefy's ground handlers flew as loadmaster. We'd have one of those on each flight from now on. Crazy Ed looked grey. He must have been on another bender. I mentioned that to Dave when we were on the ground again. He shook his head and said, 'I don't think it's the booze. I was out with him last night and he was fleeing after three pints.'

'*Fleeing?*'

'It's a Scots word that Hardisty uses. It means dancing drunk. I think there's something the matter with him.'

'Perhaps all he's doing is topping up the drink already inside him.'

'No. That's not it either. I've seen him go for a week without a drink and it still hits him as quickly.'

'It's probably time I instituted regular medicals for our flying crews anyway, instead of waiting for the Air Ministry to catch up with you lot.'

Scroton smiled, 'You're beginning to sound like a bloody manager, Charlie.'

They unloaded *Whisky*'s milk, and a similar load from a Briton Air Dakota that had come in from Southend, on to an RAF York which flew it straight on to Gatow. It would take at least two Yorks full of dried milk powder a day every day just to keep the nursing babies going. *Whisky* was then loaded with wooden crates for the Army, and was due for Lübeck . . . where she would be based for a while. Scroton would get to see his Countess every other day. I wondered where Randall was, and how I could keep them apart.

Before *Whisky* left, some RAF electrical types swarmed all over her cockpit and removed the magic box from underneath Scroton's seat. I asked the flight lieutenant in charge of them, 'Testing finished?'

'No. We're switching it to an RAF Hastings. It's an interesting box of tricks, isn't it?'

'Was there a problem with it in the Dakota?'

'No, but the Intelligence wallahs with radios tell us they intercepted some Red Air Force traffic a couple of days ago. They were asking their pilots to report sightings of red-painted Daks, so I was told to whip it out. Better safe than sorry.'

'How often have you used that thing over here?' I asked Scroton.

'Six times. Maybe eight.'

'Bollocks.'

'I will feel a bit naked without it.' He'd missed the point, hadn't he?

The station commander was an all-right type. He offered me a lift into Gatow in another Hastings the following day, which meant that I was stuck at Wunstorf for the rest of the afternoon and night. Then he sought me out at the crowded bar in the evening, walking across the room straightening his moustaches with his fingers. I've seen cats do that sort of thing. He said, 'There was someone asking for you at the gate. I know the man from a few years back, so I took the liberty of having him passed through, and brought here. OK with you?'

'Fine. It's not a Yank named David Thomsett by any chance?'

'Tommo? You know him? No. Someone who flew with one of my squadrons in the war.' He turned to look over his shoulder, and Bozey Borland marched through the door to the bar, escorted by an RAF Regiment one-striper. The escort saluted, and the station commander thanked and dismissed him. Borland said, 'Hello, guv'nor,' to me, and 'Hello, Porky,' to my companion.

The station commander turned to me and said, 'I know that you're Halton's Charlie Bassett, but we haven't been properly introduced. I'm Peter Churchill – no relation. I used to be fat once upon a time. They still call me *Porky*.'

Then he turned back to Borland. 'Hello, Bozey. Who are you with?'

'I don't know yet. Mr Bassett promised to find me a job with someone if I could get to Germany on my own . . . before we get down to business, am I allowed to buy anyone a drink in here?'

'Think we could manage that.' That was Churchill. Then he said, 'Glad to see you, Bozey.' I found that I was too.

Borland and I found our way to a small lounge with prewar modernistic furniture which was a lot more comfortable than it looked. I flagged down one of the white-clad German Mess boys and got him to bring us long whiskies and a beer. Before Bozey got into his stride I held my hand up and told him, 'I don't want to know how you got out of England. OK?'

'What the eye doesn't see the heart can't grieve over?'

'Something like that.' We sipped our beers. 'But I am pleased to see you.'

'Pleased enough to give me a job?'

I thought about it.

'Yes. Yes, I think so. Depends what you can fly.'

'Virtually anything. I've flown singles, twins *and* multis since the RAF kissed me goodbye. Anything that would pay. What will it pay, by the way?'

'I don't know. Not much: I'll have to ask my office. Bottom whack I expect, but better than sitting on your arse in Wormwood Scrubs stitching mailbags.'

'Do criminals still have to do that?'

'I've got no idea, but it seemed an appropriate time to mention it.'

He laughed, and pointed a finger. 'I met some people who knew you. They said that you could be deceptively pleasant before you pulled the trigger.' That was nearer to the truth than I wanted him to be.

'I like people to know where they stand with me.'

'Fair enough. When do I start?'

'I'll see if I can get you on a flight to Berlin with me tomorrow. You'll be the spare man there. We were supposed to have a small accommodation hut at Gatow, but we'll be lucky if we even get an office, so you have to shift for yourself. Most of the commercials just have to put up with RAF rules.'

He nodded slowly and said, 'You're right, boss.'

'About what?'

'It beats sewing mailbags in Wormwood Scrubs.'

'Tell me that again in a week.'

He shared my concrete cabin, taking the upper bunk. He snored. Maybe I'd made a mistake.

In the early hours of the morning I was awakened by an RAF corporal who shone a torch in my face, and shook me gently. 'Mr Bassett, sir?'

I felt slow-witted. Muzzy. 'Uh-huh. Yeah.' It was like being on a squadron again, and being awoken for a raid.

'Station commander's compliments, sir, and would you join him in the Watch Office?'

I nearly asked *Is it urgent?* Before realizing that no one would get me up at this time if it wasn't. Borland must have been a light sleeper. He grunted while I was dressing in the dark, and asked, 'Want me to come, boss?'

'No. I'll send for you if I need you, but thanks anyway. Go back to sleep.' I heard him roll over, and he was snoring again before I let myself out.

Churchill had left the Watch Office by the time I reached it, and I had to follow him down to the operations room they were beginning to call Flying Control. It was a large room with huge charts on three walls, and a dozen staff even at that time of night. Half a dozen pilots were receiving a briefing of some kind around a table in a corner. Two of them were obviously Yanks. Peter Churchill was standing with his back to me, looking up at one of the charts. When I joined him he nodded. No preliminaries.

'We lost your Dakota.' A vision of Scroton and Crazy Ed's faces swam before me. Then he added, 'The pink 'un. Dreadful colour for an aircraft by the way. Asking for trouble.'

Max then . . . and Red Ronson, or Lieter or whatever his name was. I still hadn't responded, so he asked, 'You OK?'

'Yes. Thank you.'

An erk wandered past, and after he had gone by there was a mug of cocoa in my hand. I took a sip. It was strong and scalding hot. I asked Churchill, 'What happened?'

'I don't know yet. What was he hauling?'

'Bulk foodstuffs of some kind: flour I think – nothing dodgy. Don't you have radar coverage of the corridor?'

'There's a gap. Your bod was in it, on the way back to Lübeck . . . apparently there was a very dense burst of Russki radio jamming . . . your bod was heard to say *Wait one*, as if something had happened, and that was it. He didn't come out the other side.'

'Any reports?'

'None. It's not as busy at this time of night. There was someone three minutes behind him who didn't see anything. We've warned all flights to look out for fires on the ground. It's been forty-five minutes now, so I decided that someone should tell you. OK?'

'I'll hang around if that's all right.'

'Fine. Do you want to call England?'

'No. Not yet. I'll wait until morning. We may have heard something by then.'

I sat in on a radio and navigation briefing for something to do. The radio beacons were simple medium-wave jobs . . . picking them out was kids' stuff, and the Eureka radar beacons were very reliable . . . in 1940s terms, that is. Navigation between them should have been a piece of piss: all you had to do was watch out for the guys in front and behind you. What would Max have been doing? I *knew* what Max would have been doing: he would have been relying on an old guy with a magnetized nail on a piece of string. It had been my mistake as much as his. Magnetized nails can't talk to radar beacons. Bollocks.

I don't know what time the sun came up, because the ops room was under the concrete. When I stepped onto the tarmac it was a step into a watery dawn. About eighteen aircraft had flown through *Pink Pig*'s last piece of air space, and nobody reported anything on the ground. Maybe they were flying too high. I needed some unofficial help from someone a lot better at flying low, so I walked back up to the Watch Office and put a call through to a pilot named Dare. I wondered if he was as good as his name.

Anyway; that's half the story of how the *Pink Pig* flew into legend. She flew into the northern corridor of the Berlin Airlift not long after it started, and forgot to come out the other end. Just like the Ninth Legion marching across the Scottish border into oblivion and history.

Peter Dare blasted along the corridor that morning at very low level, after receiving permission from a sympathetic wing com-mander. He set the fastest transit time along the corridor ever recorded, upset an awful lot of Russians, saw absolutely no trace of the *Pig*, and came back with a bit of pine tree jammed in his port engine intake. By mid-morning we'd probably managed to nudge the temperature of the Cold War up a degree or two.

Halton, of course, was his usual detached self. I put it down to that hacking cough. It always gave him time to think before he spoke. It wasn't a good telephone connection: the line crackled as if it was alive.

'The War Office has indemnified us, Charlie. They'll replace it with one of their own Dakotas.' I thought, but didn't say, *What about our bloody people?*

'Then make sure you get a good one, boss, and this time, whatever you do, don't paint it. If they think it belongs to the RAF they might leave us alone.'

'This time I shall agree with you, Charlie, but never rely on it. Speak again when you have some news.'

Neither of us had mentioned Louis 'Max' Maxwell the Third, or Red Ronson. Criticize me if you will, but that's just the way it was. What do they say? Easy come, easy go. That was Max all over.

I think that you'll understand why I was depressed when I strapped into the Hastings that was to take me and Bozey Borland to Berlin that afternoon. That old wartime question had come back to haunt me: *Was it ever bloody worth it?*

PART THREE

The Air Bridge

Chapter Seventeen

Russian Greg was out of town. I wondered if he was poking around in the bones of the *Pink Pig*, or had just disappeared for a week because he couldn't face me because of it. The Brits weren't saying much, and a call I put through to the Americans at Tempelhof didn't exactly start a bush fire. So I ended up in the Leihhaus for a couple of days.

When I'd told the Old Man I was flying out to Germany he hadn't said anything else about Frieda. Neither did I, so I left without her. In my opinion Berlin hadn't been a place for a woman for years . . . too many people dropped bombs on it. I became sorry when Magda walked into the Leihhaus with a cheap brown paper envelope she'd picked up from the BFPO post office at Gatow when she came off duty from the hotdog and doughnut machine. It was addressed to me. It had been opened.

Magda asked, 'Who's Frieda?'

'Did *you* open this?'

'Yes. Who's Frieda?'

'Do you always open other people's mail?'

'Not always. Don't you ever say thank you to people who deliver it? We do in my country.'

'Thank you, Magda.'

'Don't mention it. Who's Frieda?'

'I think that she's my boss's bit of fluff. She's German and wants to find her relations. I was supposed to bring her here with me, but deliberately forgot. I may be in for a bollocking when I get back.'

I dropped a transport manager five dollars to borrow his jeep, and picked up Frieda on the Gatow apron. Randall taxied the drab Oxford up to the admin blocks. I could see that he had applied black registration markings to it now, but they were so small that you needed a microscope to read them with. As I helped Frieda down from the door, a gust of wind lifted her dark blue dress around her waist, and a passing squaddie whistled. She was like that I think – without meaning to, she attracted attention wherever she went. Despite an antagonism I felt towards her I couldn't understand, I thought that she had nice little pins. Her stockings alone were worth as much as a Berliner's weekly pay. I smoothed her dress down instinctively, and she said, 'Thank you, Charlie.'

She rested her hand on my shoulder as she stepped down from the aircraft. I felt as if she was scalding me with her touch.

'No problem. Welcome to Germany.'

'Welcome home, you mean.'

'Yes. I suppose so. Do you want me to fix you up at one of the British clubs, or do you have somewhere to stay?'

'I have Geoffrey's flat. It's not far from here. I'll give you the address.' Geoffrey was Geoffrey Halton of course. Was there anyone on the make who hadn't helped themselves to a little bit of Germany? Randall appeared at the Oxford's door and handed me down her small suitcase and a plain raincoat.

'Decent trip?' I asked him.

'Company could not have been better.' For a moment I thought he was going to blush. Frieda smiled. She liked compliments. She took her case and coat from me, and sat in the passenger seat of the jeep. I tarried a moment. Randall asked, 'Where's my Countess?'

'She's just finished a stint on the Doughnut Wagon, and then she's going over to the Leihhaus to wait for you.'

'I may get there first. Where's Scroton?'

'He left for Lübeck an hour ago. You've got two days before he gets back.'

'I'm heading back tomorrow.'

That was the first bit of good news I'd had all week. There were three soldiers and a Customs guy crowded around Frieda, chatting her up, when I joined her. One of them gave me a dirty look as I slid behind the wheel of the jeep. I was right; she was going to be trouble. As I pulled away I asked her, 'Tell me where you want to go.'

She directed me to a broad avenue of huge houses in our zone, curiously almost untouched by the war: I might have guessed. Her apartment was an entire first floor of the largest. There was a concierge, and a gardener was busy converting a sweeping lawn into a vegetable patch. The whole set-up telegraphed money: I might have guessed that as well. I left her as quickly as I decently could – after she'd explained that a Russian squad had been billeted there, and it had taken a month to clear up after them: they'd used every room as a toilet before they left, and had decorated the walls with revolutionary slogans, and women's underwear. I saw little evidence of either now. The place rivalled Greg's in the East.

There was one moment I will remember. She sat in a two-hundred-year-old chair, framed by the light from a massive window behind her, erect and with her legs crossed. That had the effect of emphasizing her top hamper. They actually didn't need any emphasizing: maybe I've told you that before. She took a cigarette from her small leather shoulder bag, and waited for me to light it for her. I obliged without thinking. She glanced to the right where a small table with an ashtray was just out of her reach. I moved them for her. She smiled and blew out a thin stream of rich smoke. She knew that she'd created an image I would never forget.

'I will try not to make too many difficulties for you, Charlie.'

'But you will create some?'

'Probably . . .'

Her chair was on a small Persian rug, on polished boards. She deliberately flicked the ash from her cigarette on to it. I asked, 'Will madam require anything else before I go?'

'No, Charlie. I will send for you when I want you.'

No pleases. No thankyous. She didn't even ask where I hung out. I could see that this was going to be a trial of strength.

As I pulled away from the place I noticed that there was an unusual mix of uniforms and civilians strolling in the avenue with none of the usual Berlin sense of urgency or deprivation . . . and that there was an armed police patrol parked up at the end. Whoever these bastards were, they had protection. That was interesting.

I handed back the jeep and sloped over to the club: Greg was back in all his pint-sized glory. I told him, 'If I'm going to be around for a while I'm going to have to fix up some transport.'

'I know. I called Tommo. He's going to stop over with something for you.'

'I didn't know he was in town.'

'Neither did he.' Now what the hell did that mean?

Randall was already there with his feet stretched under the table, and an enormous jug of light beer before him. I asked him, 'What did you make of your passenger?'

'I'm passionately in love with her, Charlie. Love will never be the same again.'

'You mean you . . . ?'

'No; don't be an a-hole. Just wishful thinking: she's *way* outta my class, but sensational, ain't she?' I liked the way that he couldn't actually bring himself to use the word in everyday conversation.

'What about Magda?'

'Who's Magda?'

Well, that solved *that* one I suppose.

Magda came in an hour later. She had taken some trouble to tart herself up for him, so she was pretty put out to find Randall treating her like a least favourite sister.

Marthe was in the kitchen, and didn't come out immediately. When she did it was only to plant a small peck on my cheek and retreat again. The buses had definitely stopped running for me this week. I'd filled a small pack for her in the store at Wunstorf, and although she clucked appreciatively over it I slept on my own on the sofa that night. Quite like old times. Lottie came out to see me before she went to sleep. She had a long thick nightdress, and her hair was in two braids. She was clutching the rag doll to her, but gave me a peck – just like her mother had – and squeezed my hand. She looked sorry for me. There were no street lights so I didn't bother to close the curtain. I curled up on the settee and watched the black window, whilst I made up my mind to get a place of my own. If I could find somewhere close to Gatow with enough space, the boys could bunk down there between trips as well. I didn't ask Marthe why the honeymoon was over; I wasn't sure I'd want to know the answer.

This is the second part of the *Pig*'s story: how she flew back into history again.

I had mourned the *Pig* for three days, when the bastard thing turned up again. You'll often find her today in a footnote to books on the Bermuda Triangle, or on alleged timeslips. It didn't actually happen that way. The loonies say that she flew into the northern corridor during the Berlin Airlift, and flew out three days later, and nobody knows what happened to her and her crew in between. That's not exactly true either. I do; and so does anyone who was there at the time. The problem is that I suppose that there aren't that many of us left.

I was mooching around on the apron, making a nuisance of myself, when an erk hurried up and used almost exactly the same words.

'Mr Bassett, sir? The Duty Officer's compliments, and would you care to join him, sir?'

'Have I just lost another aircraft?'

'I don't believe so, sir . . . if you'd care to follow me?' I knew where the bloody man was, but the erk was only doing his job.

Déjà vu prevailed. The Duty Officer, an overweight overpaid French Letter, said, 'Fancy a cup of cocoa, Mr Bassett?'

It was mid-afternoon of a summer's day, but in Control it was cool.

'Thanks. What's up?'

'One of your aircraft just turned up from nowhere, and slotted in between a couple of incoming Yorks. I've had to stretch out the train to get a decently safe separation. I thought you'd like to be present when I give your buggers a bollocking. Saves me repeating it to you.'

This was not going to be my week, but I could see his point. Absolute adherence to the discipline of separation between the incoming and outgoing aircraft at the Airlift airfields was the key to the operation. The Air Traffic Control you see at Schipol or Heathrow today began there. They played the verbal interchange between the tower and the aircraft over the speakers, and as soon as I heard the pilot's voice I turned away and found a chair.

The DO asked, 'Anything wrong?'

'That pilot was killed three days ago.'

'He doesn't sound very dead to me.'

'Nor me. What's the little sod been doing?'

I saw him reach for a dark blue telephone handset that stood on its own. 'Who are you calling?'

'The Regiment. I think we'd better keep them away from the motley until we know what's going on, don't you?'

They wouldn't let me see them for a couple of hours; but I had a look at the *Pig* to see if she offered any clues. On the outside were some scrapes and small dents and a few dark green streaks on the wing leading edges. Peter Dare wandered over. I said to him, 'I didn't know you were here. I didn't thank you properly for going out to look for this lot three days ago.'

''s all right, squire. Thought I'd have a gander at what I was supposed to find.' Then he laughed. 'You couldn't really miss her, could you? I definitely didn't see anything like this. Why did you paint her that horrible shade of pink?'

'My boss ran out of red paint.'

That made him laugh even more. He told me, 'Do you know that the Cousins are using exactly that shade for high visibility on some of their reconnaissance jobs? B-29s flying over the North Pole and that sort of thing. I bet the Reds are worried about you.'

That put a different complexion on it: I wish someone had told me before. We climbed up inside, but it wasn't long before we were turfed out by an RAF technical team. I pointed out that it was my aircraft, not theirs. Their surly warrant officer responded, 'It's been in the hands of the Reds, sir. It's *ours* until we've established that they haven't planted a bomb in it, or engaged in other nefarious acts of sabotage. Then you may have it back.' Prat.

We were in it long enough to notice one thing: the Russians, or whoever had had the old cow, had nicked her pilot's seat. Max had flown home on an old wicker basket chair – the sort you see in hotel sun lounges – strapped in place with what looked like a number of leather belts.

DAVID FIDDIMORE

'I wonder what they wanted with that,' I mused.

'It's a relatively late mark of Dakota,' Dare pointed out. 'Perhaps the seat's more comfortable than the ones they have.' He clearly thought it amusing. 'Shall we grab a cup of coffee? The doughnut wagon has just pulled up over there, and they have a cracking bit of old Jerry in the back.'

That would have lifted Magda's morale. Maybe I should introduce them. The last thing he said was, 'Those streaks and dents, especially around the wing tips . . .'

'Yes?'

'I'd say he flew her a tad close to some pine trees, wouldn't you? My speciality you see . . .' If anyone knew that then he did.

Max and Ronson found me in the station Mess bar we were allowed to use. It was starting to bustle because Gatow was taking in a dozen flights an hour, and launching as many. Max bleated, 'Sanctuary, sanctuary . . .'and flopped into an easy chair alongside me. Red slouched into an upright one, looking over Max's shoulder.

'Did you two try to fly the *Pig* through a forest?' I asked them.

Ronson said, 'Down a firebreak for about ten mile. The bastards boxed us in.'

'What bastards? Russians?'

'I'm not sure, boss, but they were speaking German all the time they were with us. Pretty good flyers; the only space they left us was into the ground. One on either side, and one above. They were flying Russian Sturmoviks, anyway.'

'They lifted us out of the stream as neat as a dollar.' That was Max. 'Forced me down into a firebreak in a forest of enormous black pines. There was an old airfield at the end of it . . . probably a training base because it was grass.'

'It could have been anything,' I told him. 'Most of their airfields were either grass or bits of autobahn by the end of the war. You landed there?'

260

'They made their intentions abundantly clear; they shot at us whenever I turned a way they didn't like.'

'Then what?'

'They separated us, and marched us away. Lots of Kraut jubilation going on. I never saw Red again until they put us back in the ship.'

'They interrogate you?'

'Sort of; but half-hearted. During the day I was locked away in a beat-up hangar where they were working on the *Pig*. Now and again they would come back and ask me something. They weren't interested in me, they wanted the *Pig*. They turned her inside out.'

'What were they after?'

'Her radio. They said they wanted the special radio. They pulled the radio out. Then they got angry and put it back again. I didn't understand it.'

The *Pink Pig*, like most of our aircraft, could now fly without a radio operator if it had to, but I didn't think that our kit was sophisticated enough to make anyone jealous.

'What were they like when they'd put it all back together?'

'You're right. They were a bit subdued. They left the seat out though.'

'Where were you kept at night?'

'In a bunker they were also using as a horse stall. The damned thing stood on me during the night. After that I had to be careful.'

'Feed you?'

'They fed me. It was crap food, but they ate it themselves. Then some very small bigwig comes in with more medals than uniform and gives them all a dressing down in front of me, turns to me and tells me in good American that I am free to go, and apologizes for the mistake.'

'*Mistake*?'

'That's what the man said.'

'What happened to Red?' I shouldn't have referred to him in the third; I should have asked him myself.

'Dunno. He won't tell me. He won't tell you either. He won't tell anyone.'

'Is that right?' I asked Ronson. He nodded guardedly. 'They interrogate you?' He nodded again, and held out his hands, palm upwards. The palms were covered with small circular cigarette burns; particularly the soft fold of flesh between each thumb and forefinger. I asked, 'That wasn't about a radio, was it?' It was no good; he pointedly looked away.

'They took away his pointing nail,' Max said. 'He goes to pieces without it.'

'I'll get him another.' Then I told Red, 'Look. I know that you're in some sort of trouble. Can I help you at all?'

'No.'

'Will you tell me about it?'

'No.'

Sometimes the simplest questions are best. 'Why not?'

He gave me a look that wasn't unfriendly. 'You wouldn't believe me, boss.' I thought that was all he'd say, but he surprised us both by adding, 'I've told too many folk already. Maybe that's the problem.'

Max asked me when we would get the *Pig* back.

'Your guess is as good as mine. I suppose that I'd better find you two somewhere to stay, and go and find out . . .'

Accommodation turned out to be no problem because the police weren't prepared to let them off the airfield anyway. The same warrant officer gave them keys for rooms in the barrack block, and chitties for food. He'd already taken their passports and identity cards. Now he took their dog tags as well. He thought that it made moving around impossible for them. They would have to pay for their own drink so I left them twenty-five dollars each, and headed off-base to do a little thinking. I hate it when things begin to get complicated. I'd consult Old Man Halton, and then maybe it was time I brought Bozey into play. I picked up yesterday's *Sunday Pic* in the crew room as I wandered away. There was a picture of Halton with a group of other pirate airline executives on the front page. The headline was *Air Bridge*. If it was in the papers it had to be true I suppose.

I was sitting in the Klapperschlange a few hours later, drinking a little wine and talking to Alice. Talking to Alice always worked for me. Tommo was upstairs with his girl, and I had asked the barman not to tell him I was here yet. Alice flickered her tongue at me, and her eyes glinted. Her tongue was black, and in the forced light of the bar her eyes looked black as well. As black as new rubber tyres.

Something at the back of my mind was nagging me. There was a telephone on the bar. I asked the barman, 'Is that thing connected?'

'Sure is, bud.'

'Can I speak to Gatow?'

'Sure can, bud.'

He got me through. I asked to speak to the warrant officer, whose name, I remembered, was Power. Good name for a warrant officer, that. I probably sighed before I spoke to him. After identifying myself I asked him, 'You don't happen to remember what my Dakota's tyres were like, do you?'

'No, sir. Might that be important?'

'It might.'

'Wait one; I've one of my blokes in the office here . . .' After a decent pause he came back and said, 'Normal Dakota tyres, sir, perfectly standard.'

'American or British?'

I heard him relay the question. When he spoke to me again he said, 'American tyres, sir. Worn but serviceable. Can I ask why it's important?'

'Because she flew into the Russian Zone on a brand-new set of Russian tyres I had bartered with the Reds before the bridges came down, and she flew back into Gatow with a set of used Yankees. They must have had the wheels off her, Mr Power.'

He paused before he replied, but it wasn't a long pause. 'I can have her in a hangar tomorrow morning, sir.'

'Very good, Mr Power; when would you like me to come out?'

'1030 hours seems like a respectable time to begin, sir; I'll have one of my lads put the kettle on.' I didn't like the bastard, but at least he was quick on the uptake.

I put my head down close to the bar when I put the phone down, and looked hard at Alice. Snakes aren't supposed to have eyelids, but I'll swear that she winked at me.

I splashed around the peritrack in a soft mist of autumn rain. It didn't affect the flying – there was an aircraft landing every few minutes. Half of them were civvy jobs and I didn't recognize the liveries. I was driving Tommo's small Mercedes saloon: the one with a cannon-shell hole in each of the back doors. I would plug them with conical-shaped pieces of carved wood. Les had taught me how to do that years ago. Tommo was hiring the car to me: he said there would be good money to be made in the future, hiring cars out to folks. He was crazy, of course: everyone would want one of their own. They'd manoeuvred the *Pig* into a hangar that was strictly speaking too small for her. It was probably designed for a Ju 88 or Me 110 in the night-fighter days. She was already up on trestles, and they were ready to drop off the wheels.

Power came bustling over, throwing back at his people, 'The officer's here, boys, time to get moving. Chop-chop.' Then he asked me, 'Cuppa char while you wait, sir? Shouldn't take more than ten minutes to get the first one off her.'

There was a large canvas-wrapped package inside each of the tyres. They were bulky and irregular.

'Could be that Indian hemp stuff,' the warrant officer told me before we opened one, 'or penicillin. People are paying small fortunes for either.'

It was neither. The packages were full of hundreds of soft shiny black sticks, about six inches by a half – each with a flattened end – and flat thin rolls of the same material. There were also long twisted rods of the stuff, each more than a foot long. The warrant officer sniffed it. He said, 'Familiar smell somehow. What is it? Plastic explosive?'

I had the knife the Frenchman had given me. I opened it, and cut an end off a piece, and gave it to Power. Then I took a piece myself and popped it in my mouth. Power copied me, and said, 'Why: It's . . .'

'Bloody liquorice . . .' I finished for him, '. . . and I know the bastard who put it there.'

I don't often get so angry that I lose it. I did then. When I got to the Leihhaus I walked rapidly across to Greg's table, lifted him out of his chair by his lapels and flung him across the room. I was even impressed by it myself. Until then I'd always been a little leery of him: this was the first time I managed to scare him. He even spoke in English without thinking about it first. What Greg said was what you sometimes still see in word bubbles in boys' comics. He said, 'What the . . . ?' as he was trying to pick himself up from the floor. It would have sounded better in Russian, wouldn't it?

I actually saw him through a veil of red mist the way they tell you, and followed him. It was oddly satisfying to see the sudden terror flood his face. I reached for him again, but an arm pulled me back. Bloody Bozey. Then Bozey did almost the same as me, but *to* me. He lifted me up by my lapels until my feet were off the ground, and held me against the wall. As I stared at him the red mist dissipated, and incredibly we began to laugh. Then he let me down because I was safe again. I wonder if he realized that when I had put my hand into my jacket pocket I was reaching for my pistol. Greg slid away from me: he wanted space between us.

'What did I do, Charlie?'

'Kidnapped my aircrew, pinched my tyres and put me through three days of hell.'

He went white. I said as evenly as I could, 'Now fuck off, Greg. Fuck off before I kill you.'

He picked up his ridiculous dinner plate of a cap from where it had fallen and did just that: maybe I could learn to become a proper officer and give orders after all. I didn't move a muscle until I heard his big GAZ jeep fire up outside. I righted the chairs which had been swept over, and sat with Bozey at the table. I had to fight to stop one leg trembling. He asked, 'Know what you're doing, boss?'

'Not exactly. It felt quite good though.'

We both had a little laugh over that: men's stuff. He walked to reach over the bar, and returned with a couple of bottles of beer.

'Would you have pulled that gun on me?' So he knew, but he'd stopped me anyway. That was interesting.

'I don't know. You were daft to risk it.'

He shrugged. He was better at shrugging than me.

'It's still better than sewing mailbags, isn't it?' I smiled back at him I guess. It was probably a weak smile. So he asked me, 'What do you want me to do?'

'Go back to the airfield and find out where our aircraft are, and when the next one's due.'

'Aren't you supposed to know that?'

'Yeah, but I seem to have lost track . . .'

'OK, boss. Leave it to me.'

After he'd left, Marthe came out of the kitchen. I didn't know if the look on her face was anger or sorrow. She spoke in English, which was unusual these days — maybe she wanted to make sure that I understood.

'You beat up on Greg. Why?'

'Because he betrayed me.'

She got herself a beer from the deserted bar, and drew up a chair to join me.

'Is that all?'

'Yes. Isn't it enough?'

'You men are doing it all the time. What you expect?'

'In my country we have this saying: *Honour among thieves*.'

'What does it mean?'

'That even thieves should respect each other, and treat each other honourably.'

'Only an Englishman would be stupid enough to believe. Is crap.'

That was me told, wasn't it?

'I expect so. Does that make things difficult for you?'

'No, Charlie. It makes things difficult for *you*. You find somewhere else to sleep until you and Greg make friends again.'

'You mean that?'

'Yes, Charlie. I told you. I have to live here when you're away. You have another phrase about bread and butter. An Irish priest taught it to me last week . . .'

'*Knowing which side your bread is buttered on* you mean.'

'That was it. Greg is the butter on my bread.'

'What about me?'

I think there was genuine affection in the smile she shot at me.

'You're like an occasional sweet cake, Charlie. Enjoyed and not forgotten, but you don't come round often enough.'

'I told you; you can come back with me.'

'I thought about it, Charlie, but I'm a German who happens to like Germany. It's where I want Lottie to grow up.'

'Even when it's like this? Smashed up and . . .'

'Maybe *especially* when it's like this. Don't you feel the spirit in the people around us? That is very Germanic . . . I won't leave unless Lottie begins to starve. I decided that.'

'Thanks for telling me, anyway. It's hard to believe that a couple of weeks ago you were almost in love with me, isn't it?'

She looked at me as if I'd said the stupidest thing in the world.

'No. It's not hard to believe. But what's that got to do with it?'

What indeed, Charlie?

The Old Man was quiet when I told him. The line crackled when he spoke. 'You're sure they're all right, Charlie?'

'Yes and no, boss. Maxwell is fine, apart from the corns on his backside from flying the *Pig* back on a makeshift seat. But they tortured Ronson. They burned him with cigarettes. His hands are a mess.' There was a sharp intake of breath. That was interesting because I had never put Halton down as the squeamish sort. The line crackled again. I said, 'This is a bad line.'

'No it's not, Charlie . . . and the noise we just heard wasn't me: it was Mrs Curtis listening in. Put the telephone down Elaine.'

There was a click, and when Halton came back his voice was stronger. 'Why did they hurt the engineer?'

'I'm not sure. He won't tell me.'

'Get him to.'

'I won't burn him.'

Halton went into one of his serial coughs. He'd actually thought that funny. When he came back he said, 'Understood, Charlie. I expect you to be subtler than that. How's the operation?'

'Each of the Lancs is flying a trip a day, sometimes two. *Whisky* does a trip every day, but some of those are between fields in our own zone positioning cargo for the RAF. They don't pay as well . . . but overall you're making a lot of money.'

'Problems?'

'A few local difficulties that's all. Nothing I can't fix. What's *Dorothy* going to be doing?'

'UK to Lübeck and back shuttling heavy cargo. They like *Dorothy* in Lübeck.'

'We'll have to pull one of the Lancs back for maintenance next week, and the other the week after that: we're flying the pants off them.'

'What do you suggest?'

'Get another so we can relieve them.'

'Impossible, Charlie. There isn't an aircraft to be had this side of the Atlantic.'

'Get one over the other side then, boss. If you keep flying yours at this pace they'll start dropping out of the sky.'

There was a pause and a cough. I don't think he was angry when he said, 'I didn't expect you to be this good, Charlie. I didn't actually expect you to be a clever manager.'

'Nor did I, Mr Halton, but I'm getting used to it.'

I thought that neither of us had anything left to say: if I needed anything I would ask Elaine or the Chiefy . . . Halton surprised me. He asked, 'Have you seen Frieda today?'

Bollocks! I swallowed before I replied, 'Actually I haven't seen her since the day she landed, boss; I . . .'

'Then get over there now. It's one of the things I'm paying you for.' Goodbye England and good luck.

Chapter Eighteen

I put it off of course. I wanted an hour for thinking. I went to Gatow on the pretext of catching up with Bozey, who was in Operations there. I phoned James from the plywood call box in the crew room.

'Everything's fine, Charlie, but you can't talk to the boys. They're out on a tractor somewhere with Maggs. Some farmer's wife she's pally with.'

'Tell them I called.'

'Of course.'

'Anything new?'

'You don't happen to fancy retiring and learning to cook, by any chance? I need a new person in the kitchen.'

'What happened to the old one? Jules. I thought he was happy with you.'

'He was. It's just that he was even happier with Eve Valentine. They've sailed off into the sunset on the Valentines' yacht. The Captain is livid.'

'I'll bet.'

I suppose I should have seen that coming. What would he miss most, I wondered, the woman or the boat? You can always get a new woman, but the yacht must have been worth a few quid.

*

The sexiest song I have ever heard is that Joan Baez recording of 'Danger Waters' made in the 1960s. You may be unsure of what the *danger waters* were, but I never was. I was past my best by then of course. The first time I heard it a memory of Frieda from 1948 sprang into my mind.

The security at the end of the avenue was being provided by a Navy shore patrol: they looked bored. I'm sure that they were off-duty and moonlighting. They didn't fancy my old RAF jacket, and made me leave the Merc with them and hoof it. Ten minutes later I was climbing up the path to Frieda's front door. The lawns had been dug over, and planted out with winter veg I guess, but they had left a foot of grass around the edge to show what it had once been: it was that sort of place – they had to keep reminding you. The concierge who barred my way at the top of the steps had probably worked for Heinrich Himmler. She was big and squat and the marks on her cheeks looked suspiciously like duelling scars. I didn't think that girls had done that sort of thing. She didn't even try me in German. She asked, 'Yes?' That's not what it sounded like. It sounded like *yaess*?

I gave her back my best German: I was getting better. 'I have come to visit Fräulein Frieda.'

'And *you* are?' The way she asked the question said that she was disinclined to believe the answer.

'Mr Bassett, but tell her HMV and she'll understand.'

The troll didn't; neither did she smile. They don't have a sense of humour, you know – I should have believed my dad when he told me that. HMV was His Master's Voice: a gramophone company. They did both the gramophone and the 78rpm discs we stuck on them when we fancied a knees-up. I was kept waiting there until I felt the sun on the back of my head. The gardener came out with what looked like a medieval edged weapon, and proceeded to straighten the grass verge with it. I don't think that he trusted me either. Eventually the ogress came back to the door and waved me forward. She barred my way momentarily at the threshold and looked pointedly at my boots and the doormat. I complied, but made up my mind to do something about the old bat.

The huge door to the Halton apartment was open. I closed it behind me, and wandered from room to room looking for my quarry. She was in the very last one, dwarfed by an enormous armchair, and with her feet up on a sagging leather hassock exposed to the sun. The pungent smell of pear drops in the air told me that she was drying recamouflaged toenails. The shade of pink was very pale: it matched the lipstick she was wearing. Her feet were beautiful. Have you ever noticed how few people have beautiful feet?

'Geoffrey prefers darker shades,' she told me. 'I prefer lighter colours.'

'They make you look younger.'

The skin of her calves was very white.

'Thank you. I will be ready in a few minutes.'

'That's OK.' It was ridiculous: I felt shy.

She was wearing the same dress I had first seen her in: I suspected that it was silk. Dark blue, and buttoned up to a high neck. Big white polka dots. Bare pale arms. There was a pair of white open-toed flatties alongside her chair. I asked, 'How have you got on tracing your relations?'

'Sorry. I didn't understand the question . . .'

OK, so my command of German was hardly perfect yet. I tried slightly different words in a slightly different order.

'Did you find your relatives?'

She smiled and nodded, but that was only because she had understood me. Then she shook her head. 'No. They are not on your lists, nor the Amis' . . .' – that was slang for Americans. 'They won't give me access to the lists in Eastern Zone.'

'Who did you ask?'

'The Control Commission . . . and some friends of Geoffrey. You will have to help me. Geoffrey said . . .'

'I know what Geoffrey said . . .' I cut her off.

The lists were *Die Vermißten* – lists of missing people. People drifting back to Berlin after the war – particularly returning servicemen – had lost touch with their families, and were able to register them as missing with the early versions of the Control Commission. The lists were updated with addresses as people were reunited. In practice that meant by 1948 a lot of people found lost relatives by checking on the searches already carried out by others. By 1948 they were already well organized enough to expand the lists to include other parts of what had once been Germany. I had heard of the lists. In our zones they were now administered by civilian authorities, and there were stories of waiting in line for days and paying for a look at them. Of course, overdoses of money seemed to solve that problem; they usually do.

'You didn't expect to find them in Berlin anyway. Weren't they over in the Russian Zone?'

'About as far East as you can get, Charlie, without going into Hungary . . . .'

'Bollocks!'

'Sorry?'

'. . . English word.'

'I will remember that. Geoffrey will be pleased.'

'I wouldn't be too sure about that.' At least she made me smile.

The problem was that I'd fallen out with Russian Greg, probably the only man I knew who could help her. I decided not to tell her that.

She offered me coffee, and when I accepted she made it herself. She was gone about ten minutes – she probably spent most of that time transiting the vast apartment. The coffee she came back with, still barefoot, was real; and American. That was interesting. She had put me in the chair I had found her in. The sun was beginning to set. I was beginning to relax. She sat on the hassock at my feet and said, 'You will stay for supper of course.' I didn't think that it was a question.

Supper was a plate of beans. I don't know what kind they were. The plate itself was old and probably very valuable: the beans were old and probably not very valuable. They were the size of butter beans and an odd khaki colour. The taste was not objectionable, just profoundly monotonous. Frieda attacked hers with relish. I wished I had some sort of relish to douse mine with.

'I do not wish to get fat,' she told me, and placed her hand on her stomach. I thought of putting a hand on her stomach myself, but daren't take the chance.

'No. I can see that.'

'Will keep you regular.'

The romance sort of goes out of it after that.

When I left her it was after dark, and I had nowhere to go that I wanted to go. The Shore Patrol had been replaced by three tough-looking Military Policemen in a three-tonner. I reckoned I'd be OK with them, so I pulled the Merc up close to them, climbed in the back and settled for the night. After a half-hour I was roused by someone tapping on the window. It was the old Troll. She was wearing a Wehrmacht greatcoat over her nightclothes and her hair was tied in bunches with pieces of rag. She didn't look friendly and gestured fiercely – *follow me*. As I followed the shuffling mass back to the house I noticed that she was wearing an outsize pair of men's leather slippers. They would be worth a mark or two.

Frieda waited at the open door of her apartment.

'I watched for your car to leave. It didn't. Are you spying on

me?' I already told you; at least she could make me laugh. It
wasn't a loud laugh, or a long one.

'No. I have nowhere to go tonight.'

She stared at me for a moment, and then made an odd noise
which conveyed that she didn't believe me but couldn't find
another immediate explanation.

'Come in; come in . . .' That wasn't as welcoming as it
sounds. In fact she sounded cross. She waved the concierge away,
and locked the great door shut behind us. She had her hair tied
back with a plain cotton band, and had cleaned her face of make-
up. Without it I could see, even in the poor light from one bulb
suspended in the huge space, that her skin was pale, and that she
had a few pale freckles around the sides of her eyes, and on her
brow. Her undyed rough silk dressing gown was like a winding
sheet. She looked curiously vulnerable.

'Sleep here.'

'Thank you.'

'Tomorrow you find somewhere else.'

'Fine. Thank you.'

She moved through the apartment so fast that I had to scurry
to keep up with her. As we passed one door she pointed through
and said, 'My room . . .'

'OK.'

About a fortnight later we reached another. She said, 'Your
room. You sleep here.'

'Thank you.'

Here was a big bedroom decorated not unlike the one I had
awoken in at Greg's place. Second Empire stuff. The double bed
was so far above the floor I'd need a parachute. What surprised
me was the contrast with her own. The glimpse I'd had as we'd
skated past her room showed it to be as small and plain as a nun's
cell: light grey walls, and no paintings that I noticed. A single bed
with coarse brown blankets was lit by a single candle on a night

275

stand. She saw me running the comparison, and smiled. For a moment I thought she might kiss me, but instead she kissed her right index finger and touched it lightly to the centre of my forehead.

'Good night, Mr Bassett.'

'How would I find you again in this place if I wanted you?'

She frowned. I wasn't supposed to find her, or even want to. Then she grinned. 'You can always whistle. You know how to whistle, don't you, Charlie? . . . You just . . .' She was making fun of me . . .

'Yes; I've seen that film too. I know how to whistle.'

She said goodnight as she was walking away: head down. Her winding sheet trailed on the polished boards, making a gentle swishing sound. Her feet made no sound at all.

Ten minutes later I was warm, and on my back in the largest bed I'd ever slept in. I whistled experimentally a couple of times, but the noise was lost in the space around me, and came back as a reedy, quavering echo. I touched my own finger to my forehead – the spot she'd touched – and brought it down to my lips. There was a faint taste which I couldn't identify. Raw alcohol maybe. I went to sleep thinking of Bogie and Bacall: they kept our hearts beating when the world was falling to pieces. I wonder if they ever knew that.

Breakfast was hard black bread and harder black coffee. Whatever Frieda used to snare her men with wasn't her cooking. There was no butter. She dipped pieces of the bread in the coffee, and sucked it dry before eating it. I looked at her. She had put on a light lipstick, but the rest of the warpaint was still in its boxes.

'What are you looking at?'

'You.'

'You think I am pretty?'

'No.'

'You're a liar, Charlie Bassett. All men think me pretty: even those old enough to know better.'

'I think that you're beautiful . . .'

She'd won a point, and smiled. Her nose was slightly snubbed; it turned up at the end. I couldn't tell her age properly, even to the nearest ten years.

'. . . But you do not like me?'

'No.'

'Why not?'

'Because I don't want to.'

'I can understand that. I do not wish to like you either.' It suddenly occurred to me that we were speaking English. I almost hadn't noticed. 'More coffee?'

'Yes please. Would you like me to bring you some the next time I come to Berlin?'

It was her turn:

'Yes please . . . but don't tell anyone.'

'OK. What next?'

She sighed, and pulled her gown close around her.

'Do you know anyone who could check the lists on the other side?'

'I know a couple of people. So *maybe*. Do you want to know that your people are still alive, or where they are, or to make actual contact with them?'

'The last.'

'I can't guarantee that.'

'Can you guarantee anything?'

'No.' That last question actually cheered me up: I was dealing with a realist. 'Thank you for my breakfast.'

'You hated it.'

'Not quite.'

At the door to the room I paused, half-turned and looked back at her. It is really odd to look at someone and not know if they are smiling or not, but that is what happened.

She said, 'Thank you for being honest.'

'I didn't mean to be.'

This time she did smile.

I closed the door behind me, took half a dozen steps but then went back.

'I forgot to ask you something.'

Her face said that she didn't quite believe me.

'What?'

'Why did you hope to find your people listed in Berlin in the first place?'

She did believe me.

'When Germans in the East fled in front of the Russians they were driven towards Berlin. I think that was part of the Russian plan – to flood Berlin with refugees.' I nodded, but didn't butt in. 'Besides, there were uncles and aunts here in Berlin who would have taken them in.'

'You've checked up on the uncles and aunts?'

She shook her head. 'No record: not on the list.'

I found that I'd been holding my breath. I let it loose with a bit of a sigh.

'OK,' I said, 'I really *am* going now.'

She nodded, but she still hadn't moved when I pulled the door closed behind me.

I found Bozey in a tiny cubbyhole of an office at Gatow. Everyone seemed to know him already, so he was easy to find.

'What's this place?' I asked him.

'*Ours* for the time being. I won it in a card game last night.'

We had two rickety wooden chairs either side of a small desk.

The room was probably a store cupboard in the time of the Greater Reich.

'Who did you win it from?'

'A sanitation engineer. It smelt a bit niffy until I washed it and threw most of his old clothes out. I kept a pair of overalls.'

'Well done anyway. Thank you.'

There were a couple of hooks on the back of the door for our jackets. Bozey had already pinned up a couple of large sheets of paper on the wall that even I could interpret – our schedules for the next ten days.

'Think nothing of it. We get a phone in later in the day with our own extension – but that's it. You can kiss goodbye to any promises made earlier. The RAF's grabbed everything it had left for an operation on the lakes: they're going to fly Sunderlands on to them.' Sunderlands were those enormous flying boats I've already told you about – the four-poster beds of the seaplane world. They had bunks and kitchens, and somewhere to powder your nose.

'What are they going to do with them?'

'Salt. The city needs tons of salt for cooking and preserving. Salt reacts adversely with aeroplane aluminium: aircraft start falling to pieces.'

'. . . So?'

'Seaplanes are made from anodized metal to resist corrosion from seawater, so the Sunderlands can bring in all the salt we need. The Russians almost had us there.'

I turned with difficulty to examine his flight schedule. He had prepared it very neatly. 'What happens today?'

'In a couple of hours Hardisty is bringing one of the Lancs in: flour and medicines. I've chalked him in for a day off, so I'll take it back to Wunstorf myself once we turn it round. Tomorrow I'll relieve George Turton . . . Until you've got a regular slot for me, I'll work my way around the circuit giving our boys a day off at a time.'

'You seem to have it all worked out.'

'Thank you, boss. I thought so too . . . only I won't be ferrying any of our kites back to Blighty if you don't mind.'

I'd forgotten his little problem with the Customs. I grinned.

'OK, Bozey. Thank you *again*. You've done a grand job.'

'That's because I'm a grand person. Everyone thinks so, except the police and the Customs.'

'I'm sure they'll come round in the end.'

He smiled happily and said, 'There's a galley just down the corridor. Fancy a cuppa?'

I found that I was whistling as I followed him to the tiny kitchen. That made me think of Frieda. That must have been why I was smiling as I caught sight of myself in a mirror.

An RAF corporal with a technical flash fitted the telephone an hour later in fact, and ran the line down the corridor and out of sight. I was doubtful that it would work, but it rang about five minutes later. Bozey scooped up the receiver and smoothly said, 'Halton Air . . .' before I had a chance. Then he handed it to me.

Russian Greg's voice said, 'You have some things of mine, Charlie. Don' play games with me.'

'You had some things of mine for three days. I was getting ready to write the condolence letters. This is not a game, Greg.'

'Who said it was? Maybe you wouldn't have got yours back without me. Did you consider that?'

'I might have done, but the liquorice persuaded me otherwise.'

Greg didn't say anything for a ten-beat, and then he sighed and asked, 'Why nobody trust me?'

'It's your job: you don't even trust yourself.'

'We gonna fight or dance, Charlie?'

'I'm not that good at dancing.'

'I teach you.'

'When I come back, maybe. Tomorrow.'

I thought that he had gone, but then he said, 'My sister . . . are we still talking about her?' His voice definitely changed every time he spoke of her. My turn to think before my tongue rattled.

'I gave you my word, Greg. I won't go back on it . . .'

'You didn't come through with my liquorice . . .'

'You never gave me enough time.'

Another pause. I could hear him breathing. He said, 'I hate the English, you know that, Charlie?'

'Don't worry about it Greg; so does everyone else.'

After I put the phone down Borland looked at me. His face wore a question, but he didn't ask it. I liked him for that. I told him, 'I'm coming with *you*: I feel safer up in the air.' That was a first. Had Greg known the number allocated to us, or had he just called Gatow and asked for Halton?

Now: a Lancastrian is a Lancaster bomber converted for transport duties. I've already told you that too. Some of them had a passenger cabin, and were used to fly a dozen passengers at a time across the Atlantic or to the Middle East. They might even have used them on the Australia run. Our two had had their guts removed, and were filled with a cargo space over an unnaturally bulging belly – to my eye, that is. At the RAF's insistence we used ours for food and perishable cargoes, and packages that dare not speak their names for the military. *Whisky* and *Pink Pig* had been relegated to mostly hauling sacks of coal. I thought that almost redeemed them.

We were flying each of our fleet with a pilot, engineer, loadmaster and radio officer when we had one. Some of the privateers actually used navs as well, but if our pilots couldn't find their way about Europe on their own by now I didn't want them anyway. Elaine had been responsible for swelling our ranks to accommodate the new numbers we required. Most of them were ex-RAF like me, so therefore as dependable as a perished condom.

Bozey and I trudged out to the *Tin Man* with a tall thin engineer and a small thin loadmaster: Meredith and Drew. They were such an improbable coupling of names that everyone conspired to keep them together: they both had heavy, sinister Victorian moustaches and looked like Wyatt Earp and Doc Holliday. They were what we described then as *men of few words*. In fact they hardly spoke at all. They went up the ladder in front of us, and as they did I told Bozey, 'On the ground I might be the boss, but up there,' I gestured, 'I'm just the radio operator, OK?'

He nodded. 'What's the matter, boss. All the responsibility getting on top of you?' Funny man.

The *Tin Man* was going to Wunstorf to kiss and tell with *Dorothy*. She was coming out from Croydon full of potatoes, tinned whale meat left over from the war and sacks of powdered egg. Most of it would be transferred to *Tin Man*, which would haul it back to Gatow.

We flew empty out of Gatow in the early afternoon, and just like the unladen bomber she was originally intended to be, *Tin Man* flew like a dream. She was like a greyhound pulling at the leash. If Borland hadn't had to stay inside the corridor he could have had a lot of fun. Meredith grumbled about the hydraulic pressures. That was OK: engineers always find something to grumble about. We were about halfway along the corridor when the hairs on the back of my neck stood up. I had been monitoring the Soviet bandwidths. I thought that I could pick out a word or two, but Red Greg had been right: my Russian was shite. I clicked and said, 'Charlie, Skipper.'

Click. 'Yes, Charlie.'

'They're talking about us.'

'Say again.'

'They're talking about us.'

'Do you speak Russian?'

'Almost none, Skip, but I still know they're talking about us. Believe me.'

After a five-second delay Bozey clicked and came back, 'I do, Charlie, I do . . . I'm just trying to work out if I can do anything about it: always hated gossips you see.'

I could see his point. The northern free air corridor was getting crowded in both directions. If Bozey tried any sort of evasive action to mess the Reds about we would fly across the stream and cause chaos: someone would get hurt. I leaned back in my seat, and looked forward.

I could see Meredith's back, and the back of Bozey's head and right shoulder. Meredith must have had one of those built-in radar systems which tell you when someone's looking at you: he turned and looked back. Then he smiled, showed me an O with the first finger and thumb of his right hand, and then a simple thumbs-up. Whatever it was, he thought it was under control. What; *me* worry? It was only a moment, but it unsettled me.

Bozey didn't change our heading or altitude, and not much more than an hour later we popped safely out of the eastern end of the corridor like a rabbit out of a conjuror's hat. The belts of conifers looked up at us starkly black, in a screen of fine late light that cast long shadows of trees into the firebreaks and across the occasional road. Bozey was a bit heavy-handed putting *Tin Man* on the ground at Wunstorf, but I'm an old RAF hand, and subscribe to the *A landing you can walk away from is a good landing* school of flying . . . so I didn't say anything.

Once we'd signed in I asked to see the Senior Officer (Flying), who turned out to be a harassed squadron leader of about twenty-eight. He was probably one of the younger squadron leaders of our new peacetime air force: in my day we'd have thought him already an old man. He looked up from a desk piled high with flimsies of flying orders and asked, 'You wanted to see me, squire? What can I do you for?'

'I want to see the station intelligence officer.'

He tapped his pencil against his front teeth: nerves.

'Don't have one, squire. Not allowed under our treaty obligations and all that. No intelligence-gathering on friendly allies.'

'I still want to see him.'

'Can't help you squire. Sorry.'

Stalemate.

'In that case I can't help *you* either. I'm grounding my aircraft until after I've seen him – that's three or four aircraft you'll have cluttering up your airfield and not hauling freight. So when you next find your station intelligence officer who doesn't exist, tell him I'm in the bar, partying with my crews, OK?' I didn't give him time to reply as I walked away, but I knew that he was staring at my back, and I heard the pencil clicking against his teeth.

I was still on my first bottle of beer when a tall thin man in a tweed suit walked in and paused for a moment scanning the crowd. He had a thin, especially carved moustache, was carrying an old brown trilby, and smoking a straight pipe – like mine. When we made eye contact he nodded and walked unhurriedly over. I gave the lads the eye, and they moved away to another table. The new man sat in one of their vacated chairs. A German Mess boy had followed him over with a whisky and soda. Tweeds said, 'Cheers, old bean. Thanks for the drink.' He sounded upper-class, but a bit seedy.

'Cheers yourself.' I thought he looked Sexton Blake in one of those comics.

'Must say, you don't exactly look like a troublemaker.'

'I didn't know I was one. Charlie Bassett. Temporary manager with Halton Air.'

We made a handshake. Brief and not clutchy. He said, 'I know. I had the S O (Flying) bending my ear. Said we had a troublemaker on our hands. Threatening to clog the field up with unused aeroplanes.'

'Awful. Who'd do such a thing?'

'The sort of person who wanted a little chat with a person like me I suppose. 'nother drink?' His not inconsiderable whisky and soda had gone already. Fast drinker. All he did was look towards the Mess boy, and drinks moved towards us. 'So. What's the problem?'

'I was hoping that you could tell me. When I was first out here I found out that the RAF had been trialling some new equipment on one of our old Dakotas . . .'

'. . . Didn't know that, old bean.' I believed him. He was paying attention and looked interested.

'Didn't last for long. Some of your engineers removed it at the very beginning of the Airlift. Then the Russians pinched my *other* Dakota and its crew, and gave them back three days later. That Dakota came back with its pilot seat missing, and the flight engineer had been tortured. Cigarette burns all over his hands.' I decided to leave out the packages of liquorice until after I had dealt with Red Greg. My new friend frowned, but filled and lit his pipe before he responded, 'Can't be having that. Any idea why?'

'He won't tell me.'

'Interesting . . .'

'Sinister more like . . .'

'Anything else, old bean?'

'Yes. When we came back out along the corridor a couple of hours ago the Soviet fighter controllers were talking about us to their fighters.'

'Speak Russian do you?'

'No, not much. It's just a knack a radio officer picks up. You know when someone's talking about you, even if you can't speak the language. I was a wireless operator: still am.'

'. . . and you were in one of your Dakotas again?'

'No. One of our Lancastrians . . . but you can't miss the Halton aircraft; they've been painted as red as pillar boxes.'

At least he had the taste to wince when I said that.

'Interesting . . . and you suspect that all this adds up together somehow?'

'What's bloody going on?'

'Haven't a clue, old bean . . . but if you withdrew the threat to ground your kites I could try to find out for you.'

I let out a long breath. 'Consider it withdrawn.'

He wanted Max and Ronson's details. I didn't mention Ronson's other name. If the guy was any good he'd find that out for himself. He also wanted details of our aircraft: their airframe numbers, call signs – that sort of thing. He wrote them into a small policeman-style notebook with RAF grey board covers.

' 'nother snifter, old bean?'

I can pick 'em.

There was a bit of a party that night because an RAF bod dropped his York in the middle of the main runway and shut down a lot of the flying. Inbound flights – including *Dorothy* – were diverted. The RAF pilot had been faced with the same problem as Dave Scroton had a few weeks earlier: once his York was on the ground he couldn't stop it. He used the same braking effect as well: just selected *undercarriage up*, and let her slide along on her belly spitting out a trail of sparks, flame and smoke. It made a spectacular firework display in the dusk. The speed with which the crew abandoned her after she'd stopped sliding, and the distance they put between the plane and themselves before they paused for breath, left me wondering what she was carrying.

You might have thought the party was just like old times, but it wasn't. It still didn't feel like war, so the old spirit was lacking. Most of the men just sat around small tables looking shagged out and drinking. I suppose that there must have been about twenty girls to dance with, but they were hardly overworked, and before twenty-three hundred they gave up trying. I got drunk, which was irresponsible – but I *am* irresponsible, so no change there – and I saw a few of the dead guys I used to fly with. That often happens to me at parties. I spent an hour arguing with dead Marty about a bombing trip we'd done to Peenemunde in 1944. Bozey had been dancing with an ugly blonde and when he came back flopped down alongside me and asked me why I'd been talking to an empty chair. I just laughed.

An erk found me and asked me if I could spare a moment: somebody wished to speak to me. The *somebody* was the station IO, who was standing in the corridor outside the Mess hall. He said, 'Sorry to drag you away, old bean. Message for you. Sounded cryptic to me so I thought I'd deliver it in person.'

'Who from?'

'An Irish priest in Berlin. When *are* you going back to the Big City?'

'Tomorrow.'

'He says you're long overdue for confession and should look him up when you get back. Mean anything?'

'Damned if I know.'

'Thought you'd say that. 'night, old bean.'

He didn't believe me, but why should he?

Chapter Nineteen

I hopped a clapped-out old Anson to Lübeck in the morning, nursing a hangover. Despite what you might think, that was a good sign. It was repositioning empty. The pilot looked like Jimmy Edwards. I suppose that he might have *been* Jimmy Edwards, except that Jimmy was supposed to be packing them in at The Windmill. The aircraft was one of two owned by a small mob from Newcastle, and had been chartered by the government to move bods around between the airfields we were using for the Lift. I thought it was easy money for them, until a month later one crashed near Limoges. It killed all seven people on board, and an old man on the ground, sitting in his outdoor privy reading a newspaper. I hoped the pilot wasn't the cheery soul I'd flown with.

He had a regular dispersal spot at Lübeck on the far side of the field. That was one of the characteristics of civvy flying on the Airlift – the RAF had grabbed all the best hard standings near the Administration and Engineering buildings for themselves. Civvies found themselves stuck out over the Styx if they were overnighting, or waiting for a load. When the Anson's curious little propellers stopped turning, and relative silence prevailed, we climbed down on to the concrete and stretched. He said he usually had to wait ten minutes for his transport to reach him. Then he said, 'I know. I'll take you to the museum first.'

I didn't know what he was talking about, but he had gestured towards a small hangar we had parked close to. He dragged one of its sliding doors open, and me the other. There were two ancient aircraft inside: they were both biplanes, had enough wire to make a hen-coop, and big black Maltese crosses.

'Bugger me! How old are these?' I asked.

'Thirty-two, thirty-three years old.'

'First War kites?'

'That's right: where's Biggles?' He had a deep chuckling laugh. The sort that made you smile when you heard it. 'The white one's an Albatross – a fighter plane. The other one is a Roland – reconnaissance job. Want to sit in them?'

'Are we allowed to?'

'No one will stop you. The Jerries say this place is haunted, and refuse to come in here. Now one of our erks claims he saw someone here a week ago, and *our* people have come over all windy as well.'

I climbed up and sat in the fighter. It was grey with dust but I didn't mind. This was the aircraft in my head when I read W E Johns as a nipper. The small wicker basket seat might have been made for me, and my feet settled naturally on the pedals while my hands found the joystick as if they had been born to it. For the first time in my life I wanted to learn to fly for myself. My companion stood up on a stirrup-shaped piece of metal from which you climbed into the cockpit, and explained the very simple controls and instruments to me. Then he asked, '*You* believe in ghosts?'

'No. You?'

'No . . . ever seen any?'

'Yes . . .'

He paused before he replied, 'Yes. So have I.'

I scrambled down when I heard a vehicle approaching, and we were sliding the doors shut when an RAF jeep strolled up.

They dropped me off alongside *Whisky*, which was moored up in the coal yards. I shook hands with the Anson pilot and thanked him. Then I shook hands with Dave Scroton, who was sitting on the step of *Whisky*'s open cargo bay smoking. I was pleased to see him. *Whisky* was full of dirty, lumpy sacks. Coals from Newcastle: it was a joke you couldn't get away from on the Airlift. I couldn't see Crazy Ed.

'Where's Eddie?'

'Over the other side, being sick.'

'Was he on the juice again last night?'

'Not particularly. He had a fight with a Frenchman over a German girl, and his nose is a funny shape.'

'Is he really any good, Dave, or shall I get you another engineer?'

'Don't even think about it, boss!' It suddenly struck me that *boss* was the name most of my mates were using for me these days. I wasn't all that sure I liked it. 'Leave him with me. Ed's brilliant in a crisis: he might leave it to the last minute, but he always does the right thing.'

Just then Eddie ducked under *Whisky*'s nose, and leaned for a moment with his hand near the bint's pink backside. I should have got a photograph. Then he wiped his mouth on his sleeve, and broke the spell. 'Have you two stopped talking about me, or do you want me to go away and come back again?'

'You're a fucking maniac,' I told him, 'but your pilot loves you.'

'Good job someone does, boss. I'm having no luck in any other department.' That was sad, wasn't it? The loadmaster, a tough little Londoner about whom I knew little, came out from behind a coal stack buttoning his fly. Time to go.

We motored it sedately to the very end of Lübeck's long runway, and got into the queue. There was a York and a Skymaster in front of us. Our progress was sedate because we were at the very top of our all-up weight; as we rolled over the small bumps in the peritrack I could feel her bouncing right down to the stops of her undercart oleo legs. Dave didn't shoogle up after the aircraft that took off before us: he held *Whisky* back to give her the longest possible take-off run. To begin with I could have moved faster on a bicycle.

'I have a new take-off technique for when she's this heavy,' he flung back at me over his shoulder.

'What's that?'

'It's called the curvature of the Earth. When the Earth drops away from us we're airborne.'

He wasn't that far wrong. The take-off run seemed to go on for hours. I shut my eyes when I saw the far perimeter fence coming up with no sign of lift. I opened them again when the rumbling stopped, and I felt the big main wheels bump home under the engine nacelles.

'Remember how we stopped *Dorothy* when she lost her brakes?' Scroton shouted at me.

'Yes.'

'That's how I get *Whisky* to fly off with these loads. As soon as I get an ASI of ninety-five knots I select *undercarriage up*: and if she doesn't fall on her tits then she's flying, isn't she?'

'I'll take your word for it, Dave.' Maybe I could understand why Crazy Ed threw up now and again.

I've told you before that when I wake up these days there's often a tune or a song running through my mind. This time it was 'Whisperin''. The Lou Prager version I think. Then I heard the noise of unfriendly air screeching through an abused airframe. I was curled in a ball hard up behind the pilot and second's seats in the cockpit, and had a headache. I'd also hurt my ankle again.

'George Hotel Whisky. Gatow. Come in please . . .' It was a faint and distant sound: a metallic girl's voice coming through the earpieces hanging around Dave's neck and she sounded pissed off. When I looked back down the fuselage I could see Trask, the loadmaster, lying across the sacks staring at me. He didn't blink. I knelt between the seats, and was looking at Scroton when he opened his eyes.

The yoked control wheel moved gently in front of him of its own accord. Scroton reached out for it, but the left-hand side of his body didn't work. In particular, his arm didn't work. He glanced down at it. I could see that there were no outward signs of damage. I could also see that it just wouldn't work. I snapped a look forward, and down. We can't have been flying at more than a couple of hundred feet. Alongside Dave, Crazy Eddie grinned fixedly at the shattered windscreen in front of him. His open eyes would never see anything again. His hands were folded as neatly in his lap as if he was in church. I asked, 'You OK, Skip?' Stupid question. He obviously wasn't.

'OK, Charlie. Problem with my left arm. The others OK?'

'Ed's dead. So's Trasky. Ed must have banged in the autopilot when we were hit. My foot is pointing in an odd direction, but it doesn't hurt too badly yet. I saw that before, on a gunner at Bawne in the war.' My leg didn't feel wet or bashed about. Just a jangling pain.

'Stop it, Charlie. You're babbling.'

'Yes, Skip.'

The girl's voice. 'George Hotel Whisky. George Hotel Whisky. Gatow. Respond *now* please.' She was browned off enough to be using the airfield's proper noun instead of her call sign.

Dave cleared his throat before he spoke into his mic set. 'Gatow Gatow: This *is* George Hotel Whisky.'

'You're half a mile off track *Whisky*, and twenty-five seconds off ETA. Are you going to make your slot?'

My mind felt dull. We both knew that Berlin was landing and

launching so many planes that he had less than a minute either side of his landing slot to get in to. Outside that he was almost on his own. The papers were praising Berlin as the greatest airlift ever attempted. Half an hour earlier Scroton had told me it wasn't the greatest, merely the most bloody dangerous. He wouldn't be all that pleased to find himself so right.

'Hotel Whisky. Are you OK?'

'A bit bashed about, Tower. I'm in my slot . . . wish I was in yours.'

Silence.

'Are you injured, Hotel Whisky?' They must have known something down there.

'Gatow Gatow. George Hotel Whisky. I have injured on board. Five minutes to pancake.'

Her voice was lower, matter-of-fact. 'Five minutes to pancake. Confirm.' If she knew her business the sirens would already be sounding down there. Then I heard her calling out a contact sequence to the aircraft in line behind us.

Scroton said to me, 'Strap yourself in, Charlie.'

'There's nothing left to strap into, Skip.'

'Brace, then.'

I could see that his arm was rigid, but he could still use it to nudge his hand into poking switches on and off. He switched off the autopilot and we immediately wallowed sideways. He caught it. I asked him, 'Shall I get the throttles?'

'Would you, old son? So kind. Careful now. Where's all the black smoke come from?'

'It's not smoke. It's bleeding coal dust. That second MiG's cannon shells went off in the coal sacks.'

'OK. Hold on now.'

Someone had once told me that Scroton used to side-slip Dakotas in just to be flash; now he did it for earnest. There were children and civilians waving thanks to us as he heaved *Whisky* over the airfield perimeter.

Hardisty drove out with the ambulance to meet us, sitting alongside a Regular who wore a white armband with a red cross. Safety first. Hardisty looked white. Magda followed close behind in the hotdog wagon. Ridiculously I hoped that she didn't see Eddie or Trask. We had to climb over the sacks and past Trasky to get out. I could see daylight coming into *Whisky* through jagged holes that weren't part of her original design spec. Scroton got to the concrete before I did. As soon as I put my foot down I started to fall. I'd seen that at Bawne as well. Dave held me up with his good arm.

Hardisty asked, 'What now, boss?'

My brain hurt, but I managed, 'Tell them to get Ed and Trask out of there, and then taxi her round to the coal dump if she'll go.'

'Right, boss.'

'You're in charge until I can think properly again, or Borland gets back.'

'Right, boss.'

'What else?' I asked Scroton.

'MO next I should think, old boy . . . Check the damage.'

'Yeah.'

We made it to the ambulance together; a one-armed man leading a one-legged one. I managed a weak grin for Magda, who hadn't shifted from behind the wheel of the comfort wagon, and we rode in silence to the medical station with a couple of dead men. They didn't seem to mind. Ed wasn't marked, except for a smear of blood on the back of his head, matting his stringy hair. Trask had bits missing. I knew absolutely nothing about him. Was he married? A father? Were his parents still around? I realized that for the first time in my life it would be *me* writing to the bereaved family. I was composing the letter in my head when I passed out.

I awoke in a big chair in the MO's office. No music this time. Scroton was sitting on the MO's desk – his arm was moving around again. When I looked at him he waved it, grinned and said, 'Good as new. Just bruised.'

My ankle and foot hurt. When I looked down I saw that my boot and sock had been removed, and I was all bound up in wet crepe bandage. The foot was pointing the right way again. I didn't even have to ask. 'You too; but bruised and dislocated. We were lucky, they tell me. Now you're no longer dislocated. You swore in your sleep when the Doc rearranged your foot. You'll get around on a stick for a bit.'

Christ, I was tired. 'When?'

'Now. They want us off the airfield before we talk to anyone else about it.'

'Surely someone will want to know what happened?'

'Yep. But not now. They're flying a specialist in apparently, but he won't be here until tonight. Hardisty spoke to Mr Halton who says we have to go out to an apartment he's got here.'

'Then what?'

'I told you already, boss. Tell no one, and wait.'

I thanked the MO, who curled his lip and said he'd send in his bill. I curled my lip back at him but couldn't think of anything to say. Scroton helped me up. My ankle hurt like hell if I put weight on it the wrong way. After a couple of steps I learned the right way – balanced between my good leg and a stout stick which had appeared from somewhere. I hadn't had much luck with my feet recently: I'd also messed them up after a parachute jump in France the year before. A big drab staff car outside looked to be a much better way to get around. Warrant Officer Powers was driving it. As I slumped into the back with Dave he turned and said, 'Bad luck, sir. Are you going to be OK?'

'I will be as soon as you put a gun in my hand,' I snarled, '. . . and a Russian in front to shoot at.'

He laughed. I thought there was sod all to laugh at.

'Don't take it personally now, sir. These things happen, don't they?'

Scroton jumped into the conversation hastily. 'We told Mr Power how you'd stumbled getting down from the kite, and sprained your ankle.'

'Mr Power is not stupid,' I told him. 'He'll want to know why *Whisky* is full of bullet holes and came back with dead people in it.'

'No he won't,' Dave said, surprisingly firmly. 'I think we'll find that no one will.'

Power still hadn't moved us off. He switched his glance from Scroton to me, and said, 'Don't you worry, sir, I'll have her patched up as good as new in a couple of days.' Then he winked and added, 'Your company should be more careful of its Dakotas: that's what I think.' Then he turned away, and set us rolling. My toes were cold. Why is it that no one ever tells you to be more careful with your people?

The security detail at the end of the road was three men in long dark leather coats, fedoras and a black Mercedes; like mine but bigger. It had been polished to a mirror finish.

'Christ,' I muttered, '. . . the Gestapo are back!' That raised a couple of smiles.

Power said, 'Nah. It's the Froggies; being mysterious again.'

So it seemed that all of the friendly powers were providing security details for this wide street.

'How come we're all so keen on this street?' I asked him.

'This is where the embassies are going to be if we stay. They're the biggest houses this side of Berlin not too knocked about to live in. The guards are there to keep the riff-raff at bay.' The riff-raff who Ed and Trask had just given their lives for.

The Troll was on the bottom step waiting for me. She treated me like a lost chick coming home; pushed Dave out of the way, and lugged me up the steps like one of the coal sacks we'd just brought in. Outside Frieda's place she slapped her chest and barked, 'Hanna,' at me a few times as if I was an idiot.

At least it was a less wary greeting than the last time I'd stood there. She kissed me on both cheeks, and would have carried on if Frieda hadn't opened the castle door and dragged me inside. Scroton followed. I overbalanced on Frieda of course, and dropped the boot I was carrying in my free hand . . . but Dave was there to catch us, and steady me up.

'This is David Scroton, my pilot,' I explained to Frieda. She'd shut the door on Half-ton Hanna, who'd started to look weepy: maybe she loved me after all.

'Is he a good pilot?'

'He just saved my life.'

'Then he must also be a stupid one.' But she was smiling at us. 'I was brought a message from Geoffrey. He says that I must look after you, and keep you safe.'

'Too late for that. One of his aircraft nearly killed me.'

'One of Geoffrey's aircraft, or the Russian who was shooting at it?'

So the word was out anyway. Berlin was like a girls' school: nobody had any real secrets there. I went back a couple of years ago – that hasn't changed.

'Would you mind if I sat down?' I asked her. 'My foot's squeaking.' Actually what was happening was that the conversation around me was washing in and out like a bad signal. They helped me to a massive wooden chair that looked as if Charlemagne might have owned it once. That thought went through my mind again: *Christ: I'm tired!* I heard Scroton saying, 'The Doc gave him enough morphine to scuttle a horse, but he's still talking. He's a stubborn little cuss.'

'Stubborn?' That was Frieda. 'Is that good?'

'In his case, *yes*. You need stubborn cusses like him around to make things work.'

What's the silly phrase they use to describe that sort of thing these days? *Positive feedback?* Dave must have thought I wouldn't hear it; he didn't usually fling the compliments around. 'I think we ought to put him to bed, don't you?'

Night. It was the second time I had awoken in that big bed. I was wearing pyjamas which didn't belong to me. Silk. I could get used to that. The room was lit by a dim and flickering table lamp. Either the bulb or the electricity supply was about to go. A familiar figure sat by the bed: the Station Intelligence Officer Who Never Was, from Wunstorf. I recognized his tweed suit and narrow moustache. I recognized his hooded eyes and his black widow's peak. I also recognized his voice.

'Hello, old bean. Back in the land of the living?'

I struggled to sit up. 'Don't know. Ask me again in an hour.' My tongue felt big in my mouth. 'Rotten headache – I feel as if I've been on the binge.'

'Morphine. Don't worry about it.'

I'd got the events arranged in my head in the right order by then. 'You're the specialist they told me about, aren't you?'

'Spot-on, old bean. Sorry I was late. Your little excursion messed the flight schedules up a tad. Took me longer than we thought.'

'Do you call everyone *old bean?*'

'Ye-es. Upsets some bods fwight-fully.'

'Is that why you do it?'

'Yes, old bean.'

I laughed. Sometimes I think that I laugh when I don't know what else to do. I noticed that he had his little notebook open on his knee, and an expensive pen in his hand. From outside I heard a distant air-raid siren. It wasn't the same as the sirens I remembered from England − its cadence was more insistent somehow. The light flickered once and went out. I said, 'Either the bulb's blown, or we're at war again.'

After a moment he said, 'Neither, old bean. It's the ten o'clock Lights-Out. Starting tonight, they're chopping off the electricity supply at ten to save the fuel − and it will get worse before it gets better. There's a rumour that you'll all be down to six hours a day by December.'

'What was the siren for?'

'Warn people to get their candles out. I wonder how long before we start to run out of those?'

I'd thought that his voice had a sort of plummy, seedy quality: now I realize that there was a bleakness in there somewhere as well. The moon was only a few days off full, and that threw us some light.

'Can you see to write in this?'

'Just. Don't worry about it. Feel like talking?'

'OK. You've already spoken to my aircraft skipper?'

'Yes, old bean, but can't do any harm to get it from another angle. What do you think happened?'

'I think the bloody Reds tried to shoot us down.'

'Absolutely *fwightful* of them . . .' It was almost as if he was taking the mickey.

'We were on the coal train, twenty minutes from Berlin, and cleared to descend. Then I heard Ed shouting. When I looked over his shoulder I saw a little grey MiG barrelling straight at us at ninety degrees. It was flying right across the corridor: a proper kamikaze effort. Dave turned hard away from him, and dropped . . .'

'A jet?'

'No; a piston-engined job – it looked a bit like a Mustang with red stars.'

I could hear his pen scratching.

'Which took you to the edge of the corridor or beyond . . . ?'

'Guess so. Then someone was shooting at us. They must have had another one upstairs; waiting to pounce as soon as we strayed over the edge.'

'The first one was the beater, old bean, wasn't he? He drove you under the other's guns.'

'That's what it looks like to me. What were the mad buggers thinking about; did they want to start World War Three?'

'To use our ally's colourful terminology, either the Reds are playing hardball – or they have a particular grudge against you.'

'Maybe a bit of both?'

'I thought about it on the flight here. There *is* another way to look at it . . .'

'Tell it to me . . .'

'If you were a gung-ho Russian pilot – and these flying types are the same the whole world over, old bean, aren't they? – who had been briefed he could force down any aircraft that strayed out of the air corridor, and had hatched a plan with a pal to make it happen . . .'

'Yes?'

'. . . well, old bean. Say you've decided to hassle a lumbering old Mary out of the corridor. You fly a parallel to the strip for a few miles, don't you, and what do you see? You see drab green aircraft – one after the other, dull silver ones, grey uninteresting ones . . . and then in the middle of all this comes something painted as red as a letter box. Tell me, which one would you go for?'

'What are you trying to say?'

'Red rag to a bull, old bean.'

He was saying that we were being picked on because we were red. Either he was a genius or a fucking idiot. He went over my story another twice before he was satisfied. Eventually I asked him, 'You like your job? Station Intelligence Officer.'

'Not a bad screw, old bean. But not what I want to do . . .'

'What's that?'

'Stand-up comedian on the Halls. I'd like to make them laugh.'

'You'd be good at that, old bean,' I told him. 'What's your name?'

'John Thomas. See what I mean?'

I woke again in the middle of the night. The woman Hanna had been drafted in to sit with me, and she was snoring like an over-revved Tiger tank. That was probably what woke me up.

She opened her eyes as soon as I moved. 'OK?'

'Very thirsty.'

'That's the morphine they gave you. I know: I was a nurse.' She poured me a glass of water and handed it to me. I remembered all the rumours, and hoped it had been boiled. 'In the last days the soldiers called morphine *angel juice*.' She used a single word which sounded like *Engelsaft*. 'I sometimes think the war would not have lasted as long without it.' That was a novel and very professional observation.

I don't know what else she said, because I fell asleep again as she was talking.

She wasn't there in the morning, so maybe I dreamed her. The walking stick was within reach so I swung my legs experimentally out of the bed, and took my weight on them. It was a piece of piss as long as I remembered to distribute my weight between my good foot and the cane. The problem was that until I had the weight balance worked out I zigzagged across the floor like a paranoid crab. I went looking for a bathroom and found one, after opening four other doors. It was probably as big as my bungalow at home.

A large lion-footed cast-iron bath stood in the centre of the room on a raised, tiled platform. Polished copper pipes dropped down from the ceiling to its taps. I couldn't resist trying them: the water was scalding hot. Marthe would have loved this. After that I couldn't resist trying the bath itself. I was half submerged in its luxury, bandaged foot and all, when I heard the door open and close. Frieda came through the wreaths of steam that were hanging in the air. She was wearing a long sensible dressing gown belted tightly about her waist. Maybe she even smiled at me.

'You are feeling improved?'

'I'm feeling improved.'

'You can reach everywhere; to wash?'

'I can reach everywhere to wash. But you can help if you wish.'

'Of course not.' She shook her head, smiled again and turned away. Either I was hallucinating or she had a softer side as well. I didn't see her again until breakfast. I wasn't sure of the way, but I whistled . . . and eventually got one back.

It was just a pity that it came from Dave Scroton. He'd tarted himself up before breakfast as well. I felt a sudden tug of jealousy wondering where he had spent the night. Not my business, but sometimes you can't help it, can you? It was almost worth it to see his face when Frieda — fully and discreetly dressed now: a black flared dress with a wide white collar — came in with the coffee, and a tray of black bread for dippers. Almost.

After I pushed the plate back, and Frieda had poured me the

dregs of the coffee, I told him, 'If you're really OK, go back to the field and supervise the work on *Whisky*. Get her back in the air as soon as you can. Offer the erks some dash if you have to.'

'*Dash*?'

'Money: an inducement. My dad uses the word all the time.' I suddenly realized that I hadn't spoken to my father for months; he probably didn't even know I was back in Germany. 'Help Hardisty if he needs it. Hardisty can take out the next crate that Borland flies in, and then Bozey's in charge until I'm hopping around a bit. Got it?'

'Got it.'

'You're *sure* you're OK?'

'When we were in the RAF we used to get crash leave.'

'We didn't crash this time, and anyway . . . my air force is too small for crash leave.'

'Right, boss.'

'*Right, boss*,' Frieda echoed. They were both taking the piss. *She* laughed.

Dave asked, 'Anything else?' He lit a Turkish cigarette that Frieda had given him. I waved away the smoke.

'If you can speak to Elaine it would be helpful. We'll have to make arrangements for Trask and Crazy Eddie. Be careful how you bring the subject up: she may not know yet. Tell her I'll write the letters to their people, and dictate them to her over the phone if that's OK . . . she can forge my signature; she's good at that.' I had one of those bad moments: I suddenly realized what I'd said, and felt sick. I knew that I wasn't a callous officerish bastard, but I'd bloody well sounded like one, hadn't I?

'Are you OK? You've gone quite white.'

It took a moment to reply. 'Yes, Dave, I'm OK. I just heard myself speaking and didn't like what I heard.'

He blew a stream of smoke at the ceiling. 'I woke up in the middle of the night and found I was crying: just like a girl. I've known Crazy Ed on and off for years, and flown with him for nearly two. I know absolutely nothing about him. We put all the personal stuff off: plenty of time to check that later. Now he's gone, and I felt ashamed. I also feel very silly.' He was a perceptive man.

'We can give him a decent send-off somewhere: it's the least we can do.'

'Yes, boss. Thank you.' He wasn't sending me up this time.

I filled a pipe, and lit it. The smoke was always bluer than that from cigarettes. It spiralled above me to the ceiling. Frieda lit and smoked another cigarette. An American one this time. Neither of us spoke. We listened to Dave clattering around as he sorted himself out, until eventually the apartment door boomed shut behind him. We listened to the silence. It was the first time that I've liked it.

Frieda never wasted time or words. Without any preliminaries she observed, 'There is every good chance that my relatives are dead, you know, Charlie. I promised my mother that I will find them, but I may not be able to – especially if they are dead.' The word *tot* seemed oddly melodic when she spoke it. This time she had dropped naturally into German as soon as we were alone. I could just about keep up with her.

'Yes. I understand. I will . . .'

She waved me quiet.

'. . . No, you don't understand. I wanted to explain to you that I, *too*, feel guilty . . . just like you feel at this moment. Guilty at being unable to change things back for my mother, and guilty for being alive if they are now dead. We can do nothing with those guilts, Charlie, except' – she reached across the table and grasped my wrist to emphasize her earnestness, and spoke fiercely: like a schoolmistress – '*throw them away*!' . . . and when she let go, she almost threw my hand away from her. It was as if the emotion in the words was too powerful to contain.

When she started to speak again it was as if someone had switched over one of those poncy new European taps that move from hot to cold water in one motion: she was all business once more. 'That door . . .' She pointed to a pale green door about half a mile away. '. . . is to Geoffrey's study. A desk you can work at, and a telephone to use. The telephone is connected between eleven and twelve hours in the morning, and eighteen and a half and nineteen hours in the evening. Having a private telephone is a privilege.'

'Yes, it is, but I thought I'd get out of your hair, and go out. To the airfield, then find somewhere to stay maybe . . .'

'There is something wrong with my hair?'

'Sorry. I meant *get out of your way.*'

'You're not in my way. I am alone in this fortress . . . and anyway, Geoffrey told me to keep you here until you are recovered. Also, while you are here, we can talk about how to find my relatives . . . two birds and one stone. You say that?'

'Yes. We say that.'

Then she switched to English. 'Still you do not like me?'

I'd probably been smiling for half an hour, so she knew that her answer was in there.

'I do not seem to have much choice. I like you.'

Back to German again. '*Gut.*' There was a bit too much self-satisfaction in the word for my liking.

Chapter Twenty

I flipped through the pictures of her magazines, but they were in German except for *Picture Post*. The German mags were being produced on better paper again: printed somewhere out in the hinterland, and brought in clandestinely by the Lift crews. You could get a bundle for one down on the Kaiserplatz. It was amazing really: in a city where everyone was tightening their belts, expecting the worst but praying for the best, women still wanted to read fashion magazines. I said that to Frieda when she sought me out in the middle of the morning, with a brew of thin coffee in an expensive cup. I suspected that it was the breakfast grounds getting their second wind.

'It is our *religion*,' she explained. 'It shows us that there is a better world out there waiting for us to join in, and that gives us hope. Pictures of women in Paris in expensive clothes, sitting in private motor cars. We look at them and hope. Hope is just like a religion. If we have no hope there will be no Berlin. No Berlin: no Germany.'

'Do you really believe that?'

'Of course.'

'Do you want me to stand up and hug you?'

'Will that increase the bread ration?'

'No. Not at all.'

'Then don't.'

This was all delivered with a voice as flat as a flounder's, but she paused at the door, just like before, looked back and smiled as she left.

I allowed myself two telephone calls. The first was to Elaine. She knew the score because Dave had already told her, and didn't sniffle. These women can really be amazing when something needs to be done.

'We've got Ted Trask coming back on *Dorothy*. Mr Scroton will get him to Lübeck to link up.' I hadn't even known that Trask's first name was the same as Crazy Ed's. 'Mr Halton has gone up to see his family.'

'Where?'

'The Isle of Sheppey. We'll still need to do a letter. The Old Man will as well I expect.'

'What kind of family did he have?'

'Mother, father and two sisters. He was engaged to a girl who was killed in the Blitz, and never really got over that.'

'No woman in his life then?'

'Not as far as I know.' The unspoken words *That's a blessing* lay between us. It wasn't actually, not for a poor lonely bastard murdered on the way to Berlin.

I shook myself. 'What about Crazy Eddie?'

'No relations as far as I know, but a girl at every airport. Mr Halton will probably want a funeral at one of the military cemeteries.'

'Fine.' It sounded inadequate and bleak even as I said it. I wondered if his aunty had actually been related, and wondered who would come. 'Anything else I need to attend to?'

'No, love . . .' She must have been alone in the office if it wasn't a Freudian slip. 'We're doing rather well together at the minute, you and I. Mr Halton's very pleased with us.'

'How do you know?'

'Told me himself. He was looking at the profitable hours we've put on *Dorothy* since her operation, and said *Charlie's quite a find!* There you are: horse's mouth.'

'I miss sleeping with you,' I told her.

'I miss you too,' she said . . . but it wasn't the same thing, was it?

Maggs answered the telephone at the Happy Returns; I'd had to wait an age to get through.

'The Major's gone down to Somerset to find some plums he wants for one of his old recipes: he'll be back tomorrow. The kids're still at school. They'll be sorry they missed you.'

'I'll phone the boys tonight; between half six and seven, my time, if that's all right. Don't tell them in case I miss it. If that happens I'll try tomorrow. How are you?'

'My feet hurt: I'm waiting tables in the restaurant because we're short. Jules ran off wiv that soppy girl from Chichester who used to waitress fer us — I don't think you met her. Your friend Les came down with his wife and his boys last weekend. We sat around a fire on the shingle bank, and sang like silly buggers.'

'Enjoy it?'

'Bloody wonderful.'

'I thought Jules had sailed off with Evelyn Valentine?'

'He did, but they stuck the yacht on the Goodwins, an' needed to be rescued. She went back to the Captain, who gave 'er a thick ear an' then bought her another boat — the silly sod.' *No, he wasn't a silly sod*, I thought: I might have done the same myself.

'If it helps, I have a sore foot as well. I sprained my ankle again: climbing out of an aircraft this time,' I lied. 'Don't tell the boys.'

' 'ow bad?'

'Not bad. I was very lucky. What do you want me to bring you when I come back?'

She didn't answer immediately. I imagined her face – she always poked out just the tip of her tongue when she was thinking hard.

'Bring yersel', Charlie Bassett . . . that'll do.' Her voice had dropped an octave. Damn her!

'Sooner than you think, Maggs. I promise.'

There wasn't much more to say after that. I put the receiver down. It was a small room of opulent dark blues, dominated by a towering door. When I looked up there was Frieda, standing beside it.

'Which boys?' she asked in English. 'I heard you say *the boys* twice.'

'*My* boys: two boys who adopted me in the war . . . one's a German as it happens. They live in England with a good friend when I'm away. Listening in to my telephone call wasn't proper, you know. I shall have to do something improper to you in exchange . . . fair swap.'

'I was not listening to you. I was waiting to use the telephone when you had finished.'

'That's a pity; I thought for a moment you were beginning to take an interest in me. Would you like me to leave you alone to make your telephone call?'

'Yes please, Charlie . . .'

The odd thing was I felt as if I'd won that trick, even although, as usual, I had no idea what game was being played.

At the door I tried her game. I turned my head and grinned back at her. She was already seated at the desk leafing through a leather-bound address book, and didn't look up. As I walked away from the other side of the door I heard her voice murmuring; persuading, possibly . . .

Tommo turned up. You could have knocked me over with a feather when Hanna brought him through.

'How did you know where I was?'

'Magda's pilot . . . the English one. He told us. Aren't you going to say it's good to see me?'

'It's good to see you, Tommo. How long are you in town for?'

'The Russian bastard asked me to do a number on you. He wants to set things right between you two. He's got some sort of trouble and thinks you can get him out of it.'

'I know about it, and I already agreed, but after what's happened in the last thirty-six hours I keep asking myself, *Why should I?*'

'. . . for the same reason you just let other people off the hook before?'

'*Off the hook?*' That was Frieda. She'd walked in without shoes, and neither of us had heard her.

'This is Frieda,' I told Tommo, and, 'This is David Thomsett,' I told Frieda. 'He's an old friend. I helped with a bit of trouble he was in last year . . . that's what *off the hook* means.'

'Like in fishing?'

'Exactly like in fishing.'

She walked over to one of the large windows and looked out over the new vegetable patch. If we had a bad winter coming they were planting out just a little too late. She said, 'I used to go fishing with my brother and my father before the war. Every autumn. It seems like a dream now . . .'

'Tommo's going to take me to somebody who might be able to help,' I told her. 'Don't give up hope yet.'

I couldn't believe it. Tommo had driven up to the front of the house in Russian Greg's big GAZ jeep. He was driving around in his US uniform, in a Russian army vehicle, for which he had no papers. I was still chuckling to myself as we pulled away. Hanna insisted on helping me down the steps, and along through the front garden to the gate. She said, 'You come back now . . .'

'I will – in a few hours.'

'Your German is getting much better.'

I thought that it hadn't been too bad in the first place. It's the colloquialisms I pick up on. The local phrases that people use have never failed to delight me. At the end of the road I recognized the patrol for what it really was – a checkpoint. This time it was a group of laid-back Canadians. One of them asked Tommo, 'Got your papers, buddy?'

'Sure: here.' He handed over the small book with a ten-dollar bill conspicuous between its leaves. It had miraculously disappeared when he handed it back.

Then the cop asked me, 'You too? You some kind of ambassador?'

'No,' I grinned. 'I'm with one of the commercial outfits flying the Lift.' I gave him my papers, which included my discharge book. The last officer to sign it had added that I was *brave and showed initiative*, but then, he'd never flown or served with me so he didn't bloody know the half of it.

Tommo offered them some gum, which they pocketed, and they waved us on. He asked me, 'That's some place you're staying at. How come you always come up smelling of roses?'

'Because I'm a clean-living, God-fearing son of the Empire.'

'An' I'm Adlai Stevenson . . .'

We were bowling along Veltenstrasse. It had once been a wide tree-lined avenue. Bombing had reduced the trees to stumps, and had smashed a lot of the houses. Those still standing were coping with a family in every room. It reminded me of a street in London I'd seen the year before. Dirty kids turned to stare at us as we rolled past. Some of the tree stumps were missing; I wondered if that was a sign of replanting, and things getting back to normal. I mentioned it to Tommo, who laughed mirthlessly.

'Don't be dumb, Charlie. They're digging them out for the wood; even the roots. What else do you think they'll burn this winter if this shit keeps going?'

He put his arm through mine as we walked into the Leihhaus. It wasn't to help me, because I didn't need him. It was to make sure I didn't scarper. My stick got in the way. Tommo trod on the toes of my good foot, and I cursed him. The place was busier than usual for the time of day, mainly REME soldiers already having a party — sooner or later the MPs were going to get seriously pissed off about the Leihhaus. Russian Greg sat alone at one of the small round tables. Everyone in the place was drinking tall glass mugs of beer: draught beer. That was new. I pulled up a chair. So did Tommo. He asked me, 'How bad did you smash up your leg?'

'Not bad, Tommo. Just the ankle. If I keep it bound tight I'll be able to throw the stick away in a few days. Thanks for asking.'

He waved his cigar and the smoke made S shapes in the air.

'Don't get sentimental about it: I was just establishing how useful you still were.'

'You didn't rush over here to see me on account of my getting hurt then?'

'Greg asked me. He wants me to broker an armistice between you two. It's interfering with our business.'

'What is?'

'Greg's worrying about his sister, and not concentrating on the work in hand.'

'Which is?'

'Making top dollar.'

Marthe came over and put a foaming litre glass jug of beer in front of me. I said *Thanks*, and smiled. She smiled back. My sister used to smile at me like that. What did that comedian use to say again? *Jus' like that!* I knew immediately that she had decided whatever the future held for her, I didn't have a central role in it.

Russian Greg still hadn't spoken. In fact he hadn't even looked at me. I turned my attention to him, and used the word he'd taught me — even if I couldn't spell it.

'Prreevet, Greg.' It was supposed to sound like *hello* in Russki.

He smiled. It was almost like relief. 'Hello, English.'

'You fired at my aircraft. You killed two of my men . . . you even knew one of them: he drank here sometimes.'

'Not me. Some Russian did that.'

'Aren't you Russian?'

'No: I'm Georgian.'

'Isn't that the same?'

'No. Is Australia also England?'

'No, you know it's not.'

'Is the same. Georgia is a different country, though Russians don't think so.'

'Isn't Stalin a Georgian?' Tommo asked.

'Is not the same.' Greg looked around slowly before adding, 'He's a *mad* Georgian. Very dangerous for the rest of us.' It was almost the same old Greg. He gazed around, and stared down everyone who met his eye. The only one to hold out was a big Yorkshire corporal. The air crackled between them until Greg suddenly let out his bellow of a laugh, and shouted at Marthe behind the bar, 'Give him a drink.'

She did, and the Yorkshireman raised his jug slowly to Greg before he sipped it.

'OK,' I told Greg. 'Go back to the beginning. Why did you force down my other Dakota, and kidnap the crew for days?'

'Didn't. Was some other Russians.'

'You forget the liquorice in the tyres: that was yours.'

'I can explain.'

'Will I believe you?'

'Maybe. Maybe not.'

I suppose that was a step in the right direction. I waved to

Marthe, and she brought over three more beers. The beer was really rather good. I filled a pipe and lit it. The cool, sweet smoke always calmed me. I said to Greg, 'Try me . . .'

'There is a Russian intelligence officer named Spartacus . . .'

'You're right,' I said. 'I don't believe you . . .'

'I do.' That was Tommo. 'Ever since the revolution their intelligence officers have used fancy secret names; it's almost impossible to find out their real ones. All the Commies in Spain had funny names . . .'

'Were you in Spain?'

Tommo rolled his cigar from one side of his mouth to the other. 'Mebbe . . .'

I tried Greg again, 'OK. Sorry I spoke. *Spartacus* . . . ?'

''s very important. Very influential. After the war he shipped German technology back to Russia. That's his speciality.'

'OK . . .'

'He thinks you got a death ray.'

Pin-drop time. Tommo must have heard it all before because he didn't say anything. I waited for the overture before I replied. 'Did he read too many science-fiction comics when he was a boy? *Marvelman* . . . that sort of thing? He thinks the RAF has a *death* ray?'

'No, Charlie: not the RAF. *You*. Some reports from panicky pilots about nearly being brought down by red-painted transport planes some weeks ago. Maybe some nosy GI seen something in one of your planes, an' talked about it where he shouldn't. Maybe some strange radio noise been heard. I don't know . . .' I got the sense that he was treading a fine line, and telling me all that he could without ending up dangling from a piano wire.

'It's insane: fiction. Where would *I* get one if it existed?'

Greg shrugged. Moody. 'Spartacus *is* insane. Everyone knows that.'

'When did he tell you this?'

314

'He didn't tell me, Charlie. I'm too scared to meet him. I called in a favour from some other guy, an' he's prob'ly shitting himself right now for telling me.'

'So they forced down the *Pig*, ripped it apart, and tortured my engineer?'

'Sorry, Charlie, what pig? You lose me.'

'It's what we call the aircraft: the *Pink Pig*.'

'OK. But the engineer was something different.'

It was Tommo who came in again. First he waved his cigar to calm me down. Perhaps he thought he could hypnotize me with the smoke shapes in the air. They reminded me of Alice when she was really teed off at someone.

'Maybe engineer would know about death rays. Pilots wouldn't. Pilots got shit for brains.' That was probably the first time I heard those words in that order. I thought he was being a bit hard on the profession.

'Fuck the lot of you!' I told him.

'That's a very reasonable attitude to take, Charlie: I should stick with it if I was you.' He said that in such a reasonable tone that you wanted to believe him. I took a couple of deep draughts of beer. I had let my pipe go out, so I relit it. That made me think of Grace, who had given it to me in '44. It was like having a hidden supporter in the room.

'That doesn't explain away the liquorice, does it?'

'*I* got it for him,' Tommo told me. 'The problem of moving things about these days is that the Commies – sorry, Greg – have shut up their side of Berlin tighter than a duck's wad. You can't get anything into Soviet Berlin from their side without going through a ring of steel. They don't want their soldiers fratting with the Berliners any more: they don't want them having goods to exchange . . . it's something to do with stabilizing the economy now they ain't printing American money and spending it against us.'

'That's interesting, Tommo, but what's it got to do with us?'

'. . . on the other hand, getting something through the border *across* Berlin is still a piece of piss . . . it's because they smashed it up so bad – the geography is still impossible to police.'

'You mean that if you want to get something unofficially from the Soviet Zone into Soviet Berlin, it's easier to smuggle it into the Allied Zone outside Berlin first, then into our part of Berlin, and then back across the line into Red Berlin?'

'Good boy! I knew you'd get it! Tol' you he was OK, Greg.'

The Russian glowered at me, and then grinned to soften it. I could hear the boots on his short legs banging against the chair legs as he swung them. That was generally a good sign. He said, 'I'm still not sure. When I heard your plane was down, Charlie, I drove there to see what I can do. I thought that it would demonstrate my good intentions for you. It took me two days. Spartacus's people were glad I come, because they'd realized that they'd made a mistake, and by then they were talking of shooting your crew and burning the crate to hide it. On the other hand they didn't want such an openly hostile act.'

'By then I'd delivered him a load of liquorice deep in his zone, not knowing he couldn't get it to his General in Red Berlin where he wanted it.' Tommo again. The picture was coming together at last.

'Why didn't you wait for *me* to get you some, Greg?'

'I did not think you could deliver, Charlie. Sorry.' He rubbed his black stubble. It made a rasping sound. 'So I convinced them it would save considerable face if we gave your aircraft back, after cautioning your crew for flying out of the corridors . . . and sending a strongly worded complaint to the Control Commission. It was to be one of those *happily ever after* stories.'

'. . . And at the same time you stuck your liquorice in a set of tyres?'

'Yes, I confess I did. The opportunity to get it to Gatow was too good . . .'

Someone had said something like that to me recently. *Two birds with one stone*. I sipped the beer, and thought it through . . . it was just stupid enough to be true.

'. . . So I'm supposed to believe that you got me my aircraft, less the pilot's seat that is . . . and my crew back?' I asked Greg.

'Yes. I never understand why they took the seat.'

'Maybe that's where they thought the death ray was.'

I shouldn't have bloody said that, should I? You can go to jail for mistakes like that. There was a brief hiatus in the conversation. Both men glanced at me. Then Tommo said, 'But there never was a death ray, was there?'

'No, just a compact radar repeater from Philips we were trying on the navigation beacons. It doesn't even bloody work, so my boss sent it back to wherever he got it from.' I said it much too hastily. I'm not sure that worked either. Then I took a deep breath and said, 'OK, so *thank you*, Greg. Thank you for returning my people.'

'What about your *Pig*?'

'That too.'

'Can I have my liquorice back now? My General's need has become rather pressing; he is making unveiled threats.'

'I'm afraid not. I was so angry that I told the crew chief to give it to any kids he could find. There are kids all over Berlin today with black teeth and big grins. I'm sorry.' Poor Greg winced. So should I have done. That was his next promotion out of the window, I guessed. Maybe worse. 'Look. Before this all started I asked them to send me over a bundle of it from England. Sweets are making a comeback, so it could still get here.'

He just looked away from me with an expression of profound injury on his face. He blew a plume of cigar smoke into the air. it mingled with Tommo's as if the blue-grey streams were dancing. He said, 'Doesn't matter.' But it did.

'That's half the story,' I told him. 'What about the rest? I was in the next aircraft you attacked. I helped them get bodies out. I rode with them in the ambulance. What about that?'

Greg shook his head. 'Bloody Spartacus. If the ray is not in the first red Dakota it must be in the other. So the order goes out to the Soviet Air Force to bring it down . . .'

'Nearly bloody succeeded. There's no death ray in there, Greg . . .'

'We know that now.'

'How?'

'If you had one, you would have turned it on your attackers, wouldn't you?'

Tommo grinned at me and said, 'So you're off the hook too, Charlie.' The others didn't know what he was talking about, and that clearly amused him. He asked, 'We all buddies again?' I nodded and he added, 'Fancy a plate of Franks ev'ryone?'

That sounded all right to me. I finished my beer and held up the glass for more, saying, 'You know? If we get this wrong, in fifty years' time some historian grubbing through an old diary might come to the mistaken conclusion that we started the Third World War over a couple of pounds of liquorice and a plate of sausages!'

We all laughed, but no one contradicted me.

Marthe served the bar, and fetched from the kitchen when they were busy. There was something light and invulnerable about her. Maybe Mr Right had come along and cut me out. Her hair had been done, and she was wearing a yellow and red flowered blouse, and a dark pleated skirt. It swung as she walked. Later I asked Russian Greg, 'What happened to put her off me? We were almost talking about a cottage with roses around the door.' He laughed in a way that said he thought that plainly ridiculous.

'Not a cottage and roses woman, English. She's a Berliner . . . a Berliner.'

'I suppose you're right, but what did I do wrong?'

'Nothing. How much you know about Marthe, Charlie?'

What do I know about any woman? I wondered, but said, 'Only a bit. There's the child, Lottie . . . and she has relatives in the Eastern Zone . . . you fixed her up with a Freepass. She had a bad time when you invaded.'

'All the women did, Charlie: had more sex in ten days than they'd had in ten years . . . only nobody asked first. Who was Lottie's father?'

'I don't know. Some soldier I think . . .'

'So do I. She thought he was dead, and so did we, but he walked in from Russia two weeks ago. *Walked*, Charlie. He was in a camp here, only for less than a week while they denazified him.'

'Christ! What's he like?'

'See for yourself.' He nodded to a gaunt man swabbing the floor of the bar. He wore a full brown apron. He had lost most of his hair, and his white shirt and dark trousers hung on him. He couldn't stop smiling at everyone who caught his eye. He looked like the happiest man in the world. 'I gave him a job . . . so you won't make it difficult for them, will you, Charlie?'

'No, of course not. Do you *own* this place?'

'Me and Tommo are part owners: this is the US–Soviet economic cooperation zone. You really going to get me some of that liquorice?'

'I'm going to try.'

'. . . What about my sister's family?'

It was always going to come back to that. In different ways he and Frieda were looking for the same thing. I said it before, but you didn't notice: in 1948 we were all looking for a family.

'That too. I promised, didn't I?' I thought about it and offered, 'I promise to do my best.' Then I began to put it together. 'There was something else I wanted to talk to you about. I have a friend who needs to consult the lists of the Missing, Found and Dead. *Your* lists, that is, not ours . . .'

The Russian swung round, and gave me his full attention. His eyes flashed. Making deals put him on his home ground again.

The last thing I asked him was how long it would take for him to muster his sister's family where we could get at them.

'Ten days from when you tell me it's on, but it's got to be soon.'

'Why?'

'My sister's having a bad time.' I'd seen that look on his face before. He bunched his right fist several times as he replied. I guessed that someone else would have a bad time in return if he got his hands on him.

Marthe's husband was named Otto. He never stopped mopping the floor, which is why he was soon known as Moppo: our humour was pretty cruel back then. He never stopped smiling at anyone he could engage. I think he'd left something from inside his head back in Russia. I gave him a large tip as I left. I glanced at Marthe behind the bar: she lifted her chin with a proud smile. I guess she had a reason to.

Tommo drove me back again. I told him he'd make a great cab-driver and he took it as a compliment. We were both a bit sauced. I asked him to let me off at the patrol so I could try reaching the house on my own. The Canadians were still there, and their sergeant walked over to say, 'Hi, Tommo. Still gotcha papers?'

'Sure.'

The Canadian didn't even look at them, but handed them straight back. He asked, 'How yer doing?'

'I'm well, Allan. You need anythin'?'

'DDT. Our new billet's lousy with fleas an' lice an' the Doc's run out of everything.'

'I'll send someone over in the morning; OK?'

'Thanks, pal.'

He didn't even ask for mine. Tommo took a dozen steps with me to check that I was in stable flight. It was OK. I asked him, 'Do you really know *everyone*?'

'Don't know that, Charlie. How could I?'

'That's what I'm trying to work out.'

I just had that feeling he was holding out on me, but I knew that it wouldn't be personal. We said goodnight, and shook hands. Tommo always did that.

It was dark. I was a bit drunk. I got to the front gate. I got up the path, but I had to sit down on the front step. It was Hanna who hauled me to my feet a few minutes later and manhandled me through the door of Frieda's apartment. I said, 'You're too good to me, Hanna. I should marry you.'

'You're too small: you'd get lost down there.' Then she roared with laughter: it was the first time she said anything coarse. That was scary.

I limped around the place for about ten miles before I found Frieda sitting on a brocade chaise longue, darning a woolly by the light of a candle. She hadn't called out to guide me, even although she must have heard the racket I made. I leaned against the door frame and watched her.

'Why are you doing that? I bet you got dozens of them.'

'And in four months' time, Charlie? How many will I have then?' She dropped the garment on the floor beside the seat. Silence; and it's not always bloody golden despite what they tell you. She looked at me and I looked at her. She looked at me looking at her. Picking the right time to tell a woman that you find her beautiful is a matter of judgement. On this occasion I missed my cue. Eventually she shook her head: she was dealing with a child or a mental case. She also smiled. Just.

There was a small rectangular table near her, under a tablecloth that looked like a small Persian carpet. There was a square parcel on it, neatly wrapped in brown paper and string, and neatly addressed. About eight inches square I guess. She pointed to it and said, 'That came for you. A motorcyclist brought it from the airport. I had to sign a form for it.'

I hopped over and began to open it. My name and the company's were in Elaine's bold script. Frieda came to stand beside me. Her eyes widened slightly when she saw the nasty French lock knife I took to the string, and slid under the brown paper. As I turned back the inner cardboard, the scent of liquorice lifted towards us. She wrinkled her nose and asked, 'What's that?'

I imagined Red Greg's face before I replied: I imagined what he'd do for what I had under my hands.

'The answer to a maiden's prayer,' I told her.

Chapter Twenty-one

I slept well, was late down, and formed a fourth for breakfast. Old Man Halton was one of the others. I hadn't heard him arrive; he must have flown in during the night. Fergal was the other; I hadn't heard him either. I realized that I hadn't seen him since I'd got back to Berlin. I'd meant to, but he had become one of the things I was always putting off. If Fergal had come to see me he'd stayed on to eat.

My foot seemed to misbehave for an hour in the mornings, until it settled down. Frieda noticed me struggling as I crossed the room, and stood up to move the one empty chair for me. Hanna served the breakfast, which was a proper crew fry-up. It seemed a bit obscene, knowing that all over western Berlin people were beginning to scratch around for food, but my stomach won out over my conscience.

The Old Man started with a smile, a cough and a handshake, so things were probably all right there. Frieda gave me a Jane Russell smirk: you know – the knowing sort of smiley lifted lip. Then Halton coughed all over the table. It was his table, so we didn't complain. Through his handkerchief he said, 'Hello, Charlie. How's your foot?'

'Wobbly, boss, for an hour in the morning – then it seems to get stronger: better each day. When did you get in?'

'About 0300. I don't seem to need the sleep I once did.'

I was charitable enough to wonder if Frieda had had any rest either; that was interesting. Then I used her phrase on the notion, and threw it away. I informed him, 'I'm going down to Gatow later this morning to see how Borland's getting on.'

'He's getting on very well, *I* can tell you that. I spent an hour with him before I came on. You picked a useful number two there. Well done.'

I turned to Fergal, who was amiably stuffing his face.

'Hello, Fergal. How's the God business?'

'Demanding. He seems to want more for His money in Berlin than He did in Liverpool. I keep on running out . . .'

'What of?'

'. . . everything.'

Fergal was ace at making a chap feel bad. I squirmed.

'You should have come to see me earlier.'

He made it worse by saying, 'I was waiting for *you*, actually, Charlie.' Bastard. 'I didn't know where you were camping until last night. I arrived in time for breakfast.'

Nobody seemed to know what else to say after that, so I said, 'Thanks for coming to see me anyway . . .' It sounded rather weak.

'I didn't. Mr Halton's office sent me a message and asked me to drop over. Apparently you have someone you want me to bury.' Fergal always ate with his mouth chock-full, like a mincer. He chewed slowly as he spoke and there was absolutely no sense of judgement in his words. He just delivered them and let you do the worst yourself.

'. . . OK, Fergal. I feel like a louse. I should have come to see how you're doing.'

Fergal went straight to the *checkmate* with a gentle smile. '. . . if I think that God would forgive you, so do I. You're busy bringing stores into our city, aren't you? He'll let you off a few visits and a couple of Sundays.' He was already calling it *our* city: four years ago he was bloody bombing it.

Halton saved me. He said, 'We're burying Eddie this after-noon, Charlie . . . I don't suppose you happen to know his last name, do you? Nobody else seems to.'

'No, boss: don't you? He's been with the company longer than I have.'

'I don't think we ever saw his papers: sorry about that – things were a bit informal in the early days. Not even his pilot knows – Eddie used to do the paperwork you see.'

'What about his pay?'

'Always cash in hand I'm afraid. If he was abroad on pay day he had Elaine make an arrangement with the local airfield: I don't know how it worked.'

'It must be on some paperwork somewhere!' But the Old Man shook his head, which I took to mean *Not so far*. I remembered taking him to the house he said was his aunt's, but knew I could never find it again, so I asked, 'What the hell are we going to put on his stone then?'

Halton winced. I'd have to remember that he didn't like me swearing. Fergal intervened, apologetically, '*An airman known only unto God* is customary in those circumstances . . .' But even *he* seemed unsure of himself.

'Where?' I sounded curt. I didn't like that.

'Mr Halton pulled some strings at the new cemetery on the south side of Heerstrasse, out in the Charlottenburg. I went out there last week. You'd be surprised how many people we knew are out there.'

I wanted to reply *No I wouldn't*, but I bit my tongue. I said, 'He'll be in good company then.' Then I smiled because having Fergal around you always made you feel good. 'It's good to see you, Fergal. I'm sorry that I forgot about you. I can't think of anyone better to give Crazy Eddie his send-off.'

Fergal was either moved by that, or preoccupied with his meal, because he said nothing, patted my hand and carried on eating.

Halton coughed, and Frieda said, 'I'll ask Hanna for another pot of coffee.' We definitely ate better when the Master was at home.

When we finished up Old Man Halton bowled a blinder at me. He coughed, but this time it was a cough of embarrassment. 'You've done really well, Charlie. The operation's running like clockwork: thank you.'

I'm as bad at receiving compliments as he was at handing them out – it's not the sort of thing that men do. I glanced away. 'Fine, boss. I like doing what I have to do, *well*.'

'So I want you to take it easy for a few days and get your ankle mended, understand? Let Borland take the strain. He's more than capable.'

'Fine.' Actually it wasn't.

'How long have you been over here this time?'

'Two three weeks, maybe a bit longer. I've lost count to tell you the truth.' And some bastard tried to kill me.

'. . . so once you're up and around properly, come back for a week. Everyone else has managed a few days back . . .'

Because I'd scheduled them that way.

'Bozey Borland hasn't . . .'

'He's still a wanted man; you're not.' It did occur to me to think *How did you know that?* He jogged on with, 'Spend a couple of days with your own people, and a few days in the office before you come back to Germany again. Berlin will still be here. The Crew Chief and office staff probably both need to feel a steady hand on the tiller.' He delivered this last with a twitchy little smile: I've told you before that you never quite knew where you were with him; the little devil didn't miss much.

The reason that this was all a bit of a blinder was that I'd reckoned on spending the next few days organizing Red Greg's family exodus and getting Frieda into the Russian records, and maybe even me into Frieda. I hadn't worked out a running order for the tasks yet, but I was getting there. Don't look at me that way: I told you before – it's the way the world works and we were all at it in Berlin.

'How about if I take it easy for a few days. Go for some walks with Frieda to strengthen my foot – then spend another couple of days setting the schedules up – I'm worried about the maintenance programme and engine hours: we're overflying the aircraft.'

'So is everyone else.'

'. . . and then I'll hop a flight home. I'll call Chiefy and Elaine this morning.'

Frieda looked as thrilled as a bucket of blood at the prospect of walks in the park. Her eyes went blank, but Halton agreed. 'Fine, Charlie.' Have you noticed that some words become catching: like measles? 'I'll expect you back in a week.'

'How long are you staying this time, boss?'

'I'm not. I'll trot soon after the funeral – not stay for the party if that's all right? There's a debate on the Airlift in a couple of days, and I promised to brief a committee of their Lordships.'

'Do you do much of that sort of stuff?'

He coughed, and finished with a wry grin. 'Where did you think our contracts came from?'

Fergal put on a horrible expression of suffering innocence. 'Is that what they call corruption in some untutored circles, sir?'

The old man was up for it. 'No, Father, they call it grease: greasing the wheels of commerce. You know what grease is, don't you? Isn't that what you called your pilot during the war?' and he chuckled. Again I asked myself, *How the hell did he know that?*

A big armoured-looking staff car with an armoured-looking driver came for them half an hour later. Halton was taking Fergal out to inspect the chapel and the grave site. They would return for me before the event. One of the last things he told Fergal to do was provide me with a shopping list for the orphanage. He was good at shopping lists: I was in no doubt that it would be filled. I was also in no doubt that none of us would know where the stuff came from. It was the way the Old Man worked.

Frieda looked at me and I looked at her. Across the table. That's what we were getting quite good at. She let out a long breath with a low hiss. Maybe I should introduce her to Alice.

'So: I am to take you for walks, like a dog?'

'Looks like it. Sorry.'

'You are serious?'

'No. I just said it to buy myself some time. There are things I have to do before I go back.'

'With your crooked friends?'

'My crooked friends have the lists of survivors in the Soviet Zone that you wanted so badly to see. It's time to see if I can get something right.'

There's no pleasing some folk: she stood up without another word, flung her napkin among the breakfast crocks and stalked out.

The telephone didn't help me much. Red Greg was out of town. The Leihhaus barman said that Marthe and Lottie had taken Moppo to see a doctor out near the lakes somewhere.

I called Tommo's bar. He was upstairs with his whore and a *do not disturb sign* on the door. I tried that in my language box and it came out as *bitte nicht stören*. I'd have to ask Frieda when she was speaking to me again. After that I told the barman at the Klapperschlange to dangle the receiver into Alice's box, and heard her warning rattle when I spoke to her. It was good to know that someone still loved me.

At Gatow Bozey Borland yawned, and told me that we had only two deliveries, the Lancastrians, due in for the day: they had flour, powdered milk and powdered egg – and after that he was going back to bed: the boss had kept him up half the night, he said.

That's why I ended up standing on the top step outside the front door with my stick in my hand, wondering where to go. It was a sharp, late autumn already, it seemed, and the sun was weak in a sky streaked by high, thin cirrus. Autumn is my season: I always have the edge in autumn. I'd only made a half-turn at the sound of the door opening and closing behind me before Frieda's arm was through mine — on my good side. She said, 'You want to walk? We *walk*.' *Wir gehen*. Well, that's what I thought she meant.

She'd put a light mackintosh on over her clothes. We patrolled in angry silence up one side of the road and down the other: her heels rattled on the cracked pavements like rifle shots. Just like any other happy couple weathering a squall. We were as tense as springs, and I pushed away her helping hand going back up the steps.

Back inside the apartment she unbuttoned her coat as soon as the door closed behind us . . . but that's as far as she got before I threw the stick away, pushed her up against the wall and kissed her. Her body seemed to relax completely, as if her bones had suddenly become rubbery. That's how mine felt. She leaned into my neck and said, 'You can't even wait for him to leave town, Charlie.' I got the feeling that what she had just said about me, she was saying about men in general. Then she pushed me off and walked away without a second glance. She must have known that I was watching her until she disappeared. Even then I couldn't move. I could still hear the clack of her shoes on the wooden floors.

I bloody hate bloody funerals. It's something my generation is good at because we've staged so bloody many. It's what happens when half the bloody world goes to war. The first funerals I attended were with my mum and dad. They were of relatives: men, whose deaths in the First War had been long-drawn-out affairs – bullets that killed them ten years later. I clearly remember a neighbour saying of me, *Poor little mite: he doesn't know what's happening.* What did she know? Even at six I recognized that if you put a favourite uncle in a wooden box and buried it, you weren't going to see him again. Not unless you were unlucky that is.

By the time we buried Ed a fine cold veil of rain had blown down from the Baltic. Fergal and the Old Man picked us up in the four-wheel-drive staff car – some kind of big Chevy. They were as grave as the situation required, but their pink cheeks betrayed the fact that they had drunk lunch. The driver was a full lieutenant from the Gloucesters – which I mention just to show you the sort of pull Halton had. Frieda wore a black wool coat which fell to below her knee, and carried an umbrella. I let her get aboard first, so I was a little damp by the time I squeezed in alongside her. We were all quiet for the twenty-minute drive – lost in our own thoughts I guess. Like them or not, there's nothing like funerals to concentrate the mind.

My leg worked all right going up the path to the small makeshift chapel across the road from the war cemetery: I could almost have managed without the stick. Some people from the bar were there, and Marthe, Lottie and Moppo. And Dave Scroton with Magda, and a dozen of the REME guys I'd met partying at the Leihhaus the last time I'd been there. The service was short – nothing like the mumbo-jumbo Fergal was accustomed to – and he led us through it at a merciful trot. The chapel door remained open, and the damp in the air seeped around us. There was only one hymn, 'Oh God Our Help in Ages Past', chosen, I suspect, because most of us knew it: Marthe's voice, singing the refrain in German, rose above the rest like an angel's. I was the one who didn't know the words and *la-la'd* along with the tune. When Frieda realized that she turned and gave me a little glance; it was the first time she'd looked at me since our close encounter. In the early days she had this knack of making me feel judged and found wanting. She also sang in German of course, and her voice was lower – perfect counterpoint to Marthe. Eddy would have been proud of us. Fergal invited us to say a few words about Ed, but only Scroton took him up on it. He shuffled forward, his old pilot's cap twisting nervously in his hands, turned to face us and said:

'Ed was a great engineer.' He paused and then added quietly, 'He shouldn't have died like that.' That was all. The corporal with the REME crowd said Amen, very loudly, and we all copied him. The odd thing was that Dave's words, and our echoing responses, sounded almost like a threat.

The corporal led the coffin, borne by six of his engineers, across the road and into the graveyard. The road was potholed, and one of the pallbearers stumbled. The others were practised at this sort of thing and held him up. We followed; I brought up the rear with Fergal . . . Halton was with Frieda. Marthe's family, Magda and Dave were in front of them. Marthe and Magda had cried but they were very restrained about it: most of the women in Berlin in '48 were just about cried out. Marthe and Moppo were wearing old grey Wehrmacht greatcoats, and had found scraps of black material to twist into armbands. Lottie walked between them like a bridge, holding on to their hands as if she would never let go again.

Then we did the business all over again at the graveside. No flowers. No flowers in Berlin since the Airlift had started: even the great parks had been dug up and replanted with scraggy vegetables. There was no bugle either and no rattling volley of rifle fire. That seemed wrong. Fergal handed Halton a trowel of muddy earth to sprinkle on the coffin. His mouth made soundless words as he did so. Frieda reached across him, took some earth with her fingers and dropped it onto the coffin. It made barely a sound. That seemed the right way to do it to me, so I copied her when my turn came round, and murmured, 'Goodbye, Ed.'

Maybe she heard me. She made eye contact again. There was nothing angry in there this time.

The Old Man dropped Fergal and me off at the Leihhaus; Frieda went on with him. If she was going back to Blighty she hadn't said. Fergal didn't stay. He gave me a written list of stores – mainly food and blankets – swallowed a couple of glasses of cheap schnapps and pushed off. He said that he didn't like leaving his kids for so long.

It wasn't a bad party, but not one that you would remember. Dave Scroton got horribly pissed and Magda took him away. The REME guys enjoyed themselves; they'd only come because someone had paid them to be pallbearers, and they'd been promised a party afterwards. I found the whole thing vaguely depressing. The radio churned out incongruously optimistic music from the American Forces Network. Marthe sat on my lap and gave me a smacker when Moppo wasn't watching, but I could tell that her heart wasn't really in it. I think that it was just a *thank you* for all the things that might have been. In the middle of it all I recalled again that I'd once met someone Ed called his 'aunty', and if I could remember where she lived I'd find out what to put on his headstone. Then I felt sorry for myself, and had that flat feeling of another day of your life wasted, so I tried to get drunk. That didn't work either, so I sloped outside and hopped on the first tram I saw.

It was the last one of the evening, even although the evening hadn't become night yet, and it took me near enough to Halton's place for me to limp there. The last mile was the worst. I had taken a wrong turning, and the ruined city had suddenly a brooding, threatening air. I could feel unseen people watching me stumbling along in the gloom. My ankle had started to ache again, and felt weak, and along a smashed-up, unlit, cobbled street I became aware of shadowy shapes moving around me, like a pack of wolves. When I stopped, turned and challenged them with a shout, they froze – and I began to wonder if I'd been imagining them. Then one of the shadows moved before I did, so I pulled my small pistol and put a shot a couple of feet over its head. That dislodged a small fall of bricks in the wrecked house the bullet struck. I kept moving, limping with some urgency now . . . aiming for the end of the street dimly illuminated by a couple of domestic windows. All I managed to do was keep them at bay . . . they must have sensed my weakness from my gait.

I stopped at the light, and leaned against a house wall – momentarily blown: I needed to get out more. Shadows moved into the light, about six or seven of them, and stopped about ten feet away. They were children. The eldest, a raggedly dressed boy with a soldier's grey forage cap, was only about twelve, the youngest, a girl with a torn dress and a bruised face, was no more than four. For Christ's sake! The leader spoke a word in Berliner which sounded like, 'Spicer?' Probably *Speise* – food.

'Nein.' *No.* I kept my pistol in my hand, and visible to them. I felt incredibly tired. A girl of about eight shuffled into the light; she was carrying a bundle which whimpered. A baby. Where in *hell* had they got a baby?

'*Kindernahrung, bitte.*' Babyfood, please. Then she began to cry big tears, but made no sound. It was the stuff of nightmares, believe me.

I told the older boy, 'I have dollars. If I give you money, could you buy food for the baby?'

'Yes. Of course, if it is enough.'

'Of course it's enough!' I threw a handful of US dollars on the ground before him, maybe fifty. Probably a small fortune for them. The boy bent slowly and picked them up, straightened them, folded them and put them in a pocket. Then he said, 'Thank you, mister,' paused, and asked, 'You are injured?'

'Just a little.' I felt my hand tighten on the revolver butt.

He said, 'You will not need that. Where are you going now?'

I could actually see the checkpoint at the end of Frieda's road: two jeeps huddled under a storm lantern they'd fixed to a dead lamp post. I used the pistol to point.

'There.'

'This is a dangerous road; many bandits. We will walk with you. You will be safe with us.'

That was the second time in a year that kids had seen me home, wasn't it? I suppose that I just went on a hunch: I put the pistol away, and moved to lean on his shoulder.

'OK, chum, lead on.'

The Canadian patrol was on duty again. The big senior asked, 'These little bastards bothered you, sir?'

'No. These little bastards rescued me I think. If I gave you an address could you arrange a lift for them? It's to a kind of shelter.'

'Y're a pal o' Tommo's, right?'

'Right.'

'Then I guess it'd be in order.'

I turned to the older boy again, and moved back into Kraut. 'I have a friend who will take you in. The baby will die if it is not cared for.'

'We can care for it.'

'I know. You can care for it even better with my friend.' I showed him the address on the top of the shopping list Fergal had given me.

'Is that the Irish priest?'

'Yes: the Irish priest.'

'He has no room: his school is full.'

'He will take you if I ask him. He has babyfood. I promise he will take you.'

He turned back and consulted the others. They were shadows again, on the edge of a circle of light. Every child had its say. When he came back he nodded, and asked, 'You want your dollars back?'

'No, keep them.'

I waited until a one-tonner arrived, and saw them lifted into the back. I gave the driver a message for Fergal, and the orphanage address: he knew it anyway. The kids waved as it pulled away, talking animatedly. The word *food* seemed to crop up in every sentence. You'd have thought they were going on holiday.

'How many of them are there?' I asked the Canadian.

'Thousands.'

'Where are their parents, relatives?'

The Canadian didn't answer. He shrugged. He could have said *Killed by people like you*, I suppose. I still couldn't let it go. 'What about the baby? Where would they get a baby? There wasn't one of them old enough . . .'

'Abandoned probably. The twelve- and thirteen-year-olds are dropping them now. We hand one in to the hospital at least once a week. They probably heard it crying and picked it up . . .'

'Christ! What a city!'

'It was once, sir. Would you like a lift up the road?'

I nodded, and by the time I stood at the front door waiting for Hanna to let me in I was no longer sorry for myself. I suppose that that was something.

Frieda's kitchen was an exercise in futility. It was the largest, most luxurious kitchen I had ever seen. My mum would have thought she had died and gone to heaven. That was a bad thought, because she had, of course, and I kept on forgetting that. It was a futile place because it was almost empty of food. I helped myself

335

to some of her black bread, and drank a glass of water. I was stone-cold sober. In a couple of hours, unless I kept my socks on in bed I would be just stone cold.

I set off to find my bedroom anyway: Wee Willy Winkie carrying a candle. There were draughts in the apartment, so I had to cup a hand around the flame, which meant that I couldn't use my stick. My ankle felt not so bad again, but I still lurched along like a drunken sailor. I remembered the words of the song and they made me smile. I may even have been humming the tune. There was one long gallery room, which had probably been full of furniture once and had pale rectangular patches all along one windowless wall where pictures had hung. I wondered what they had been. Halfway along that wall there was a panelled door I hadn't noticed before, and before the door the stub of a candle gleamed in a jamjar. I moved it carefully to one side with my foot, and opened the door.

The room was high-ceilinged – the whole apartment was – but small; it must have been an antechamber or serving room in headier times. There was a small tiled stove which still radiated the heat of its last burning. On the floor on one side of the room, close to the wall, was a candle in an old-fashioned candle holder. On the other side was a comfortable three-quarter-sized bed, half in shadow. It had rich covers and heavy pillows . . . and it had Frieda, of course. The flickering light of the candle didn't reach far into the room, so she was part of the light and part of the darkness. The candlelight gave her body a million shades of colour . . . she was half upright, propped against the pillows. Her face was in shadow. I could see her shoulder, a breast, her hip and her splayed-up knee and leg . . . and the arm and hand which held a cigarette. The smoke was blue-grey against the dark.

I muttered the first stupid thing that came into my head. 'Frieda, I'm paralysed. I don't know what to do.'

She did: 'Idiot,' popped out with a low-level laugh. It was

probably the first time I heard her laugh at something which genuinely amused her. 'Take off your clothes and come over here. I'm getting cold.'

It wasn't a dream because she was still there in the morning. We underlined the memory with a rematch.

'How's your ankle?' she asked later. You know what it's like when two people have so large an area of their skins touching that you feel like one creature.

'I don't know. I can't feel it . . . the only part of me I can feel tells me I want you again: you're amazing.'

'I think you're mad,' she told me. But she was smiling, so maybe she didn't mind my kind of madness.

When we got up at mid-morning we were starving, but we shared a bath before we dressed, and that took longer than I anticipated. The black bread dipped in coffee seemed like the finest food I had eaten. Sometimes I reached across the small breakfast table to touch her hand. And we smiled a lot, and didn't stop looking at each other.

She observed, 'You were late last night. I thought that you were not coming home.' *Home* was a strange word in Berlin, but it seemed to fit.

'I thought you'd flown to England with Halton. I expected to be alone. On the way here I took the wrong road, and was saved by some street kids. So I saved them in return. They had picked up a newborn baby.'

'How many did you save?'

'Six or seven. Does it matter?'

'No. One would have been enough.' She let that odd thought hang in the air between us for a minute before she asked, 'What did you do for them?'

'I sent them to Fergal.'

'He might not be so pleased: more mouths to feed.'

'He won't turn them away; besides he has us on his side now.'

I telephoned the bar and Marthe answered. Russian Greg was still out of town. I told her that I had a private parcel for the Red but hadn't the transport to get it out to them – Bozey needed my Merc. She said that she would make arrangements, and that she missed me. There is a definition of *contrary* in there somewhere. An hour later Hanna showed a postman in: he was moonlighting of course.

Every time I looked at Frieda I found she was looking at me. The last time I had felt like this I was ten years old, with half a crown in my hand, standing in front of a sweet-shop window. That night we slept: facing each other, with one of her legs hooked over mine. We were still joined at the hip. It was the first time I understood what that really meant.

Chapter Twenty-two

We left the apartment late: almost dusk, and got a beat-up cab to a place, near Tegel in the French sector, which Frieda knew. That was one thing about Berlin: you could always get a cab if you had the moolah in your pocket. She didn't say much on the way there: she seemed to have gone back into herself. Most of the folk in the joint knew her as well. She made it plain that I would have to pay because she was short of dollars. We shared an immense dish of marinated sliced cabbage bleached almost white, and washed it down with a cheap white wine for which I had to pay top dollar. Guys would call out, 'Ho, Frieda!' as they walked past our table, and she would wave back – sometimes reach out and squeeze their hand . . . but she didn't stop eating.

A caricature Frenchman played sad songs on a squeeze box. He wore a blue and white striped vest, and a pencil moustache. His waiflike singer was a girl in tight black trousers and a black sweater: she looked young and serious, like a university student. She had long straight black hair and a very pale face: no make-up. Her clothes clung to her like a second skin, and all of the men gave her rapt attention as soon as she began to move. When she opened her mouth her voice was a million years old, and deep. You could catch the vibration of her low notes on your diaphragm.

'Interesting, isn't she?' Frieda said. 'Wouldn't you rather sleep with *her*?'

'No.'

'Idiot. She's rather good.'

'How do you know?'

She waved her fork dismissively. A piece of anaemic cabbage caught on its tines waved like a banner. 'Someone must have told me. Geoffrey brings me here.'

'What's her name?'

'Julie something or other. Do you need to know a woman's name before you sleep with her?' The question threw me. There was an edge in Frieda: I didn't know what I'd done to deserve it.

'Stop it, Frieda.'

'Stop what?' She stopped eating. That wasn't what I meant.

'Stop sounding as if you want to pick a fight.'

'No, Charlie: I pick a fight if I want to.'

'. . . are you punishing me for something?'

'No. If I wanted to punish you I would sleep with that Frenchman: there – the tall good-looking one at a table on his own . . . over there.' She used a fork full of cabbage to indicate the guy. He was in washed-out pale blue overalls, and had a sheepskin jacket draped around his chair. Pilots get all the luck. Then she said, 'In fact, I think I will.' She pushed the plate of food towards me, stood up, walked over to the Frenchy's table and pulled him up to dance. The song was a groany chanson about lost love, and they danced slowly. Her eyes were closed.

I got up and walked out.

It was a clear night, but not freezing. The street had huge paving stones, but they had been cracked and tilted where armoured vehicles had stood on them. I had to watch my step. She caught up with me, running, after I'd gone less than fifty yards. She was still pulling on the coat she had worn to the funeral. I stopped and turned as she grabbed my arm. The Frenchy was silhouetted in the light spilling out from the club doorway. He raised an uncertain wave as I looked. I waved limply back. Frieda didn't even look at him.

'He had an erection like a donkey,' she said.

'I thought that's what you wanted.'

'No. I wanted you. We should get a taxi or a lift, it's dangerous out here.'

'*You* can. I'm going to walk.' I was still stung.

'Then I'll walk too. It will take us more than an hour you know.'

It took us longer because my damned ankle started to ache. What was good was that I could do more on it each day: nearly back to normal. Eventually I saw a cabbie in an elderly DKW putting off a passenger at a roofless building on a corner, and waved him over. In the back of the cab Frieda wanted to be affectionate, but I couldn't throw off my anger so we sat apart. The driver took us a longer route than strictly necessary, avoiding a bad district, and I paid over the odds.

We sat on the outside steps and watched the stars. I ticked off the stars and constellations I knew and pointed them out to her. Then she pointed out even more to me. We spoke quietly. She smoked one of her cigarettes. I filled and lit a pipe. I had thought that after I had had her once I would be in charge. That's how things with women had always worked for me in the past. After that I could take it or leave it. I was wrong, of course – story of my life. I said, 'You don't like men much, do you, Frieda?'

'They're OK.' She blew out a stream of smoke. It drifted away on a breeze. 'Ask me about people instead.'

'Then you don't like people much, do you?'

'No.'

I decided to challenge that, instead of asking why. 'In a way that surprises me. Mr Halton gives you his house, and his money . . . and a Russian friend I'm going to take you to will take a big

341

chance to show you the things you want to see. They're both people, and they seem to be on your side.' I had carefully not included myself among her benefactors.

'You mean I should be grateful?' She whispered it, almost a hint of amusement in her voice.

That embarrassed me. It wasn't exactly what I meant, but maybe it was close.

'Why not? It doesn't cost you anything.'

'How would *you* know?'

'I'm going in, and going to bed,' I told her. 'But before I do I'll tell you this. I've never had more joy of anyone in my whole life than I've had from you in the last twenty-four hours . . . but it doesn't matter, and I don't care if you believe me or not. You don't have to do it again.'

I went up and left her sitting there. Back to my first bedroom where I slept as alone as if I was a stranger. That was the point she was making, of course. I *was* a stranger; so was every other man in the world. She had already gone out by the time I surfaced in the morning, but I didn't breakfast alone because there wasn't a scrap of food left in the place to eat. I went down to Hanna, who lived in the basement. She gave me half a glass of precious milk and a couple of small pancakes made from flour and water. I promised to get her some jam for them. I waited until the telephone was on, phoned Bozey, and told him to come and collect me.

He skilfully steered our small Merc around a pothole in the cobbles. The potholes were no longer being repaired, and people were stealing the cobbles to repair their houses and shelters. A yellow-thatched mangy dog crossed the road in front of us, running for its life. It was being pursued by at least a dozen feral cats. I didn't give much for the dog's chances: it was missing a back leg. Bozey steered the Merc between them and the cats scattered, screeching with frustrated anger. I hadn't heard that before.

I can't explain what I said next. 'Stop near the dog.'

In fact he stopped alongside the dog. It was a small one, and wouldn't have made much of a meal anyway. I leaned over behind him, and opened the car's rear door. The dog sat on the road looking exhausted. It panted, and its pink tongue lolled from the side of its mouth. It looked like a pretty old dog to me. Someone would eat it this winter, no mistake. The cats hadn't given up altogether: they had spread out and were waiting for us to leave. You could almost hear the dog's thought processes: it looked around at the cats, and then up at us. It made eye contact with me before it made up its mind. Then it hopped in the car and I pulled the door shut.

Bozey asked, 'What do you want with an old dog?'

'I dunno. Maybe someone will give me a leg-up one day, when I'm an old dog.'

Bozey laughed. I suppose the idea of giving a three-legged dog a leg-up could have been funny. As we pulled into the queue for the Gatow gate he told me, 'Those cats are a problem. Someone told me they stole a baby a few days ago.'

I thought about the abandoned newborns the Canadian had told me about, and shuddered at their fates.

The yellow dog hopped after us into the small office, and sat under Bozey's chair. It had the gait of a demented grasshopper. Every time it pushed off on its back leg the torque threw its rear end sideways, and it had to correct before opening up with its forelegs again. It whined so we fetched it a saucer of water. It drank the water and whined again, so Bozey fetched it a saucer of milk. It drank the milk and then went to sleep under him.

'I think you made a friend,' I said.

'What we gonna do with a three-legged dog, boss?'

'Mascot. A three-legged dog for a three-legged airline. What are we going to call it?'

'If you don't mind my saying so, boss,' Bozey told me, 'you're in a very odd mood today.'

'I know. Sorry . . .'

I must have stared off into space. He continued to talk to me, but I didn't hear him. When I came out of my daydream I told him, 'We could call it *Just Like That!* That comedian is always saying it.'

'It's a silly name, boss.'

'Three words for three legs.'

'It's still a silly name.'

'. . . Spartacus, then. Someone was telling me about Spartacus recently.'

'Wasn't he a fighter? This dog just runs away.'

'This dog's too bright to stick around and fight . . . *Spartacus* will do. Put him on the payroll.' My instinct had told me that it was masculine: I hadn't checked yet.

'Where's he going to live?'

'Dunno. Here if you like . . .'

Bozey was right. I was in a strange spiky mood. One of the duty officers dropped in to see us. He had his nose in the air, and stood at the door as if he expected us to spring to attention. Spartacus slightly lifted his only rear leg in his sleep, and farted. It was atrocious. I thought of Mortensen for the first time in days, and I knew I'd picked a good dog. The duty officer – he was a squadron leader – turned his head away. Bozey said, 'Sorry about that, chum. What can we do you for?'

Our visitor visibly winced at the word *chum*, but knew he couldn't do anything about it.

'Are you Bassett?' he asked me.

'Yes, Squadron Leader. What's the problem?'

'Nothing, Mr Bassett. Quite the contrary really – you know that your mob is putting in about ten per cent more flying hours than we'd counted on?'

'No. Is that good?'

'Matter of fact it is. Corridor Controller has been able to use you to fill the gaps when other kites go tech.'

'So we get paid more?'

'Expect you do: not my department. What I came to tell you is that your damaged Dak is ready to go again, but it's your call. Be grateful if you could tell us when she's available to call forward.'

'That's a pity; I was hoping I could write her off and throw her away. I hate that bloody crate.'

'Don't worry, chum,' Borland told him. 'The boss is in a funny mood this morning. I'll handle it.'

The D O actually saluted before he left: almost as if he couldn't stop himself.

'You know these bastards are in awe of you?' Bozey asked me. 'You really ought to be pleasanter to them. Your reputation scares them to death.'

'There's nothing to be in awe of,' I replied grumpily – although I was secretly pleased.

'*You* may know that, boss, and *I* may know it, but they don't . . . we might as well get what we can out of it while we can.'

'Such as?'

'Free dog food from the kitchens perhaps, now that you've landed us with this horrible thing.' Spartacus let out a great snort in his sleep. He and Borland were definitely on the same wavelength.

I sat at the bar at the Klapperschlange. I was the only un-American in the place. Tommo had rented it out to the US Navy for the night. They were staging a men's thing for about fifty senior rankers, and the joint was crowded. He'd borrowed people from the Leihhaus to do the catering and Magda and Marthe to serve. That was as well as his local staff. He was in his *Casablanca* outfit.

I said, 'This place is looking good.'

Alice was close by and must have recognized my voice; she lifted her tail into the air and gave us a quick rattle. I said, 'Hello, Alice,' but a couple of guys in Navy whites took a couple of steps away from her.

Tommo slipped back through the bead curtain to the small space from which they were producing an improbable feast.

'. . . be a minute.'

They were playing Shanghai Sailors' Golf at the other end of the narrow bar. Three small tables had been pushed into line, and one of Tommo's girls stood at the end of them. She was only clothed from the waist up. The sailors roll coins along the tables and bet on how many she could catch. That wasn't with her hands. Tommo nodded at her and said, 'Good, ain't she?'

'I've heard of that game, Tommo, but never seen it before. Make sure none of the Mateys holds his coin over a lighter before he bowls it.'

'Make no difference; she's made of asbestos, that one.' The girl was about thirty I'd guess, tall and severely beautiful. She had long straight blonde hair, and a bakelite emotionless smile. 'I brought her along from Poland.' He might as well have been speaking of a side of pork.

'Have you been off buying diamonds again?'

'Don't believe all you hear,' he told me. His mouth had set in a straight line. He didn't like people knowing his business.

When I left half an hour later he was outside, smoking a cigar and sheltering from the nine o'clock evening drizzle under the bar door's small awning. I paused, and didn't ask, but he told me anyway. He said, 'Could be I'm wrong, but I seem to remember you stayed up later than this. You gettin' old?' He was right.

Something was the matter with me, but I was damned if I knew what.

The only difference from the morning was that there was some food in the kitchen. A box on the table contained some bread, and some of her black bread, a couple of PX tins of bully, a tin marked coffee, with the name of some Arctic expedition stencilled on it, and a dozen eggs. I wondered where those had come from. I still hadn't a key so I had to get Hanna to let me into Halton's apartment. She smelt the brimstone in the air and didn't follow me, but curtsied when I gave her the big tin of raspberry jam I had wheedled out of the kitchen at Gatow. I had promised the quartermaster a couple of pairs of woollen socks from my next run back, in return.

The jamjar with its stub of candle was still outside the small room's door, but the candle had burned out the night before: there was nothing left. That might have been a metaphor. I opened the door. The room was in darkness, but it wasn't cold. That meant that the stove had been on for a while during the evening. If I strained I could just hear her steady breathing in the darkness. I don't know how long I stood there; it seemed like hours. Her low voice when it came was still shockingly loud.

'Did you see your Russian?'

'What Russian?' Then I closed the door. Bit bloody cruel of me I expect. I wondered how long it would take for her to have second thoughts and become Little Miss Sunshine again.

I should have realized that the sort of bird I knocked about with never had second thoughts. She had already left when I awoke. I stole one of the eggs, and had it boiled for breakfast: Berlin black bread makes acceptable soldiers . . . then I mooched about waiting for the phone to come on. I was going to phone Bozey again. The phone actually beat me to it. I answered it because I thought it might have been Old Man Halton. It wasn't: it was Russian Greg. His voice had that laughing quality that said he was on top of his game. He spoke English.

'Good morning, English. I wake you up?'

'No, Greg. I've been up a couple of hours. I was getting ready to go out. How did you get this number?'

'I'm an Intelligence Officer, Charlie.' His voice expressed sad outrage.

'Now tell me the truth.'

'A little bird tol' me.' I didn't respond, so he said, 'Ask me what kind of little bird.'

'What kind of little bird, Greg?'

'A little bird with tits as big as footballs. Where you get these women, Charlie?' Ah.

I ignored the question,

'Is she with you now?'

'Yes. I tol' you . . .' He hadn't, but never mind.

'Where?'

'In the Neutral Zone.' The club.

'What's she doing there?'

'Negotiating access to some records she thinks I can get her.'

'What's she offered you?'

'Tits as big as footballs.' Then he couldn't keep it up any longer, and laughed for about a day. When he got himself under control he said, 'She said she got me a box of sweets from England as a down payment; that you were jus' the delivery boy. That true?'

The clicking noise I could hear might have been Greg picking his teeth.

'What do you think?'

'No. I think she never did that. I already delivered it, and I am a Hero of the Soviet Union. Thank you, Charlie. What should I do with this woman? Cut you out, and negotiate direct perhaps?'

I thought quickly: never easy for me before the first drink.

'That all depends on your sister, doesn't it?'

There was the full five-beat wait before he replied.

'You getting too good at this game, English, you know that?'

'You'll kick her out then?'

'I'll send her back with a flea up her arse.'

'You mean in her ear.'

'I mean what I say, Charlie. I know the difference. I can speak English.'

I sat in the office and studied the schedules. Things had moved on. They covered one complete wall. Bozey had separate sheets for each airfield: arrivals and departures, and a master sheet which integrated the lot. Any pilot could stand in front of them for five minutes and see his scheduled routes for the whole week.

I was alone because he had taken a Lancastrian back to Lübeck. Hardisty had brought it in with blankets and winter clothes even this early in the year, and I was shocked by the state of him – pasty yellow face and hollow eyes. He had a mug of coffee in one hand and a doughnut in the other when he slouched in. I took one look at him and stood him down for twenty-four, telling him to get a bath and a meal then go to bed. He hadn't even the energy to disagree.

After he'd signed out I'd asked Bozey, 'What the hell are the rest like?'

'The pilots? Not much better. I did one or two trips to keep them going, but there's not enough of us. The engineers and loaders seem to be able to take it better – you know we're still flying radio ops on the Lancs?'

'Christ! We're going to wear the people out quicker than the kites at this rate. Time to get some more pilots, or slow everything down.'

'That mad Yank is the exception. He's been checked out on

Lancs now, and even flew out a C-54 for the RAF when they ran out of pilots. When the others are dropping like flies around him he asks for more. I think he can fly anything.'

'So can you.'

After Bozey had rounded up *Tin Man*'s crew and taken off into the overcast I put a call through to Lympne. Halford wasn't there. Elaine was. She had two or three telephone numbers for the boss and said she would try them, and get him to call me back. My telephone rang an hour later.

'Morning, Charlie. Ankle healing?'

'Almost as good as new, boss . . . we just gave it a fright. Give me a couple of days.'

'I'm speaking from the House: I have fifteen minutes between committees.'

'We'd better talk about the pilots then: they're exhausted . . . everyone is in the same state as far as I can see – both the privateers out here, and the Air Force crews. We're going to have people landing on houses soon if we're not careful . . . we're flying them to death.'

'Solution?'

'Slow things down, or get more pilots.'

He coughed his thoughts together before answering, 'Get some pilots then; there are hundreds of unemployed ones knocking about. Fly less until they come on stream if you have to, but every flight we complete puts money in the bank. I thought you were going to ask me for more aircraft.'

'Not much point: the pilots would just have to fly more trips, and we'd be on the merry-go-round again. I'll tell you when you can handle more capacity, OK?'

'You're the boss, Charlie.' No; I wasn't actually. That was *his* job, but I let it pass. Then he asked me, 'How are you getting on with that inquiry for Frieda? Helping her out . . .' Ah.

'I'm getting something sorted out. It's taking longer than I thought . . .'

'She was on to me this morning. Seemed to think that you weren't pushing enough . . . something to do with a Russian officer who might be able to help?'

'Was she *complaining* about me, boss?'

A two-beat. I could tell he felt uncomfortable because for once he forgot to cough.

'Possibly.'

'She's not the easiest person in the world to deal with, is she? Look, she tried to go over my head to someone, and may have messed up the whole deal. I'll see her later, and try to straighten things out.'

I couldn't believe that she was still using Halton to pressure me. He chuckled, so that was all right. As usual it finished with a cough.

'When are you coming back?'

'I thought the end of the week.'

'Leave it until Saturday. Claywell's in Berlin on Friday after-noon with some special cargo. You could hop back with him; bring Frieda if she'll come. I don't know why she kicks around an empty flat in Berlin when there's London . . .'

'I'll tell her, boss – OK?'

I heard someone call out his name in the background, so we cut the rest short. He hung up first, and I was left looking at a buzzing handset. I replaced it slowly in its black cradle.

I tried Elaine again. I could tell she was eating. I said, 'Pilots.'

'How many?'

'Five for starters. They've got to have had current hours on Daks or Lancasters.'

'By when?'

'I want the first ones out here by next week.'

'I've had a couple phone up looking for work. It shouldn't be impossible.' Then she giggled and laughed, 'I love it when you're being masterful.'

'Stop taking the Michael. I'm coming back on Saturday, and going straight on down to the boys; then I'll be back in the office for a few days.'

'. . . anything you'll need?'

I thought of saying *Norwich*. That was the acronym that lonely servicemen used to put on the back of the envelopes of their letters home: it meant *Nickers off ready when I come home*, or some such. Poor lonely buggers. Then I realized that it wasn't what I really wanted at all. I wanted company and I didn't know how to ask. I said, 'You could learn to make a decent cup of tea . . .' She began to splutter, so before I got the thick end of her tongue I added, 'Finish your sandwich now, and go back to work,' and hung up.

I waited to see *Dorothy* in; that was Dave Scroton. He didn't look too bad. He had Mortensen with him. Mortensen didn't look too bad either if you discounted the vague yellow glow in the air that seemed to frame his body like an aura: I'm sure that I imagined it. Magda had parked up the happy wagon, and was going to get a lift with them out to the Leihhaus. When they asked me if I would join them later on I told them the truth.

'Maybe. I got things to do.'

'Don't work too hard, boss. All work, no play makes Charlie a . . .' Scroton of course.

'Get lost, the lot of you,' I waved them away. There was a big grin on my face: I loved them really, and they knew it. Spartacus had been under my chair in the office when I arrived. He followed me out to the Merc, and hopped straight over to the front passenger seat when I let him in. Bozey had left it full of gas; I wondered who he'd got it from. I also wondered if Frieda would be back in the apartment when I reached it, and what she'd say about a three-legged dog.

What she said was, 'Oh!' and then, 'If that's a dog, I used to like dogs.'

'It's most of a dog,' I told her. 'We call him Spartacus. He's adopted me.'

'Like your boys did. Things like adopting you.'

Why don't you try it, I thought, and limped across the sitting room – one of at least three – to the large round table she was sitting at, and slipped into a chair opposite. I placed my stick on the floor beside me. Spartacus lay on it.

'What were you trying to do at the Leihhaus?' I asked her softly. 'You could have really sodded things up.'

She was playing solitaire with an old set of cards, and kept on laying them down one after the other. She didn't look up at me.

'What does *sodded* actually mean?'

'Sodomized: biblical stuff.'

She didn't answer me, but this time she glanced up from her cards and looked at me from under an eyebrow which was cocked up. Bad choice of words, come to think of it. Then she asked me, 'So. Is it all off? My search is stuck?'

'No; it is not all off, neither are you stuck. But if you go off rattling around my friends again I'll . . . I'll . . .'

'What, Charlie?' Bloody incredible! She was smiling at me as if we were the best of friends again. I couldn't help smiling back – it's the way that signal works. '. . . You'll do what?'

'Never you bloody mind, but you'll have bloody deserved it! What happened to you at the club anyway?'

'They made me sweep out the floor before I left. With a dustpan and brush. A cook said it was a penance, and that I was lucky it wasn't worse. A man named Otto grinned at me all the time. He followed me around and dribbled.' I suppose that it was time Otto had had a slice of luck.

'I also spoke to the Old Man . . . your Geoffrey . . . you complained to him as well: if you get me fired you'll never see those records.'

'I thought you had changed your mind, and I was angry after what they made me do in that club. I felt like a maid.' *Might have been a lot worse*, I thought, but I didn't say it. I went for tact; it was a skill I was learning.

'Look, I don't understand how this bad feeling you have for me started up. I thought that maybe we were getting on OK. Then I woke up one afternoon, and you suddenly hated me. Why?'

She glanced out of the window. 'No. I won't tell you that, Charlie . . . but I can remember to be more careful in future. All right?'

Our war hadn't ended, she was telling me, whatever it had started over – but at least we could declare a local truce.

'All right. Is there any more food in the house?'

'More eggs. You like English eggs scrambled, with real toast?'

'I'd love that.'

I thought that it stretched her culinary skills, but I hung around her in the kitchen, and made her laugh. Then I took her back to the small room with the bed and the stove, and tested her other skills. I came nowhere close to exhausting those, and nowhere close to finding out what I'd done to annoy her in the first place.

Russian Greg was wearing a new medal on his uniform. It had a livid red and silver ribbon. I asked him what it was.

'The Medal for Patriotic Sacrifice . . . pretty, yes?' We were speaking our usual make-believe German.

'What did you sacrifice for it?'

'Sacrificed half a kilo of liquorice to my General. It reminded

him of his secret bourgeois childhood. Nobody seems to know
how I obtained it. Possibly it was a miracle.'

'Do communists still believe in miracles?'

'Not often: but Georgians do,' and he roared with laughter.
The Leihhaus was going full swing, and they were serving a
medley of any food you liked as long as it was potatoes. The
REME blokes were back again, off duty from putting a new cross-
runway into Gatow. Now all they had to do was repair the roads
to the food warehouses in the centre and we'd be in business.
The noise of people enjoying themselves washed across the table.
I'd brought Frieda, although after her last appearance there she
wasn't too keen on it. Two guys cut in to ask her to dance as we
walked across the club, but as soon as we were sitting at Greg's
table they let her alone.

I leaned towards her and said, 'If you want to dance with
anybody it's no business of mine.'

'Last time I did that you walked out on me.'

'I'd do it again.'

'Why, Charlie? Jealous?'

'Yes,' I said shortly. I never had been before: I suppose there's
a first time for everything.

'Are you Charlie's woman?' Russian Greg asked her. 'He needs
a woman of his own. We want him to be happy.' That was a
difficult one.

A small combo in the corner launched into 'On Green Dolphin
Street'. People were suddenly playing it a lot. I tilted my chair
back on two legs and hummed along with the opening bars.

'I *am* happy,' I told them. 'I couldn't be happier, but Frieda's
not my woman. She's my boss's woman. He told her to nurse me
when I bent my ankle, so she's probably my nurse.'

'Is she a good nurse, Charlie?' Red Greg almost had to shout
to make himself heard.

This time it was more difficult to duck the issue, so I turned to her instead, and said, 'One of the very best.' Then I said, 'Thank you, Frieda.'

'Eat your potato,' she told me. 'We need to keep your strength up.' That seemed to suit everyone.

Dave Scroton and Magda walked in. They were holding hands, but she immediately settled down to business and began to work the customers. He sat at the bar and chatted to Marthe. She looked over his shoulder at me, and smiled. Otto had graduated to emptying ashtrays and wiping them with a damp cloth. He waved to me from across the room when I caught his eye. The REME corporal danced a solo rumba with a broom balanced inverted on the bridge of his nose, and his arms outstretched. Frieda reached for my hand under the table and squeezed it. I think that she was scared that the broom was coming in her direction, and that she'd end up sweeping the floor again.

Before the alcohol addled my brain cells I explained to Red Greg, 'In two days' time I'm going home for a week's rest. Before I go we need to understand the arrangements we have for Frieda to look up her relatives, and for the parcels you wanted transporting. I need a picture in my head.'

He understood that, and sobered immediately. 'In two weeks you gonna be asked to visit the Soviet Zone, Charlie. They expect an important man like you to take his secretary with him.' He nodded towards Frieda.

'Why should I go? How do I know I'd be coming back?'

'The British occupying authority will be asked to present you to give evidence in the People's trial of the pilot who exceeded his orders and fired on your company's aircraft. Just because we're trying to starve you out doesn't mean we ain't talking.' He seemed to find that funny. I wondered who'd taught him *ain't*. 'Your little aeroplane may have been out of position, but that was

no excuse: he had not been released to fire on you. He jumped
the gun: funny, yes?'

'Funny, *no*. He almost killed me. He *did* kill two friends of
ours.'

'. . . and that has severely embarrassed my much maligned
Socialist Republic . . .'

'Only because some of us lived to tell the tale.'

'My government is regretful. This is the second time we have
unintentionally inconvenienced your airline, and this time the
criminals will be made an example of. We wish you to see justice
done, and report that back to your own people of course . . . as
a voluntary witness your safety, and safe return, will be guaranteed.' I missed the plural there. I wish I hadn't.

'You expect me to believe that? By whom?'

'By my General of course.'

'How will this help my secretary?'

'The new East Berlin People's Hall of Records, containing the
latest East German census record, was completed a month ago. It
is next door to the courthouse. Your secretary will be chaperoned
separately while you are giving evidence in the court. Her
chaperone will be an archivist at the Hall of Records. He will
probably insist she visits his new facility.' Ah.

'Would we return immediately?'

'Not necessarily. If you wished to inspect the sites of major
Soviet victories in the East I am sure that can be arranged.' In
other words we might be free, in a limited fashion, to follow up
on anything Frieda found in the census. Anyway, I hoped that's
what he meant.

I leaned back in my chair and looked at him. It seemed like a
practical deal. Frieda followed the conversation like a linesman
watching a tennis match, although she didn't pick up on the last
bit of Greg's chit-chat. '. . . and the export cargo for your aircraft

will be ready within fourteen days of your return from giving evidence. Favour for favour.'

'Favour for favour,' I confirmed, and we shook hands across the table.

It sounded even more dangerous for him than for me. I wondered what would happen to Greg if we got away with it.

The REME corporal came out of the kitchen wearing a dirty white apron over his khakis. He said, 'There's an old three-legged dog in there, stealing the kitchen scraps. It says it's with you, Charlie. That right?'

'It's my new bodyguard. It's been trained to throw itself in front of the bullet if the Reds try to kill me again.'

'What yer call it?'

'Spartacus.'

Red Greg looked away and pursed his lips. I was probably smirking. Frieda squeezed my hand under the table again. I thought it was time to round up the dog and go.

Chapter Twenty-three

The flight back was awful. The thick weather kept us only a couple of hundred feet above a massive grey sea, and at that height every major upsurge of a wave seemed to throw the small aircraft upwards as well. Even Randall looked white when we landed at Lympne just after noon. Frieda sat behind us. For most of the flight I heard her retching into the brown paper carrier bag Randall had thoughtfully provided. Behind her, Spartacus howled and moaned for most of the trip, but managed to keep his breakfast down. Randall had told me, 'We'll be in big trouble if we're caught bringing in a dog: they're supposed to go into quarantine for six months.'

'He *will* be in quarantine: Elaine will keep him on the airfield.'

'She'll kill you!'

The grass at Lympne was wet, which slowed us down to a walk quite quickly. Randall kept that speed on her until he pulled on to the concrete, alongside the offices and Halton's Roller. The grey chauffeur came out to the Oxford, helped Frieda down the narrow steps, and carried her suitcase. We followed. Spartacus whined. I hoped that he hadn't been heard. At the open rear door of the car Frieda turned, gave me a sisterly peck on the cheek and said, 'See you in Berlin, Charlie. Next week.'

'See you in Berlin,' I agreed.

We watched them drive out onto the road, and then until they were in the village and out of sight. Randall sighed and said, 'What a little cracker! What I'd give for a night with her – wouldn't you?'

I squirmed: only mentally I think.

'No: I've heard she has a shocking temper. Life's too short to spend on girls like that. Besides; there's never a future in chasing the boss's woman, is there?' I had my fingers crossed behind my back.

It had stopped raining, but there was still dampness in the air. Elaine was belting up a short mac as she came up to us. She was wearing a great smile.

'What did you bring me, Charlie?'

'Nylons, cigarettes, a nice old bracelet and a three-legged dog.'

'Stop being daft!'

'I bought you a silk scarf,' Randall told her.

She stretched up on her toes to give him a chaste kiss on the lips.

'Let me see,' she said.

Spartacus whined from the aircraft behind us, and we all turned to look.

Flying had finished for the day, so we sat around in Elaine's office, which was bigger than mine anyway, and sipped whisky. Randall had brought a case of it back; he always seemed to have his sources. Spartacus made himself at home and curled up to sleep on a pair of old boots in the corner. He had this preference for sleeping on irregular surfaces.

'This scotch was exported from Scotland to the US in 1945,' he told us, holding up his glass to the light and squinting at the colour. 'Where it was sold on into the PX, which sent it to Germany, and now it's back where it started.'

'Not quite.' That was Elaine. 'The Scots wouldn't thank you

for lumping them in with the English: I had a Scottish boyfriend once. In fact they're very touchy about it.'

'Like the Injuns,' Randall sniffed. 'Sign of insecurity, isn't it?'

I said, 'The Indians have every reason to feel insecure. Didn't you kill most of them off?'

'Stop insulting my wonderful country,' Randall grinned, 'and take us both down the pub for a warm beer.' He gave us a bottle each from his case before we left.

The bar was crowded. Well, it was Saturday after all. I still wore my flying ovies and jacket, and felt decidedly underdressed . . . most of the younger men were in cavalry twills and tweeds; with a smattering of smart cravats. I don't know where they all came from. An hour later a screech of tyres on tarmac announced the arrival of a fast or bad driver, and a film star battered through the saloon-bar door. That's what she looked like to me, anyway – Veronica Lake – and she made straight for our table. Before I had time to glance at the ceiling, thank God and ask what I'd done to deserve her, she was past me and smearing her lipstick all over Randall. Everyone stopped to watch. She said, 'Hello, baby. Been here long?'

Randall made her comfortable on his lap, and nuzzled her ear. 'Doesn't matter, hon. It's always worth the wait.'

Then she looked at Elaine and me for the first time.

'Introduce me to your little friends.'

I don't think that the Scots would have liked her either.

I drove west about an hour later. That was a bit stupid because I had drunk too much, and I caught myself nodding off behind the wheel a couple of times. Someone had filled the Singer up, so I got to Bosham on one tank. The lights were on in the prefab, and Maggs was playing Farmyard Snap with the boys; she'd kept them up to wait for me. In the sitting room there was a large old leather chair that I hadn't seen before. The boys dragged me to it, and then climbed all over me when I was seated. Dieter said,

'This is your chair, Dad. We got it from the Emporium. I chose it.'

'Where did you learn words like *Emporium*?'

'School. I won a prize for English. I'm going to be a writer when I grow up.'

I ruffled his hair. I've told you that people did that to me. It was odd to find I did it myself. I thought about a German refugee kid winning a prize for English at an English school. It made me smile.

'I'm very proud of you: I chose a good 'un when I chose you, didn't I?'

'No, Dad; Carlo and I chose a good one when we chose *you*.' There was a deadly serious side to him that could be unnerving. 'Are you getting married yet?' He also had a memory like an elephant.

Maggs told them to leave me alone to get ready for bed. Carlo, as usual, didn't say much to begin with. He sat on my lap and hugged me around the neck until the air supply was cut off. I had to carry him into their room to get changed. I'd brought them two of the white-metal aeroplane models the Americans were shipping into Berlin for the German kids. There was a large silver C-54 Skymaster, and the smaller C-47 Dakota. Mortensen had given that a careful coat of red paint. They were astonishingly accurate. Dieter immediately handed the larger toy to his brother. It wasn't altogether an altruistic gesture. He asked me, 'You still fly red Dakotas, don't you, Dad?'

'Yes. We still fly those.'

Carlo asked, 'Do you fly in mine as well?'

'Yes, sometimes I fly in yours. Usually as a passenger – then I can go to sleep.'

Carlo ran around the room in circles making aircraft noises until Maggs chased him to bed. She made me a cup of cocoa after I turned down a drink. I felt suddenly absolutely drained. I sometimes used to feel like that after I'd come back from Germany in 1944. She said, 'You look buggered.'

'Thanks!' But there was a smile behind it.

'You know what I mean.'

'Yes I do, Maggs. Thank you.' I stood up and gave her a long hug.

'How long are you back for?'

'Until Wednesday. I'll go out with the boys tomorrow if it's fine.'

'We'll all come with you. Fancy a day up on the Downs? The Major's become very fond of flying kites, silly old bugger, an' Dieter'll want to fly his glider . . .'

Then she left me. When I looked into the boys' room before I turned in I saw that they'd both gone to sleep with their new planes in their bunks. Carlo was still holding his. *Definition of a lucky man?* I thought. *Me.*

I'm not going to tell you about a perfect day flying kites on the edge of winter. It's one of the memories that I shall keep for myself. Go away and try it for yourself.

We came back at dusk with rosy cheeks, and a new chill in our bones. Maggs had left a mutton stew in the slow oven and the boys fell on it like ravenous wolves. They were in bed before seven, and were asleep within minutes. When I was sure they were settled I walked over to the Happy Returns in time to help James open the bar. The Valentines were there, looking as if they were still together. I wondered what their new yacht looked like. Then I wondered how they'd paid for it . . . it was not as if the country was exactly drowning in money.

The bar was often quiet on a Sunday night: the London yachties were all on their way home. I found myself talking to a young man named Monty who played clarinet with an amateur jazz band, and promised I'd approach James about giving them a monthly spot for a jazz club: I wasn't sure that he would go for it because James's sort of music seemed to be about a thousand musicians in big concert halls . . . but he liked military band concerts as well, so I suppose that there was always hope.

When Eve came up to the bar for refills she said, 'Haven't seen you around for a while, Charlie.' Was there regret, or maybe a little resentment behind that? No: not a hope. I was kidding myself.

'No. I was working. This is my first time back since the boys did a bunk. Did I thank you for what you did then by the way?'

'Several times; but you can always say it again.'

Maybe we looked too matey. Whatever it was prompted her husband to walk over.

'The hero returns,' he said, and raised his brandy glass to me. Oddly there wasn't exactly a note of mockery in his voice. I looked a question at Eve. She said, 'You were in the papers.'

'Oh Lord! That was ages ago . . . and they made most of it up. Load of tosh.' I had a gulp of beer to drown my embarrassment.

'No.' She looked puzzled. 'Last week, in the *Chichester Observer*.'

'*Three heroes of the airlift*,' Valentine explained. 'That was the headline. You and two others; one's a pilot from Arundel, and the other has something to do with the cargo . . .'

'A loadmaster? . . .'

'Probably . . . anyway, you all live nearby, so they did a local story – you know the sort of thing.'

Yes, I thought, *unfortunately I do*. Why didn't these bastards talk to you before they wrote? Why hadn't Dieter or Maggs told me about it?

'Thanks for the warning. If people start looking at me as if I have two heads I'll know why. Excuse me a minute, there's something I have to do. I'll catch up with you later.'

I found James in the kitchen looking very smug over a huge pot of livid green soup. It seethed as if it was full of crocodiles. I'll tell you about crocodiles one day: I've never liked them much. I don't like animals that look on people as snacks.

'James. Why didn't Dieter say anything to me about the newspaper article? – it's just the sort of thing he spots.'

James carefully stirred the pot and didn't catch my eye.

'We kept it away from him.'

'Why?'

'It said you were recovering from injuries received when your aircraft was shot down by the Russians. We thought it best not to say anything until you were back.'

'Damn! Why do they print such rubbish?'

'Didn't some Yank say that if you have to choose between the truth and the legend – print the legend?'

'Bollocks.'

'Were you shot down?'

'No. I wouldn't be here now if I had been, would I? I'd be in some Russian prison.'

'You *were* over the other side then?'

'They chased us over, then the bastards shot at us. They're worse than the Jerry.'

'Was anyone hurt?'

'Yes.' He didn't ask any more, but I did. 'Does everybody else know?'

'Work it out for yourself, Charlie. It was on the front page.'

'Balls. I've been back two days, why hasn't anyone said anything?'

'They probably like you too much. Who told you?'

'Evelyn Valentine's husband hinted at it: just now.'

'I've always thought that man was an idiot.'

That seemed to be about it.

'Did you save the paper?'

'Mrs Maggs kept it. We can give the article to Dieter now; for his scrapbook. Be prepared for a dozen questions.'

I went back to the bar and chatted with the Valentines. He left after ten minutes to sit in a corner with a cabal who could have been from the local Lodge, but were, in fact, members of his yacht club's committee who hadn't left yet.

'Impromptu board meeting,' Eve confided in me. 'They wait for the awkward squad to go home, and then make the real decisions.'

We had one of those wonderful twenty minutes of chat which aren't about anything important. She told me about their new boat, and at some point I might have moaned about none of my relationships ever really lasting. She mocked me.

'Poor Charlie: always coming second.'

'I'm getting used to it. It's not so bad.'

Before she could say anything else the party in the corner broke up, and Valentine led them over to the bar with an empty glass in his hand. He asked, 'You chatting this lady up, Charlie?'

'Wouldn't dream of it, Captain. Her husband's much bigger than me.' Honour satisfied. He found it funny anyway. A couple of the others laughed as well.

'Fact is,' Valentine said, 'the Committee's asked me to put something to you . . .'

I packed my kitbag on Tuesday night so that I could get away as soon as the boys left for school the next day. Maggs had laundered everything I'd brought down, but flying clothes always smell like flying clothes. That's probably why I had the dream.

I always sleep with the bedroom as darkened as possible. Light wakes me. Even so there's enough light to see for anyone with half decent night vision. I always had A1 night sight. I dreamed that I awoke in the early hours and sat up in bed. Marty Weir was standing at the end of it in his flying gear. The dark stuff on his face was probably blood, but he was smiling away, so the afterlife can't have been all that bad. He was talking to me. His mouth and lips were moving, but I couldn't hear a word.

'I can't hear you, Marty.'

He frowned, grinned and tried harder. I could see that he was shouting now, although that didn't wipe the silly grin off his face.

'Marty. I still can't hear you. Try harder.'

But he didn't. He shrugged, grinned again, and turned away to walk back into the darkness. I lay down again, and went back to sleep as if nothing had happened. That was odd, but in dreams your behaviour often *is* odd. The first thing I thought of when I awoke in the morning – I could hear the boys skylarking in the bathroom – was that I'd have to speak to Fergal before the day was out. Maybe that was the message.

Lympne's little admin block consisted of a dozen courses of WD bricks, with creosoted weatherboarded offices slapped on the top. There were thousands of sheds like that all over Britain after the war. They were what we were building in the Forties when airfields needed a quick upgrade. I sat outside making the most of the last of the sun, balanced back against the woodwork on two chairlegs; Elaine sat alongside me doing some knitting, and Scroton beside her. Spartacus was inside somewhere. The office window above us was open so that we could hear her telephone. Across the field we could see *Scarecrow*. Her arse was inside one of the hangars, but her front half was out in the air. Two of her engines were in pieces on the portable benches beneath one of her wings. The Chiefy wandered over with a half mug of char in his hand. It would be cold. The ground crews I knew always let their tea get cold for some reason.

'When will she be ready, Chief?'

'I've said Saturday, OK, sir? She's got a load of medical stores for the Yanks in Frankfurt. That means she'll be back in the Lift proper for Monday.'

I didn't mind that. The Old Man made a lot of these one-shot deals with the American military: they paid much better than the much more dangerous runs into Berlin.

'Good, Chiefy. You can tell their pilot that he's got a radio op for the trip: me.'

'You'll go as a passenger, Charlie, and like it! They'll need their own man once you've abandoned them over there.' His master's voice.

'Yes, Elaine.'

There was a very late hatch of small flies: the heat left in the sun had woken them up two seasons too early: the air teemed with them.

'Pity the swallows have flown,' Scroton observed. 'They would have loved this lot.'

'When are you flying?' I asked him.

'Tomorrow. Your Yank, Padstow, is dragging the *Witch* over from Leeds with sugar and hospital blankets. Then he gets a few days off while I take them on to Germany. His name's not Padstow, by the way: he got very drunk last week and told me.'

'I shouldn't take too much notice if I was you. Some people I know change their names as often as their socks these days. You still like *Whisky*, even after Eddie and Trask . . . ?'

'Wasn't her fault was it? She's just an aircraft . . . you know who I saw yesterday?'

'Tell me, or do you want me to guess?'

'One of those Hungarian Joes we fetched back. He was washing dishes at The Parachute.' I know that it's a phrase that I use too often . . . but that was interesting. I know that Elaine was bursting to ask us about the Joes, but her telephone began to ring and she ran inside.

'Did he see you?'

'Don't think so. The kitchen door was only open for a mo, and I saw him side-on. It was him all right.' Another thing about pilots is that when they say they've seen something they *have*. Sight's one of the senses which keep them alive up there.

'We still have the Spitfires the Customs seized?'

'Yes, boss. They were all still there the last time I counted them.'

For how much longer? I wondered. 'When was that?'

'Monday: I had a walk round in the evening.'

'You stay in the sun and make the most of it,' I told him, 'and maybe we'll grab a beer later on. I've a couple of calls to make.'

I sat on my desk and thought about it. I could call Holland or I could call Dolly. The question I finally asked myself was who it would benefit most, and I called Dolly. I had an old number for her office in London: it had once almost been mine. The man who answered the call definitely wasn't her. He barked, 'Bowser.'

'I'm looking for a Miss Wayne.'

After a ten-beat he asked, 'Exactly how did you get this number?'

'From a year or so ago. We worked together.'

'. . . and you are?'

'Pilot Officer Bassett.'

'Wait one . . .' There was a pause, and I could hear a curious scliffing noise in the background. I closed my eyes and immediately recognized it: he was riffling through a card index. When his voice came back he said, 'OK, squire, what can I do for you?'

'Nothing. I'd like to speak to Dolly.'

'She doesn't work in this office any longer: posted. You can tell me anything you'd tell her.'

'No I can't.' Neither of us spoke for a moment, then I said, 'Look, I'm sorry I bothered you. I'll leave it at that.'

But he said, 'Oh, all right, I'll transfer you.'

The phone went dead, and I was about to hang up when it went live again. Dolly's voice said, 'Motor Section. Section Officer Wayne.' Posted. Back downstairs more like. Poor Dolly was back where she'd started: driving men around London in staff cars. She sounded a bit sniffy as we made all the *hello, and how are yous* – I can't say I'm surprised: I hadn't brought her much luck.

'You're back downstairs again?'

'Yes, Charlie. I told you my promotion was only temporary.'

'Whoever unpromoted you made a big mistake, but don't take it personally: anyone can make mistakes. Look what happened to me.'

'You should have never been let in the RAF the first place. Bevin should have bunged you down a mine, and left you there.'

I don't think that she meant to give me the opening, but I took it. 'Talking of Mr Bevin, do you remember those two unpleasant visitors he was expecting earlier in the year?'

Pause, then, 'Yes. Of course.' Her voice had dropped two registers.

'A pal of mine saw one of them a couple of days ago.'

'No! Where?'

'Less than a mile away.'

'Are you in England, Charlie?'

'Of course I am. Back at Lympne.'

I could almost hear her thinking. She was suddenly my favourite old girlfriend again, but that was for the benefit of whoever else might be hearing the conversation.

'Charlie, why didn't you say so? We've so much to talk about. Can I ring you tonight when I'm off duty?' I gave her the office number, but told her it was my digs – you can't be too careful.

'I'll be there at about seven, OK?'

I sat in Elaine's office and waited for Dolly's call. The office cooled quickly after dark, and I pulled her small new electric heater close to me. The call from Dolly never came because she did instead. I heard a car nosing down from the Lympne Road and went out to the office door to watch. One of Dolly's big brown staff cars rolled to a stop under the light above the door. Her face looking at me through the windscreen was pale and expressionless. I realized immediately that all the rehearsal in my mind was going to come to nothing: this was going to be a difficult interview. Dolly followed me into the office, and hung her big leather coat on the coat stand. She looked tired but didn't thank me for saying it.

'You look fagged out.'

'Thank you; a girl always likes to be told when she's not at her best.' See what I mean?

'A cup of tea?'

'Do you have any scotch?'

'Yes; I have a bottle of scotch.'

'What are you waiting for then?' Then she saw the notice on the outside of my own office door, and gave a mirthless little laugh. 'I don't think you told me you were actually running this outfit.'

'It probably didn't come up.'

I poured us each a couple of fingers of scotch and raised my glass to her. She made no effort to meet me halfway. I said, 'Chin chin.'

She just nodded. Then she said, 'Begin at the beginning. Pretend I'm a copper you've just met . . .'

So I told her the lot, including my part in smuggling them into Lympne in the first instance, and waited for the jangle of handcuff keys. Eventually she leaned on the visitor's side of Elaine's desk, made a steeple of her hands, and rested her chin on them. Piers, our old boss, used to do that. Maybe she'd caught it from him. She said, 'When you found out that those two Stern Gang members had killed Gus in Berlin you realized that they were probably the same two refugees you'd smuggled into England soon afterwards.'

'Yes, it suddenly added up . . . but when we flew them we didn't know they'd done anything wrong. They were just two lost Jews heading for the Holy Land.'

'You might have told me . . .'

'I thought about it. I decided not to tell you.'

'Why?'

'Does that matter?'

'I suppose not. Damn you, Charlie!' She thought for a little and added, 'Then you saw them again, at an arms fair buying Spitfires, and you informed some friend in the Customs.'

'He isn't a friend . . . just someone I've met through my job. I thought that was a way of getting something done about them without having to confess to you like this: I didn't want you involved. I didn't see that it would do any good.'

'But now they're back?'

'One is, at least. Trying to work out how to steal his Spits back no doubt.'

'You realize that we'll both be lucky to get away without being arrested?'

'I've thought about that . . . I suppose that sex is out of the question?'

She threw Elaine's heavy glass inkwell at me.

'I'll take that as a *No*, then.'

I can't remember which of us began to laugh first . . . then she said she'd have a cup of tea after all, if I knew how to make it. She had some telephone calls to make. She used the switches on Elaine's telephone to put the line through to my office, and went into it to talk to someone – shutting the door firmly behind her. I don't think that she was all that pleased with me.

When she reappeared she still looked tired, but the tension had seeped away. She reached for the mug of tea, which was still warm, and said, 'Thanks, love', as she slumped into the chair opposite me. *Love.*

'OK.'

'Do you know that you're a jammy little bugger, Charlie Bassett?'

'We're all right then?'

'That's right, Charlie. I keep forgetting not to underestimate you.'

'What did they say?'

'Who?'

'The people you telephoned . . .'

'Oh them? . . . Very pleased, surprisingly. They'll ask Special Branch to deal with it I suppose; the bottom line is that they're glad to get another chance at those two, and they won't press me on where the information came from. You're in the clear.'

'What about you?'

'Me too.'

'But you won't get your old job back?'

'It was never mine in the first place. I was just keeping the chair warm.'

'But you were booted back to the Transport Section because you failed them in Berlin.'

'No, Charlie. I was booted downstairs for being the wrong shape.'

'Sorry, I don't understand.'

'A *man* wanted the job, that's all. My mother told me that exactly the same thing happened after the First War: our *land fit for heroes* is actually a land fit for *male* heroes: the girls don't actually get all that much of a look in. It doesn't matter if a woman has a brain the size of a battleship – if she doesn't have the dangly bit, a man is always going to get a job over her.' *The dangly bit.* Dolly was herself again.

We slept in adjacent beds in the hut and didn't touch each

other all night: it wasn't the first time that we'd done that either. She woke me at about six, even though she dressed quietly – I moved my head just as she bent down to kiss me so she got me on the nose, and giggled.

'Goodbye, Charlie.'

'Goodbye, Dolly. See you soon?'

' 'spect so.' And then she was gone. Minutes later I heard her car fire up. I lay on my back, and studied the rust marks around the bolts through white-painted corrugated iron sheets above my head while around me England woke up. Better late than never.

Elaine arrived at half past eight dragging Spartacus behind her on a piece of rope. They didn't look as if they were enjoying each other's company

'Don't sulk, Elaine.'

'Maybe I won't, if you put the kettle on.'

On my last night in Blighty I lay on my back in the dark, and thought about women. I was getting it all wrong, wasn't I? If Maggs was right maybe I didn't try hard enough. I thought about Eve Valentine, Dolly and Elaine in England, and Marthe and Frieda back in Germany. Smashing people, but stepping stones to nowhere. The truth was that I'd been useless with women ever since I'd failed to pin Grace down in 1944 – and it was time I grew up, wasn't it? I mentally crossed off the ones who had probably had enough of me. That left Dolly and Frieda as current possibles. I didn't mean anything to Frieda, I thought – no one did. No future there, I was pretty sure of that. Which left Dolly . . . maybe I should try to sign her up before someone else did. I was already packed, even though I would have bags of time before *Scarecrow* took off for Germany the next day: I've told you – that's a habit of mine. I think that the RAF taught me it, but it could always have been the Boy Scouts. You know: *Be prepared*.

The temperature in the hut dropped sharply; maybe Marty was

coming back for another visit – Spartacus, lying across my feet, growled at something I couldn't see. I'd lifted the bedclothes from the bed Dolly had occupied, and piled them over my own – they smelled faintly of her perfume. I self-consciously muttered, 'Go away, Marty. I'm going back to Germany tomorrow, and need to get some sleep.' Then I turned over and closed my eyes.

Chapter Twenty-four

Told you before: God sends me these little messages, but I never work out what they mean in time. The auguries for me in Germany were never much good from the start. The *Scarecrow* was shitty about the start-up of one of her serviced engines which, when it fired up, eventually blew out a plume of black smoke before it settled down. The engineer's dials said that everything was OK, but you should never completely rely on what an aircraft is telling you. Even less on engineers: they are the world's last optimists. This engineer, Giz, had a three-way confab with Chiefy and Hardisty, and eventually they decided to go. Giz had had a French father somewhere down the line and had been named Giscard: I only ever heard him called *Giz* or *Gizzy*, the same as everyone else. He was tall, slow-speaking, deceptively well read and reliable. He always wore an immaculately clean pair of white overalls: to be honest, that sometimes irritated me a bit . . . for an outfit at our end of the market it was a trifle dandyish.

The engine had another strop half an hour before we raised Frankfurt, so we arrived with a feathered propeller freewheeling in the stream. It wasn't that bad; Lancastrians could always fly on three engines, it's just that you'd rather not.

We had to go into the circuit and hold for an American Skymaster that was coming in from somewhere far away. I was up in the office behind Hardisty and Giz, and watched its approach

low over the miles of dense black pine: it occurred to me that I'd
been watching bloody aeroplanes for half my adult life. It looked
OK to me, but then about a mile from the Frankfurt field it began
to slow-roll. You don't slow-roll a four-engined job that close to
the ground when you're getting the air speed off her. The only
thing I could think was that something had gone terminally wrong
with the pilot. When she went through ninety degrees of roll we
all began to talk at once.

'What in hell's name is . . . ?' Hardisty.

'What the?' from Giz, and just,

'No,' from me.

Spartacus whined: he must have known what would happen
next.

When they hit the tarmac just inside the airfield they were
fully inverted. There was an immediate huge detonation: the sort
that no one walks away from. I saw a main wheel flung high
into the air, and could momentarily see the shock wave from the
blast. Hardisty was wrestling with *Scarecrow*, which was thrown
up and sideways by it. Giz held on to the combing below the
cockpit glaze to steady himself. He said, 'Whoa!' Then, 'They
must have been ferrying munitions.'

Behind me I could hear our radio op talking to the Control.
They told us to stay in the circuit. When we told them that our
fuel situation was iffy, and we were down to three engines
anyway, the Controller diverted us to an emergency field at
Nierstein, about ten miles away. There they had Hardisty taxi
Scarecrow into a dispersal area and immediately had a group of GIs
come up and throw a camouflage net over her. Once I was on
terra firma I looked around and noticed that she wasn't the only
camouflaged hump on the ground, there were lots of them –
although most of them were smaller . . . probably fighters. I
suppose that if you are trying to pretend that something is not an
airfield a fat red monstrosity like *Scarecrow* sitting in the middle of

it would have been a bit of a giveaway . . . not that the troublesome port outer's casing was red any longer anyway: it was glistening black with oil which had also streaked back across the wing . . . and made a nice shiny puddle on the concrete underneath.

'Oil seal,' Giz told us. 'I've seen that before. We'll have to have the bugger out again.'

'How long?' I hated sounding like a manager, but it was my job.

'Two days, boss, if I can get replacement gaskets. You can have her back on Tuesday.'

Even though we had messed up their airfield the Yanks were very hospitable: they always are. They arranged transport for us back into the city centre and the army of occupation administration buildings. We left Giz behind organizing a makeshift ground crew to work on an unfamiliar airframe . . . bloody funny folk these engineers: he was in his element, and grinning from ear to ear. Hardisty and Spartacus made for an SAC club.

I paid off the cab outside the club in Kaiserstrasse. Even although it was only late afternoon there was a party going on, and a bouncer on the door. He was about eleven feet high and broad and had polished dark brown skin. It looked like the brown Americans had graduated from carrying boxes since my last visit. The hand he placed against my chest was bigger than my head – and he had to bend forward slightly to do it.

'Private party, son.' I've already told you about people calling me *son*.

'Is Tommo around?'

'Never heard of him. Who's asking?'

'Charlie Bassett.'

'What we do have, Charlie Bassett, is a book with the names of acceptable people in it. Excuse me for turning my back to consult.' It wouldn't have mattered anyway: his back was as large as his front, and I couldn't have wriggled around him. When he turned back he was less hostile, 'I think you'd better go through to the office, Mr Bassett; you know the way?'

They were having what I thought of as an American party. What happens at an American party is that the booze doesn't stop coming, the music is loud, and the dames don't keep their clothes on. They had redecorated the place, and had papered the walls with Allied newspapers from the last six years. I stopped to read a page from the *Daily Mail* from a couple of months after D-Day. *7 Shillings for a Loaf of Bread in Brussels* one headline shouted; *'Witch' Trial of Widow, Aged 70* said another. The paper was already yellowing, and I could smell cigar smoke from it. I glanced back at the bouncer. He was still watching me, and waved me on. I nodded. I could smell sweat and make-up from the dancing girls I had to push between. The brassy jazz music to which they moved clapped at my ears like thunder. What Dolly would have called their *jiggly bits* jiggled, and they were pretty, but somehow the whole thing was sad. Someone explained to me once that the audience at a striptease was more degraded by the performance than the performer. I was beginning to get that.

I remembered the office door as being around the end of the bar and through a bead curtain into a small corridor. There was another big fellow behind the curtain. He was in a civvy suit, but wore a Luger pistol in a grey canvas holster openly at his waist. He patted me down as I passed him, and relieved me of my little piece.

'You get it back if you come out again, bud. OK?'

I shrugged, although the word *if* had not escaped my attention.

The inside of Tommo's office was dangerous to your health, heavy with yellow-grey tobacco smoke. The aroma was wonderful, but it stripped the lining of your lungs inside of five minutes. The small room was crowded because Tommo and three other guys sat around his desk playing poker. Each had a personal cheer leader behind him, and most of the cheer leaders were missing a bizarre variety of items of clothing. The chips these people were playing for were cut precious stones – I couldn't believe the size of some of the gems. Tommo was wearing a croupier's eyeshade, and one of his fat black cigars. He looked up as I was let in, grinned . . . and folded the hand he was holding.

'Hi ya, Charlie. When d'yer get in?'

Before I could answer an older sergeant opposite growled at the girl behind Tommo, 'Let's see yer legs, honey . . . get 'em off.'

'Chip an' strip poker,' Tommo explained to me. 'Ya lose twice when ya lose: you lose the stake, an' someone tells ya girl to get her clothes off.'

'So the girls lose as well?'

'Don't get picky with me, Charlie; I told you before not to get picky.'

The other two guys in the game were also sergeants. They had a small fortune in stones in front of them, and didn't look best pleased to see a stranger in the camp. They probably didn't like picky people either.

'This is Charlie,' Tommo told them. 'He's English, an' he's been my partner since I was in England in '44.'

That seemed to do the trick. The players relaxed, and even the girls looked at me in a different way I thought. One of the sergeants asked, 'Fancy a hand or two, Limey?'

I laughed and shook my head. What I meant is *I'm not that stupid*. What I said was, 'I'm unlucky with cards. Besides, I don't have a woman.'

'We'll sell you one,' one of them offered.

They would have too. I shook my head again, and said to Tommo, 'I can see you after the game if you like. Mind if I sit outside and read the papers while I wait?'

The party outside was beginning to bop. The men, a mixture

of rank, nationality and service I couldn't put a name to, had imbibed enough to overcome their inhibitions. Many of them were dancing with a mostly naked woman in their arms, driven around the small dance floor by the noisy jazz combo blowing out a storm. They didn't seem to mind bumping up against other couples. Nor would I.

There was a scantily dressed brown girl on a bar stool not five feet from me. She wasn't wearing much other than an expensive smell, and was smoking a long untipped American cigarette in a tortoiseshell cigarette holder. She was pretty, but snooty-looking, and looked as much out of place as me. She asked me, 'Want to dance?'

'No thanks.'

'Want to do anything else?'

'No thanks, but I appreciate the offer. I'm Charlie, by the way. I'll buy you a drink if you like.'

The barman must have been able to lip-read: he was over with a bottle of pretendy champagne. She waved that away. 'Scotch,' she told him, and then asked me, 'That all right by you?'

We drank scotch. A quick one each, followed by a slow one. It was the real thing. She said, 'Don't mind me asking, but why did you say *No?* I don't make those offers every day.' Then she laughed, and added, 'Shit, that's a lie. Of course I do . . . you catch something?'

'No, nothing like that. I've just never been with a black woman before . . .'

'*Ah.* I see . . . you're one of those.'

'One of what?'

'You have prejudice, don't you?'

Laughing was probably the wrong thing to do. I did it anyway, and used the words I'd said a few seconds earlier.

'No, nothing like that. I'll just keep you for later. You're a pleasure I'm holding back for another few years. Cheers.'

She took minutes to digest that, and spent it sipping whisky. Then she said, 'What if you get *yours* just this very minute? *Blam!* Just like that? You step out of the club, a truck gets you and you're absolutely dead. What then?'

'Then I go to my maker with the knowledge that I stayed true to my principles until the very end. What's your name?'

'Lucy. I'm a nurse with a black outfit. I don't know why I started doing this.'

'So you could meet nice people like me, and make money.'

She laughed this time. She sounded as if she meant it.

'I'll never understand you English.'

I stretched over and touched her shoulder just to see what she felt like. She felt smooth and dry and cool. I waved the waiter for another couple of drinks.

'You should put some clothes on,' I told her. 'Winter's here: you'll catch your death.'

Tommo had the strangest house I'd ever seen. He lived in a couple of railway carriages on rails in a forest clearing. It took us an hour to get out to them. His girl slept in the back seat of his Horch limousine for most of the journey.

'Private train to a general in da war,' he told me. 'Makes a nice home.'

'Unusual anyway.'

'Stay here while I make us safe won't ya.' Then he looked at the girl and said, 'You too. Don't move.' She yawned and smiled and nodded. I don't want to be cruel – because she was an exquisitely beautiful, nice-natured girl – but I was beginning to suspect that we'd almost reached the limit of her vocabulary. Tommo was halfway across the clearing, in the car's headlights, before a large black bear hurled itself out of the forest and attacked him – rearing up on its hind legs. That's what it looked like anyway. I grabbed for the door handle but the girl pulled me back.

It was actually a huge shaggy German shepherd dog that was happy to see him. When it stood up it could place its forepaws on his shoulders. I thought that Tommo was going to put his head in its mouth, like lion tamers do. The dog seemed to think that Tommo's face needed a lot of licking. He chained the animal up to a boxlike kennel by a carriage, and then beckoned us over. The dog had orange eyes and looked at me as if I was supper. Tommo bent below the carriage and came out with the end of a stout electrical cable with a bayonet junction. 'I got eight Kraut Teller mines under these babies, an' a pressure pad under my big chair. Anyone who breaks in an' sits down uninvited goes into orbit: one-way trip.'

'But they're *safe* for now?' I asked him.

'You wanna live for ever, Charlie?' He'd asked me that before, hadn't he? The woman obviously knew her way around, because as soon as we climbed up into the carriages she started to fire up a large wood stove: I hoped it wasn't above the mines. Tommo opened a couple of bottles of wine, and she produced some shaped pieces of toasted bread topped off with smoked cheese and a fishy paste. They were like an old married couple. She kissed him on the forehead before she left us, and gravely wished me *a peaceful night* in laboured English. Tommo asked, 'Fancy a game of chess before we turn in?' He never failed to surprise me.

'If we can keep our clothes on.'

He won. I think he cheated.

The second carriage had been split into two bedrooms with a bathroom between them, so I suppose that I slept about thirty feet away from them. I could still hear them through the two walls between us; maybe they were actually more like a *newly* married couple. The dog heard them too and set up a mournful howl. I pulled the pillows over my ears and went to sleep.

In the morning the early sunshine didn't lift the frost from the grass. The floor of the clearing was like a multi-faceted mirror.

Tommo never did breakfast at home; we sat at a rustic table twelve feet from the carriages and drank terrific coffee. I asked him, 'Was I sleeping over one of those . . . what did you call them? . . . *Teller* mines last night?'

He laughed. I always liked the sound of Tommo laughing. It made you feel as if someone was actually in charge of the world.

'Two actually. Freak ya?'

'I don't know. How much is it in explosive terms?'

'Each one would do the same as a 250lb bomb. Y'd never feel a thing.'

'Why are they there?'

'I got some stuff stashed here that shouldn't fall into other hands. Know what I mean?'

'No. Just tell your dog to stop looking at me like that.' It hadn't taken its eyes off me since we'd reappeared. It lay with its head on the ground between its paws and watched my every move. 'What do you call it?'

'Magda, after that Goebbels woman who poisoned all her kids – Magda's got a bad attitude.' We didn't say we knew a Magda in Berlin.

'Like your snake.'

'Alice: yeah. I'm gonna take Alice back to the States with me.'

'When will that be?'

'Next month; month after maybe . . . that's what I wanna talk to you about.'

I gave an exaggerated sigh but we were both still smiling.

'OK, Tommo. What do you want me to do now?' It was good to be back.

What he wanted me to do was take a bag of diamonds back to Berlin for him. It was an old sugar sack: he said it only weighed a quarter of a kilo – say ten ounces – and, naturally, he'd prefer it if I told no one else about it. When I asked him why he could bear to have it out of his sight for a minute, he told me it was something to do with not putting all of his eggs in one basket. That reminded me that I had been with him when he closed a black market deal for fresh eggs. A year later he was doing diamonds. People move on I guess.

That was what we talked about on the way to the Urdenvald, which was another hour away. I already told you I had a house there that I'd never seen, and Tommo had been rather insistent of late that I inspect my German responsibilities.

I liked the country I saw when we turned off the main road and onto a straight narrow way lined by pines. After half a mile we met a couple of iron gates with a couple of white-tops behind them. The MPs seemed to know Tommo – I shouldn't have been surprised by that by now – and opened up for us. There was a gingerbread house just the other side. It was a nice house, but Tommo didn't stop to let me see it.

'Why can't I stop and see my house, Tommo? Isn't this why we came here?'

'It's the gatehouse, dummy.'

'But it's mine?'

''course it is. Ev'rythin' you seen since we left the main road is yours.'

'Even that?' A big block loomed on our right.

'That's the *stables*, Charlie.' He sounded a bit tired of me. 'You gotta start thinkin' big.'

'How big?'

We drove out of the end of the straight avenue of trees and I saw a mad red-brick castle in front of us. It was as big as St Pancras station, and could have suffered from the same bloody architect.

'That big,' Tommo said.

My brain told me that I was having a heart attack. I said, 'Stop the car.'

'Why?'

'Stop the car: you'll see.'

He stopped the car, and I got out and threw up on the verge. You'll laugh at this, because you've probably dreamed of winning the Pools all your life, but what I could see scared the living daylights out of me. When I got back in the car I whispered, 'Stop messing around, Tommo. Turn the car round. This can't be mine.'

' 'course it is. Relax: you'll get used to it. I got three like this. Quarter a Germany belongs to the Yanks these days.'

'Please can we turn round, and go back?'

'Nope. A bunch of folk over there has turned up to see you. You can't disappoint them now.' *There* was a small mixed group, including a couple of kids, waiting by a detached coach block. Tommo knew what I was going to ask when I nodded at it. He beat me to the draw – 'Yep, that's yourn too.' He looked supremely pleased with himself, and lit one of his cigars. 'Come and meet your subjects.'

He meant my tenants.

His laugh at me was almost a giggle; as if he had played a silly joke.

'Do you think they saw me being sick?'

'Don't matter. You're in charge: sooner they get used to yo' mucky little ways the better.'

Tommo's German was suddenly astonishingly good, because I'd never seen him as a linguist before. The local pastor had come to act as intermediary between me and my people, and was pleased he didn't have to. After an initial bit of awkwardness I squatted down to shake hands with a couple of kids: one of each. The little boy asked me a question, and I didn't get it the first time round, because he mumbled. A man went red in the face and stepped forward, but the pastor pulled him back. I explained to the children that I was still learning to speak German, and asked the boy to repeat his question slowly. His hands were shaking, so I held one of them. He said, 'May we stay on our farm? Please.' *Bitte*.

Pin-drop time.

'Of course you can. Why would you want to leave?'

'We do not want to go. My Mama and Poppa think you might want it for yourself.'

I shook my head. 'You must all stay. I need children I can trust to live here.'

There was just a slight pause before he made his response. His chin came up. '*Sie können uns vertrauen.*' You can trust us.

'I know I can. You and your family can live there for ever if you want.' He threw himself forward and hugged me; I hope that he didn't notice the residual odour of vomit. When I stood up everyone was smiling, and wanted to shake my hand. Fergal had a phrase for moments like that: he used to say, *God Bless Ireland!*

I had to visit two farms and admire their livestock and fields. I had no idea what I was looking at. We were given a tour of my ersatz castle by a chatty Administration lieutenant with a stores branch somewhere – his two star general, who was the temporary resident, was temporarily back in the USA so everyone was relaxed and stood down. He explained that it had once been a hunting lodge enlarged by some important Nazi. Moving rapidly from room to room of my German residence took me more than an hour . . . I couldn't wait to bring my dad over and show him. We stopped at the gatehouse, where an old lady too frail to move far hugged me and told me the estate now had the master it had waited for. They were good people: there wasn't a Nazi among them of course. I had to keep reminding myself of that.

I drove us back to Frankfurt because Tommo had drunk too liberally at each of our stops: as soon as they learned that their current rent arrangement was to be continued indefinitely, and that I was prepared to give them squatters' rights, a bottle came out. For some reason they seemed to like us.

'What *are* their current rents?' I asked Tommo in the car afterwards.

'Zilch. Nozz-ing. They don' pay. The rent you get for the big house more than makes up for it, and the service wants that until 1960 they say . . . you bought yerself a money tree. The Army'll pressurize you to sell: make sure you say *No*.'

'I don't know what to say, Tommo. I'm a bit overwhelmed.'

'Say *Bravo*, Charlie.'

I said, '*Bravo*,' and Tommo tossed the end of his cigar out of the window, closed his eyes and went to sleep.

Spartacus was so pleased to see me that he pissed himself. I'll bet you've never had that effect on animals. Luckily I'd met Hardisty outside at a coffee kiosk at the railway station, which was less ruined, I guessed, than when the Allies arrived. I couldn't believe that we'd left it standing. Spartacus's corrosive-smelling urine ran across the cracked cobbles and into the gutter. A plain woman in her forties, wearing a fine fur coat, stepped delicately over it. To hang on to a coat like that she must have been an officer's lady: an American officer's lady I mean. She smiled at us, and I smiled back. It seemed like a civilized thing to do.

'Is the *Scarecrow* feeling any better?' I asked him.

'No: we can't get the gaskets. Avro's are flying some out to us today with some spares for the Flight Refuelling people. They won't get down here until Wednesday or Thursday.'

'Bollocks!'

'Giz did his best.'

'I know. It's still bollocks.'

'I got you on a flight to Tempelhof this afternoon. That was the best I could do.'

'What will you do?'

'Wait for *Scarecrow* with Gizzy. Someone will have to fly her out.'

'What about the cargo she was supposed to be hauling?'

'Borland has switched the others around. They're being over-flown, but he says he's coping. You can see for yourself tonight.'

My people seemed to be managing OK in my absence. It's the sort of thing that can make you feel unappreciated.

'OK. What time am I out of here?'

'14.00 local. We could run over there now, and catch a free lunch.' He held up his hand without looking, and a taxi from the station cab stand sidled over. You've got to hand it to the Americans: whenever they move into an area the first thing that happens is the sanitation systems start working again, and then, miraculously, there are cabs everywhere.

We shared a table with a couple of Yankee air accident investigators who had come in for the C-54. They sat at a big table and it was noticeable that none of the regular aircrew would sit with them: they would rather double up on crowded tables or miss lunch altogether.

'They think we bring them bad luck,' the older of the two told me. He was soft-spoken, wore thick-rimmed spectacles and was losing his fair hair: tough for a thirty-year-old.

I asked him, 'Do you know what happened yet?'

'Officially no. There's a lot of sifting to be done. Unofficially, the last two we looked at crashed because the pilots went to sleep. People are getting tired. They fly straight into the ground.'

'So what do your reports say?'

The other one was small and dark, maybe my age. Even although he was close-shaved his chin was dark. He spat out, 'Pilot error. What else?'

Hardisty pushed a hamburger around his plate, suddenly not hungry I guess.

'Why don't you point out that the schedules they're flying are pushing them into the errors that are killing them?'

'Blame the colonels who sign the orders? Nope, son; not our business. They can work that out for themselves if they care.' It was the way things were then; nobody would put up with it today. An hour later I walked out onto the tarmac for a reunion with an old friend. *Camel Caravan to Berlin* stood there with her inadequate-looking props just turning over. She still looked brand-new. Inside she still smelt it.

Things must have hardened up in the week I was away, because when we were in the corridor to Tempelhof I counted three patrolling pairs of Russian fighters prowling along the boundaries. It wasn't going to make what I planned to do any easier. *Camel* felt good: when an aircraft is new it feels tight – nothing rattles. You felt that she wouldn't think twice about doing anything her pilot asked of her. Unless he fell asleep that is. Spartacus slept the whole trip: he had no such worries.

Bozey drove up to the *Camel* to meet me in a jeep. It was khaki, but had old RAF serials.

'We have a jeep?' I asked him as I flung my kitbag in the back and climbed in.

'I won it in a card game. It's good for moving around off-station. Better than your Merc.'

'How's that?'

'Anyone in a jeep is one of the gallant Allies these days: feeding a beleaguered city. They leave us alone. Anyone in a private car is either a rich hoarder or a racketeer: sometimes they throw stones at you. The back window of your Merc is cracked.'

'Doesn't take long for things to change, does it? There were Red fighters all over the corridor.'

'It's not as bad in ours. The Russians seem to have taken a very personal dislike to Uncle Sam. They're giving him a very hard time.'

'Stands to reason, doesn't it? Although they put up a good scrap at Stalingrad, and smashed the Wehrmacht to smithereens in the East, the truth is that without American weapons and supplies the Russians couldn't have fought off the Jerry for another five minutes. America saved Russia, so naturally the Russians hate the Americans.'

'I'm not sure that I understand that, boss.'

'Mr Truman does. That's the important thing.'

The flying and maintenance schedules on our office walls at Gatow were now on blackboards freshly painted up with aircraft, crews, destinations and cargoes. I made a decision: it was time that Bozey's administration skills were recognized, but I wouldn't tell him yet. I asked, 'Is any other private airline allowed its own office around here?'

'Shouldn't think so, boss; the military is really pushed for space – and the other airlines are bloody awful with the cards, the lot of them, they couldn't win at snap.'

'What do you play?'

'*Anything*. Bridge, chaser . . . poker of course. If you can bet on it I can play it.'

'I never played poker.'

'Technically it's a bit tedious, but the tension really gets at you.'

'What else have you won?'

'A nice girly with nice pins with an even nicer little flat in the Charlottenburg. I don't really think I ever want to go home again.'

'I think I understand you, but I don't understand why. How can a city as shitty as this one grab you the way it always does? I look forward to coming back here for God's sake.'

'*For God's sake* is probably the reason in your case, boss. Your Irish priest has called asking for you a couple of times.'

Bugger it! I'd forgotten him again. I'd forgotten Him as well.

It was OK. Fergal had called to say *Thank you*. He had flour, milk powder and sugar enough for a couple of months, and a mysterious Australian dropped by every week to top up their paraffin storage tank. He said that he believed in miracles. I told him, 'It's not me, you know. Old Man Halton must have arranged it.'

'He arranged it *because* of you. God is very pleased with you, Charlie: he told me so last night . . . you must be part of His great plan.'

'Tell Him I'm pleased He's pleased.'

'Why don't you do it yourself, Charlie? All you have to do is get down on your knees.' When I didn't respond to that he asked me, 'When are you coming round to meet my children?'

'In a few days, Fergal: after I have a few things sorted out. OK?'

'No trouble. They'll sing some songs for you, and break your heart.'

That reminded me of something. 'I saw Marty the other day.'

'Where?'

'He was standing at the end of my bed and shouting at me, but I couldn't hear what he was saying. He had blood on his head.'

'That would be right. He was in a hard landing on the training squadron and the aircraft stopped before he did. He went out through the Perspex and broke his neck. Did he look troubled?'

'No he was grinning all over his ugly mug.'

'That's all right then.'

'No it isn't, Fergal: I still don't know what he wanted.'

'You'll find out, Charlie, won't you? All in good time.' Why do we say *good* time, when nearly everything about it is bad?

Spartacus was on that pair of old ovies that Borland had left for him. He had rolled over on his back, exposed himself the way dogs do, and gone to sleep. He farted when I replaced the telephone receiver. Dogs do that sort of thing as well. I hadn't the heart to shift him, so I left him with Bozey when I went out. My new head of station didn't look exactly ecstatic about that.

The barman at the Klapperschlange was polishing glasses. Alice lifted her head an inch and had a little squint at me. There was already another small cloth bag inside her box. It was smeared with what looked suspiciously like rattlesnake shit. I told the man that Tommo had asked me to deposit his sugar bag in the Bank of Alice. I didn't say anything about diamonds.

'What's in it?'

'Some kind of chemical that keeps her calm,' I lied to him. 'She needs a lot of it at this time of year.'

He opened the lid of her clear box and I carefully dropped the bag in. Not carefully enough, actually. I dropped it on her rattle. Alice struck savagely. I hadn't realized that she could strike almost vertically: she came up at me like a V-2. Her pink gaping mouth must have come a clear nine inches out of the box before she dropped back. Then she went into a tight coil around the new bag, and rattled her bony tail like an epileptic mambo band. I was just quick enough: I reckon she got within an inch of me.

'Cow! I thought she liked me,' I complained to the barkeep, as we dropped the lid back on.

'I think she does: it's just the way she shows her affection.'

He didn't know the half of it. In that micro-second of blurred action I had seen the drops of venom flicking away from her fangs. She'd bloody tried to kill me. Maybe she was going stir-crazy after all these years: the sooner she was back on a hillside in the States the better. When I looked at her kill markings on the box I realized that there was a new little matchstick man since my last visit.

'Who got unlucky?'

'The Kraut.' The Kraut was the bouncer who used to stand

behind the curtain. He was from Southside New York, but had a German name. 'He said your bag of chemicals in there with Alice must be valuable, so he tried to get it out when she was sleeping. She got him on the cheek – right through to the eye socket. Both his eyes swelled up like baseballs, and bled before he died. You shoulda heard him scream.'

'Bloody Alice. We should have got rid of her years ago.'

'Who'd take her, bud? Anyway . . . I kinda like her.'

After a pause I said, 'I probably like her too; when she's not biting people.'

'You wanna drink?'

'Please?'

'Bourbon?'

'That would do: thanks.'

He gave me three fingers of bourbon in a heavy glass and said, 'I got the key to the boss's office behind the bar. He said to tell you to use it whenever you wanted.'

'Thank you.'

'Don't thank me, thank Tommo. Us poor mortals jest do as we're told.'

I looked at Alice. Her head was resting back on her coils; her black tongue flickered in and out. Then she did the trick again: she winked. Snakes aren't supposed to be able to wink. Whenever she winked it was just like Tommo was looking at you out of her eyes.

I went back out and got in our new jeep. It was untouched. Five months earlier if I'd left it unattended the vehicle wouldn't have been there when I returned. But Bozey had been right: now anything associable directly with the Airlift flyers was more or less immune. The Berliners realized that we were all that was going to stand between them and starvation, and they weren't going to bugger it up. I could live with that. When I drove up to what we were beginning to call Nobs Row the cops at the end of the road just leaned into the jeep, shone a torch in my eyes and then waved me on. As I climbed the steps to Halton's place the only thought I had in my head was, *Lord, I'm tired!* Fergal would have been pleased. I was talking to the Old Fellah at last, wasn't I?

The apartment was dark and cold: it didn't occur to me that there was anyone at home. Hanna greeted me with a homely peck on the cheek, gave me a candle and let me in to the Halton flat. She was wearing that vast grey greatcoat over her nightclothes, and had her hair tied up in a dozen bunches with bits of rag. She looked like the ogress from a Grimm's fairy story. I found my way to the room I had originally slept in, stripped off and lay down wrapped in one of those huge German eiderdowns that smell of scent and herbs. Five minutes later Frieda dragged it from me, and climbed on board like an Arab mounting a camel.

Chapter Twenty-five

'What are we going to do?' We were cuddled up in bed, swaddled in that eiderdown which had been useful after all. I could never cope with questions that imply joint responsibility with a woman for a shared future, even a future measured in hours or days. Play dumb; she may just mean breakfast.

'About what?' I replied.

'About finding out if any of my people are over on the other side.'

'You know that. My nice small Russian is going to help us. I'm going to be invited to a little party in Red Berlin, and you're going to come with me as my secretary. When I'm at the party you will be given a tour of the new East German People's archive: it contains the lists you wanted to see.'

'Not sure I like that, Charlie. We're almost at war with the Reds. The English newspapers are already calling it the Cold War. It feels just like that Phony War in 1940 to me.'

'Were you already in England by then?'

'No: that's when I reached there.'

Dunkirk? I wondered.

'A lot of people whose opinions I respect tell me it won't come to that this time: we're exhausted, and the Russians are exhausted. The Airlift is just like two bullies shouting at each other across the school playground, but never coming to blows.'

'You believe that, Charlie?'

'I *want* to believe it. If enough Reds want to believe it as well we could be all right.'

'How are you sure they'd let us back, if we crossed over there?'

'That Russian officer you went to see will stand our guarantee. I have to trust him.'

'But he doesn't like me.'

'He likes you well enough: he just didn't like you jerking him around, that's all.'

'I thought all you men liked a bit of jerkin' aroun'. ' She tended to drop the last letters of words in English when she was being funny.

'Stop it, Frieda. Now you're just being arch.'

'Oh. I can do that as well. I can do the *arch*.'

. . . and you can learn something new every day; because she showed me what the arch was . . . and I don't want you to think for a moment that she was a Freemason. When Frieda was in a bad mood she was impossible, but that wasn't the end of it, because when she was in a good mood she was *absolutely* bloody impossible.

There was damn all food in the place of course, so I took her to the Leihhaus. No reason to keep her away from it any more. The only two people in the joint were Marthe and Otto. They looked shagged out. I suppose that's not a bad way for a newly reunited married couple to look. Otto mopped with more authority: if anything his happy smile was happier. Marthe ruffled my hair when she brought us two large mugs of coffee and a couple of slices of rough bread with PX jam. Both the mugs had a USAF stamp on them.

'You doing all right, Charlie?'

'I'm doing all right, Marthe. How about you?'

'We're doing fine. We have food and work, and Lottie is at school. Otto found his mother and father yesterday: we didn't know whether to laugh or cry. Is this your German girl who Greg told us about?'

How did I answer that? 'Maybe: she's German, but she isn't mine. She's my employer's ward. That's what he told me anyway.'

Marthe suddenly launched into German that was so fast I couldn't follow it, except to know that it was about me. Frieda came back at her as fluently. They both laughed and giggled a lot . . . and five minutes later finished the conversation by shaking hands. I sipped my coffee.

After Marthe had left us I asked Frieda, 'What was all that about?'

'You. Couldn't you tell?'

'If that was secrets about me, what did *you* say?'

'I said *Thank you* to her, Charlie.'

'What for?'

'That was the secrets.'

Cow. When I put the mug down empty I asked her something that had been rattling around my brain for a week or more. I couldn't make my mind up. I grinned. She smiled. It was a good morning for truth and reconciliation.

'You *are* Halton's mistress, aren't you?' I tried to make it sound everyday and conversational. She looked down at the table, put down her coffee, looked up at me – the old eye lock – and replied, 'No, of course not.'

'Oh . . .' I had to think a while before I knew how to go on, '. . . but you're not his ward either, are you?'

'*Are you; aren't you?*' She waved the questions away, and then quietly said, 'No.'

'So?'

'I am just the social partner when he needs one, Charlie. I go to dinners and dances with him – the theatre sometimes. I jive and flirt with his business contacts . . . because his wife can't.'

'I didn't even know he was married.'

'No: it never comes up in the press – but his wife never goes out, and he needs to.'

'Why doesn't she go out?'

'Ask him yourself. My mother became their housekeeper in 1941: I was seventeen. It was a brave step then, taking two German refugees into your house.'

'Yes. It must have been. I . . .'

She held up a hand, palm facing me.

'No more questions today, Charlie.' She wore a sad smile, but it was still a smile.

'No more questions,' I agreed. 'You ask *me* some, and get your own back . . .'

Her eyes gleamed like Alice's, and like every other woman I've known, she went straight for the jugular.

'OK. You will have loved one woman in your life better than any other. Tell me about her now, Charlie. I want to know . . .'

I suppose I asked for that, didn't I? I was uncomfortable, but I told her about Grace and I told her about Dolly. Talking about Grace embarrassed me because she's always outplayed me. I was on surer ground with Dolly: she went out with visiting servicemen in need of partners so she and Frieda had something in common. I didn't tell her about the others, but she asked anyway.

'I don't talk about anyone else,' I told her.

'So they will be married women,' she smiled wickedly. 'Charlie takes his ease with married ladies because that way he doesn't have to take responsibility. I should have guessed.'

'I'm not saying any more; you'll only twist my words . . .'

She reached over and laid her hand on mine. 'I'm making fun

of you, Charlie. This is *Berlin*. A man can have sex with a different beautiful woman every day of the week just by handing over a bottle of milk. It means nothing.'

'It's easier than that, but no one seems to have noticed.'

'You mean?'

'These last few weeks it's easier to find a woman than a pint of milk. You live off Old Man Halton so you wouldn't notice: everyone else around you is beginning to starve.'

'You're making fun about me now?'

'No.' Suddenly I wanted to get out of there: do something. Anything. 'I think I'll go to work.' I didn't want to fall out with her again, so I picked up her hand and kissed the back of it when I stood up. 'Au revoir, chérie.'

'Will you be back tonight?'

'Maybe not. I ought to go to Lübeck and see how our people there are holding up. Don't worry: I'll keep in touch.'

I took the jeep and drove out to the cemetery and Ed's grave. He had a stout temporary wooden cross. It occurred to me that we'd better get him a proper stone fast: in a city running out of fuel his wooden marker wasn't going to last long. His details had been punched out on a strip of metal nailed to the cross arm. They read, *'An airman known only unto God as Crazy Eddy'*. It made me smile: Dave Scroton must have had the last say.

It was cold, although the morning frost on the grass had turned to moisture which seeped through my boots. I stood at Ed's feet, looked down and talked to him. Small still banks of vapour standing like sentries in the air almost made it seem private. I said, 'Sorry, Ed. Everyone seems to think the Lift is going OK, and that I'm doing all right . . . but I feel as if I've made a mess of things again: I don't know why.' I felt as if I was being watched, so I looked up and looked around. There was no one there; any patches of mist weren't thick enough to hide anyone. I went on,

'I don't think Old Man Halton really gives a toss about you, or even the Berliners; he's just raking money in . . . and whatever's going on between the nobs in Russia and the nobs in the West is not worth anyone dying for, but nobody seems to realize that . . . and my latest girlfriend is a cracker, but I don't think she thinks about anyone but herself.'

I paused there, because it was almost as if I could hear Ed's voice in my head asking, '*OK, Charlie. What about* you? *Who do you think about other than yourself?*' That was the sort of question that my mother could have asked, or Maggs, and I didn't have much of an answer.

Time to go. I whispered, 'I'll come back and visit you again, Ed. I'll find your name from that woman in London, and bring it back for you.'

I had that feeling again. That prickling of the hairs on my neck. So I looked up and found myself staring at Marty standing at the head of Ed's grave, six feet away. He mouthed some silent words, and then shook his head and smiled, as if he was amused. Then he held his right hand out, thumb up, and faded away. Just like that. I imagined him of course. It was suddenly chill. I shivered, turned, and walked back to the road and the jeep. Some ungrateful bastard had nicked the jerry can off the back: I'd have to tell Bozey about that.

Bozey told me that it was because Berlin's third stage of desperation had set in. In the first stage of desperation the Berliners stole just about anything from just about anyone. He said that there was some dispute about whether that was because of the war, or because that was what Berliners were like anyway. The second, short stage was when they started to run out of food and looked upon us as their only salvation . . . so they stopped stealing from us as a sort of quid pro quo: because they wanted to keep us flying. Everyone seemed to agree that the third stage had started yesterday, he told me. Once the Berliners realized that a total blockade was on they began to grab anything that wasn't nailed down. They wouldn't steal the jeep because they couldn't afford to run it, but they would drain it dry of petrol given half a chance. He opened a desk drawer and pulled out a petrol cap with a couple of keys on a key ring in the middle of it.

'What's that?'

'Locking cap for the petrol pipe. I got one for your Merc as well.'

I started with, 'Where . . . ?' and then asked, 'You won them in a game, didn't you?'

'Yes, boss; and a new tail wheel spare for one of the Oxfords. Randall will be very pleased.'

'Are you serious that things are getting worse?'

'Very. Did you hear about the Dak crash over in the American sector last night?'

'No. What happened?'

'Ploughed into the bottom of a block of flats in the suburbs. When the rescue teams got there the locals had stripped out the cargo already, and were busy cutting up and hauling away all the trees it had knocked down on the way in. They were stepping over the bodies of the crew where they'd fallen just as if they weren't there. Didn't give a damn.'

'Maybe they did give a damn, but had bigger things on their minds.' Oddly enough, as soon as I said that I began to think about Frieda, and wonder if I was too hard on her.

'I'm going to *choose* to believe they don't give a damn about us, boss.'

'Why, Bozey?'

'Because then when we walk away, and leave them to starve, I won't feel so bad about it.' That hadn't occurred to me either.

I hitched a lift on a beautiful silver Skyways Lancastrian. She can't have been far off brand new. The name on her schnozzle was *Sky Path*, and she bore the registration G-AHBU. Her crew called her *Abu*, as if she was a friendly Arab, and talked about her with immense pride. I liked that. She'd arrived with foodstuffs and was going back with a load of evacuees. Did the Reds know that we were secretly reducing West Berlin's population on the quiet and relieving the pressure on the Airlift? They flew with a pilot, a second, an engineer and a nav, and a W/Op like me. I spent the flight standing behind the pilot, exactly where I'd stood in our Lanc sometimes during the war. I liked that too. That was interesting.

Sky Path was directed to a remote hard standing on Lübeck Airfield where there was a motor coach waiting for the DPs. The poor buggers had just a cardboard suitcase each; the kids had school satchels. The sum of their worldly possessions.

The large red thing squatting on the dispersal next door was *Dorothy*. Her paint was already worn and peeling, showing aluminium skin beneath, and she leaned significantly to port because she had a flat main wheel tyre. In fact it was in shreds, so the wheel was probably buggered as well. *Bollocks*. I must have said it out loud, because the Skyways pilot looked back at me with pity, and asked, 'Yours, old boy?' He was a moustachioed Aussie, and the *old boy* was as close to an insult as he could get it. His second pilot smiled, and looked away.

'Yes; unfortunately. Sorry.'

'It's a heap of junk. Get rid of it.'

'Thanks. Why?'

'Tell yer later in the bar if yer like?'

'OK. If I see you.'

His name was Mickey and he was demob happy; so were his crew. Skyways generally flew out of Wunstorf. They were only at Lübeck for a crew change. By tomorrow they'd be strolling down Regent Street looking for a bar and some off-duty shop girls, at the beginning of a seven-day furlough.

I couldn't find any of my people, so it looked as if *Dorothy* was laid up again. A busy French Letter in Flying Control told me that the RAF was providing a new wheel and tyre for her, but they couldn't be fitted until the next day.

'What about my Dakota? It will be here in about three hours expecting to collect some cargo from the York: there won't be any.'

'Don't panic, old son, I've linked it up to a 47 Squadron Hastings. It can feed from that when they're synchronized. When they're not, it can just pick up from the coal yard. We've built up a pretty hefty stock now, and the DPs are bagging and loading it for us. OK?'

He was better at this game than I was. I said, 'Sorry, I was away for a week. Things change all the time over here.'

'Know what you mean, old son. Anything else I can do for you?'

'No. Thanks. I'll grab some char, and see if I can find my people.'

'I think they've gone off station: a crazy little American and an older guy with bad hands.'

It was an unmistakable description, wasn't it? They'd got themselves more organized at Lübeck. There were Messes for service personnel, and separate facilities for civvies like me. I found the Skyways people trying to start a party. I asked their skipper, 'What was the problem with the York you wanted to tell me about?'

'Design flaw. She's got a Lancaster's flying surfaces, right? Modified, but essentially the same wing and tail feathers as a Lanc.'

'Right.'

'Only they've moved the wing up to the top of the fuselage to accommodate passengers or cargo . . . it was never meant to be there. The Lanc, and my Lancastrian, is a mid-winged job, the way they were supposed to be. The York is a high-winged job.'

'OK, so?'

'Same wing but different C of Gs. That wing and spar were never intended to take the load a York puts on them at landing. Whenever a York full of cargo sits down too fast she tries to break her back. Go and look up the AIBs . . . there are Yorks in bits all over Germany. We got rid of ours. I should do the same if I was you, old fellow.'

The AIBs were the Accident Inspector's Bulletins. They usually hung on boards in the ready rooms or at briefing. What had the Old Man told me about *Dorothy* months ago? *She's proved to be a bit of a disaster*. You could say that again. Maybe Yorks were proving to be a bit of a disaster in the cargo role for everybody else as well.

'Thanks for the tip. I'll tell the boss.'

'I thought you *were* the boss.'

'I'm just the little boss. I meant the owner.'

'*Little* boss. I like that,' the Aussie said and slapped me on the back, spilling my beer. He must have been a foot taller than me, and his slap was like being charged by a rhino. Sometimes I like the Aussie sense of humour, and sometimes I don't.

He wasn't far wrong either. The number of landing accidents involving Yorks was becoming scandalous.

I found my crew in the U-Boat hotel. The little corporal was pleased to see me. He asked, 'Shall I put you in the same room, sir?' Then he saw my face and answered himself, 'No, I'm sure I can find you somewhere more convenient.' Somewhere without the shades of dead sailors sloshing about.

Ronson was sitting at the bar. Maybe this was my opportunity to tie off another little loose end. There was a man standing at the end of the bar in a sailor suit; that is he was in navy blues, wellingtons, an old white sloppy joe and a plain reefer jacket. His flat-top cap was tipped to the back of his head, and he stood with his back to us. I slipped into the seat beside Ronson and waved the bar boy to bring a drink over. It was the boy who'd called himself Reiny. He now had a Hitler moustache and floppy dark hair, which took a bit of nerve in 1948. The drink was that sharp cold beer you get in Northern Germany.

Ronson said, 'Don't mind him, boss. He does a dead Führer comedy act at the club next door.'

'Doesn't he upset people?'

'His problem. Do you want Max? He's gone for a little lie-down.'

'That's all right. I was going to fly back with you tonight, but now I'll have to stay. Can we talk about why the Cousins have a wanted notice out on you, and why everyone seems to know what it's about but me?'

'You can talk, boss. It may not be wise for me to.'

'Try.'

'Why haven't I been arrested already?'

'They're willing to leave you alone while you're flying Operation Plainfare. Once you stop they'll want to take you home.'

'. . . and into a loony bin I 'spect: never to be heard of again.'

'What for? What did you do?'

'You heard of flying saucers?'

We all had. The papers were full of them from time to time. The government said that they were no danger to anyone, and you've got to believe the government, haven't you?

'Did you make one?'

'Maybe I saw one once. Do you know what the Air National Guard is?'

'No.'

'It's like your Auxiliary RAF squadrons. Gentlemen flyers. The state provides their aircraft and a bunch of amateurs and reservists flies them around. It's a way of avoiding conscription, so the rich kids get to stay at home and go ter university, when everyone else is sent to dig latrines over here or in Japan. I was a ground-crew chief in Kentucky Air National Guard. I took care of Captain Mantell's aircraft.'

'Was there a problem with that?'

'There was after he flew it into a spaceship. You ever seen what a Mustang looks like when it's fallen in from twenty thou with bits coming off her?'

'You're losing me, Red. What spaceship?'

'One of those flying saucers. The National Guard was scrambled to intercept it over Godman Field in Kentucky.'

'There's no such thing as spaceships. Was it something the Russians sent over?'

'Not unless the Reds are flying things the size of aircraft-carriers which can also hover like a helicopter.'

'This Mantell intercepted a spaceship. That's what you're trying to say?'

'Mantell an' his flight. The other two dropped away because it was too high. Captain Mantell carried on.'

'. . . And he collided with it?'

'That's what I think.'

'That's amazing.'

'What's amazing, boss, is that it never happened after all. The top brass say that Captain Mantell made a mistake and was chasing the planet Venus when his P-51 broke up. People that agree with them get to go home; those that don't get the bin.'

'Then agree with them . . .'

'I can't, boss.'

'Why not?'

'Because I know what I heard. I was in the Tower listening out to the Captain. He *described* what he was going up against: it sure weren't no planet Venus. It was a huge silver metallic thing just sitting there. It didn't even bother to run away.'

'I don't know what to say, Red.'

'That's because you can't believe it either. I told you that.

Don't say nothin'. Maybe the row will all die down an' I can go home sometime. If people keep seeing these flying saucer things they'll have to let me go. They can't lock up half the US, can they?'

The sailor at the bar turned, and smiled a very drunken smile at us. He had a full black beard. He tried to lean an elbow on the bar, but missed, and slid along it a foot before he recovered. The black and gold cap tally bore the name of his ship. Ironically it was HMS *Venus*. Just one of God's little jokes I expect.

I took a bath: it was nice to be staying somewhere without water restrictions. As I lay there I listened out a couple of times but there was no *yo ho hoing* in the corridor outside. When I went back to the bar the English sailor was sitting on the floor propped up against it, snoring. The German barman stood up from his stool and found me a tall glass of beer. It was ice-cold. About the sailor he said, 'Nine of them here last night.'

'From the *Venus*?'

'Yes, she's in Kiel. They assure me she's a good ship.' He didn't smile but I was sure he was having me on.

'What are they doing down here?'

'Being victorious. It's what the winners usually do.'

I wanted to explore that further, but Ronson and Max walked in with a coloured radio man they introduced as Dreyfuss. That put four of us around the table. Ronson said, 'Max knows about Mantell. I told him.'

Dreyfuss looked mystified. He could bloody stay it.

'Change the subject,' I told them. 'I'll talk to someone about it, and try to sort something out. Where we gonna eat?'

We found a small place down in the docks. You've got to hand it to the Germans, they have almost as many recipes for cabbage as they had concentration camps – and that's a helluva a lot. This place had brown walls, a brown ceiling and served brown cabbage in a brown sauce which once may have been diarrhoea. It was vile. Max got into a cabbage-flicking match with a group of Icelandic whalers who threw us out. They were huge bearded men who smelt of fish oil. Red reckoned that if you set fire to one of them he'd burn like a candle until there was nothing left of him but ash. I thought about it, but they all looked too big to me. After that we went looking for a drinking place.

Back in the hotel I phoned Lympne from an old upright telephone on the reception desk. Elaine was still there.

'Is the Old Man in, love?'

There was a lot of interference on the line and I thought I heard *he's gone up in smoke*.

'Christ, not another! What happened to him?'

'What are you talking about, Charlie?'

'Another one up in smoke . . .'

'Get your ears syringed, dear. *Up the Smoke*, not up in smoke.' *Dear*.

'Oh . . .'

'Can I give him a message?'

'Tell him I found out what the problem was with that American engineer he took on.'

'Do we need to do anything about it?'

'I don't think anyone can. It's nuts. I'll tell him the next time I see him if I remember.'

'Two more pilots, an engineer and another nutty radio man will be out with you by Friday, and that's your lot! Bozey's dealing with them.' The line deteriorated further. I found that I was shouting, 'He's rather good, isn't he?'

'So am I.'

'I know. But do you mean anything else?'

'I'm pregnant, Charlie: I'm going to have a baby.' It must have been OK with her because she was laughing. It was as if she was brimming over with it. At that moment the line failed altogether.

So did my heart. For the second time in a year someone had said something on the telephone which had scared me half to death. Max was slouched in an old leather chair across the room. He must have seen something in my face because he asked, 'Boss?'

'Get Red and Dinsdale, or whatever he's called, down here now.'

'Dreyfuss. Why?'

'Yeah, that's him. We gotta go out again.'

'Why?'

'To get absolutely pissed; and don't ask me any more questions.'

His mouth opened again and made the shape for *Why*, but no sound came out. Max was learning. We went out and got very drunk, and I managed not to tell anyone.

I had another war dream that night. I wasn't in a burning Lancaster; it was worse than that. I was back in the Sergeants Mess at RAF Bawne sitting down to aircrew breakfast, and all the men tucking in around me were men I knew to be dead. There were even a few I hadn't known to be dead; until that moment of course.

In the morning Max and Red were both asleep in the downstairs bar. I didn't have to ask them why. Max woke up and yawned when I walked in. He said, 'The next time we're back in Lübeck, boss, we don't stay in this spooky dump. OK?'

'Fine, Max. How do you feel?'

'What you mean is *Can you fly this morning*? The answer is *Yes*, the sooner the bloody better. I want to ged outta here.'

'And Red?'

'Red's gotta new nail. He's as sharp as a new-minted dollar.'

'OK, Max, round them up. I'll get you breakfast on the way.'

The barman with the Hitler moustache and hairstyle was waiting for us outside. He was dressed in the Führer's brown jacket and grey trousers. His tongue was sticking out, and had gone as black as Alice's. That's because someone had hanged him from a lamp post with a piece of telephone wire. He rotated very slowly in the morning light, this way and that. His shadow danced gently on the pavement in front of us.

Red said, 'He doesn't look very well, does he?'

'His jokes can't have been much good.' That was Max.

Dreyfuss stifled a belch, 'I feel sick.'

'Save it till later, bud.' That was Max again. 'We still got some puke bags in *Dorothy*.'

Dreyfuss and I scrambled into the back of the Chevy wagon we'd borrowed. He *did* look a couple of shades paler, come to think about it. Max asked, 'Which way back to the airfield?' from behind the steering wheel, which was on the wrong side of course.

Ronson held up a magnificent rusty nail on a piece of string and spun it. 'That way,' he said, and belched. I could suddenly smell last night's thin beer from him, and felt a bit queasy myself.

Two days later I was back at Celle arguing a flight engineer I hardly knew out of a Military Police cell. He was one of ours, a fighter, and he'd broken an off-duty RAF copper's jaw in a fight at a shebeen near the wrecked railway marshalling yards. I went down to the cell to meet him before I spoke up for him. His bloodied and scabby face looked as if he had leaned too close to a propeller, and he was missing some front teeth. You can forget all the tales of archetypal scrappers you've read about who're supposed to come from Glasgow or Tiger Bay: they're pussy cats compared to the real thugs I've met. The really bad ones all come from nice little places like Selsden or Pollockshaws. This guy came from sweet suburban Barnes but the old healed scars on his face said he'd been fighting all his life.

'Hello . . . Bo . . . tth.' He smiled like he'd seen the light.

'Don't say any more; the rest of your teeth might fall out. Just nod or shake slowly. OK?'

He nodded.

'Was this your fault?'

He nodded again: but too vigorously.

'Shit. Will you behave yourself if I get you out?'

He shook his head.

'Can you fly?'

It was the nod again this time: equally vigorously, but holding up his left hand, two fingers of which were clearly broken.

'All right. I'll see what I can do.'

Out in the fresh air of the front desk again I asked the Station Officer, 'Why hasn't he received medical attention yet? His face is all smashed up and he's got broken fingers. What sort of show are you running here? . . .'s bloody disgraceful.'

'Sorry, Mr Bassett, but I can't get anyone to go into the cell with him. He's a fucking wild animal. We were rather hoping you'd take him away with you.'

Well, that hadn't been so difficult had it?

'What about the charges?'

'There won't be any. He'd only smash up the courtroom, wouldn't he? Just get him out of Germany, and don't bring him back.'

I went down to the cell with a pretty, plump nurse from the RMC. I got our man to put his hands through the bars and handcuffed him, and then I hauled on the cuffs while she gave him a hefty injection of a pale straw-coloured juice. His eyes glazed very quickly, but he stayed on his feet.

'How long will he stay docile?' I asked her as we trailed him upstairs.

'About four hours . . . it's a veterinary anaesthetic. I'll give you another couple of shots for him. Will that be enough?'

'I think so. I'll have him back in Blighty by about six, with a bit of luck.'

She did a double take: like a quick Joe Loss intro. 'Any chance I could come with you? I'm up for a ninety-six, and if I fly with you I can claim that I didn't go off duty until you get him home. I'd get another half-day.' I looked at her again, and liked what I saw. She wore a wedding ring, and looked friendly without being stupid about it, if you know what I mean.

'What's your name?'

'Lesley.'

'Your hubbie back home?'

'Yes.'

'Then signal him to meet you at Croydon tonight. I'll see you under the Watch Office clock at two. OK?'

'Me too . . . th?' my charge lisped very slowly, and dribbled. His voice faded away. Lesley gently mopped his chin.

'Shut up, and go back to sleep,' I told him. 'I'll wake you up when you're free again.'

So that was how I got an unexpected trip home. It only happened because of that fool, and because Randall was flying in three civil servants in the red Oxford. They were going to inspect the Airlift. Like most civilian inspectors of the Airlift they had probably never seen the inside of an aircraft in their lives before. I hope they enjoyed the adventure.

I borrowed a phone line in the dispatcher's office at Celle, sat down and hunted around for Tommo. It was the first time it had actually occurred to me that you could telephone someone's haunts one after the other until you caught up with them. I caught up with him at Tempelhof, where he was squiring some Yankee bigwigs around the airfield for his boss.

'Can you talk, or are you busy?'

'I can talk. They're swallowing a champagne and caviar reception with the Mayor.' It wouldn't have occurred to him that there was anything odd about a champagne reception in a city that was starving to death: I don't think he'd ever gone short of anything in his life.

'Can you contact the guys in the Neutral Zone, and tell them I have to go away for a couple of days; but not to worry – I haven't forgotten them.'

'Why can't you tell 'em yersel'?'

'They might not believe me.'

It made him think. Then he said, 'Yeah; I can buy that. Gettin' twitchy, ain't they?'

'That's what I thought. That Red Greg makes me nervous.'

'Where ya goin'?'

'Home. Prisoner's escort.'

'One o' yours?'

'Yes, Tommo.'

'What's he do?'

'He breaks up people and places, especially policemen and police stations. I'm going to take him home and fire him. Then I'll kick arse when I find out who took him on in the first place.'

'I like that,' Tommo told me. 'Y'almost speakin' American. What's it like where you are?'

'As cold as nuns' tits.'

'Same here, buddy. It's going to be a long cold winter. Time I went home . . .' The line crackled. That was never a good sign. 'You want me to look out for that German girl o' yourn?'

'No thanks, Tommo: she'd only get you into trouble . . .' He was laughing when the phone went dead. He may have hung up on me. Not like me to be possessive, I realized.

Randall wasn't that keen on the cargo. He made me borrow another couple of pairs of shackles. We put the jerk as far back in the aircraft as we could, snapped both his arms to his seat separately, and hobbled him. Then we gave him another sqwoosh of vet's juice for good measure. He slept all the way. Pity he was a snorer.

The VIPs had left a couple of magazines on the Oxford. Nurse L had the *Picture Post*, and I read *Lilliput*. They'd done something to the cheeky photos in mine, and the naturist girls had somehow lost their genitalia: their abdomens ended in – well . . . nothing really. If Dieter was like most boys he'd already seen a few of these already, so he was in for a surprise when he met the real thing at some time in his life. Odd; that was the thought that did it.

I suddenly missed Maggs, the Major and the boys and wondered if I could slip away to meet them. I'd put what Elaine had said to me to the back of my mind of course; tried to pretend she hadn't said it. I tried to talk to Randall on the trip, but something was bothering him and he wouldn't open up. His replies were short and factual. No malice there, but he wasn't saying anything either. Eventually Lesley leaned her head on my shoulder and dozed. It was actually quite a sweet way of telling me that there was nothing much doing.

Her husband met us at the aircraft. He was part of a ring of about a dozen people who surrounded the door. The rest of them were bloody policemen. I had noticed a couple of cars and an ambulance, but didn't suppose that they were waiting for us. Lesley went down the small step first, went over and hugged a thin boy in a long mac. Randall and I manhandled our drowsy passenger out between us, and the engineer was bundled away surrounded by coppers: he was still smiling his broken smile. I noticed a couple had small wooden truncheons in their hands.

'Don't worry. He's safe with us now,' one said. He turned away. So did I. I turned to Randall, who looked decidedly iffy.

'What the hell's going on, Randall?'

'I got Control to signal them before you boarded, Charlie. His

415

picture's in the English papers. He's wanted for killing someone in Nottingham. The papers say he's a nutcase . . .'

I was angry, but I held my tongue for once, and thought about it. There were one or two photo flashes as they wrestled the ambulance doors shut. I tried to ignore them. I looked around for the nurse and her old man, but they were five hundred yards away and walking with their arms around each other. A brief flash of envy? *Yes*, if you like.

I looked back at Randall and said, 'Don't worry. You did exactly the right thing. Thank you . . .'

What were going through my mind were pictures of Bozey and Ronson and the question, *How many other buggers do I have who are wanted by the police?'*

You know, I've spent my whole life keeping my head down and trying not to be noticed. You know another thing? It's never bloody worked. The next morning Randall and I were on the front pages of some London papers, photographed with the alleged Butcher of Nottingham between us as we pulled him from the plane.

I didn't mess around in the morning but hopped on a rattler first to the south coast and then turned right for Chichester, and Dieter's school. I walked into the playground when the kids were on their mid-morning playtime. Dieter detached shyly but immediately from a game of miniature cricket; the wicket was chalked against the school wall. There were no hugs in front of his mates, but he held my hand as we walked into the school and asked, 'Why are you here, Dad? Is everyone all right?' He was still that kind of kid; still waiting for the next blow.

'Everyone's fine as far as I know. I haven't been home yet. I only have a day or so down here so I thought I'd ask your Beak if you could play hooky.' Dieter's face went blank because I'd used words he hadn't understood, so I explained, 'We used to call the headmaster *the beak*, in my school days, and *playing hooky* was taking a day off. I thought we could go to a cafe, and then maybe take a wander around town.'

'*Really?*'

'Really. Now, where do we go?'

The oddest thing about the school was how small its proportions seemed. The schools I remembered all seemed to have corridors a mile long and thirty yards high. Now I could almost reach up and touch the ceiling. The corridors were as claustrophobic as some of the aircraft I'd flown in. It took me half an hour to disengage, but not because wangling Dieter a day off was a problem. The head wanted to talk, and I finally got away by promising to come back to talk to his senior year about flying the Airlift.

We had tea and a bacon sandwich in the Cathedral Tea Room fussed over by a talkative matron, then we walked over to the cathedral itself and Dieter took me round before we rode the bus to Bosham. He'd recently been taken on a school visit to it, and delighted in lecturing his Old Man. The first time you know something that your father doesn't is always a turning point for a boy.

Two days later I was back flying down the corridor looking over my shoulder for the Reds. If I could have caught up with the lyricist who wrote *Life Is Just a Bowl of Cherries* this time, I would have throttled the bastard.

Chapter Twenty-six

As it happened Ivan wasn't doing all that much: he didn't have to. Winter was beginning to show its teeth, and overflown aircraft and crews were falling out of the sky without their help. Our very own Berliners were also cold and starving, so the international effort to supply them went into overdrive. When you look back you tend to see the Airlift as a huge humanitarian effort with lives lost and broken in support of it. It didn't feel like that to me; it just felt like bloody stubbornness – we hadn't let the Jerry get us down, and neither would we the Reds. So we flew where we were asked to, when we were asked to and with what they asked us. Sometimes we took DPs back on the outward trip. If we'd been flying coal in the Dakotas the DPs would get off the other end as black as miners, but they didn't seem to mind. I flew some trips. Bozey flew a few more. Our aircraft and crews rotated occasionally back to Lympne. Spares were produced when and as we needed them, and none of my people did anything new to be arrested for. God was in his heaven.

I went to the Leihhaus to talk about Frieda's fur coat. Marthe and Magda were there. Magda said, 'It's not fun any more, is it?'

'What isn't?'

'This isn't: *Berlin*. On the radio they said that even Dietrich is on her way back. How boring can that be?' Marlene was singing on the radio at that very moment: it must have reminded her.

'Don't you like her?'

'Germans should be proper Germans; not pretend Americans.' Then she said, 'I'm not supposed to talk like that. The Denazification people would call me in if they knew: they're worse fascists than the fascists.'

'I thought you were Czech or Hungarian or something?'

'Polish, but only since the war. Before that I was a good German.' She looked uncharacteristically down in the mouth. 'You won't tell them, Charlie, will you?'

'No reason to. Where's Greg anyway?' I couldn't keep his transport hanging around for ever, and when was his famous court martial going to happen?

'He's over in the East recruiting civil judges I think. What did you want him for?'

'Frieda's been a cunt.' I immediately regretted my crudeness, but couldn't take it back.

'Isn't that what we're supposed to be?' Magda could still get it back over the net when she wanted to.

'No. Sorry. I mean she's been really stupid. She went down to the market wearing a fur coat, and nearly caused a bloody riot. Some poor woman ripped it off her back, so Frieda clouted her with a lead and leather sap she always carries. The police released her after a couple of hours, but still say they want to question her.'

'Do all your women carry offensive weapons, Charlie?'

'Thinking about it; most of them seem to have. I wonder why that is?'

'What happened to the coat?'

'It was taken into custody, and now seems to have disappeared. Frieda's shouting the house down and is demanding an investigation. I need her to attract less attention, so I thought your Greg might be able to oblige me with another one: there's none to be had over on my side.'

'Nor here, lover. They all ended up in Moscow. Why don't you ask your pal Tommo?'

'He seems to have disappeared. I don't suppose you know anything about that?'

'His snake bit a Belgian diplomat. Might that have had anything to do with it?'

'I dunno, Magda. What's the matter with you people? Every time I'm away you get into trouble.'

'That's why you love us. What y' wanna do?' That was nice, but I realized that she was someone that I genuinely thought of as a friend, and this time I wasn't going to mess it up. I got my wallet out.

'Scroton'll be in later. Why don't we get drunk and wait for him?'

Marthe came out on cue. She was carrying a tray with two bottles of wine and four glasses. The labels on the wine bottles were overstamped PX, and they appeared to have originated in Sicily. Otto followed her. I'd stopped calling him Moppo because Frieda had told me it was cruel. She was right. Time I bloody grew up.

Frieda had also been out of Berlin again, and returned the day before me. Halton had fixed her a lift with Flight Refuelling. She told me that it had been 'an interesting interlude', which could have meant anything. I wasn't jealous at all, which was a bit of a relief actually. She had been sitting on her bed in the only heated room in the icy apartment, wearing what Hollywood stars call *a negligee* and you and I call a long nightie. It wasn't large enough to contain all her assets, if you see what I mean, so opening the door and looking in was like coming face to face with a couple of old friends. It was after coffee and black cardboard the next morning that she had told me about her fur coat, and threatened to call the Old Man down on me. I promised to see what I could do. Then she asked me what was the situation with *the other thing*, and I promised to see what I could do about that as well.

You already know that what I did about both was get drunk.

That didn't go down too well either, but for the moment I was almost all she had, so we circled each other like a couple of boxers looking for an opponent's weakness. I used to drag myself into the office or Flying Control in the mornings feeling as if I'd done ten rounds with Freddy Mills. Love with Frieda could leave you hurting in places that love had never been before. I'm using the word *love* euphemistically of course. I wouldn't want to offend anyone. The one thing I never tired of surprised me. We often slept with the door of her small windowless room open so that I could listen for intruders. I never tired of the play of the early daylight through that door on her curves: I could have spent hours just looking at her. I didn't tell her that. She would have only made fun of me.

Fergal telephoned me, and asked me to visit. Red Greg called as well, and asked when I'd be back in the Neutral Zone. I saw no reason to deny either.

I'd been putting off visiting Fergal; I guess you realized that. I'm not really all that good with kids. I took Frieda with me. She was even worse, which made me feel better. I parked up in the street and gave a group of urchins hanging around outside a dollar to watch the jeep, promising another couple if it still had all its wheels when we came back. You entered the orphanage through a large street door, up a couple of wide steps. It looked like any other door in the terrace, but the terrace was just a war-damaged façade. Once through the door we found a cloister on either side, and a quad in front of us. The noise was tremendous because the quad was full of shouting children playing games. Frieda suddenly held my hand; that was nice. A nun who looked too pretty by half to be a nun hustled up to meet us. She had a toddler in her arms. He was whooping it up in no uncertain fashion. The nun was laughing, and tickling the kid. The little girl pushing a small pram behind her was the girl I'd once met in the street – it seemed months ago. There was a child sleeping peacefully in the pram. Was she still caring for the same one? The girl looked fed and relaxed – the way kids should – and her cheeks had colour. They were no longer pinched. She smiled, and said in grave formal German, 'Good morning, sir,' and after a correct pause, 'Thank you for sending us to your house.'

I squatted down to get eye-level. 'This is not my house; it is the priest's house. I am glad that he is looking after you well.'

'I think that is your house also.' She smiled, and turned the pram back to the melee. The playing children parted to let her through, like the Red Sea parted for Moses. I thought that Fergal would have liked that simile. The beautiful nun took us to Fergal's door, but then spirited Frieda away; to do the woman-to-woman stuff I presumed.

I'd never thought of Fergal as an executive or an organizer, but there again, what did I know? I hadn't expected to end up running an airline, had I? He had a large office full of shelves. It had probably once been a study or a library. Many of the shelves now hosted neatly stacked and laundered children's clothes, and there were a few wooden crates of vegetables. He got up from the trestle table that served as his desk and came round to greet me. He said, 'I sold the books. You can't eat or wear them.'

'From what I can see you don't have to. You've done a grand job with these kids.'

'*We* have. I couldn't have survived without you and Halton. Thanks for the clothes.'

'What clothes?'

'The ones that your secretary puts on your flights back from England. I think she organizes a collection in the nearest towns.'

'I didn't know . . .'

'They probably don't bother you with every little thing. That's what good staff are for.'

'What are yours like?'

'The sisters? They're wonderful. I couldn't run this show without them.'

Another nun put her head around the door to offer us tea, of all things! She was also improbably beautiful.

'Are all your women that good-looking? The two I've seen so far are.'

He still hadn't let go of my hand, but looked away as if embarrassed.

'There's something beautiful in all women, Charlie.' Then he looked back; the old Fergal. 'Yes. They do seem to be corkers, don't they? I have five working with me; all volunteers. One was in Spain before the war. She can nurse.'

'Which side was she on?'

He looked pained, but it wasn't real.

'There are no winning sides in war, Charlie, only losers.' It was the sort of guff that he must have been taught in the Seminary.

'You know that's bollocks, Fergal. She was a bloody fascist, wasn't she? All your lot were, over there.'

'I've learned to forgive, Charlie.'

'I'll forgive her if she's . . .' I managed to stop it before it came out – as the gardener said to the art mistress. Maybe I was learning after all. I suppose the pause before he spoke meant that he was deciding how much to tell me.

Whatever else they teach them in convents they teach them how to make a fair cup of char. It was the best I'd had in Germany all year. They were short of neither milk, tea nor sugar. In fact I remarked later, as Fergal showed me around, they didn't seem to be short of *anything*. This was a very un-Berlin situation that winter. I wondered what he wanted me for. Eventually he told me.

I'd said, 'You appear to be managing very well here, Fergal: your people in Liverpool must be proud of you.'

'They don't know all that much. I don't tell them.'

'Why not?'

'They'd only interfere and bugger things up. I prefer to be left alone to manage in my own way. I suspect that my methods are a bit rough and ready for the dear old Church.'

'Is that where I come in?'

'Yes please.'

'What?'

'I want you to fly a planeload of children back to Blighty. The Church will take them on once you get them back.'

'Why? Your kids seem to be fine to me. They're the happiest kids I've seen in Berlin for months.'

'That's the point, Charlie. I need to take in more, and haven't the capacity. Those kids you saw at the door will wait out there day and night until I take them in, or they die there. How many of them were there this morning?'

'About a dozen.'

'One less than before, anyway: a boy froze to death on the steps yesterday. He can't have made a sound – we didn't hear a thing. I phoned you when we found his body because I had to do something. I need you to empty the place, so I can move more in. Do you want to see his body?'

'Don't be daft!' We were pacing around the cloister now. His kids were at lessons. There was just the girl with the pram. She was sitting on a stone bench, rocking the pram and crooning a childish lullaby. 'There must be a snag?'

'The government won't want you to do it. England's up to its ears in DP children already. They won't want any more. It would also send a message to the Reds that they're winning. I'm afraid that if you tell anyone, some bugger will try to stop you.'

I found I was talking as if I'd already made up my mind. 'Will you tell *your* lot?'

'Only when you're in the air. They won't have any choice then – the papers would eat them alive.'

'What about the kids at the door?'

'If you say you'll do it, I'll get them in right away. I'll fill the place to bursting with the little sods.' I could hear that not all of his training had taken yet. I thought about it and grinned.

'You'd better get them in then, hadn't you?'

Sometimes God simply doesn't give you a choice. He wanted me to see the boy who had died. When we went to find Frieda she was in a small cold room off their chapel washing down the small body with the sister who had taken her away. The child's skin was a sallow yellowish colour. His ribs and breastbone stuck out like those of the creatures I had seen in a small and hardly noticed concentration camp in 1945. He had lifted his chin as if in defiance as he died, and it had remained that way. He would have been about the same age as Dieter.

I didn't share the thought I had with Fergal before I drove away. I was in the jeep. So was Frieda. She was powdering her cheeks to cover up the tear streaks; that was interesting. I held my hand out to Fergal, but he clasped me wrist to wrist the way men sometimes do when there are things that are too important to say. Then he stood on the steps and watched us leave. I could see him getting smaller and smaller in the round wing mirror. His new gang had disappeared: they were already inside. The thought I had was that old thing again; *two birds and one stone* – it was as if the notion fell fully formed into my lap.

*

'I asked you if you wanted to go the Leihhaus, and get a lot of hassle . . . or would you prefer me to drop you off at the flat?'

'I heard you.' That was Frieda. 'I think I'll be hassled at the Leihhaus. It will save putting the stove on until later.' She was actually starting to sound like a bit of a *Hausfrau*, but I dared not tell her that. I parked the jeep alongside Red Greg's big GAZ thing, reckoning that it might scare off the scavengers. I needn't have bothered. There was a fully paid up member of the Lootwaffe on the door: white helmet, nightstick and all. He nodded to me and said, 'Sir,' as we walked past him. I almost expect him to say '*Evening all*' like PC 49.

Greg was playing cards with Tommo and the REME corporal – he was beginning to look like a fixture. He stood for Frieda, and found her a chair. She made up a fourth and started to deal – with a suspiciously fluid motion.

'Are we being raided?' I asked them.

'Naw,' Tommo said. 'He's the new doorman. We got a patrol o' them workin' overlappin' shifts. Very good rate.'

'What are you playing?'

'Strip poker?' Tommo asked hopefully, and eyed Frieda. She smiled back. I've already told you; Alice smiled like that.

'If you do,' I told him, 'she'll have all the clothes off your back before she's even shed a glove. I thought you were away?'

'I wuz. Now I'm back.'

'Bought any new countries lately?'

'What's the matter, Charlie?'

'I don't know,' I admitted. 'Maybe I'm falling out of love with Berlin; it's getting too much like hard work. I came to see your partner. Can I drag him away while Frieda strips the rest of you?'

'What will you bet me that I have duds off her 'fore she gets any of mine?'

'Twenty-five dollars?'

'*Done*,' he told me. 'I'll take it.' He stuffed one of his horrible cigars in his mouth. That reminded me to fill and fire up my pipe. I watched them start off, and told Tommo, 'The cigar doesn't count as clothes,' before I wandered away with Red Greg to a small table in a corner. I looked back as we did so. Tommo scowled at me. A hungry-looking civilian with his hair in rats' tails moved from another table and joined us. He was wearing a cheap blue suit that might once have fitted, but was now two sizes too large for him. It had greasy cuffs.

'Charlie, this is *Judge* Horst Molly.' Red Greg did the introductions.

'Hello, Horst.' Horst had a soft handshake that didn't go with his hard hands.

'Hello, Charlie.'

'He's your judge,' Red Greg said. 'I found him yesterday.'

'I'm not really a judge,' Molly said. 'I'm a cobbler.' *Ich bin . . . ein Schuster.*

'Not any more,' Greg said. 'You're a judge in the People's Court; you've no idea what privilege awaits you.'

'I was a cobbler yesterday,' Molly explained, 'when this officer stopped his car. I was delivering a pair of repaired boots. He told me to get in, and then told me I was a judge.'

'The simplest ways are best.' That was Greg again. 'Last year I found a mayor in exactly the same place. It was better for him than being a park keeper. His park was full of large holes.' Then he asked Molly, 'Are you sure that you know what to do?'

'I find for the Englishman, *yes*?'

'Yes. Good. You find for the Englishman.'

'Hang on a mo.' I dropped back into English because the nearest German phrase I knew sounded like a fire alarm. 'What's it got to do with me? I thought I was just a witness?'

'Witness yes; complainant also. Communist courts are very democratic before they execute people: we need a complaint first.'

'Is anyone going to get killed, Greg?'

He thought for a min before replying, and swung his little legs happily. 'Possibly not.'

When I asked if we could speak in private he sent the cobbler back to his corner. I asked, 'Is he really a judge?'

'He is now; I signed the papers this morning. Don't worry about it.'

'Everything about you worries me, Greg.'

'Good. Keep you alert.'

'Is there a Russian word for that?'

'Yes, but you wouldn't like it. Ask me another.' That was a catch phrase from a British quiz show that was doing the rounds. It had spread into every European language like smallpox.

'What have you got me into, Greg?'

'Nothing. Nozzinc. Don' worry about it. Ask me anuzzer.' He laughed. He thought that it was funny.

'Do you want to know how we're going to get your people out of Germany?'

The transformation was alarming. That guy Holland could do the same when he wanted to. They were all policemen when it came down to it, and all coppers are bastards – or so the old song goes.

'Is difficult.'

'Not any more.'

'How so?'

'You plan to smuggle your people into *your* Berlin, across the line into *my* zone, and then on to one of my aircraft at Gatow. Right?'

'Of course.'

'But we know that smuggling *anything* into Eastern Berlin from your side is very dangerous. Look at all the fuss you went to over a kilo of liquorice. It could have cost you everything. How are you going to hide a family of four? Remember that your side of Berlin is surrounded by a ring of steel not under your control. If any of your family is stopped they'll round up the bloody lot of you. Firing squad next stop?'

'Maybe better than where they are now.' His face had taken on that dark, sentimental moody look that I'd seen before.

'I've got a better idea,' I told him.

He took some convincing. I wasn't a professional smuggler after all. After I explained the deal we went back to the card players. Tommo was squinting at his cards through an overcast of old tobacco smoke. Frieda was smoking one of his cigars as well: she'd probably won it. Tommo had one of Frieda's stockings draped around his neck. Other than that, and a pair of startlingly purple boxers, he was stark naked. He was beginning to grow a gut. The REME man had disappeared, but as far as I could see all of his clothes were neatly folded, and in a stack alongside Frieda's chair. It looked to me if the stocking was the sum of her losses.

'Told you,' I said to Tommo.

'You owe me twenny-five bucks, kiddo.'

'How come?'

'I got the stocking first. You lost.' Seeing the state of him it was almost worth it, but I didn't tell him that.

Back in the jeep I told her to put her stocking back on.

'Why?'

'Because I want to watch you do it.'

She did it by feel, not taking her eyes from my face. She didn't smile but there was something there. The back of the jeep was full of men's clothes – she had refused to let Tommo buy his clobber back.

'What do you want to do with these?' I asked her. 'Raffle them?'

'Let's give them to that clothes relief centre for the DPs.'

'Tommo will get pretty mad when he sees someone walking around in his hundred-dollar tailored uniform.'

'Teach him a lesson then, won't it? Just like I taught you.'

'How did you teach me?'

'You don't think I needed to lose a nylon do you? Cost you twenny-five dollars.'

'He gave it back to you.'

'He's a gentleman; it always shows.'

'It was worth the money to see you put it back on.'

She smiled this time, and gave a soft little laugh. There was definitely something for me in there.

'Then maybe you taught me a lesson as well, Charlie.'

'I want to sleep with you.'

'That's a pity.'

'I mean now. I want to drive you home, and sleep with you.'

We'd have to stop doing this.

We went through the new checkpoint into East Berlin at four o'clock in the morning. A soldier in an odd gaudy uniform was driving Russian Greg's big jeep. I think he was a bandsman. He looked very impressive; or like the cornet player in a colliery silver band – suit yourself. A GAZ jeep was like the sumo equivalent of the original thing – for which, by the way, I still have a soft spot.

The Soviet checkpoint guard put his head into the jeep, scanned the passengers and started to shout and bawl. When the guard started to turn out, fumbling with rifles, bayonets and submachine guns, I was sure that we'd got as far as we were going to get, and were bound for the pokey. But I needn't have worried. They sorted themselves into the best kind of line you're capable of at four in the morning, and Russian Greg got out to inspect them. They were all six-footers, which kind of put him at a disadvantage.

Finally someone was dispatched to come running with a chair for him to stand on, and from it he harangued them for ten minutes. There were smiles all round when he finished.

As we drove into the Soviet sector he said, 'You the first Westerner passed through that checkpoint in six months who didn't have to wait for twelve hours, Charlie: maybe they'll name it after you, if I tell them to.'

'What about *me*?' Frieda was muffled in coats and blankets, and her voice came out in a squeak and a steamy plume.

'Nah, honey,' the Georgian told her. 'Checkpoint Frieda? It don' scan.'

I'll bet that's something you didn't know until today.

'What did you tell them from that chair?' I asked him.

'That if they stuck by me they'd have their back pay next week. I'd kick arse in Moscow and get it here for them.'

'Can you do that?'

'Don't see why not. It's been in my safe for two months already.'

He took us to his apartment, and put Frieda and me in the room I'd occupied before. She delighted in the subtropical temperature of the place, and the fact that heating didn't seem to be a consideration. The form her delight took was walking around our room without any clothes on. It took my mind off other things.

The only court I had been in before that was a coroner's court in Gloucestershire. It was like a parish council meeting in a village community hall. This place was different. It looked just like the courts you see at the pictures . . . except there were three nervous-looking judges up on the bench, and no jury. Horst Molly sat in the centre, slightly elevated from those on either side of him. He looked more comfortable with his role than the others – maybe they'd just been pulled off the street that morning.

They'd separated me from Frieda as we had walked up the steps into the building. It was a bit banged about on the outside, but OK where it counted. Story of my life I suppose. Frieda had walked off escorted by two pretty-looking German boys with cow's-lick blond hair styles . . . I wasn't sure I liked that, because she glanced at me over her shoulder as she moved away. Her face was wearing the *I'm all right, son* expression of the platoon card sharp, and I heard her laugh at something one of them said.

Russian Greg walked me into the court and down to a long table at the front, with his arm through mine. If one of us had been wearing a skirt we could have been going to a ball. He told me, 'Each of the accused will be represented by a spokesman.'

'Will I be represented?'

'No. The prosecutor will speak for you. He will ask you seven questions to which you will answer only with the word *Yes*. Do you understand?'

'In what language?'

'Russian of course: Adam is the master now. You know that story?'

'What story?'

'English revolutionaries three hundred years ago: *When Adam toiled, and Eve span, Who was then the gentleman?* You should know your own history better than you do, Englishman. No room for gentlemen this side of the line any more.'

'OK. He asks me seven questions in Russian, to which I answer *Da*. Does anyone else ask me anything?'

'The defenders also ask you seven questions each, and you reply *No*: *Nyet*. Can you do that?'

'Of course I can, Greg, but I feel very uncomfortable. My Russian is shite: I won't understand what's going on.'

'Don' worry.' He waved his hand as if he was waving a troublesome fly away. 'Neither can the judges. They do as they're told.'

The prosecutor was an oily, thin colonel who seemed scared of Greg. His hands trembled as he shook ours and seated us. The two public defenders were wearing very new lieutenants' uniforms. The defendants wore badly fitting civilian clothes: one was a scared young boy, and the other an elderly man. They sat with their team at the other end of our table. Their faces bore the signatures of their interrogators' fists and boots, and expressions of resignation.

The proceedings were conducted in Russian.

There were about ten rows of public benches like church pews – and they were full; that was probably something to do with how warm the courtroom was. From the muted buzz of conversation behind me I gained the impression that the audience was wholly German. They probably hadn't much Russian between them either. They applauded wildly each of the questions the prosecutor apologetically asked me . . . and then applauded my answers. They hooted and howled at each of the questions the defenders asked me, but then applauded my responses. I was finished in a half-hour. I whispered to Greg, 'Who's next? The next witness?'

'None. Just you.'

'Oh.'

The prosecutor made a speech in Russian. It took him nearly two hours. He perspired heavily as he spoke and stopped from time to time to mop his brow and his thinning hairline with a brilliantly white handkerchief. The audience applauded enthusiastically for fifteen minutes afterwards. They didn't stop until Molly motioned them to. Then Greg stood up on his chair and told everyone to go to lunch. It was nearly the first German I'd heard spoken aloud in the room all morning.

We had lunch with the judges and the prosecutor. Nobody mentioned the war – which was a line I'd remember later in my life – and no one mentioned the Airlift. Molly had begun to grow into the role of chief judge, which meant that he dominated the legal team's conversation, and we talked about shoes most of the time. He favoured high insteps and double stitching.

'What you think?' Greg whispered to me. I felt like one of the Guy Fawkes conspirators.

'Alice in fucking wonderland,' I told him.

His face suddenly embraced an expression of unexpected and wild delight.

'You understan'!' he said. 'You understan' the modern Soviet state. You are a Soviet in your heart, Charlie.'

I replied completely by instinct, without thinking, 'No, Greg. No heart. Not me. I don't have one.'

Greg went grave on me. I'd told him the truth without meaning to. He turned his words back on me. 'So you *do* understan', Charlie. You truly understan' modern Russia. I am sorry for you, English.' Then he turned away to give Molly his last briefing.

The court reconvened at fourteen-thirty with the defenders' pleas: the audience had got the hang of things by then, and drowned them with cat-calls. They never stood a chance. Molly pronounced guilt and sentences less than fifteen minutes later. He read it in Russian from a paper that Greg had given him earlier. His Russian sounded no better than mine.

'Good,' Greg said. 'That's finished. Let's find a bar.'

The bar was a wrecked house about a hundred yards from the court. When Greg walked in, the half-dozen grubby soldiers there before us ran away . . . literally. The aged barman sniffed, wiped down a small round table for us, and produced a bottle of vodka and two glasses. After we had swallowed our first drinks the three judges trooped in. Greg waved them to a table the other side of the room, where the barman served them. I noticed that he failed to wipe the crumbs from their table, and the greasy bottle he put before them was only half full. No glasses.

'They show promise, don' they?' Greg asked me. 'But they must learn their place.'

'Adam is the master now?'

'You got it. I tol' you. You get my job one day.'

'I wouldn't want it, Greg.'

'I ask you again in ten years. In my office in London.'

'You believe that?'

He picked at his teeth with a sliver of wood he'd pulled from the table top.

'No. Actually I don'. Also I don't unnerstan' why all those other Russians do.'

We did what we were good at: we got drunk. I had forgotten Frieda. That was OK: she'd probably forgotten me. I know that at one point I asked him, 'What happened to the defendants? What were the sentences?'

'The pilot got Siberia. He thinks Siberia is better than death. Big mistake.'

'. . . and the old man?'

'Death by shooting.'

'Will he appeal?'

'No point, Charlie. Dead already. They shot him behind the courthouse ten minutes after we sat down here. One-bullet job.'

'Who was he, Greg?'

'I like you, Englishman. You're very lucky for me.'

'Who *was* he?'

He waved his arm. I'd seen that gesture before. He was waving off an awkward question.

'An old man, Charlie. Ol' man called Spartacus. You safe now and you owe me.'

'. . . pay you in your office, Greg, in ten years' time.'

'That will be in London.'

'No it won't, Greg.'

I'd dropped my tobacco pouch on the floor and, bending to retrieve it, fell off the chair. Greg laughed. The three judges across the room laughed. Greg looked at them and they stopped laughing like the gramophone needle lifted from a 78. Then I laughed. The laugh was on everybody except me, and I'd just realized it.

It must be something to do with my lack of height: I'm always in the company of people who think they can change my plans without consulting me. That's why we flew further east instead of driving back to the West. Bollocks. Frieda had found an uncle registered in a town a long way to the east, and having trusted Greg to get us this far it seemed daft not to make the effort to go for a goal. He made out a different set of passes for us and got Molly to sign and stamp them. Then he gave the German some sort of ration card as a reward. I thought we were chancing our arm, although it didn't feel like that: it felt as if I was chancing my neck.

We flew into the winter's sunshine from a farmer's field, after passing through Greg's 'ring of steel' close outside the old Berlin Ring Road. The field still had a couple of smashed tanks in a corner: one Russian and one German – locked head to head in an embrace of death, like dinosaur carcasses. How many men had died in them when they clashed? Eight? Ten? Greg hadn't lied about the ring of steel because we passed through two more checkpoints, although I thought the attention paid to Greg's papers was perfunctory at best. They had a good shufti at mine and Frieda's though. The young officer commanding the second barrier reached into the car towards Frieda. I'll swear he was going to squeeze her tit. Russian Greg slapped his hand away, and bawled the man out. Eventually he said, 'Apologize,' in German.

The guard looked at Frieda hopefully, and spoke quietly in Russian. Greg exploded behind the wheel and screamed, 'In German; apologize *in good German!*' *Entschuldigen Sie sich auf guten Deutsch!*

Frieda was gracious. She told him, 'That's all right. I like them myself. So does my husband.'

The Russian officer looked at me and muttered an apology, but quickly broke eye contact. Russian Greg had the last word.

'Be careful,' he told the young man. 'In future you be very careful.'

'*Jawohl, Herr Kommissar. Jawohl.*' He was so scared that he'd stayed in the language into which he'd been ordered.

I began to breathe again. I'd noticed a word used in the incident. It was one I'd have to think about.

The aircraft was a brand-new Me. 108. How did the Reds get a brand-new Me. 108 in 1948? – well, they'd *made* one. They'd just started making them in Czechoslovakia on old jigs taken from the aircraft factories in Germany. This one had that nice new smell inside, like a new car, and was flown by one of Frieda's blonds, while the other one navigated. The Czechs had managed to cram four small passenger seats into an airframe originally designed for two I think. I sat alongside Frieda, and Greg sat behind us. He went to sleep. I looped an arm around Frieda's shoulder and concentrated on not being airsick: I've never liked small aircraft.

Frieda's Uncle's *Heimat* turned out to be a market town that looked, from the air, as if the war had passed it by. Most of the buildings still had roofs. Three big Russian Josef Stalin tanks stood in the market square. Their crews waved lazily to us as we circled them. A haze of exhaust smoke drifted up into the still air from one of them. It was obvious that Europe wasn't going to be short of tanks for a long, long time. We landed on yet another field of short grass: the flattened brown wheel ruts we rumbled over said that we weren't the first. We were met by a civilian in a requisitioned VW Kübelwagen. What surprised me was that Russian Greg turned down the immediate prospect of a lift. He pushed Frieda and me towards the little jeeplike car.

'I will find the hotel,' he told me. 'We will wait in the bar.'

'Aren't you coming to make the introductions?'

Russian Greg gave me a wise little smile, and whispered, 'They will talk more freely I suspect, Charlie, if I am not there.'

We scrambled under the canvas and into the rear seats of the little car. Its driver was pale enough to be an albino. He wore the ubiquitous black leather trench coat, clear rimless spectacles and a wide-brimmed felt hat. His plump lips smiled, but his eyes were expressionless. He turned and offered me his hand, saying in accented English, 'Welcome to Free Germany, comrade. We are pleased to welcome a friend of the Free State.'

Frieda told him the address she had found in the archive. His hand was still waiting for me, and when I grasped it it was cold and very soft, like a dead thing from the sea. When I get to the River Styx at last, Charon will be like this man. It was all I could do to mutter *Gut!* and wave him on before I threw up. He smiled again, as if he had won a point, and slipped the vehicle into gear. Behind us the air-cooled engine screamed as the car began to slip and slide across the grass.

An ordinary house in an ordinary suburb. Untouched by war. A crazy-paving path up to the front door. Crazy paving: that's a phrase you don't hear often. A lot more crazy people wandering the streets thanks to Care in the Community, but not much crazy paving any more. Anyway, I thought that Crazy Eddie and his auntie would have been at home here. The man who opened the door for us was almost as small as me. Thick white hair, and rimless spectacles like the animal who had brought us, but who had stayed with the car. He was directly in front of Frieda, and for at least a minute he said and did nothing. Then he smiled and opened his arms. They stepped towards each other, and he said, 'Frieda,' and, 'child,' and began to cry. I didn't cry, but I did turn away so that they couldn't see my face.

Frieda said, 'I have come for Elli,' and he replied, 'Of course. Please come in. Bring your companion with you. Is he an American?'

'No. English.'

The old man turned to me as we followed him into your everyday middle-class house.

'You started this war,' he told me. 'Without the English everything would have been all right.' *Gut ausgehen*.

I could have told him a million things about the London and Glasgow Blitzes and the concentration camps, *Tuesday's Child* and Bremen in 1945. Instead all I said was, 'I know.'

Frieda shot me a quick glance. It had a smile, and it had comradeship . . . and for the first time, I believe, it had gratitude. Everything changed right there. In that moment. It was as if a door had opened.

She introduced me after I had met the other people who lived in the house: a woman the man's age, another a lot older, and a teenaged girl who might have been a maid – it was that sort of place. There weren't supposed to be any servants in the East any more – that's what the propaganda told us, but old habits die hard.

Frieda said, 'Charlie, this is my Uncle Matti. We always called him *Beppo* in the family, after a famous clown.'

Uncle Matti wasn't clowning now. He shook his head. He took both Frieda's hands in his and said, 'Elli is dead, little one. I'm very sorry. She died in 1946. In the spring . . .'

Sometimes I get it right. I think that I did this time. I told her, 'I'll just go out to the garden, and smoke a pipe. You and your family have a lot to talk about.'

I smoked two pipes through, and was beginning to get cold

and nauseous when they remembered me, and called me back into a big kitchen that smelled of smoked meats. They gave me a glass of sweet wine, and I followed them in heavily watering it to make it last. Russian Greg had given me a quarter of a pound of coffee beans to give them as a present. You would have thought the paper poke had been full of gold.

Frieda told them, 'Charlie smokes far too much, but he's going outside to smoke his pipe again. I will stay with him, and smoke a cigarette.' The old folks exchanged knowing glances which weren't exactly appropriate.

When we were outside I noticed that I had been right the first time: the temperature was dropping. I said, 'Who was Elli?'

'My sister. My little sister.'

'What happened to her?'

'She had a Russian baby. It killed her.'

'I'm sorry.'

'It's OK, Charlie. I think I always knew it.' She had her arm through mine, and I hugged her, because that was what she really wanted.

Back in the kitchen I said clumsily to Beppo, or whatever his name was, 'I'm sorry about what happened to your niece. It must have been very hard. The bloody Reds were undisciplined when the war ended. I met some then . . .' If you believed everything people told you the Reds had raped anything that moved.

The old man looked at me, and shook his head. He must have been good at shaking his head. 'You know nothing, Englishman.' It took a moment for him to decide to tell me any more. Then his lip stiffened and he said, 'Elli's young man was an honourable officer. He did everything he could to look after her. The baby grew in the wrong part of her womb, or somewhere else . . . that was all. He took her to the Russian hospital and they fought for her for days . . . for the life of a *German* girl remember. Then the baby killed her; it would have killed anyone.'

'I'm sorry . . .'

'. . . and if it wasn't for the Russian doctors the baby would not have lived.'

'Did he take it away with him?'

'No, he did not go anywhere. The day after Elli was buried he shot himself. Such a waste. Romeo and Juliet. Poor little baby . . .'

'What happened to it?'

As if on cue a thin crying came from a room somewhere above us. The old man shrugged.

'Little Elli. She's just two.'

Frieda looked at me, and I knew what was bloody coming next.

Chapter Twenty-seven

The two blondies made a great fuss over the child, and flew us as gently as if they'd had a cargo of finest porcelain. Once we were in the back of the GAZ again they insisted on tucking a greatcoat around her before we set off. The first checkpoint was OK because the same young officer recognized Russian Greg and jumped like a doomed jackrabbit. The second one took longer. We kept the engine ticking over to keep some heat in the vehicle but it all blew out around the canvases.

I got out and flapped my arms about, and jumped up and down on the spot, to get warm. A couple of the Russian guards looked on with amusement. Greg had an earnest conversation with the captain of the guard, who made a couple of earnest telephone calls. Then I think that some earnest money changed hands, and we were driving into the US Zone. The American white-tops weren't in the slightest bit interested in us once they spotted Russian Greg riding shotgun. They looked over their shoulders to see that their officer wasn't watching, and waved us through – there wasn't anywhere on our side that he hadn't an entry to.

We pulled chairs close to one of the pot-bellied stoves in the Leihhaus, and held our hands to the heat. There was a heap of coal in the corner that could have kept a family warm for a month . . . for once I didn't feel bad about it. Russian Greg leaned

towards me and held out his hand for a manly shake. I obliged.
He said, 'That was my side of the bargain, English.'

'*More* than your side,' I admitted. 'We came out with one
more than we went in.' The child had a chair of her own between
Frieda and me: she was still swaddled in a Russian greatcoat and
looked a bit bewildered. I suppose that I'd feel the same.

'It's your move now,' he told me.

I nodded to him. Something touched my left hand. I looked
down to it – the child was trying to take hold of my little finger.

Scroton and the Countess blew in. The cold blew in with
them, into a momentary silence. Dave knew my complicated
domestics in England. He took in the tableau and said, 'Christ,
boss: you've done it again, haven't you? Another addition to your
bleeding menagerie.'

'No, Dave. This one already has a family of her own. Ask
Frieda. We just have to get it back to Blighty.'

Frieda said testily, '*It* is a girl . . .'

Scroton ignored her. 'Shouldn't be too hard.'

'Wanna hear the rest of it?'

I told him what I'd planned. He said he was up for it. I may be
wrong, but I fancied he was a shade or two paler by the time we
were finished.

I suppose that I was too: by the time we were ready to go I
hadn't slept for two days – I just hoped that my pilots were in a
better state. They said they were, but you never can tell.

Chapter Twenty-eight

It cost me five hundred Occupation dollars in bribes to get Fergal's orphans airside at Gatow.

Tommo had conjured up an American GMC six-wheeled truck from somewhere, and then let his tough-guy image down by offering to drive it himself, kitted out like a simple PFC. In the back we had thirty-eight kids, and two peculiarly glamorous nuns. I sat up front alongside Tommo, and Frieda sat alongside me. Elli was on her lap, swaddled in a blanket and already asleep. The night was cold, and frost glistened on the smashed pavements as Tommo gently rolled the big wagon through the city. We didn't see a living thing on the streets the whole trip. He drove the truck as if he'd been driving things that size all his life, with an elbow resting on the window frame, a cigar in his mouth, and the peak of his soft olive drab cap angled up. The only thing he said to me as we rolled up to the manned side gate and killed the lights was, 'Gimme the dough.'

I passed him the plain brown envelope of dollars. He'd told me beforehand not to seal it. The barrier was up because we were expected, but the arrangement had been that we'd stop at the gate office. An English sergeant stood up on the GMC's running board and carefully looked at neither Frieda nor myself. Tommo must have passed him the envelope upside down, and they fumbled it, because the Englishman swore, hopped down, and I was aware that some banknotes were falling free. As soon as he was off Tommo killed the lights, hit the big lorry into gear, and we were clear. I could hear the Englishman swearing at our disappearing tailboard. Tommo whistled. I think that it was that American march they call 'Dixie'.

'They're only kids,' Tommo explained. 'The bastard should'a passed us through for nothin'.'

We'd only done fifty yards in the dark before an unlit van pulled out in front and led us around the peritrack to the far side where the *Witch* and the *Pig* were waiting. It was the Countess, of course, driving the chow wagon the way she always did. Unlike Tommo she knew her way around the airfield in the dark, and all he had to do was follow her. We didn't want lights showing near the Halton aircraft: I wanted our activity hidden from the tower for as long as possible. Magda never simply drove things, she wrestled with them, so not running into the back of the doughnut wagon was one of Tommo's triumphs that night. Otto and Marthe were squeezed in alongside Magda – so in a way what followed was the Leihhaus's finest hour. That drive through the dark seemed to take for ever.

The kids had been briefed to be quiet, but there was that whispered excited buzz, and a couple of whimpers: you know what kids are like. They each had a small bundle, bag or satchel – all that was left of their lives in Germany. We put them all into the *Witch*. I think that Marthe kissed each one as they were lifted up. Dave had flown in the day before with sacks of coal, but somehow he had managed to get the *Witch*'s stomach as clean as a BEA passenger job. You could have eaten from her aluminium floor and sideskins . . . which was just as well, because there were no seats this time – the children sat on the cargo floor in short rows, shoulder to shoulder. When I looked in at them all I could see were rows of pale little faces: some scared, some excited. One of the nuns sat cross-legged in the middle of the foremost row; she was as beautiful as Jane Russell. The small girl I had last seen pushing a small pram at the orphanage was alongside her, holding her arm. The baby was against the nun's shoulder: even now the girl and the baby hadn't been parted.

Bozey drove up in my Merc, parked it on the back of the pan and locked it before he walked away. I asked him, 'Come to see us off?'

'No, boss. I decided to fly the first leg alongside Dave. His navigator and engineer.'

'I'm not sure I like that. I thought I put you in charge here.'

'You did. That's why I make the flying decisions today – not you.'

'I suppose you think you're better at that than me anyway?' I guess we were all a bit keyed up.

'I didn't say that.' Borland spoke very carefully.

'I will,' Max said cheerfully. He and Ronson had wandered over from under the *Pink Pig*'s wing. 'You can't sack me the way you can the others. You're crap at picking who flies with whom.'

Dreyfuss was with them. He hadn't met Scroton before, but now he introduced himself and shook his hand. He was flying this trip on Dave's radio: everyone knew by now that I was in the *Pig*.

'Who's left in charge?' I asked Bozey.

'Hardisty. He'll stay in the office until we've all touched down.'

'Is he any good at telling lies?'

'Top-hole, boss. I thought that was what this outfit was looking for when you took us on.' He grinned, and held out his hand. I had to smile back as I took it. 'See you in Lübeck . . . *Hals und Beinbruch* . . .' he said as he turned away to climb up. *Break a leg* – the good-luck wish of one flyer to another from the old German Imperial Air Service. Before he went over to check and close the cargo door – he would lock it from the inside – he bent to his feet, picked up an animate mass, and pushed it in ahead of him. That was Spartacus. No matter what language they are speaking *delight* always sounds the same on children's tongues, doesn't it? Their squeaks and giggles were the last noise I heard from them as the door was closed.

I should have sent Frieda and her niece with them of course, but she was having none of it, and we'd had that argument a few hours earlier . . . they were sticking to me and the dangerous bit. I had conjured up every persuasive power I had. Not a bloody chance.

'I think you're lucky for me, Charlie. I stay with *you*.'

'I'm lucky for everyone except myself,' I had told her. 'I'm fed up with it.'

'We have time to go to bed before Hanna brings Elli back.' That was that. I lost myself in the morphia of her curves for half an hour. As we had driven out to the airfield one of the things that had occurred to me was that I hadn't taken the cover of telling the Old Man that it was partly *her* idea, in case everything went tits-up.

Max and Ronson had already preflighted the *Pig*. I fired up her radio rig — the old-fashioned one. Scroton fired up *Whisky* alongside us. All her cabin lights were on. Max copied him, but all our lights remained off. Dave waved. Ronson waved back from our darkened flight deck. *All set*.

As we taxied away in the *Witch*'s wake I looked down through my small square port, and could see the women and Marthe's man huddled together in the front of the Hotdog and Coffee Wagon. Tommo and his truck were already on their way back. I hadn't even said *Goodbye* to him. I waved. I think they must have seen me because Magda flashed the lights. Then they were in the dark. I remembered Frieda and Elli were sitting back close to the tail. It would be cold and dark back there as well, but at least she had a seat to strap into: I would go back and check on them later.

Scroton lined up on the right of the runway. He still had all of his lights on. Max lined up to his left: he still had none of his.

There was just enough room for the two Goonybirds alongside each other, Max slightly behind Dave. If Gatow was running Control from the terminal we were out of sight of them in the gloom: and even if it had transferred to the portable cabin, that was at least seven hundred and fifty yards away.

The idea was that Gatow would launch only one *Halton* Dakota, whilst we would launch two – I'm sure that you've worked that out yourself by now. As long as there was no flight nipping at our tails to get off after us, no one else would know. That's why we were climbing into the sky at 0230. Over the radio I heard Dave's clearance and chat with Flying Control. When he got the green he looked across at us. I saw the pale flash of his hand as he chopped it forward giving us the signal, and we began to motor together.

I monitored the waves as we pulled away as one like a couple of fighter planes. Scroton kept us low until we were away from the city. A couple of times Control came back at him and urged more height, and then we started to put clean air between us and the ground about ten miles from Gatow. I heard Gatow preparing to clear a Hastings for take-off – we hadn't seen it in the dark, so there was every chance its crew hadn't seen us either – things were slightly, but only *slightly*, less frenetic in the early hours. Then I heard this exchange between two ground stations. The woman's voice was whoever was awake in their emergencies service centre. She asked Control, 'Was that one or two aircraft which just lifted off, Control?'

'One of Halton's old Dakotas. Why, honey?'

'Don't honey me. I thought I saw two.'

'Can't have done. You sound tired, honey. Like you need a warm bed . . .'

'Bugger off, Arthur!' Then there was a very obvious click. I'd met that Controller myself, and hadn't fancied him much either.

I checked our station-keeping on the *Witch*. Max had us in so close, and almost underneath her, that I had to crane my neck back to see her. Then I went back to check on Frieda. The kid was still asleep, despite the noise, and in my square masked torchlight I could see there were two cigarette butts on the floor beneath her seat.

I shouted, 'You OK?' She didn't reply, but nodded and reached out and squeezed my hand. I told her, 'When you light a fag cup your hand over the light.' I cupped my hands to demonstrate, the Dakota staggered for a moment in the cold air, and so did I. She reached out and steadied me, almost as fast as one of Alice's strikes, and nodded she'd understood. 'Thanks. I'll come back later.' She nodded again. It wouldn't be too long before things got technical.

I was actually back up in the cockpit, squeezed between and behind them, when the turn came up. Ronson had been holding up his nail on its bit of thread for about ten minutes when its point began to twitch inexorably to the north. I don't know why his arm didn't cramp. He glanced ostentatiously at his wristwatch, clicked and said, 'Skip. Turn in four minutes and thirty seconds from . . .' he paused, '. . . now.'

Max nodded. He dropped us under the *Witch*'s tail, and put us into the descent which should have terminated at about a very twitchy five hundred feet above the Father Christmas trees below, before he commenced his turn. Hopefully Dave would stay not too far above us throughout the approach, and hide us in his radar profile until we split – it would only work if their buggers were half asleep down there. *Ours* would be, I knew, and I just hoped that the Russian squaddies manning their mobile radars were as tired, cold and homesick as ours were. I couldn't hear any opposition radio traffic that sounded even vaguely urgent, or to do with us – but I'd got that wrong before, hadn't I?

Max put us into a flattish banked turn above the trees. At precisely the four minutes thirty Ronson had held his left hand up between them, four flat fingers and thumb pointing directly to the right. They must have done this before because they didn't exchange words. As the bank to the right came on, and I got that slightly unnerving sense of one side of the aircraft beginning to feel just a tad lighter than the other, Ronson's hand started to jerk gently back, almost degree by degree, until it was pointing directly ahead through the windscreens. Max had been counting the seconds. When he reached seventy-five he reached forward and switched on the instrument and navigation lights. The altimeter read four hundred and fifty feet, and it must have either snowed out here, or been subject to a hard frost, because we were flying above a white firebreak between the giant black pines. Max had told me that if we had to get down into it there was room for the *Pig*, with about a yard to spare at each wingtip. It was an option I wasn't keen to test. I put my hand on Red's shoulder; he turned and lifted his earphone.

'How long before we see it?'

He glanced at his watch, then back at me. 'Twenny or twenny-five minutes. That's if I found the right firebreak.'

That was something else I didn't want to think about. I went back to the radio rig. I heard nothing to indicate that there was anything alive out there. I even had time to go back and check on Frieda before I felt Max throttle back. She pulled my head forward for a quick kiss. Her nose was as cold as ice: little Elli whimpered in her sleep.

When I got back into the cabin the old slapdash Max had disappeared. The one in the pilot's seat had tense, set shoulders and both hands on the wheel. The bottom of the screen had frosted over, and he was leaning forward to see over that. I could even sense the minute movements he was making with his feet. The landing lights were on, and gaunt treetops flashed past. Red muttered, 'He hates flyin' slow an' low in cold weather . . . you can lose it too quick.'

'He hates flying slow at any time; it's not in his blood.'

'Shut up, gents,' Max spat. 'Where's your hand, Red?'

'On the throttles, Skip, just like the "Wreck o' the ol' Ninety-Seven".'

That was a song the Americans were singing. I guess that none of us found it funny. Just when I thought that the firebreak went all the way to the Baltic because Red had picked out the wrong one, there was a field in front of us, and Max slapped us onto it. Poor old *Pink Pig* bounced twice, like a lobbed tennis ball, and the noise was tremendous. I only just stayed on my feet.

'Ground frozen,' Max grated through clenched teeth as he tried to get the speed off her, then, 'Welcome to their bit of Germany, boss.' When he audibly exhaled I guessed that we were all right.

'I was there a fortnight ago. Didn't like it.'

Max rumbled the *Pig* around the grass; he obviously knew where he was going. He should have – it was the strip that the Soviets had shanghaied him onto weeks before. I went back to Frieda, found that Elli was crying, and Frieda was trembling. It wasn't with the cold. When she asked me, her voice shaking, 'Does that boy actually know how to fly this thing?' I squatted down and hugged them.

'He's one of the best. No one else could have found this place in the dark and got us down on it.'

She stopped shivering and said, 'You can say *I told you so* if you like, Charlie.'

'*I told you so*. What about?'

'We should have been on the other aeroplane, shouldn't we?'

'Too late for that. Don't worry; not long now.' Then I got up and left her. Elli had put her thumb in her mouth and had stopped whimpering. She regarded me with huge brown eyes. *Pretty kid*, I thought as I walked away.

I opened the cargo door and hopped down. Then I closed it to keep in whatever heat was still in the *Pig*. Max was keeping the engines ticking over – probably scared to shut them down. Their exhausts made soft blue plumes in the black night, and I could see steam rising from the engine covers. The idling propellers seemed to make a lot of noise in the still air, but they probably didn't. Apart from them, I could hear nothing. I could see nothing. Bloody Greg had let me down, hadn't he?

Ronson joined me. He lit a fag. I asked him, 'This is where they burned your hands?'

'Yeah; in an old brick machine-gun post alongside the hangar.' I followed his glance. I could just make out a fractionally lighter hump at the edge of the black mass of the hangar which stood between us and the lower stars.

'And you didn't mind coming back?'

'Yeah, I *minded*, boss. But I goes where the skipper goes.'

'Simple as that?'

'Life generally is. Wanna smoke?'

'No. I'll fill a pipe.'

There was no wind, so his smoke hung around us in the air; a wonderful toasted tobacco smell. He asked me, 'Am I in the clear over that *Mantell* thing yet?'

'I'm working on it,' I lied: I had completely forgotten it. 'I think that Old Man Halton will be able to fix it.'

'Good. I wanna go home. I wanna work on a farm, an' never see another goddamned aircraft as long as I live.'

'You really mean that?'

He paused for a long time before he said, 'No.'

I lit my pipe then, and left him there. The hangar was locked, and Ronson's machine-gun post smelled of piss. When I climbed back into the *Pig*, waving at Frieda and Elli before I turned my back on them, I moved up to sit alongside Max in Red's chair.

'Just as you remember it?' I asked him.

'Yeah. Can't see all that much though.'

'That small pillbox stinks of piss.'

'Sounds like the same place.'

'That was some navigating.'

'I've told you before, boss. Red's some navigator.'

'I'll believe you from now on. How long can we afford to wait?'

He must have been running the time in his head because he replied immediately, 'About seven minutes.'

'You always that precise, Max?'

'No. I reckon it's about as long as them lights will take to reach us.'

I saw them as soon as he pointed them out to me: two sets of lights moving slowly through the trees to the east of us. They flickered behind the foliage, but kept station on each other, so I guessed they must be on vehicles moving along a track. It was time for me to get down again to greet our guests. Either it was going to be Russian Greg, and I would be a hero again, or it was some significant other, and we'd all end up in Siberia.

All Russians are bastards. They kept me guessing until the last minute: the lights burst out onto the field and drove straight for the *Pink Pig* . . . even crossing the tracks she'd made across the frost-crisped grass. That would have prevented us changing our minds and taking off before they reached us. At the last moment they pulled over around her port wing and came to a halt near where I was standing. Their lights dazzled me, but in the minutes before they skidded to a halt I made out a small armoured car leading an army lorry with a tilt cover. In my mind I rehearsed the Russian words for *We surrender* I had idly learned from Greg months before. If they were Krauts I could always try *Kameraden*!

The iron lid of the armoured car clanged open. It was a shockingly loud sound. I could just make out the shape of a head and shoulders levering itself out. The turret and its heavy machine gun traversed slowly towards me, and I lost my nerve and held my hands up.

'*Kameraden*!'

'No you're not,' Red Greg's gravelly voice said. 'You're a fockin' Englishman.' Then he laughed. I didn't see what was so bloody funny.

We didn't do the introductions because we ran out of time. The driver didn't leave the small truck. Greg unbuckled the canvas tilt and helped out two children and a man and a woman. The children were so wrapped up you couldn't tell their sexes. The man looked about sixty – he was probably about thirty – it was a common look then for people who came out of the Eastern Zone. I knew that the woman had been a fighter pilot in the Russian air force, so I had expected someone glamorous like Amy Johnson, Queen of the Air. This woman was small and sort of pinched-up looking, and in my torch light I could see that there was a scattering of grey in her cropped dark hair. She smiled uncertainly at me.

'I'm Charlie,' I told her as I helped her into the *Pig*. 'Your bus conductor.'

She paused momentarily, which was something I didn't want.

'I don't understand.' Her voice was just as I remembered it. Low-pitched and weary.

'Sorry, English joke. I'll explain later,' and I urged her on.

Ronson had boarded in front of the passengers, and settled them onto a short bench the *Pig* had down one side of its aluminium inner skin. It had been designed for the Paras, and had useful lap belts. When I turned back to speak with the Gregs Ronson suddenly barked hoarsely at me, 'Max says there's more lights in the forest, boss . . . a couple of miles off. We gotta go.'

Red Greg said, 'Yes. You gotta go. Border patrol.'

'They'll get you. Come with us.'

'. . . an' spoil a promisin' career? No. Goodbye, English.' He was still bloody laughing.

No shake of the hand, no kiss on the cheeks – he ran back to the Dinky Toy armoured car. With legs that short he always looked funny running. Ronson dragged at my arm, pulling me back into the aircraft. Max was already winding up the engines. The Russian driver waved laconically from behind the wheel of the truck: did he know what his boss had got him into? Then we were moving in one direction and them in another. They drove straight for the track they'd arrived on, with all of their lights on. Max pointed the *Pink Pig* at the place he thought the firebreak was, and let her go: I was still checking the cargo-bay door was dogged shut when our wheels left the ground.

I may have been wrong but I gained the impression that Max had us away from there with more height than we'd come in on: I suppose he was right. If it *was* a border patrol down there the time for subterfuge was over – our only chance was to barge our way into the neutral corridor before the Reds sent nasty things with red stars on their wings to find us. I spun the dials for twenty minutes but the only thing I heard was a lonely American C-54, which had wandered off track and off schedule, being chided by his Controller. It was only after I sat back and thought about it that I realized that it was all a bit odd.

I stuck my shoulders through the bulkhead door space into the cabin. Ronson was doing the hand-signal game again. His left hand with its vertical palm was pointing right, across his body. He held his right hand up – fingers splayed – and was using them to count off the seconds: a finger came down with each second. I couldn't see the nail. When he said, 'Zero,' at his clenched fist Max pulled us into a nice climbing turn. He had known I was there without looking. He said, 'Spot for the other traffic, Charlie. I want to find us a gap to slot into.'

He had one eye on the altimeter, and the other on Ronson's

left hand, which was ticking like a clock towards the centre frame of the windscreens in front of them. When Ronson's hand pointed dead ahead he centred his controls, and settled the *Pig* into level flight. It was getting on for five in the morning. There was a dawn somewhere lighting up part of the east, and the sky train to Berlin was winding up for the day's effort. The navigation lights of a stream of aircraft heading for Gatow and Tegel twinkled relentlessly above us. The westbound stream wasn't much less dense, but Max edged us up closer and closer to it, and eventually found a couple of guys who were crap at station-keeping and managed to slot us in between them without giving anyone a heart attack.

That's when I asked him, 'Why didn't that border patrol tell their air force? I don't understand it. They could have roasted us.'

'Perhaps they figured they owed us one.' It was a lazy reply. Then he yawned.

Ronson said, 'Don't go to sleep on us, Skip. Not now you've nearly done it all right.'

'I'll go and ask our passengers,' I told them. 'Maybe they can tell us what's going on.' As it happened they couldn't, because they were all asleep and holding hands, and I hadn't the heart to wake them. Frieda was awake. She smiled and put her finger to her lips. I went back to my radios and stayed there until I was sure of the beacon at the northeastern end of the corridor, and it was time for me to make up a story for Lübeck.

Red stuck his head through the bulkhead door and said, 'Just thought you'd like to know it, boss.'

'What?' My eyes snapped open. How long had I been asleep?

'We just got into free air. Downhill all the way now.'

I didn't like to say it, but the problem was, I suppose, that *downhill all the way* is always a fair description of how an aircraft works when things go wrong.

Chapter Twenty-nine

That used main wheel tyre which Russian Greg had put on the *Pig* failed as we touched down at Lübeck. The heavy night landing an hour or so earlier, on a frozen grass field, probably hadn't helped. The tyre shredded immediately against the runway, and then the wheel began to break up. Then one of the undercarriage oleo legs gave out, and the wing slammed into the deck. There was no way back after that, even for Max.

What was left of the wheel bounced gaily down the runway ahead of us, shedding a spark or two each time it hit the concrete. The *Pink Pig* immediately slid into a series of enormous ground loops to port which probably saved my life. Thank you *Pig*. The huge horizontal gyrations took us out into the grass. We must have lost the tail wheel just about then. The first big bang was half a port prop blade coming through the fuselage about three feet behind me. The second was the outer section of the port wing detaching, and flipping over to slam back down on the cabin roof above me. I saw it physically distort and then split.

I could see that because I was lying on the floor . . . and I wondered why. At some point in the dance I had been spun off my seat, and had thumped my chin on my radio table on the way down.

After that there was silence. I've told you before about how quick violence is – the whole of the *Pig*'s death dance didn't take much longer than it has taken to write this. After the silence there was the distant – or so it sounded to me – cries of the children, and a steady dripping sound from above me. Then I smelled aviation spirit, and decided to split.

'That was a pig of a landing, Max.' That was Red's voice. He sounded shaky.

'This is your captain speaking. Ow! I think I broke a rib!' Max. 'The Brits would say I'd made a pig's breakfast of it.' He sounded even shakier.

'. . . or a pig's ear?' Red again.

'Stop fucking about you two, and get out!' I roared at them. 'Can't you smell the petrol?' Anyone who flies will tell you that they are precisely the five little words you never want to hear.

I staggered back down the fuselage to find that the poor old *Pig* had broken her back about ten feet ahead of our passengers, and, conveniently for me, had left her wide cargo door thirty yards away in the frosted grass.

Frieda was OK but staring ahead. She looked slightly pop-eyed. Elli was crying. I put my hand on the kid's head, and unbuckled their seatbelt. My hands and legs were shaking, and my chin hurt. I told Frieda, 'I'll say it now: *I told you so.*'

The little smile I got back, as she struggled to her feet still clutching Elli, said that her brain still worked. I helped them through the door and said, 'Start walking in *that* direction. Go as far as you can. Stop if you reach the road . . . You have to go quickly.' There was a moderate crosswind: it got inside the poor ruptured *Pig*, who creaked and groaned, and moved gently as if she was dying.

Max had slid past me with a moan, and over the door sill. Red had stopped to help the Russians out. The man spoke sharply to the two children, who stopped crying as if a tap had been turned off. When we were all outside and staggering away the Russian began to laugh, and then the woman copied him. So did I, and so, eventually, did Ronson. When we caught up with the others they looked at us as if we'd lost our minds.

We sprawled on the frozen field a hundred yards from the wreck, and saw and heard two excited fire trucks and an ambulance dash past about half a mile away, going in the wrong direction.

Max observed, 'They don't know where we are, do they? They don't know where we ended up.'

I told him, 'That aircraft always was a contrary bitch.'

That was when the *Pig* agreed with me, and set herself on fire. At first all I noticed was a blue light, like a gas flame, outlining her one good wing, which was tilted up into the halflight of dawn. Then she blew with a great yellow flash as the fuel left in her tanks went up. We felt her warm breath on our faces. Max grunted with pain, and sighed. Then he said, 'They can't friggin' miss us now, can they?'

Red Greg's sister began to sing a sad song in low tones you could scarcely catch, but the rest of us just watched the *Pig* burn. I heard the same song years later in a Russian Orthodox church in Paris, and someone told me they always sang it at funerals. Maybe, like me, she just hated to see aircraft die. I reached over and squeezed her hand.

'They'll find us soon,' I told her. I almost believed it myself.

Dave found us first. He'd grabbed a bicycle and hared around the peritrack in the direction he'd last seen us. He was on the runway when he saw us huddled in the grass outlined against the *Pink Pig*'s fire.

He threw the bicycle down and knelt by me.

'Did everyone get out, boss?'

'They did. God is being particularly friendly this morning.'

'You're only saying that. Any damage?'

'Max has hurt his chest. Probably stove a couple of ribs. That right, Max?'

Max groaned. He had a good groan. Then he said, 'I'm dying.'

Scroton said, 'He sounds all right to me.' He produced a leather-covered flask that must have contained a pint. 'Drink, anyone?'

Now you know that when a person is hurt, or in shock, alcohol is the worst thing you can give them . . . and I guess that we were all hurt or in shock.

'Thought you'd never ask,' I replied, propped myself up on my elbows and held my hand out. It was a very good whisky. I took a swig. Then I turned on one side, and offered it to Frieda. She took a pretty respectable swig herself before she passed it on. I stayed on my side looking at her. Everyone else was watching the burning wreck. The flickering light of the Dakota's distant flames on her face reminded me of the shadowy patterns on her body in our little room in Berlin. The *Pink Pig* crackled and popped, and we could feel the heat of her passing from where we lay. Bells in the distance, approaching, signalled that the emergency crews had reoriented themselves.

My sense of timing has never been good, you know that, but I felt driven to speak – me and my mouth – and found myself saying something odd.

'Frieda,' I said, loud enough for her to hear above the fire, 'will you marry me? Please.'

She paused before she replied, and then shook her head before saying, 'That would probably be a very silly thing for me to do, Charlie.'

Scroton sighed. I think that he was disappointed . . . there had been a smile in her voice though.

The first of the fire crews drove straight past us, and frantically began assaulting the *Pig* with foam and axes. They wanted to rescue the survivors. Ronson wandered over, narrowly avoiding being run over by the second, and advised them not to bother. I lay back, put my hands behind my head, and closed my eyes.

When I opened them again I could see Borland's boots and legs close by, and a three-legged dog was pissing on my foot.

Max complained when we stuffed him in the ambulance. Red accompanied him. That didn't seem to make it any better for him; I think that he was feeling a bit abandoned . . . so I bundled Spartacus in with them and told Max to see he got back to Gatow. Thinking about it later I wondered how he had got that far with us that morning – I think he just couldn't bear to be left out of things. A second ambulance trundled us around to the far limits of the airfield where *Whisky* and *Dorothy* were chumming up to each other – it was where we were supposed to have met them.

Dave had perked up. He said, 'Glad you're here, Charlie.'

'Why?'

'*You* can tell the Old Man that we've burned one of his aeroplanes having a private party. I wouldn't want to do that myself.'

Max had been supposed to take *Dorothy* on to the UK for maintenance; he was due a rest – so was she. We hadn't told anyone she was full of children and refugees of course, and now we all took it for granted that Scroton would step up to the plate. They made room for the four Russkis, Frieda and Elli in the York among the children and the nuns – it was beginning to look a bit crowded in there – while we stood between the two aircraft sorting out who was going to do what. Bozey and Dreyfus would take *Whisky* back with them in a couple of hours; a load of coal had already been earmarked for her. Bozey would then run things until I got back. What was left of the *Pink Pig* was still burning in the infield . . . the fire crew seemed to have her under control.

Bozey pointed out, 'They won't like it if you just sod off, and leave that bonfire out there without giving them a report, boss.'

'Max was flying it. He can tell them.'

'You're Max's boss – they'll expect you to cooperate.'

'I know,' I told him. 'Let me think for a minute; I'm trying to work that one out.'

Several excuses came to me, but none sounded very convincing. The only saving grace was that the *Pig* hadn't shut the airfield down. Flights were arriving and leaving with the regularity of a metronome. 'What if you told them I had to go back to fix up a replacement kite ASAP? . . . that I was more worried about getting the job done than completing the paperwork?'

'Anyone who didn't know you well could believe that.'

'Would you?'

'Not sure, boss. Try it on these buggers, and see what happens.'

These buggers: a sedately driven jeep which disgorged a stocky sergeant in khakis, wearing a sleeveless leather tank jacket over his uniform, and an officer who looked like that comedian-in-waiting John Thomas. Because it *was* John Thomas. He saluted negligently with his swagger stick as he strolled up.

'Morning, squire. Somebody told me it was you.'

'What was . . . or who was?'

'The leader of the shower that just left a burning aeroplane in the middle of our nice tidy airfield. Demned thoughtless of you.'

'Main wheel tyre blew as we touched down. We were lucky.'

'I know, old chap . . . and I'm very pleased that no one was hurt. I've already had a quick word with your pilot.'

'How is he?'

'Swearing very colourfully. The MO wants to hang on to him for a day . . . apparently he was going on leave.'

'Don't worry. He'll still get it.'

'This'll crimp your style a bit. Losing an aircraft must be hard on a small outfit like yours.'

'Yes. I'm going back with the York now; see if we can get another one quickly . . . we've got to keep the operation running.'

'The station commander won't like that very much, old boy.' He hadn't said *You can't do that*, which was very interesting.

'You've got my pilot and my engineer – isn't that enough? I can't tell you anything they can't. One moment we were in the middle of one of Max's usual sweet landings, and the next we were falling to bits in the middle of a ground loop. Anyway, I got a knock on the chin, and might have been out of it for a few minutes.' If I looked browned off it was because I felt it.

Thomas said something that sounded like, 'Hmph,' and stroked his chin. 'Wait one, won't you . . .' He strolled back to his jeep. I watched him reach in, pick up a radio mic, and begin to speak. His sergeant gave me a friendly smile and said, 'Don't worry, sir; the Captain will sort things out – it's what he's good at.'

It was just his manner: it had *Regular* written all over it. I felt better already. When Thomas came back he was whistling perkily, and slapping his stick gently against his knee.

'He's inclined to let you off this once, provided you make a statement to the AAIs when you come back: matter of ticking the right boxes . . . all crew witnesses accounted for, that sort of thing.'

'And what are *you* inclined to do, Captain?' I assumed that the matter rested with him.

'I'm *ectually* inclined to get you off my patch as soon as I ruddy well can, old son. To be honest you've been a pain in the proverbial from the moment I clapped eyes on you.'

'It's nice to be wanted.'

'As far as I can make out, old son, about half your mob appears to be wanted – but I don't think we're talking about the same thing, are we? It just so happens that everyone requires you to keep flying for the moment . . . otherwise you'd all be facing a spell talking to my sergeant here.'

There was the way he spoke which made you smile.

'. . . but you're saying we can go?'

'Bravo. I'm saying you can go. I'd do it now if I was you, before I change my mind.'

'Thank you.'

'. . . but first you wouldn't mind my man having a quick shufti in Red Rover over there . . . just to make sure it's not full of contraband . . .' I shrugged. Bollocks! The bastard had me, and he knew it. We'd been far enough away from *Dorothy* for no sound from her to travel, but she was full of little people and nuns, wasn't she? Thomas nodded to his sergeant and said, 'Carry on, Mr Staggers.'

The sergeant walked smartly over to the rounded door under the York's wing, and rapped on it. Someone opened it from inside. I immediately heard the murmur of the kids – it swelled and died. Staggers was looking at more than forty people. Thomas eyed me. I couldn't hold his gaze: I hated letting Fergal down. Staggers closed the door, and came back. He said very clearly, as if he was making a report, 'Empty, Mr Thomas, just as you thought. Not a blessed thing. She's going back as clean as a whistle.'

Thomas stared at me, and then turned on a dazzling smile.

'Very well, Sergeant. We'll leave it to them, shall we?'

He touched the sergeant's elbow as they turned away to their transport, but he said to me, 'Say hello to Blighty for me. I miss the lights.'

'I will, Captain . . . and I will remember you; both of you.'

'Just remember us the next time we ask you a favour, that's all, old fruit.'

At least he was telling me where we stood.

Scroton waited until their tail lights were fifty yards away before he said, 'Blimey. What was that all about?'

'It was all a charade. He was just showing me who was in charge, that's all. Shall we go back to England now?' Then I had a thought. 'Who's your engineer?' I wondered if the nuns had a prayer against farts.

For once in her evil life *Dorothy* flew like an angel: she seemed to slice across the sky like a huge red toboggan – no bumps, jumps or little skids. No shudders or misses from those tired old motors. Now, I know that the pilots among you will deride this thought, but from the viewpoint of an outsider looking in, a pilot's skill sometimes appears to move from essentially a technical performance to an art form. That was what Dave did with *Dorothy* that morning: he flew the big old cow as if he was intimately attached to her.

We picked up the new London Traffic Control just off Gravesend, and with their blessing skated west down the Channel for home. The Goodwin Sands were showing, and the red lightship bobbed on a dark blue sea like a toy boat. There wasn't a cloud in the sky, but it was cold out there . . . anyone glancing up could have seen our contrail stretching for miles. I didn't know what to expect when we made landfall; my planning sequence had ended with getting the circus airborne from Lübeck. Fergal had told me to leave the rest to him, remember? What the hell I was going to do with the Russians and Frieda's niece was anybody's guess. Frankly, I didn't care all that much. I was just glad to have got them this far.

Something very curious happened at Lympne. My brain stopped working. It was as if I had run into a brick wall.

There was a cream and red motor coach parked up alongside the admin building. Two priests stood alongside it. One was that villainous old sod I'd met in Liverpool – Fergal's mentor: he looked like a dog with two tails. I have rarely met someone who looked as pleased with himself. The other was a tall ascetic-looking guy who had *administrator* written all over his face. He had two expressions which chased each other around his features: *pissed off*, and *alarmed*. I liked neither.

Father Leakey said, 'Welcome back, Mr Bassett. I would say *Well done*, but my colleague is very nervous about it all. If the opposition had a College of Bishops handy they'd all be in a pet.'

'Am I going to be blamed for this?'

'No; why don't we blame God? He has broad shoulders. Do you care?'

It took me ages to frame an answer for him.

'I don't know.' I was telling the truth.

The children were helped out of Dorothy's capacious gut one by one, and led over to the coach by one of the glamorous nuns. At the coach's door a stocky woman in a dark blue uniform I didn't recognize was checking the luggage labels that Fergal had attached to each kid's coat, and writing their names in a hard-covered exercise book.

I asked, 'Who's she?' without having realized that the action had moved away from me. I was temporarily alone.

Holland, the Customs guy, must have heard me, because he wandered over from somewhere and said, 'Mrs Search. I thought you'd already spoken to her?' I hadn't noticed that he was part of the reception party.

'I may have done,' I told him. 'Years ago. What's happening?'

'The children are being taken to an orphanage up north. That was the idea, wasn't it?'

'I don't know.' I was still telling the truth.

He squinted at me and said, 'When did you last sleep, Charlie?'

'I don't know that either.'

He beckoned someone over. When she turned up she was

Elaine. I couldn't see the bump in her belly yet. Bob asked her, 'Is there anywhere we can tuck this sad specimen up before he falls asleep on his feet?'

'We have one of the old crew huts . . . aircrew sometimes overnight there.'

I thought *That's not all we do over there*, but the words didn't get as far as my mouth.

'It will have to do; won't it? Come on.'

They told me afterwards that I insisted on taking Frieda and her niece over there with me, and Frieda reported that I'd ordered, 'C'mon. We're all going to bed.'

'It's still afternoon, Charlie.'

'Doesn't matter; I'm shagged out.'

She didn't argue. We put Elli in one of the old iron-framed beds; I took the one next to her, and Frieda the next. Elaine was OK to us; she fired up the stove and pulled down the blackout blinds. I remember I let all of the air from my lungs in a huge sigh, and Frieda's voice asking, 'Are you all right, Charlie?' The words came from a thousand miles away.

'It all became too complicated. I'm a plain man really,' I told her, and then I closed my eyes.

I had a bad moment when I awoke because I thought that I was back on the squadron. I opened my eyes to see the curved roof of a Nissen hut above me, and heard a gentle chorus of sweet snores. Scroton and Mortensen had crept in and bagged the two beds nearest the stove. The stove contributed to the smell of the place; burned logs and coaldust briquettes – once you've smelled that combination you never forget it. I got up, banked up the stove – its fire was on its last legs – and slipped outside. It was evening and chill: there was already a frost on the grass. It even glistened on *Dorothy*, reflecting the light from Elaine's office window.

Elaine wasn't there, but she was around somewhere because her coat was still hanging from a hook on the back of the door, and there was a trace of her scent in the air. She came in with a mug of Bovril in her hand.

'You didn't sleep long. Want one of these?'

The rich beefy smell from the mug was delicious.

'Yes please. You OK?'

'I'm fine, love. Never better.'

'Still . . . ?'

'Preggers? Yes; two months. Can I come back to work after I've had the baby?'

'Of course you can. We'll never manage without you. What does your Terry think?'

'Like a dog with two tails. I've never seen him this happy.'

'Who's the father?'

'*He* is, of course. What do you take me for?' It was a dumb thing for me to ask straight out of the blue, wasn't it? It was the first time she had completely blanked me. The temperature in the room fell by about ten degrees. '*Here*, have this.' She thrust the mug of meaty water at me, 'I'll make myself another.'

I followed her through to the small galley to apologize. 'That was really stupid: I'm sorry. I just wanted to . . .'

She kept her back to me. 'There are some things we won't talk about any more. OK?'

'OK I understand.'

'You *don't* actually, Charlie, because you're not a woman – but I won't argue with you: I still want you to be my friend . . .'

'A friend who's allowed to cop a feel now and again?'

That put a grin back on her moosh. 'I think that's a definite *no*. All right?'

'It will have to be, won't it? Story of my life.' It was a terrific way to end a relationship and begin another . . . still smiling. 'So tell me what's been going on. Who was arrested while I slept . . . ?'

'No one. Everything's running very smoothly. The Old Man is

flying to Holland tomorrow . . . if KLM won't sell him another Dakota he'll try to lease one from them.'

'Did Bozey check in?'

'Yes: he says the dog misses you. He's moved one of the Lancastrians over from food from Wunstorf, to coal from Lübeck, and the dog got back with him on the first flight. But he still wants to know when he can get *Dorothy* back.'

'I'll speak to him. Anything else.'

'An American Flying Fortress has crashed in Scotland. It was on the news.'

'Bloody Yanks can't fly for shit.'

'What about *our* Yanks?'

'They're the exceptions that prove a rule. Randall's a genius. So's Max: how is he, by the way?'

'Who?'

'Rufus. His real name's Louis Maxwell, otherwise known as Max.'

'Oh *him*. Didn't he do rather well?'

'Yes he did. I told you, he's probably a genius too.'

'Bruised ribs. They'll let him loose tomorrow.'

'Get him back here: he's due some leave.'

'*Jawohl, Herr Kapitän.*'

'. . . and put the wireless on; they may say something about that crash . . .'

Elaine threw me a mock salute. I took a step towards her but then thought better of it, and turned away. She noticed and smiled: it was probably going to work. I asked her one more thing. 'What happened to that Russian family I brought in?'

'They had no contacts over here so the Old Man arranged for them to be taken away to some charity for DPs. He's not angry, but the Foreign Ministry is being a bit humpy. Mr Halton said to ask you to tell him in advance the next time you're going to take the country's foreign policy into your own hands . . .'

'He's not angry, you said?'

'He laughed. I think he rather enjoyed it.'

'I'm surprised he hasn't whisked Frieda away before now.'

'He asked, but she wanted to stay with you.'

'I wonder why.'

'Wait until she wakes up and ask her, you stupid man.'

Chapter Thirty

What else do you need to know? I suppose that I could tell you about the photograph. I was looking through my old photograph albums about a week ago. I came across a snap that was taken about ten days after I brought those children home – which would probably be called *people trafficking* today, and have a bunch of social workers running around with smoke coming out of their backsides.

The photograph was taken on a chilly morning on the strand at Bosham, and it wasn't a classic: all of our feet are chopped off below the knees. James had bought one of those new-fangled cameras that gave you a timer setting for a delayed exposure. He made us all huddle together, balanced the camera on a fence post, and then scuttled round to get into the picture himself. There's James and Maggs, me and the two boys . . . and Frieda with Elli Junior on one arm. Dieter is between Frieda and me, holding our hands tight: you probably get the picture. If you look carefully at the grins on the faces in the photograph it sometimes looks as if they merge into one great smile. Was it Max or Red who'd told me *downhill all the way*? Maybe the old fellah upstairs had decided I was due for a bit of downhill after all.

I didn't get to see any more of Operation Plainfare – they did the rest of the Berlin Airlift without me, and it worked out rather well for them. Maybe I should stay away from wars, or the things that pass for them, more often. I stayed at home, and learned to run an airline instead. It wasn't wholly my choice, or the Old Man's either. It was something to do with the War Office sending us a telegram withdrawing permission for me to be in Germany: apparently I caused too much bother. I showed it to Holland months later. He told me, 'I've seen a couple of those before. They were handed out to a couple of black marketeers they couldn't prosecute. You haven't been buying or flogging the stuff they don't want you to, have you?'

'Not so much as you'd notice.' I thought I'd lied rather smoothly. 'Nylons for the ladies, and a few fags. I smuggled a couple of pounds of liquorice into Berlin once for a Russian with a sweet tooth.'

'It must have been all those kids you brought back then. I wonder who you upset most.'

'Everyone, probably. I noticed you moved your Spits. What did the government do with them this time?'

'Sold them to a rather charming South African with an export licence, who will no doubt sell them on to where they were going in the first place; so everyone will be happy.'

'So what was the point of seizing them?'

'Because that's what the law tells us to do.'

'Well, the law's an arse!'

'. . . and people like me are its bog paper. Let me worry about the law while you keep the birds flying.'

I could see that he was even more downcast than me.

'What's the matter with you, anyway?'

'That Israeli smuggler of yours they captured in The Parachute. He was sentenced yesterday.'

'What did he get?'

'Four years, then we'll send him back to Hungary. They still don't like Jews over there, so they'll probably try him all over again, and swing him.'

'I had a friend called Tommo once. He used to say *Shit happens*. What happened to the other one?'

'We never saw him again; maybe he lost his nerve. Part of me hopes he reached Israel.'

We were whingeing on like a couple of girls, and someone had to break the spell. I asked him, 'Fancy a drink? The pub's shut, but they'll open the back door for me.'

Because you are reasonably attentive you'll have noticed that I referred to Tommo in the past tense, which wasn't a mistake.

I went north more than a year later. A sort of pilgrimage I suppose. Randall, Max and Dave Scroton all knew the score, and came to me separately to offer to come with me. I turned them down, and went on my own. Apart from my father and his brother I didn't know anyone who had the fortitude required to live in Scotland. Old Father Leakey did, and he called in a couple of favours to ease the way for me.

It had all started when Elaine mentioned that Flying Fortress crash in Scotland the night I got back. I had shivered immediately. I knew that it was nothing to do with me, but I shivered all the same. What's that phrase? *Someone just walked over my grave*. I look back on that first Boeing crash now as if it was a pebble tossed into the sea of time. The ripples of its warning came forward, and came forward and came forward until they reached out and touched me weeks later – because weeks later was when Tommo was strapped into another Fortress that met a fiery end in one of those high Scottish glens.

Dolly called me: it was the first time we had spoken since my return – she had the crew and passenger list for an air crash the day before. She said that Tommo's name didn't figure on it, but nevertheless he'd been on the flight, and she was sorry. I asked how she knew, but all she did was say *Sorry* again, and put the phone down. When she had begun to talk about the crash I was aware that we were talking about Tommo, long before she said his name. It was as if I already knew, as if I had known for ever; I believed her as soon as she said it.

It wasn't a Flying Fortress this time, it was a Superfortress – one of those big B-29s – and it's gone down in legend as *The Diamond Bomber*, on account of the stones that some of the passengers and crew were alleged to be smuggling back from Germany. Nobody walked away from it. That was the way it was in the Forties: miracles or disasters.

I took the night train to Glasgow, and was awoken in the morning by a smart-looking steward offering me a mug of char. When I opened up the window blind all I could see were rolling miles of marsh and wasteland, with jagged mountains in the near distance: Rannoch Moor. I'd flown exercises over the same damned place in 1943, and had hated it even then. It's an inhospitable dump. I'm not one of these foolish Englishmen attracted to desolate wastes: I get insecure if I can't see a pub sign swinging in the breeze. We rolled into Glasgow Central at twenty past eight. For the first time I loved its blackened walls, and the smoke in the air.

My old man met me in the station hotel lounge there, and we caught up with each other over a pot of tea and a plate of cakes. He scoffed most of them, just like I remembered from when I was a kid. He'd never approved of cakes and biscuits at home when my sister and I were young, saying that they'd make us fat. There was never any chance of that, because on the few occasions that they appeared he ate his way through them like an army of soldier ants on the march. He was one of those sugar-addicted folk who couldn't bear to leave anything sweet on a plate, or in a packet or tin. The old prayer, *Lead me not into temptation*, had never worked for him, which is why he never bought any cakes for us. There's logic in there somewhere.

We talked about his brother, who lived with him now, and agreed we both missed my sister and ma. After that we didn't seem to have all that much to say to each other. He asked me, 'Where d'ye say you were going?'

'A place near Lochgoil, which is up in a place called Argyll. Wild and woolly.'

'An air crash, you said?'

'Yeah. One of my pals: an American going home.'

'Would ha' thought you'd seen enough air smashes in your time. How many was it now?'

I did the arithmetic in my head. I only counted the real ones.

'Three and a bit.'

'Want me to come with you?'

'No; but thanks for offering, Dad. I'll stay with you on the way back, and tell you all about it then.'

'How do you get there?'

'Believe it or not the quickest way is by sea. I've got to get down to the docks before midday, and get on a small cargo ship that goes around the islands and coastal villages. It will set me off at the nearest pier sometime tomorrow. I understand that I'll have to hoof it from there, but someone's arranged for a local chap to guide me. It's not too far.'

'Make sure he takes you to the right crash – there's bloody dozens of them up there. The Yanks are calling Scottish mountains Boeing Magnets because of the number of planes they seem to attract.'

Not exactly encouraging about anything, my dad. I often wonder where I got my irrational optimism from. Then he gave me his famous sideways look, and added, 'Wouldn't have minded a wee sailing trip though.'

Ah well. It had always been on the cards.

That night I found out three things about the old man: he could win any card game you could name, he could play a squeeze box he borrowed from the engineer, and had the largest repertoire of dirty songs a man was capable of learning.

'It was the Great War that did it,' he explained to me. 'We had to find something to do with our time when we were waiting to fight.'

'When were you waiting to fight?' the little skipper asked him – we were alongside Dunoon Pier for the night, and the bottles had come out.

'Most of the time,' my dad told him, and broke into a wheezy laugh that led into another stuttering obscene ballad. When I looked around the small day cabin it was like being in the company of pirates. Maybe I was.

They dropped me off on another small pier, and promised to pick me up again in a few days' time. The tide was dropping, so the skipper just nudged the end of the pier with his puffer's straight bow, and expected me to jump down with my pack on my back. My old man stayed with the ship: I think they wanted him for his entertainment value. They'd even signed him on articles to make it legal. No matter what the old bastard did, he always seemed to come up smelling of roses.

The sea loch was like a mirror as the old ship backed away, its thin whistle quaking. I could already hear the concertina squeaking away below. I thought they'd probably got the bottle out as soon as my back was turned.

I needn't have worried about making contact with my guide, or finding the hotel. A small dark blue Fordson van was at the land side of the pier. It had *HM Coastguard* in white letters on its doors, and a Coastguard officer leaning back on the bonnet smoking a big black pipe. He stuck out his hand.

'James Gillies, Coastguard. We're expecting you. Duncan asked me to collect you.'

'Charlie Bassett.'

'Of course, Mr Bassett . . . and who else would you be?'

I counted the houses, and reached eleven. I counted the churches and stopped at one. There was also only one hostelry . . . and the small stone Coastguard office. Sure, who else would I be? He drove me the hundred yards to the hotel bar. Inside there was a smouldering peat fire even although it was early summer, and a reception party of half a dozen men. I quickly got the impression that it was going to be a jolly afternoon.

I got to meet Duncan Galloway, my mountain guide, about four hours later. He was actually a local shepherd. I was drunk by then, and my pack was at my feet. I still hadn't booked in or seen my room. I had imagined the guy would be about nine feet tall, red-haired, bearded and wearing a kilt; one of those supermen who rub cold porridge into their muscles to keep them toned. Galloway was actually about the same size as me; clean-shaven, and had a small sun-browned, lined face. He wore an old navy sweater that was so darned and out of shape that gravity had begun to have her say. The scrawny neck that poked from its top was white. After a while I realized that he reminded me of a tortoise. Oh yeah; and he was about a million years old . . . I wondered if he could make it upstairs at night, let alone take me up a mountain.

He collected me at six-thirty the next morning. The hotelier had woken me an hour before, and I'd lain in a bath until the hangover began to relent. I was still halfway through breakfast of Loch Fyne kippers and scrambled egg when Galloway arrived for me. He sat in the sun and smoked his pipe until I showed up. Then he just nodded along what passed for a street and we began to walk.

Where the street ended an unmetalled forestry road began: it wound up into the heights like pictures I've seen of roads in the Swiss Alps.

Galloway told me, 'Don't fret, Mr Bassett; we'll be up the hill long afore noon. It's just a wee scramble for a man as fit as yersel'.'

The hill, he called it. As far as I could make out I had about five miles of Alpine pass to climb, onto a hundred miles of rough scrub, and then *the hill:* great grey crags like rotten teeth . . . it looked about as high as bloody Everest. A cloud actually touched one of the peaks.

'We going up there?'

'Most of the way.'

'Any tips for me?'

'Keep your pipe going, sir, against the midges.'

My old man had told me about the midges; he said they'd bite you to the bone.

'Will that prevent them from biting me?'

'No; but it might help keep your mind off them.'

'Would you mind slowing down a bit, Mr Galloway, so I can keep up with you?'

'I'm trying to outrun the midges and the ticks for us . . . if you put the work in now, Mr Bassett, you'll find it easier going later on.'

Seconds later I felt the first midge grab me by the nape of the neck, so I hurried to stay up with him.

We weren't troubled by midges at the crash site. Duncan told me the strong smell of aviation spirit in the air disagreed with them, although we'd still have to run their gauntlet on the way down. The big silver Boeing had iced up above the mountains, clipped one of the peaks and created its own Viking funeral in a high glen named Succoth.

'What does *Succoth* mean?' I asked him.

'Buggered if I know. A lot of places up here have damned silly names.'

'Aren't you a local?'

'I am now. I came up from Manchester when I was a teenager, after the First War. I never went back.'

An area the size of a football pitch of heather and coarse grass was burned and scorched. The fuel soaked into the ground ensured that it would be years before the secondary growth re-established itself. Interestingly it was already pitted with freshly dug rabbit holes, and piles of their fibrous pellets. There were pieces of aircraft everywhere – most of them small, so she must have hit the ground very hard indeed. The first thing I recognized was the distorted tail turret, under a small section of fin. Then I picked out engines, wheels and small sections of airframe. Bullets were strewn around; the local lads could have had a field day up there – they probably did.

Duncan told me, 'I was the third man up here that day. We'd heard the aircraft, you see; awfu' low . . . And then the crash; it was a hell of a bang. With two other hill men we made up two parties of two, and climbed the hill to look for her. The other group got there first; we searched too low to begin with.'

'What was the weather like?'

'Bloody cold, sir. Exceptionally bloody cold as I remember. There was a light covering of snow – which had melted with the fires of course – but the ground was still as hard as iron.'

'It must have been ghastly . . .'

'You ever saw an air crash, Mr Bassett?'

'Yes. I've even been in a couple.'

'So I don't have to tell you what it was like.'

'No you don't.'

Time for reflection. Neither of us spoke for a minute or two. Then he resumed. 'We checked for survivors, but all we found

479

were bodies everywhere. They'd been thrown around, and smashed up. They were all dead before they burned, I'm sure o' that.'

'Good.' I'd always had a morbid fear of burning; still have, come to that.

'The nonsense started the next day when the Yanks arrived.'

'What nonsense?'

'All the pretending that things were other than they seemed to be, sir. For instance, they said that the passengers were all low-ranking soldiers, but we'd been picking up solid gold wings and generals' stars all morning. At least five of them had general's uniforms in their kit. I saw a full dress uniform come out of a split kitbag. Then there was an army padre going round picking up any loose papers he found, and pulling papers out of briefcases and spilt bags, and burning them. Right over there.'

'Didn't he say a prayer for the dead?'

'No. He just told me to fuck off when I asked him what he was doing. Funniest damned preacher I ever met!'

'Can you remember if there was a big man among the dead?'

He sighed. 'Mr Bassett . . . there were big men, small men, middle-sized men, and bits o' men. Scattered all over the hillside. Some o' them pretty, and some o' them not. It took us all the next day to recover them . . . I can't remember any one man. Except the one who wasn't there, o' course: we didn't find him till spring.'

'How was that?'

'Oh: people come up here – you know. A hundred years ago the poor folk took the bounty of the seas when wrecks came up on the coasts; now we collect pieces of airplanes when they fall on our mountains – you've no idea how useful some things are. One of my neighbours took a bit of an aircraft's body down the hill with his tractor and trailer: it's his garden shed now.'

'From here?'

'*No*, man. There was nothing up here that size.'

'What happened to the bodies?'

'They were taken off the hill the next day. 'orrible day that was: freezing fog. We had to take them down on stretchers. They say that from Lochoilhead you could see the line of lanterns and torches, bobbing down the hill in the fog and silence. Then there was the Yanks collecting everything up, and burning the papers like I told you.'

'Did they take the dead away then?'

'Not at first. They laid them in the church hall for identification. The place stank of petrol and burnt people for months afterwards. The Boy Scouts who meet there now say the place is haunted.'

'Do you believe that?'

He looked off into the distance. The cloud had lifted, and the peaks were granite grey and magnificent against the blue of the sky.

'I don't know of anywhere that's not – haunted, that is. It's what happens to you as you get older.'

'What about the man you found later?'

There was a long pause again before he said, 'He'd been thrown hundreds o' yards away by the crash. That's why they missed him. He'd been up here for months by then, and even although it had been freezing he was messed about a lot. Foxes and wild cats had been at him. Maybe some birds as well.'

I shuddered: that echo through time I told you about. 'What did you do?'

'We emptied his pockets, and buried him over there.' He nodded to where the scorched earth and shallow crater ended, and the green scrub started. '. . . about twenty paces over there, and put him under two slabs o' rock. We dug him a good grave, but we couldn't write on it of course.' *When you don't know what to say, don't say anything*: one of my dad's rules, and not a bad one. So I said nothing, and Duncan went on, 'I still feel bad about

481

that. Some of the bodies are still down in the burial ground: he should be down there wi' them.' Then, from his pocket, he handed me Tommo's Swiss wristwatch. It had been scrupulously cleaned, and was still ticking remorselessly. Tommo had been very proud of it. 'I took that off him; I always knew someone would come for him one day.'

I took the watch and walked away – as far as the patch of ground covered by two granite slabs. It actually looked like a pretty decent grave to me; I wouldn't have minded it myself. I pulled out the half of Johnny Walker I had taken with me, and had a decent couple of swigs. As I tipped the bottle the sun made my eyes water. Duncan left me alone: I don't know what he was thinking. I don't know how long I stood there. When I eventually walked back to him he said, 'They told us that there were twenty people on the plane, you see: four crew and sixteen passengers . . . all on their way home to America. They took twenty down off the hill that second day, so this last man was never there.'

'So you robbed him?'

He sighed before he told me, 'Aye: I've already said, Mr Bassett. I don't feel proud about what we did.'

He must have thought I was slightly crazy when I grinned and said, 'Don't worry about it; he would have found the idea really funny . . . and I don't suppose he'll mind being up here on his own either. Anyway, he won't be alone . . . you and your pals will climb up from time to time and toast him, won't you?'

I didn't say it, but the implication that that was the price of my silence was deep in there somewhere. Duncan nodded. That would do. I told him, 'I'd like to keep the watch.'

'Fine. I was jest minding it fer ye.' Then he said, 'If we started out now we could be down again fer opening time. It always takes longer going down.' I've never figured out why, but he was absolutely right.

As we picked our way down in the sunlight the midges began

to savage me again. Duncan didn't seem to notice. I rubbed some whisky on my exposed neck. I don't know if that helped, but at least I smelled better. Part of the way down he said, 'The way of it with these high-ground aircraft wrecks is that you find something new every time you go up there. I picked this up while you were thinking about your pal.' He dived into a pocket, and held his hand out. '. . . one of them must ha' been taking back a doll's house for his kiddy; that's very sad to think of.'

He handed me what looked like a miniature hand-painted pub sign. It read *Alice's Restaurant*. Poor Alice. She must have been on her way back home too. I told him, 'I know who this belonged to. Can I keep it as well?'

'Sure. It will make a nice keepsake.'

The road, when we got back to sea level, was uneven and dusty, and my ankles were sore. There were a lot more people in the bar when we reached it. They must have known what Duncan would tell me, and I suppose everyone was interested – if not anxious – to see how it panned out. I didn't see Duncan again until later in the evening, and we were all pretty lit up by then. That's when I got what I now think to be the real end of this story. I found myself crushed up to the small bar when Duncan shoved in with two glasses of whisky. He gave me one, and said, 'These folk think I'm touched y'know.'

'*Touched*?'

'Not all there.' He tapped his forehead with a finger.

'Why?'

'I told them that I saw a big fat snake up on the hill last month; thick as my arm it was. No bugger believes me.'

I probably laughed, because he winced. I told him, '*I'll* believe you. What did it look like?'

'Like one o' them poisonous things in Randolph Scott Western films, but bigger.'

'Did it rattle at you?'

'It surely did, sir. I think it must have escaped from a zoo, or something like that . . . but no one believes me here.'

'Then that's their misfortune, isn't it? Tell the kids to run away if they hear the rattling sound: better safe than sorry.'

I tried to engage him with the eye-to-eye lock, to communicate that I knew more than I was saying, but his attention was already elsewhere, his head turned away. He was looking across at one of the few women in the bar; the only one under fifty.

Much later I was very drunk. The Coastguard, James Gillies, steered me to a chair at a small table. Duncan was in another alongside it. Gillies asked me, 'So tell us . . . how long will you be gracing us by your presence, Mr Bassett?'

'. . . another couple of days I expect. I have to wait for the boat. My dad's still on it.'

'Well, Englishman . . . why don't we walk up another hill tomorrow, with my friend Duncan here. You can meet his ewes, and he can instruct us in the finer points of shepherding. The exercise will do you good. Then we can drink some more.'

'Why not?' I asked him.

The last person to call me *Englishman* had been Russian Greg, and I suddenly realized that I hadn't thought about him for weeks. I raised my glass and said, probably in a bit of a wobbly voice, ''bye Tommo: 'bye Greg.'

The Coastguard asked, 'What was all that about?'

'Just closing a book,' I told him.

Epilogue

Behind our grey stone house there's an overgrown Victorian garden I never got round to, but years ago we opened up one of the old paths. We cut a large round glade in the rhododendron forest which had swallowed everything. The glade is framed by high, lanky larches and firs, and we planted large boulders around it like a Neolithic stone circle. That was my horticultural joke; something for the archaeologists to puzzle over in years to come. We've managed to keep it open, and it fills with bluebells and snowdrops each spring. It is my favourite private space. I love it because it's cool in the summer, and one of the last spots to succumb to the frosts of autumn.

I saw Tommo there last week. He's taken up a pipe, which is quite odd, because he was always a cigar man when I knew him. He was standing in the last of the autumn sunlight, but throwing no shadow of course. He was telling a joke when I hobbled in, and turned and waved idly to acknowledge my presence. Russian Greg was sitting on one of the stones listening and laughing, and swinging his legs in his polished cavalry boots. He appeared to be chewing on a stick of that awful liquorice.

I guess that he must have gone at about the same time as Tommo, because he looks no older than when I last saw him in 1948. He looks chipper enough these days, but his head is crooked slightly to one side, so maybe it had been the old bullet-in-the-back-of-the-neck job for him after all.

What really pisses me off about these ghosts from my past is that they seem to be no older than when I last saw them; whereas I'm as crook-backed as Richard III, walk with a stick, and have a face as lined as a zebra's arse. I'm also annoyed that I can't hear what they're saying. I can see that they're talking, or laughing – sometimes it's about me; I can see that in their eyes – but I can't hear them. There's something both substantial and insubstantial about them at the same time: I saw a bat fly right through Marty last year – he looked momentarily startled, and then began to laugh. These dead bastards seem to spend a lot of their time laughing, although once you're dead it probably isn't *time* any more, is it?

Sometimes I lie awake at night and simply long to know what happens next. But it's selfish to want to be dead when there's nothing essentially the matter with you except the batteries running down. Anyway, then I feel the old lady warm alongside me, and hear her snores and her occasional mutterings, and know that I have to wait for the proper time. That's what most folk do. I imagine that one day I'll walk out into the garden, into the sunshine, and find that I'm dead just like everyone else. All the boys will be there and up for a big party. Maybe the girls will be there too; I'd like that. You never know.

Afterword

The ravens of Succoth . . .
and some mislaid history

I have a problem with UFOs – apart from the fact that I don't actually believe in them, that is. The problem is that when I was about ten years old I actually saw one, spinning slowly and silently above Muschamp Road Junior School playground, in about 1952. I am reasonably certain that the authorities would have explained it away as a runaway weather balloon, a planet – suddenly and uniquely visible in a clear blue sky – or offered some other such flaky misdescription that no one in their right mind should believe.

What I saw during that morning break – we still called it 'playtime' in the 1950s – was a stationary, slowly rotating, shiny metal disc, which tipped gently from side to side occasionally, as if maintaining trim. Having seen silver barrage balloons aloft, and silver metal aeroplanes, I knew the qualitative difference in the images they fed back to the eye – and I still do. This was a shiny metallic disc, and although there was a noticeable breeze it did not tack.

What I remember clearly is that our teachers also came out and watched it with us for more than an hour. It finally departed vertically, and with incredible speed it was gone, in maybe less than 15 seconds. By then it was too close to dinner time to go back into class. So what I remember is a single magical playtime which seemed to go on for ever, and the staff of the huge Sunlight Laundry opposite coming out onto the road to stare up at the sky.

When I told my parents they were mildly interested; the press reported flying saucers regularly in 1952, and everyone knew what they were. Oddly, no one was particularly worried about them. Looking back, both our almost passive acceptance of them then, real or not, and our total denial of them now, is a little disturbing. So, there you have it – I am a man who cannot believe his own eyes: just like the rest of you I do not believe in UFOs, but I saw one once . . .

Unfortunately so did Captain Mantell, and I borrowed him. The real Captain Thomas F. Mantell was the leader of a section of F51 Mustang Fighters being moved between airfields in the USA. It was his bad luck that his flight was crossing Godman (Air)Field in Kentucky on 7 January 1948, when an alert was received concerning an unusual object in the sky. He was asked to investigate, and two of his flight went with him.

There is no doubt that Mantell climbed his flight to a height above which the aircraft couldn't operate without oxygen equipment for the pilots – and they had none – and this contributed to the disaster that followed. Both Mantell's wingmen dropped out of the climbing chase, but Mantell did not. Among the transcriptions of his radio transmissions can be found the reports, 'the object is above me, and appears to be moving at about half my speed', and later 'it is metallic, and is tremendous in size'.

Mantell began his pursuit at 1445hrs. At 1515hrs all visual and radio contact with him was lost, and there are reports of his aircraft being seen spinning to destruction minutes later. The wreck was found on a farm near Franklin in Kentucky. Mantell's body was in it, and his wristwatch had stopped at 15.18. The air accident enquiry which followed concluded that Mantell had been affected, maybe even killed before the crash, by *hypoxia* from oxygen deprivation. This is where it should have ended, except . . .

The Air Force first announced that as a result of misidentification Mantell actually chased the planet Venus. They subsequently changed Venus to a weather balloon, then back again, before plumping for two weather balloons. In some reports they also moved on to Venus *and* two weather balloons. But, intriguingly, that's not quite the end of the story either.

In 1953 one Richard Miller circulated a self-published *Prologue* in which he claimed that he was in the US Air Force in January 1948, serving at Scott Air Force base near Belleville, and listened live to the Mantell interception transmissions as they came in over a closed communications link. He agreed that the transmissions from Mantell which had already been reproduced were accurate, but then added:

> This is where the official Air Force account ends. However, there was one further radio transmission at 3.18 that afternoon. His last statement has been stricken from all of the official records. He said, 'My God. I see people in this thing.'

I don't think Miller's account has ever been corroborated, but it makes a great story, doesn't it? Every time I read Mantell's alleged last message I get goose flesh!

There are probably several identifiable mind maps that writers use to create their geography. I try to describe places that I know or have seen but occasionally find myself, like a small boy standing in front of a pick'n'mix sweets counter, moving buildings, farms and landscapes around a bit. The Parachute cafe I have put down on the edge of Lympne Airfield in Kent was actually outside Drem Airfield in East Lothian, not half an hour from where I am sitting. It was famous for dangerously huge fried breakfasts. Drem is where the Drem Lighting System for recovering aircraft at night was developed, which in turn evolved into the airfield approach lighting system which now safely guides down to landing virtually every night flight made . . . so the next time you are making a night landing, mouth a quiet *thank you* to the people at Drem in the 1940s. The airfield was transferred from the RAF to the Navy, but quickly returned to agriculture after the war ended. Many of the airfield buildings were simply civilianized, and remain in use. If you are lucky, employees at the restaurant, farm shop and kitchen centre will tell you of the persistent and unnerving wartime ghosts with whom they share what was once the Wren's quarters.

The reference Charlie makes to 'a maniac with a horse and cart' around the narrow lanes of Kent and West Sussex is a reminder I wrote myself of my grandfather, 'Kiki' Owen. A chauffeur to wealthy families for much of his life, he had the privilege to be fined twice in magistrates' courts for the offence of speeding on the open road: once on a pedal bike, and once with a horse and trap!

War surplus aircraft *were* smuggled to the emerging State of Israel, and there *was* an unsuccessful Israeli plot to blow up Ernie Bevin. Israeli terrorists perceived him as opposing the establishment of Israel, and anti-Semitic to boot. I don't know if they were right. I find that historical footnotes like this drop almost accidentally into my stories like pieces falling into place in a jigsaw.

I have CAMRA London to thank for finding me again The Canterbury on Fish Street Hill. It's long gone now, but in the 1960s it had stupendous beer, legendary barmaids and was a drinking haunt of the Customs Officers who worked the Pool of London. Some of those, at the end of their careers, maybe, were WWII ex-servicemen, and they taught me my trade, and how to be a man. I always think of them, particularly Johnny, with gratitude and admiration. John Swift of the Folkestone Classic

Cinema Club told me where Charlie went to the pictures in 1948, and what film he saw. My thanks to him and all of the others who help me to research and build my stories: I am constantly amazed by the help I receive from complete strangers.

Air accidents feature prominently in this narrative, but don't let it put you off flying. Anyone nervous about commercial flying as a passenger today should really look at the air accident statistics and reports for 1947 and 1948: aeroplanes were falling out of the air all over the place. The casualty statistics for aircrew, passengers and aircraft in that period simply would not be tolerated today. The only saving grace I can see is that the passenger aircraft of the 1940s carried far fewer passengers per flight than modern aircraft do, which means that the accidents – greater in number than today by a factor of maybe as much as ten – killed far fewer people. There is no doubt in my mind that air passenger travel today is (fingers crossed: I'm about to fly off to Kuwait) safer than at any other time in history.

One British European Airways (now BA) passenger flight was lost in Germany in 1948 in the way I describe, and the Radio Operator whom Charlie knew was lost with it . . . doing his duty to the very end.

The Avro York flew with the RAF from 1942 to 1957, and I haven't been able to obtain at first hand a pilot's opinion of it as a type, although I'd love to hear from one, and be put right if I have erred. However, there are several air accident investigation reports of catastrophic undercarriage failures, and of pilots stopping runaway aircraft on the ground by simply raising the wheels. The York had a flat belly, and must have skidded like a sledge until it began to come apart. As well as the RAF, it was operated by BOAC, Dan Air, Skyways and several foreign air forces and airlines . . . and even as I write I am looking up to a beautiful little metal model of one. It looks a bit of a tyke actually.

Of the other aircraft with which Charlie became acquainted on Operation Plainfare it is the Avro Lancastrian that the general reader will be least familiar with. It was essentially a civilianized Lancaster Bomber. Those flown by Flight Refuelling Ltd can take a lot of the credit for keeping the engines of aircraft, vehicles, boats and generators running throughout the Berlin Airlift: they shipped in millions of gallons of precious fuel. The friendly Lancastrian I describe, registration G-AHBU, really existed. She was flown by Skyways, and bore the romantic name *Sky Path*. Sadly she died in flames at the delightfully named Nutts Corner Airfield in Northern Ireland some time later.

I can't adequately summarize the Berlin Airlift in a couple of paragraphs, so I'll just try to give you a journeyman writer's flavour.

Operation Plainfare – the British part of the Berlin Airlift – began in July 1948 when the Russians closed the road, rail and canal links to western Berlin through which it had been supplied since 1945. The air corridors, covered by international agreement, stayed open, and the air supply proposal by the British Air Commodore Reginald Waite, although initially rejected by the Americans, eventually saved the city. It was the Americans who made the first move: on 26 July a number of war-weary C47 transport aircraft (we called the type the Dakota) flew 80 tons of medicines and supplies into Tempelhof Airfield a day after the blockade began. They coded their ongoing action Operation Vittles, and after that they never stopped flying. Neither did the British, who centred their Berlin operation at Gatow Airfield. Nor did the numerous private operators who were contracted to support the air forces: fortunes were made and lost, and airlines were born and died between July 1948 and May 1949.

The American pilot who started dropping chocolate and sweets, on handkerchief parachutes, to the German children was

Gail S. Halvorsen. His aircraft was quickly identified by the young Berliners, who dubbed it 'The Candy Bomber': I like that. Such was the positive publicity it generated that he received official sanction, and before long Halvorsen had other pilots involved, and dozens of people who collected sweets and attached them to small parachutes. He called his private airlift 'Operation Little Vittles': I like that too.

Berlin, the most international of European cities, survived. It's a city which knows how to do that. So, after much deprivation, did the Berliners. If there is such thing as a *character* in the population of a city I always think that that of the Berliner is typified by an intelligent, indomitable stubbornness which gets them through the hard times. They don't bang on about their survival. Survivors rarely do: they survive – they've nothing else left to prove. There are many fine books on the Berlin Airlift, that written by Ann and John Tusa particularly springs to mind. My own favourite is *City Under Siege* by Michael Haydock (Brassey's, 1999). It is, necessarily, mainly described from an American point of view but, of all of the Airlift books I have read, it seems to convey something of the *feeling* of the Airlift: the urgency, weariness and a spirit of defiance. It's the one I would recommend.

In my first novel, *Tuesday's War*, I described a bombing raid on the German town of Celle in 1944. I was delighted to receive a letter from an ex-service policeman who had been posted there in 1948. He was able to tell me that although the town itself had largely managed to avoid the intimate attention of the RAF, its railway marshalling yards had been severely smashed up by RAF Typhoons at the very end of the war. I am pleased this novel has given me the chance to modify my earlier observations.

*

The Diamond Bomber also existed. Her airframe number was 44–62276, and you'll find her, and a cairn to honour her dead, at Ordnance Map Reference 56/161022. She's on a high mountain glen named Succoth above Lochgoilhead. Pieces of the aircraft are scattered all around an impact crater still bare of vegetation after sixty years. She was a Boeing B29A Superfortress – the same type that delivered the atom bombs to Hiroshima and Nagasaki, and one of two B29s which left Scampton on 17 January 1949 en route for Kansas in the USA, via Iceland – they would refuel at Keflavik for the long hop over the pond. The pilot, Sheldon C. Craigmyre, had a crew of three and sixteen passengers. These people were all on their way home, their deployments to Europe completed: many had worked on the Berlin Airlift. When the weather over northern England deteriorated, the other Superfort turned back, but *The Diamond Bomber* battled on. Her wings iced up over the first mountain ridges of the West Highlands, and she plunged into history taking everyone inside with her . . . but, like the tale of Thomas Mantell, that's not quite the end of the story . . .

She's become known as *The Diamond Bomber* because of stories repeatedly told of her pilot carrying a fortune in cut and uncut diamonds, sourced in Germany before his trip home. People go up there looking for his diamonds – supposedly sealed into a tubular glass Alka-Seltzer bottle – to this day. It is alleged that he intended to start or buy into a family jewellery business. I hope that the story is true, because it is regularly resurrected by the press, and if it isn't it still must cause pain to his family. As mysterious are the contemporary reports alleging that General's insignia were found on the bodies and in the luggage of apparently enlisted men. The aggressive, vulgarly abusive chaplain who maybe wasn't a chaplain – I'd love to know what documents he was burning – features in several of the contemporary eye-witness accounts, and there *was* a twenty-first body found later in the year, when the crew and passenger manifest bore only twenty names. This was tailor-made for Tommo's exit, stage left.

You might have noticed as Charlie tells his tale, that life's natural attrition has caused some of his friends or enemies – mainly his friends – to drop out from time to time. This was Tommo's turn, and I'm going to miss him a lot. I was just beginning to enjoy writing about Crazy Eddy when he popped his clogs. What I found I couldn't do was kill off Alice, the rattlesnake. In four books she has become, after Charlie, my favourite character, so I left her rattling her wicked temper on an Argyll hillside, with plenty of rabbits to live off. I reasoned that in her native US she would have coped with freezing winter temperatures, and hot summers . . . not unlike some parts of Scotland, so she might be OK.

I climbed the hill to catch up with Alice and find *The Diamond Bomber* a few weeks ago. After the finest kipper breakfast in the world in The Creggans Inn on Loch Fyne we made a seven-hour climbing march on forest track and rough hillside. You can see the remains of the aircraft glinting in the sun from a full mile away, like a field of mirrors. Nothing, however, can prepare you for the utter devastation of a giant aircraft reduced to its component parts in a violent crash, and the concentrated debris field that is still there 60 years later. My first thought as I broke out of the trees was, 'This must be what the *Titanic* feels like.' She sits up at the very edge of the tree line, surrounded by the dark peaks which claimed her and guarded by soaring ravens which call eerily over her grave and warn the unwary, *this is where people die . . . this is where people die.*

And why did Lympne Airfield figure so prominently in this story? That's an easy one: 44 years ago I took off from there for Beauvais in France in a piston-engined Dakota aircraft, just like

Charlie does. It was my first commercial flight as a passenger, I was spectacularly hung-over and I was holding hands with my new bride on honeymoon.

I'll finish on the note of speculation which always haunts me as a volume of Charlie's memoir draws to a close: will he fly again?

I don't know. Publishing is a refreshingly brutal business, so it will all come down to sales in the end. Anyway, maybe Charlie and I deserve time away from each other.

Whatever happens, I *am* going to take him to Suez and the Canal Zone some day. My brother was there in the early 1950s, probably at the same time I was watching my first flying saucer. So were thousands of other brave men whose stories seem to have been forgotten or overlooked. It will be good to open the book on a few of them after all this time.

David Fiddimore
Edinburgh
September 2008

Visit **www.panmacmillan.com** to read more about all our books and to buy them. You will also find features, author interviews and news of any author events, and you can sign up for e-newsletters so that you're always first to hear about our new releases.